CURSED COMMAND

Professionally Published Books by Christopher G. Nuttall

Angel in the Whirlwind

The Oncoming Storm
Falcone Strike

ELSEWHEN PRESS

The Royal Sorceress

The Royal Sorceress (Book I)
The Great Game (Book II)
Necropolis (Book III)
Sons of Liberty (Book IV)

Bookworm

Bookworm
Bookworm II: The Very Ugly Duckling
Bookworm III: The Best Laid Plans
Bookworm IV: Full Circle

Inverse Shadows

Sufficiently Advanced Technology

Stand Alone

A Life Less Ordinary
The Mind's Eye

TWILIGHT TIMES BOOKS

Schooled in Magic

The Decline and Fall of the Galactic Empire

HENCHMEN PRESS

First Strike

CURSED COMMAND

ANGEL IN THE WHIRLWIND

CHRISTOPHER G. NUTTALL

Published by 47North, Seattle

www.apub.com

Amazon, the Amazon logo, and 47North are trademarks of Amazon.com,
Inc., or its affiliates.

ISBN-13: 9781503943971
ISBN-10: 1503943976

Cover design by Ray Lundgren

Cover illustrated by Paul Youll

Printed in the United States of America

CURSED COMMAND

PROLOGUE

"Mission accomplished?"

"Yes, sir," Crewwoman Julia Transom said. She smiled rather coldly. "Captain Abraham is dead."

Senior Chief Joel Gibson smiled back. It hadn't been hard to arrange for Captain Abraham's death, even though the IG would almost certainly go through the entire series of events with a fine-tooth comb. Captain Abraham wasn't—hadn't been—*precisely* aristocracy, but he'd had connections at a very high level. Yet there had been no choice. Captain Abraham had also been far too effective. Given time, he might have turned *Uncanny* into a *real* wreck, and *that* Joel could not allow.

He leaned forward, warningly. "And the evidence?"

"Gone," Julia assured him. He didn't miss the flicker of fear, swiftly hidden, in her eyes. "If they manage to recover the black box, it'll look like a random fluctuation in the shuttle's drive field. They can take however long they want to sift through the debris. They won't find anything incriminating."

"Good," Joel said. "And so we are without a commanding officer. Again."

Julia nodded hastily. "You'd think they'd grow tired of losing officers to this ship."

Joel shrugged. *Uncanny* had been in active service, technically, for three years. The first of her class, she'd been intended to serve as both a squadron command vessel and an independent command for a fire-eating captain. But she'd had a run of bad luck that had left her relegated to lunar orbit, well away from anywhere *important*. Spacers believed—or chose to believe—that she was cursed. Given just how many *accidents* had befallen her crew, they were right to be reluctant to serve on her. Joel and his allies hadn't been responsible for *all* of the accidents.

"They'll want us heading out to the war, sooner or later," he said reluctantly. Though the information was classified, he'd long since spliced a hack into the command network. Given how much time the XO spent in the lunar fleshpots, Joel could honestly say that he read his superior's mail long before Abraham did. "And that gives us our opportunity."

He smirked as he turned away from her. He'd honestly never expected to stay in the Navy, not since a judge had given him a choice between taking the oath and serving his planet or going straight to a penal world. Joel had expected to put in his ten years as an ordinary crewman and then leave Tyre for good, but it hadn't taken him long to see the possibilities inherent in his new position. There was something to be said for being the only effective man in a crew of drunkards, morons, near-criminals, and people the Navy bureaucracy couldn't be bothered to discharge. There were all sorts of other possibilities for a man with imagination and guts.

Julia coughed. "Our opportunity?"

"Why, to take our fate into our own hands, of course," Joel said.

Julia's eyes went wide, but she said nothing. Joel nodded in approval. He trusted Julia about as much as he trusted anyone, which wasn't very much. Julia would sing like a bird if the IG found proof she'd assassinated her commanding officer. The less she knew the better.

He'd considered disposing of her in another accident—and he would have done so if he hadn't *needed* her. How such a remarkable talent for hacking computer networks had escaped being put to better use was beyond him, but he had no doubt of her loyalty. She'd done enough to more than prove her credentials to him.

He turned back to face her. Julia's red hair, cut close to her scalp, shimmered under the bright lights. Her uniform was a size too tight, showing every last curve of her body. There was a hardness in her face that warned that anyone who tried to take advantage of her was going to regret it, if he survived. Joel had taught her more than enough dirty tricks to give Julia an unfair advantage over those who thought that mere strength and brute force would be enough to bring her down.

"Keep a sharp eye on the XO's personal channel," Joel ordered. "If the Admiralty wants to send in another CO, they'll notify him first."

"Unless they know what he's doing with his time," Julia reminded him.

Joel rolled his eyes. The XO wasn't very smart—there was only so far that aristocratic ranks and titles could take a person—but he'd shown a certain low cunning in assembling his protective shroud. Unless the Admiralty decided to make a surprise inspection, they shouldn't have any idea that the XO was enjoying himself rather than doing his duty. If they did . . . Joel found it hard to care. The XO would take the blame for everything and the plotters would pass unnoticed.

Unless they break up the crew, he thought.

He shook his head. *Uncanny* had served as the Royal Navy's dumping ground for the past two years. Even her couple of combat operations in the war hadn't changed that, particularly not after the . . . *incident* . . . at Donne's Reach. Breaking up the crew would force the Admiralty to distribute over a thousand unwanted crewmembers all over the Navy while facing stiff resistance from everyone else. No captain in his right mind wanted a crewman or an officer who had served on *Uncanny*. The ship wasn't known as *Unlucky* for nothing.

3

Julia cleared her throat. "Sir?"

"Keep an eye on his channel," Joel ordered again. "Alert me if anything changes."

Julia nodded, then turned and hurried out of the compartment. Joel watched her go, thinking dark thoughts. They were committed now, no matter how much he might wish to believe otherwise. Whatever he'd said to her, he knew that the IG would not take the death of a commanding officer lightly. And if they started digging through *Uncanny*, they'd uncover far too many oddities to look away . . .

But by then, we should be ready to move, he told himself firmly. *They won't have time to stop us before it's too late.*

CHAPTER ONE

HMS *Uncanny* looked . . . faded.

Captain William McElney wasn't sure just what had prompted *that* observation, but he couldn't escape his first impression of his new command. HMS *Uncanny* was a blunt white arrowhead, like HMS *Lightning*, yet there was something about her that bothered him. Her hull was painted the same pure white as the remainder of the fleet, but it was obvious that no one had bothered to—that no one had *needed* to—repaint the hull. The network of sensor blisters dotted over her exterior looked new, too new. Her point defense weapons, which should have tracked his shuttle as it approached her hull, were still, utterly immobile.

"She doesn't seem to know we're here, sir," the pilot said.

William sucked in his breath sharply, feeling a yawning chasm opening in his chest. A command, his *first* command . . . he'd served the Royal Navy faithfully for years, hoping for a command of his own. And yet, the more he looked at the heavy cruiser, the more he wondered if he'd been *wise* to want a command. On paper, *Uncanny* was a dream; in practice, the First Space Lord had made it clear that the heavy cruiser was trouble.

"Send a standard greeting, then request permission to dock," William ordered finally.

He cursed under his breath. The Theocracy had shown itself more than willing to use suicide missions to target the Commonwealth, even before the tide of the war had started to turn against them. A shuttle crammed with antimatter, exploding within an unsuspecting starship's shuttlebay, would be more than enough to vaporize the entire cruiser. Even a standard nuke would be enough to do real damage if it detonated inside the hull. These days, no one was allowed to dock without an elaborate security screening to make sure they were who they claimed to be. Even civilians were included despite endless protests. He couldn't help wondering if the Theocracy had deliberately set out to ensure that the precautions caused more economic damage than their attacks.

Careless, he thought grimly. *And dangerous in these times.*

"No response," the pilot said.

"Send it again," William said. He didn't want to try to force a docking, certainly not on the day he boarded his first command. But if there was no choice, he'd have to try. "And then find us a docking hatch."

"Aye, sir," the pilot said.

William nodded, then glanced down at the shuttle's tactical display. *Uncanny* should have been running a low-level sensor scan at all times, but she clearly wasn't doing anything of the sort. The vessel was *technically* within regulations, given how close they were to the network of fortresses guarding Tyre, yet the lack of forethought was careless. *Really* careless. If the ship had had to bring up her sensors in a hurry, it would have taken far longer than it should have . . .

. . . And he'd seen enough combat to know that bare minutes could mean the difference between life and death.

"Your commanding officer has written a glowing recommendation, Sir William," the First Space Lord had said. "And so has Rose MacDonald. I'm afraid the combination of recommendations has *quite* upset the bureaucracy."

William had kept his face impassive. He'd been promoted to captain; he'd been promised a command . . . yet he'd forced himself to keep his expectations low. He was too senior to command a gunboat, he thought, and too junior to be offered a cruiser or carrier command. He'd expected a destroyer, perhaps a frigate. Yet, with so many conflicting recommendations, he wasn't sure *what* he'd get. There were hundreds of officers with better connections and only a handful of commands.

"You're being given a heavy cruiser," the First Space Lord had added, pausing just long enough for his words to sink in. "You're being given *Uncanny.*"

"Thank you, sir," William had stammered. He had expected a sting in the tail and hadn't been disappointed. He had no reason to be given a heavy cruiser, not when he'd just been made a captain, save for the simple fact that *no one* wanted to serve on *Uncanny.* The ship had a notorious reputation. "*Unlucky?*"

"That's what they call it," the First Space Lord said grimly.

He'd said a great deal more, William remembered. *Uncanny* had lost *two* previous commanding officers to accidents, but that was only the tip of the iceberg. The ship had been deployed to a cloaked fleet lying in wait for a Theocratic vanguard, only to have her cloaking system go offline at the worst possible moment. If *that* hadn't been bad enough, there had been a whole string of incidents culminating in the starship launching a missile barrage towards a *friendly* ship. The events had all been seen as glitches, but they had cost *Uncanny*'s commanding officer his career.

And matters weren't helped by the missiles being unarmed, William had thought when he'd reviewed the file. *If she'd been shooting at an enemy ship, she'd have inflicted no damage at all.*

"We need to get *Uncanny* into service as quickly as possible," the First Space Lord had concluded. "And if you succeed in sorting out the mess, you'll remain as her commanding officer permanently."

It wasn't much of a bribe, William thought. There was no shortage of captains willing to compete for a post on *Lightning*—the heavy cruiser was *famous*—but *Uncanny?* He'd be surprised if there was *any* competition for her command chair. And yet, he had to admit, his appointment was a hell of a challenge. A heavy cruiser command was nothing to sneer at, even if she *did* have a reputation for being unlucky. He'd be on the path to flag rank . . .

Assuming I survive, he told himself. He hadn't felt comfortable airing his concerns in front of his superior officer. *Those accidents may not have been accidents at all* . . . "Captain," the pilot said. His voice shocked William out of his memories. "We have received permission to dock at Hatch One."

William felt his eyes narrow as the shuttle altered course and sped towards the hatch. Hatch One was located near the bridge—it was the *closest* shuttle hatch to the bridge—but it wasn't where a new captain would board his command for the first time. Normally, a captain would be met by his XO in the shuttlebay, allowing him time to meet his senior officers before formally assuming command. And the XO *was* supposed to be on the vessel . . . he'd checked, just before he departed Tyre. Commander Stewart Greenhill was currently in command of HMS *Uncanny.*

"Dock us," he ordered, wondering just what sort of hellhole he was about to enter. "And remain docked until I give you leave to depart."

"Aye, Captain," the pilot said.

The hatch looked normal enough, William noted, yet he couldn't help tensing as the shuttle mated with *Uncanny.* Captain Abraham had died in a shuttle accident—the IG had found nothing suspicious in two weeks of careful investigation—but Captain Jove had died in a freak airlock accident. A component had decayed, according to the engineers; the airlock had registered a safe atmosphere when it had actually been open to vacuum. William had been in the Navy long enough to know that accidents happened, but he'd also learned that accidents could be *made* to happen. Losing two commanding officers to *accidents* was more than a little suspicious.

He covertly tested his shipsuit and mask, hidden in his shoulder pockets, as the hatch hissed open. Everything looked normal, but the inner hatch took just long enough to open for him to start feeling nervous. The hatch should have opened at once, unless the sensors registered vacuum or biological contamination. William took a long breath as he stepped into his cruiser and had to fight to keep from recoiling in horror. *Uncanny* stank like a pirate ship after a successful mission of looting, raping, and burning.

Fuck, he thought.

He felt a sudden surge of anger as he looked up and down the corridor. No one had come to greet him, neither the XO nor his senior officers. What were they playing at? Even a *very* busy XO should have come to meet his CO for the first time, if only to explain any problems that caught the captain's eye. And to explain why his ship smelled worse than an unwashed outdoor toilet. It wasn't as if replacing the air filters required a goddamned shipyard! He took another breath and tasted faint hints of ionization in the air, warning him that dozens, perhaps hundreds, of components had not been replaced for far too long. Every trained spacer *knew* that that smell meant trouble.

A hatch hissed open in the distance. William braced himself, unsure what to expect as someone hurried down the corridor towards him. He rested his hands on his hips—it was hard to resist the temptation to draw his sidearm—as the welcome party came into view. A very *small* welcome party. It was a young woman wearing a steward's uniform; she was young enough to be his daughter, yet with a hardness in her eyes that shocked him. Whatever military bearing she'd had before leaving Piker's Peak was long gone. Her salute, when she finally gave it, was so sloppy, her instructors would have cried themselves senseless.

"Stand at ease," William curtly ordered. He took a moment to match the face to the files he'd studied during the flight from Tyre.

Janet Richmond, Captain Abraham's personal steward. Blonde enough to remind him of Kat Falcone, but lacking Kat's poise and grim determination to prove herself. "Where is the XO?"

Janet quailed. William suddenly realized that he might have been too harsh. "I . . ."

William took a breath. Janet was a *steward*. She wasn't in the chain of command. Hell, he doubted she had *any* authority outside her CO's suite. What the hell was she *doing* here?

"Calm down," he ordered, forcing his own voice to calm. "Where is the XO?"

"He's not on the ship, sir," Janet said carefully. She cringed back, as if she expected to be slapped. "Commander Greenhill hasn't been on the ship for the last ten days."

William felt his mouth drop open. "What?"

"He left the ship ten days ago," Janet said. She sounded as if she were pleading with him for . . . what? Understanding? "He ordered the communications staff to keep up the pretense that he was onboard."

"I see," William said.

He had to fight, hard, to keep his anger under control. He hadn't thought much of Commander Greenhill after he'd read the man's file, but he'd promised himself that he would keep an open mind. Now . . . Commander Greenhill would be lucky if he was *merely* kicked out of the Navy. Going on unauthorized leave when he was meant to be in command of his ship? Dereliction of duty was a shooting offense in wartime.

"Please don't tell him I told you," Janet pleaded. "He'll get angry."

"He'll get dead," William snapped. Shooting was too good for Commander Greenhill. *Far* too good for him. William had been raised to do his duty or die trying, no matter what curves life threw him. Commander Greenhill didn't even have the decency to resign his commission and totter off to spend the rest of his life in the nearest bar. "Who *is* on this fucking ship?"

Janet cringed, again.

"The chief engineer is in command," she said finally. "But he's in his cabin . . . the bridge crew are scattered . . . the crew . . ."

"Let me guess," William said. He hated himself for taking his anger out on her, but it was so hard to remain focused. "They're currently too drunk to notice that they're steadily poisoning their own fucking atmosphere?"

He saw a dozen answers cross Janet's face before she nodded, once.

William shook his head, feeling an odd flicker of sympathy for Commander Greenhill. He might have had a good reason to throw in the towel, after all. Offhand, William couldn't remember a ship and crew falling so far, certainly not in Commonwealth history. A handful of UN ships had turned pirate, he recalled, after the Breakaway Wars, and quickly fell into very bad habits.

And most of them were small ships, he thought numbly. *This is a heavy cruiser.*

"Take me to the bridge," he ordered, meeting her eyes. "And *don't* call ahead to say I'm coming."

"Yes, sir," Janet said.

She turned and hurried down the corridor, moving so quickly that she was practically running . . . as if, William reflected grimly, she wanted to get away from him. He hadn't paid much attention to her file, he recalled; in hindsight, that might have been a mistake. A captain had considerable authority over who served as his steward, after all. Had Captain Abraham been motivated by something other than efficiency?

He followed Janet, feeling his anger simmering as he took in the condition of his starship. A dozen maintenance lockers had been left open, their contents scattered over the deck; a handful of overhead lockers had been torn open; the strange smell only grew more unpleasant the farther they moved into the ship. He winced inwardly as he smelled the telltale presence of rats and cockroaches. He'd been wrong, he reflected, as they passed through a pair of solid hatches and entered Officer Country. There were pirate ships from the edge of explored space that were in better condition than *Uncanny*.

Janet stopped and turned to face him. "It wasn't their fault," she said. "Sir . . ."

William scowled at her. "*What* wasn't their fault?"

"Everything," Janet said. She turned back and opened the hatch to the bridge. "You'll see in a minute . . ."

William followed her onto the bridge . . . and stopped, dead. A single officer sat in front of the tactical console, smoking something that smelled of burning grass. William stared at him, and then realized, to his shock, that there was no one else on the bridge. Regulations insisted on at least *three* officers on duty at all times, even when the starship was in orbit around the safest world in the Commonwealth. Where were the other two? It struck him, a moment later, that *Janet* might be one of the other officers. Was she even *qualified* to stand watch?

He pushed the thought aside as he surveyed the compartment. The holographic display that should have showed the system was gone; five consoles were deactivated, four more dismantled for parts. He'd never seen anything like it, at least not outside a shipyard putting the finishing touches on a brand new starship. Creeping horror threatened to overcome him as he keyed the nearest console, demanding a status update. The internal sensor net was down . . . completely. He'd never seen *that* outside starships that had been battered into hulks by enemy fire.

"It's nonfunctional," Janet said.

"I can see that," William snarled. He strode over to the smoking officer and tore the cigarette out of his mouth, dropping it on the deck and grinding it under his heel. "What happened to the bridge?"

The officer stared at him. "Who are you?"

"I'm your new commanding officer," William snapped. Up close, the man's breath made him want to reel. He had no idea what the man had been smoking, but it couldn't be good for him. Or anyone. "Who are *you*?"

The officer's mouth opened and shut for a long moment. "Lieutenant Rodney Graham, sir," he managed, finally. "I'm officer of the watch."

"Glad to hear it," William said. "What happened to my bridge?"

"The engineers cannibalized it to keep other starships running," Janet said quietly. "They were practically stripping out the entire hull . . ."

William understood, just for a moment, why one of his uncles had drunk himself to death after his farm had failed. It hadn't been the old man's fault, not really. He'd just seen his investments fail, one after the other, even before the pirates had arrived to threaten his homeworld. Maybe the remainder of the ship's crew—*his* crew—felt the same way.

The First Space Lord couldn't have known, William thought grimly. *Even if they hadn't stripped out essential components, they'd been vandalizing their own ship and rendering it unserviceable.*

He cursed under his breath savagely. It was difficult, sometimes, to get spare parts from the bureaucracy. Even during wartime, the bureaucrats insisted on having the forms filled out before they released the components, despite the best efforts of supply officers. Having a source of supplies they could tap without having to fill out the paperwork would be wonderful, as far as the supply officers were concerned. God knew, he'd rewarded a couple of officers for being excellent scroungers . . .

It may not be as bad as it seems, he told himself. *Or that could be just wishful thinking.*

"Right," he said, pushing the thought aside. "I want you"—he glared at Graham—"to recall each and every officer and crewman who is currently not on the ship. If they are back before the end of the shift"—he made a show of glancing at his wristcom—"nothing further will be said about their absence. This time."

Graham looked as if he wanted to object but didn't quite dare. "Yes, sir."

"Good," William said. "I *suggest*"—he hardened his tone to make it very clear that it wasn't a *suggestion*—"that you get rid of any drugs and anything else that could get you in hot water before I hold a search. This is your *one* chance to clean up your act."

He turned and met Janet's eyes. "And *you* are to take me to the chief engineer."

Janet paled. "Yes, sir."

"Good," William said. He wondered, suddenly, what Kat Falcone would make of a ruined starship and a wrecked crew. "Let's go."

CHAPTER TWO

"You gave him *Unlucky?*"

"*Uncanny,*" the First Space Lord corrected. "Her *name* is *Uncanny.*"

Kat closed her eyes in pain. She owed Commander William McElney—*Captain* William McElney—her life and career. He'd been her XO on HMS *Lightning* and she knew, all too well, that she would have lost everything without him. She'd called in every favor she was owed and made promises of future favors to ensure that the delay between his promotion and his assignment to a command was as short as possible. Still, she'd never expected that he might be offered *Unlucky.* *That* ship had killed two of her commanding officers and ruined three more.

"Might I ask," she said in a tone she knew would get anyone else in trouble, "why you gave him *that* ship?"

"Politics," the First Space Lord said dryly.

"*Heavy* politics," King Hadrian added.

Kat swallowed, hard. King Hadrian had sought her out more than once since her return from Theocratic Space, but she'd never been sure why. Perhaps he just wanted the benefit of her experience. The monarch had vast power in wartime, but King Hadrian had no military experience. He'd never been allowed to leave his homeworld, even after being crowned.

"Politics," she repeated finally.

"It's a delicate balancing act," the First Space Lord said. "On one hand, we have noncitizens of Tyre who want postings to the very highest levels; on the other hand, we have the existing power structure complaining about outsiders being allowed to compete with insiders. And you *know* it. We have to navigate this political storm before it tears the Commonwealth apart."

"We don't have enough ships to go around," King Hadrian said.

"Yet," Kat countered.

She shook her head, irritated. The Commonwealth had a formidable industrial base, but the demands of wartime were pushing it to the limit. Her father, the Minister of War Production, had told her that production was still being ramped up even though countless new starships, gunboats, and missiles were rattling off the assembly line. According to the latest projections, the Commonwealth wouldn't achieve a decisive tonnage advantage over the Theocracy for another two to three years.

But we now know that we overestimated their industrial base, Kat reminded herself. *They're already running hot, while we're still increasing our production rate.*

"Yet," King Hadrian agreed. "But we do not have enough stability, not right now anyway, to risk upsetting the political balance of power."

"And *not* allowing outsiders to be promoted will *also* upset the balance of power," Kat pointed out tartly.

"Quite," the First Space Lord said. "So we promote your XO and offer him a chance to put an . . . *unlucky* . . . starship back into active service. If he does well, we can use him as a test case to prove that outsiders should get their chance; if he doesn't . . . well, at least we have good reason to justify turning down other promotions."

Kat managed to keep her face impassive, but not without effort. The Kingdom of Tyre had never intended to become a multistar political entity, not when everyone had *assumed* that the UN's hegemony over humanity's growing domain would last indefinitely. However, the UN had fallen into war, leaving chaos in its wake. Tyre had created the Commonwealth, a union of stars and planets, with the intention of integrating the newcomers slowly and carefully. And yet the war had blown all of their careful plans out the airlock. The Commonwealth had to square the urgent need for manpower with the political requirement not to sacrifice the ethos that had made the Commonwealth great.

But William deserved his promotion, Kat thought. *How many others also deserve promotion?*

"I am not an all-powerful ruler," King Hadrian said. "We cannot ram through such changes without paying a stiff price."

He cleared his throat. "In any case," he added, "we did not call you here to discuss your former XO."

Kat leaned forward, stiffly. She didn't share her father's obsession with political games—no one had really expected the tenth child of Duke Lucas Falcone to wield political power—but she knew enough to expect trouble. King Hadrian wouldn't have called her to the palace's war room, knowing that it would have displeased some of his ministers, if he hadn't *wanted* her here. And if he wanted her here, he had a reason. He wouldn't have summoned her on a whim.

The First Space Lord tapped a switch. A holographic star chart materialized in front of them, hanging over the table. Kat devoured it, noting with interest the handful of stars that had seen raiding parties from the Theocracy sweeping through in hopes of delaying the Commonwealth's mobilization. None of those raiding parties had taken or held territory, not since the first thrusts into Commonwealth territory. The war seemed to have stalemated.

"As you are aware," the First Space Lord said, "Admiral Junayd defected six months ago, after you embarrassed him in front of his superiors. Since then, he's been singing like a bird. We've learned a great deal about the Theocracy's industrial base, its long-term plans for conquest, and most importantly, how its government actually *works*. Our analysts have been able to confirm enough of the data to discern that Junayd's been telling the truth."

Kat nodded. Admiral Junayd would have to be *insane* to lie. She honestly couldn't imagine the Theocracy choosing to sacrifice an entire superdreadnought, perhaps more than one, in a vain attempt to prove Junayd's *bona fides*. There was the vague possibility, her father had warned, that the whole thing *was* a con, but Admiral Junayd had been checked and tested extensively.

"Admiral Junayd did not know just what his former allies had in mind to break the stalemate," the First Space Lord added, "but he does know some of their long-term plans. Despite waging war against us, the Theocracy has continued its aim to subvert nearby star systems and eventually bring them under its control. Admiral Junayd believes that the Theocracy intends to continue those plans."

Kat blinked. "Even now?"

"They're committed to spreading their religion," King Hadrian reminded her. "Even if they lose the war, even if their homeworld gets blasted from orbit, their religion will survive."

"Maybe," Kat said. "But they could be wrong."

The thought made her shudder. She'd seen thousands of refugees fleeing the Theocracy and knew there were hundreds of millions trapped on a dozen occupied worlds. She rather doubted that the Theocracy would survive if it lost control of the high orbitals. The level of hatred the Theocracy had unleashed promised bloody purges once the war was over. The Theocracy had meted out savage treatment to their helpless prey and, once the boot was on the other foot, savage treatment would be meted out to them in turn.

"They could be," the First Space Lord agreed.

He pointed to a cluster of stars near the Commonwealth's border. "The Jorlem Sector," he said by way of introduction. "I believe you've been there?"

"I visited briefly, when I was assigned to HMS *Thomas*," Kat recalled. "But I only had a couple of days leave on Vangelis. I never saw Jorlem itself."

King Hadrian looked surprised. "You are not familiar with the sector?"

Kat shook her head. Groundhogs never really comprehended the sheer immensity of interstellar space. The Jorlem Sector held over fifty stars and over a hundred settled worlds, ranging from tiny farming settlements to Jorlem itself. She hadn't really seen much of Vangelis, save for a few tourist traps near the spaceport. The idea that her limited experience made her an expert on the sector was absurd.

Although quite a few analysts claim to be experts without ever having left their homeworld, she reminded herself. *At least the king is trying to talk to people who might know better than himself.*

"I couldn't call myself an expert," she said.

"Very wise," the First Space Lord said.

He gave her a half smile as he pointed to the star chart. "The important part, right now, is that the Theocracy is planning to . . . *seduce* . . . a number of independent planets within the sector," he told her. "Our defector believes that the Theocracy intends to offer all sorts of incentives to its potential allies, ranging from protection from Theocratic incursions to honored positions within the Theocracy."

"They wouldn't fall for *that*," Kat insisted.

"They might," the First Space Lord said. "There's a great deal of resentment and suspicion of the Commonwealth in that sector, Captain. They may see the Theocracy as the lesser of two evils."

"They'll regret it," Kat said. She shook her head in disbelief. "How can people be so *stupid*?"

"Poor trade policies," the king said. "A number of worlds have expressed interest in joining the Commonwealth, Kat, but their local rivals have been much less enthusiastic. They've actually been trying to arm themselves to the teeth for the last couple of decades. Not enough to be a threat to us on their own, of course, but allied with the Theocracy . . ."

Kat nodded as his voice trailed off. The Theocracy had poured its resources into building the largest fleet of warships it could but neglected the sinews of war. She'd known, long before Operation Knife, that the Theocracy was trying to buy up freighters and hire merchant spacers in a desperate attempt to solve their problems, yet that hadn't been enough. The Theocratic advance into Commonwealth space might well have gotten farther if its logistics system hadn't collapsed mere weeks after the war began.

"They could tip the balance back in their favor," she said.

"That's not the only implication," the king confirmed. "If the Theocrats open trade links with the Jorlem Sector, they'll have access to markets and traders from right across the human sphere. It wouldn't be hard for them to purchase military-grade gear from a dozen potential sources, mil-spec gear that might be enough to neutralize our advantages. There would be nothing we could do about it. Diplomatic protests won't be enough when vast sums of money are at stake."

"We could buy the gear ourselves," Kat pointed out.

"Measures are underway," the First Space Lord said.

He leaned forward, resting his hands on the table. "HMS *Lightning* and HMS *Uncanny* are being posted to the Jorlem Sector," he informed her. "Our regular patrols through the sector have been withdrawn with the advent of war, so the normal trade routes have become increasingly lawless. Intelligence believes that pirate and smuggler consortiums have relocated themselves after pickings in our territory became rather slim."

"Or the Theocracy may be trying to put pressure on the locals," Kat offered.

"It's a possibility," the king agreed.

Kat scowled as she contemplated the situation. Theocratic forces hadn't hesitated to sponsor pirate activity within Commonwealth space, hoping to weaken their targets before the war actually began. There was no reason they couldn't do the same in the Jorlem Sector, with an additional nasty little twist. If the Jorlem Sector joined the Theocracy, those raiders could be sent elsewhere . . . but if the Jorlem Sector joined the Commonwealth instead, the Navy would have to divert patrols to protect the sector, putting yet another demand on the Navy's very limited time and resources—just the sort of scheme that would appeal to the Theocrats. Whatever happened, whatever the sector's governments did, the Theocracy would come out ahead.

"Ideally, you'll be doing nothing more than showing the flag and assisting the locals in hunting down pirates and other threats," the First Space Lord told her. "Six months of patrolling should do wonders for our reputation. If you *can* forge a set of alliances, we'd be delighted . . . but we're not expecting it. Right now, it's more reasonable to simply foster warm relations in the sector; we can worry about convincing them to apply for membership later."

"Because we can't defend them now," Kat said.

"Yes," the king said. "In the long term, yes; we'd like them to join. But for the moment, we'd prefer to keep them at a distance."

"You'll be given specific orders in the next couple of days," the First Space Lord added. "Do you have any questions for the moment?"

"Yes, sir," Kat said. "Why me? Why us?"

The king smiled. "There are several reasons," he said. "First, you have a growing reputation for military skill—you saved an entire fleet at First Cadiz, practically won Second Cadiz singlehandedly . . . and then raided deep into enemy space, throwing them back onto the defensive."

"Admiral Christian might have a few things to say about *that*, sire," Kat said. "I *didn't* win the battle singlehandedly."

"No, but that's what the media is saying," the king said. "Are you suggesting that . . . that they're *fibbing*? I am *shocked*."

He went on before Kat could come up with an answer. "The point is that you are a military hero, a *genuine* military hero, and you have *very* close links to the aristocracy. Sending you to the Jorlem Sector is an excellent way of showing how important we consider the sector to be. You talking to their rulers on equal terms is a sign of respect. *And* you can talk to their militaries, discussing the exact nature of the enemy threat and how it can be defeated. Your reputation will precede you."

The media will make sure of it, Kat thought darkly. She *loathed* the media.

"Your former XO, your fellow captain, is also an advertisement for social advancement within the Commonwealth, even though he wasn't born on Tyre," the king added. "He was knighted six months ago, which makes him a *de facto* member of the aristocracy, and he was given his own command. A *heavy cruiser* to boot. He's living proof that noncitizens can and do advance within the system."

"Of course, sire," Kat said. "The fact that it was a struggle to get him promoted, after *years* of loyal service, is neither here nor there. The fact that *Unlucky* is on the verge of falling apart . . ."

"Of course not," the king interrupted. He shot her an annoyed look. "We are trying to fight a war, Captain, while trying to patch over the holes in the Commonwealth's structure. It needs to be handled carefully."

"It does," Kat agreed. "And what do we do if we encounter a predatory merchant?"

"Whatever you see fit," the king said.

Kat resisted the urge to rub her eyes. There was no escaping the simple fact that a number of Tyre's merchants had established trade links that effectively exploited stars and planets *outside* the Commonwealth. Their behavior was technically illegal, but it was difficult to prosecute them when they also tended to have allies in high places. The kingdom's determination to protect its people, even at the risk of war, didn't help. There was no way she could stand back and watch as a crowd threatened to lynch a Commonwealth citizen, but she didn't want to risk her ship and crew to save someone who only deserved a quick trial and a one-way ticket to a penal world.

"I want *carte blanche*," she said flatly.

"Already in your orders," the king said. Kat had the uneasy feeling that someone had anticipated her demand. "We're at war. The normal rules don't apply."

And they just dumped a hot potato in my lap, Kat thought. She was starting to suspect that there were other reasons for her appointment. No one could say she didn't have ties to the merchant sector, not when her father ran, or had run, one of the largest corporations in the sector. *But which way am I expected to jump?*

"Thank you," she said. She'd consider the problem later. "When do you want us to depart?"

"Ideally, a week from today," the First Space Lord said. "But organizing a convoy to Vangelis may take longer. Spacers . . . are none too happy about the convoy requirements."

"They wouldn't be," Kat said. She'd never served on a merchant freighter, but thanks to her family, she understood the logistical problems facing civilian skippers better than most military officers. "If they miss their due dates, they face fines . . . perhaps even the loss of their ships."

"We've introduced emergency legislation to tackle the problem," the king said. "But it's stalled in the House of Lords. Too many people are suspicious of how it can be misused."

Kat sighed. "Is there any *evidence* it *will* be misused?"

"Of course not," the king said. "But who needs evidence when there are political points to score?"

"Touché," Kat said.

She shook her head. In all fairness, she could see both sides of the debate. A merchant skipper in danger of losing his ship would run terrifying risks, if necessary, to make his scheduled deadlines. Even with stasis fields, certain cargos were all too perishable; they might arrive too late for anyone to want to buy them, but introducing legislation to override contractual requirements would open up a whole new can of worms. Either deadlines would no longer matter, in which case the merchant skippers could and would cheat at will, or each and every case would have to be decided individually, tying up the courts for years. It would be a political nightmare.

But a collapse of interstellar trade would be a nightmare too, she thought.

"You'll receive your formal orders soon," the First Space Lord said. "Good luck with your new XO."

Kat had to fight a frown. She'd requested that her former tactical officer be promoted, but she'd heard nothing. Somehow, she suspected that the bureaucracy had found a reason to turn down her request. And *that* meant her new XO would be transferred from another ship . . .

"Thank you, sir," Kat said. She had no trouble recognizing a dismissal. "I won't let you down."

CHAPTER THREE

William couldn't help feeling, as the hatch started to hiss open, that he was stepping into the lair of a wild animal. The stench of alcohol and unwashed human body drifted past his nose as he took a step forward, peering into the darkened cabin. He would have wondered if the compartment was empty, if he hadn't heard the sound of heavy breathing—it sounded almost like snoring—coming from within. The chief engineer didn't *sound* healthy.

And he's suicidal, William thought, darkly. Problems with the air filters suggested that, sooner or later, the atmosphere would become toxic. The crew would die before they realized that something was horribly wrong. *He certainly isn't doing his fucking job.*

"Stay here," he ordered Janet. "And *don't* go anywhere."

"Yes, sir," Janet said.

William walked into the cabin and paused long enough for the hatch to hiss closed behind him. The lights should have brightened automatically as the room's sensors registered his presence, yet nothing happened. Some officers disabled the sensors if they had to share a sleeping compartment with another officer, but the chief engineer slept alone. William allowed himself a moment of frustration, then touched the switch by the side of the hatch. The lights brightened sharply, revealing a truly *filthy* compartment. Clothes, tools, and items William couldn't identify, items he didn't *want* to identify, lay everywhere. Bottles, *empty* bottles, were littered all over the compartment, leaving it smelling faintly of shipboard rotgut. From the next room came the sound of breathing, breathing that was growing increasingly loud.

Bracing himself, William strode up to the open hatch and peered through. A man—the chief engineer, he hoped—was lying on the bed, dozing. His face was unshaven, his uniform was a mess, and he was clutching a half-full bottle in one hand. He turned slowly and blinked owlishly at William, as if he didn't quite register his commander's presence. Then he started to lift the bottle to his lips.

"No," William snapped. He moved forward and yanked the bottle from the engineer, tossing it across the compartment. It struck the far bulkhead and shattered. "No more alcohol."

"Fuck off," the engineer said.

William felt his temper snap. He caught hold of the engineer by the lapels and hauled him to his feet, holding him a centimeter above the deck. The engineer stared at him in shock, clearly unable to formulate a response. William shook him violently, then half dragged him towards the medical kit on the wall. Unless the crew was *truly* suicidal, they'd have left the medical kit alone. There should be a sober-up spray inside. It wouldn't be the first time some unfortunate officer had needed to sober up in a hurry.

"No," the engineer protested, as William opened the kit and found the injector. "I . . ."

"Be quiet," William snapped. He was tempted to smack the engineer, but he had the feeling the man was too far out of it to notice. "Take your medicine like an officer."

He pushed the injector against the engineer's neck, then pulled him into the washroom as the drug worked its magic. The man's body convulsed violently. William barely managed to get the engineer's head over the toilet before he threw up, spewing out everything in his stomach. Shaking his head, William poured the engineer a glass of water, but waited until the man was finished throwing up to offer it to him. Dehydration would be a very real threat for the next few hours.

"That was dirty," the engineer protested as he downed the water. William passed him another glass without comment. "That was *really* dirty."

"That was really dirty, *sir*," William corrected sharply. "Name and rank. Now."

The engineer stared at him. "Chief Engineer Calvin Goodrich, sir," he managed. "Chief Engineer of *Unlucky*, and goddamn all who serve on her."

"No, you're the chief engineer of *Uncanny*," William snapped. "And you're going to do your job."

Goodrich blinked at him. "Or what?"

William picked Goodrich up and shoved him against the bulkhead. "Shut up and listen," he growled. "I don't give a damn about your problems. I don't give a damn about this ship's reputation. I don't give a damn if you think I'm a complete bastard who's been sent here because he pissed someone off. I am going to get this ship into working order before we leave orbit, and *you* are going to help me."

He allowed his voice to harden. "And if you *don't* help me," he added threateningly, "you'll be wishing that you were merely tossed out of the airlock when I've finished with you."

"I've done nothing," Goodrich protested.

"That's the point," William snarled. "The air filters are clogged, risking the certain death of the entire crew. Half the consoles have been stripped or removed, rendering the ship unsuitable for anything but the scrap yard. I hate to imagine what would happen if we tried to pick a fight with a fucking *gunboat* in this condition! A civilian freighter with a couple of popguns could probably kick our asses!"

He took a moment to calm himself. "Right now," he warned, "the only thing keeping me from tossing you out the airlock is the simple fact that everyone deserves a chance. This is yours! Help me get this ship back into fighting shape and I'll overlook your . . . earlier problems. Or, if you decide to be a useless piece of shit, I'll throw you out the airlock myself. Do you understand me?"

"Yes," Goodrich managed.

"Yes, *what?*"

"Yes, sir," Goodrich said.

"Good," William said. He glared down at the engineer. They were about the same age, he realized slowly. But Goodrich had really let himself go. "Take a shower and get dressed, and then join me outside. We have work to do."

"Yes, sir," Goodrich said.

William gave him one last warning look, then stepped back into the main cabin. Once again, he took in the mess: bottles everywhere, dirty clothes lying on the floor. A cleaning crew was supposed to wash the crew's clothes. Clearly they hadn't been bothering. Or perhaps they'd decided the endeavor wasn't worth the risk of entering Goodrich's cabin. The man was a mean drunk.

I need to get some extra crew in here, William thought. He rather doubted he could get any permanent crewmen, no matter what inducements he offered, but he should be able to borrow some temporary workers from the shipyard's manpower pool. *I must determine just how many crewmembers will need to be tossed off this ship.*

He shook his head. He'd need more than just temporary workers. Marines would be nice. A company or two of marines would be just what he needed to keep the rest of the crew in line if he couldn't distribute them over the rest of the Navy. But he knew he'd be lucky to get a platoon of marines, not when there were so many demands on their manpower too. Perhaps he could talk Kat into lending him a platoon. Shaking his head, he strode over to the desk, pushed a dozen bottles off the chair, and sat down in front of the terminal, keying a log-in screen. The computer was password-protected, but his command codes unlocked it, allowing him to check the maintenance reports. He wasn't too surprised to discover that they hadn't been updated in months.

They weren't updated even before Captain Abraham died, he thought numbly. *He might have died because he couldn't be bothered forcing the crew to do basic maintenance tasks.*

On impulse, he flicked through a handful of other files. No one had filed a readiness report for over six months, something that should have drawn attention from the IG. Filing a readiness report was a legal requirement, particularly when the starship was attached to Home Fleet. Crew reports hadn't been updated either, another legal requirement. Goodrich, it seemed, hadn't even been delegating the task of writing them. Nor had any of the other officers.

Leaving the terminal open, he rose and strode over to the hatch. Janet was standing outside, leaning against the bulkhead. She straightened up sharply when she saw him. William wondered at the strange mix of relief and fear that flickered across her face, then put it aside for later contemplation. Right now, she wasn't his immediate problem.

"Clean up this compartment," he ordered, beckoning her into the cabin. "Put the bottles out for recycling, send the clothing to be washed, mop the floor, and do whatever else needs to be done to make the compartment livable."

Janet saluted. "Yes, sir."

William allowed himself a moment of relief. He'd expected an argument. The captain's steward often, at least in his experience, considered herself too grand to clean *other* cabins like a common steward. Janet went right to work, though, gathering up the bottles and placing them to one side. William made a mental note to have a few sharp words with whoever was producing the rotgut—they'd clearly stepped well outside the conventional bounds—and then waited, as patiently as he could, for Goodrich. The engineer took nearly thirty minutes to freshen up and emerge into the main compartment.

"Captain," he said, jabbing a finger at Janet, "what's the Captain's Whore doing here?"

Janet flinched. William cursed, inwardly. *That* explained a great deal.

"She's here to clean up the mess," he said. "And you will *not* talk about her in such terms."

"But . . ."

William ignored the protest. "*You* are going to give me a tour of my ship. We'll start with engineering."

Goodrich looked as if he wanted to argue further but didn't quite dare. "Yes, sir."

"Janet, finish the job," William ordered as Goodrich headed for the hatch. "And then report back to me."

"Yes, sir," Janet said.

William followed Goodrich through the hatch and down the long corridor towards Main Engineering, silently tallying a list of problems that needed urgent attention. A number of cabins looked uninhabited, their interiors stripped bare; a couple of storage compartments were empty, their contents removed and sent . . . somewhere. The handful of crew he passed looked sullen, or resentful, or even *fearful*. He wondered, grimly, just how badly the lower decks had decayed. Instead of cleaning up the ship, the Admiralty had sent every rotten apple it could find to *Uncanny*. The results had been disastrous.

"We lost one of our power cores two months ago, sir," Goodrich told him as they walked into Main Engineering. "Captain Abraham didn't bother to have it replaced."

"Fuck," William said. Replacing a power core took ten days, assuming nothing went terribly wrong during the procedure. "And no one thought to report it?"

"No one dared cross Captain Abraham, sir," Goodrich said. "He was a right fucking tyrant."

And he wound up dead, William thought. Sabotage? It wasn't impossible . . . and any evidence would have gone down with the shuttle. Or perhaps it had been just punishment for neglecting his ship. *But he wasn't the only one who had died.*

"Right," he said instead of revealing his suspicions. "What else needs to be fixed before we can leave orbit?"

Goodrich stared at him. "We *can't* leave orbit."

William stared back. "Why not?"

"They say this ship is cursed," Goodrich insisted. "Sir . . ."

"Cursed," William repeated, straining to keep the sarcasm out of his voice. "I suppose the effects of poor maintenance, not bothering to do any repairs, and general carelessness *would* seem like a curse."

He rounded on the engineer. "We are due to leave orbit far too soon," he snapped. "So tell me, Mr. Goodrich, what needs to be done?"

"The power core needs to be replaced," Goodrich said finally. "Our air filters need to be replaced . . . it's possible that the system has been clogged in several places. Our internal sensor network needs to be reconfigured, our external sensor blisters need to be replaced completely. And a number of . . . ah . . . *transferred* components need to be replaced too."

"*Transferred*," William repeated.

Goodrich flushed. "The captain okayed it . . ."

"I'm sure he did," William snapped. "And how long do you think it would have been before someone *noticed*?"

He rubbed his forehead, telling himself—again—that cuffing the chief engineer would be pointless. Transferring, perhaps *selling*, components from *Uncanny* wouldn't have lasted long, not when someone noticed that the serial numbers of the components in place didn't match their records. The entire scheme would have unraveled the moment the inspectors compared notes and discovered that all of the components came from the HMS *Uncanny*. Even if they'd been sold to civilian ships instead, something that was *definitely* against regulations, the scheme couldn't have lasted forever.

Someone would have noticed the parts missing, if the IG ever did an inspection, he thought grimly. *And putting in a request for replacements would have tipped them off.*

"Captain Abraham okayed it," Goodrich said. "It was his order . . ."

"Perhaps his scheme," William said. Perhaps Captain Abraham had wanted the money more than he wanted his career. But Captain Abraham was dead. "Leave it for the moment."

Goodrich looked relieved. William had a nasty feeling that that wasn't going to last.

"I want you to put together a *complete* list of everything that needs to be replaced or repaired," William ordered. "*Everything*. I don't want to find a single item left off the list. Go through the entire ship with a fine-tooth comb."

"That could take a while," Goodrich said.

"You have forty-eight hours," William stated, bluntly. "If you have been doing your job, Mr. Goodrich, it shouldn't take you *that* long. Err on the side of caution, if you have to—I'd sooner replace an intact component than run the risk of having something fail on us."

He gritted his teeth in fury as he looked around the engineering compartment, which actually looked to be in better condition than the bridge—but only a couple of crewmen were visible, both clearly pretending that they weren't listening. At least a dozen engineering crewmen should be in the compartment at all times, even when the ship was in orbit around the local moon. It was impossible to escape the simple fact that Goodrich simply *hadn't* been doing his job.

"If you need additional crewmen," William added, "put in a request to my terminal."

"Yes, sir," Goodrich said. "But they won't be forthcoming."

"We will see," William said. "Now get to work."

He turned and strode out of the compartment, walking around the engineering section before heading back towards Officer Country. *Uncanny* followed the same basic layout as *Lightning*, a vessel he knew like the back of his hand, but there were quite a few differences that worried him more than he cared to admit. *Lightning* had always felt warm and welcoming, even though he'd never been her commanding officer. *Uncanny* made him feel as if he needed eyes in the back of his head, as if someone was sneaking up behind him with a knife. He hadn't felt so . . . *concerned* . . . since he'd served on a cloaked starship slipping into enemy territory, knowing that the slightest mistake, the faintest emission, would betray their presence.

And Captain Abraham had died, he thought.

Perhaps his passing *was* an accident. The IG had certainly thought so when they'd chalked it up to yet another manifestation of the ship's bad luck. If Captain Abraham had been as bad as Goodrich suggested, his death may *not* have been an accident. If someone on the crew had been willing to assassinate their commanding officer, there was no reason to assume they wouldn't want to kill a *second* CO. Unless he managed to turn the crew around.

He paused. His feet had led him to Officer Country. Bracing himself, he stepped through the hatch and strode down the corridor to his cabin, taking a long look at Commander Greenhill's hatch as he passed. It would have to be sealed, at least until Commander Greenhill was formally remanded to the shore patrol for investigation. William knew he was short on officers and men, but he was damned if he was keeping Greenhill around. The man was either staggeringly incompetent or insane.

Just like Admiral Morrison, he thought. *But at least there isn't an entire fleet at risk here.*

There should have been a marine standing guard outside his hatch, but the entire section seemed deserted. William hesitated, unsure if he truly wanted to proceed, then pressed his hand against the access panel.

There was a long pause, long enough to make him wonder if someone had sealed the compartment, before the hatch ground open. A faint whiff of . . . *something* touched his nostrils as he stepped inside, the lights coming on automatically. He started to look around. The cabin was surprisingly neat.

Tidy, he thought. He glanced into one of the lockers and saw a number of fancy suits and ties. A couple were standard uniforms while a third was an expertly tailored dress uniform; the remainder looked expensive enough to be beyond William's price range. He'd been advised to buy a formal dress outfit after he'd been knighted, but he was too frugal to buy something ridiculously expensive. *How much money was Captain Abraham spending?*

He scowled as he searched the remainder of the cabin. Captain Abraham hadn't left any notes behind, save for a private computer that refused to accept William's command codes. He'd have to hand it over to the IG in the hopes that one of their hackers could break through the encryption without wiping out the entire system. Then . . . he supposed it would depend on just what they found. A list of contacts for a smuggling ring, enough blackmail information to ensure that no one took a close look at *Uncanny* or . . . he didn't know.

Shaking his head, he sat down in front of his terminal and began to compose a message. He would need help, additional manpower as well as security, or there would be no hope of meeting the departure deadline. He would fail . . .

. . . and he knew all too well that he couldn't fail.

CHAPTER FOUR

"Katherine," Duke Falcone said as his daughter hovered at the door to his office. "Come on in."

Kat forced herself to walk forward. She'd always had mixed feelings about the office back when she'd been a child. She and her siblings had been banned from their father's workspace save for the times when they got in trouble and the household staff marched them to one of their parents. She'd spent far too long listening to her father's stern lectures, knowing deep inside that she wasn't receiving *all* of his attention. He'd always been a very busy man.

"They gave him *Unlucky*," she said curtly. "Did you *know* they'd give him *Unlucky*?"

"Officially, the decision was made by the promotions board," her father said, motioning for her to take a chair. "Unofficially . . . the decision was hard fought."

"I'm sure it was," Kat said.

She leaned back in her chair, wondering why her father had never changed the room's decor. With no window, the only source of illumination was a single light hanging above a massive desk. Three of the four walls were lined with bookshelves; the fourth displayed a large portrait of the family, painted when Kat had been five. Her mother had had to bribe her to sit still long enough to let the artist make the preliminary sketches, Kat recalled with a flicker of shame. It was almost as if they'd never heard of a *camera*.

"You are aware, of course, of the political realities," her father said. "And really . . . *Uncanny* is better than he had any right to expect."

Kat didn't miss the irony in his tone. *She'd* been given a heavy cruiser too—and far too many people had rightly believed that her powerful father had pulled strings to make sure she got the command. It had made it much harder for her to gain respect, at least until the war began. And now her former XO, one of the people who'd been slow to warm up to her, faced the same problem. And . . .

"Father," she said, "the ship is . . . *unlucky*."

"We need her in service," her father pointed out. "Give us two more years and we'll drown the Theocracy in starships, gunboats, and everything else we need to make war. But for now . . . we need every ship we can get on the front lines."

"Or *en route* to Jorlem," Kat said. She would have been astonished if her father *hadn't* known the content of her orders. He'd probably been informed long before she'd been told. "What happens if we're needed back here?"

Her father lifted his eyebrow. "If the enemy puts together an assault powerful enough to crack the planetary defenses," he said, "what difference will two heavy cruisers make?"

He looked up at her. "Katherine, the political situation is unstable," he reminded her. "Right now, it would probably be a bad idea to make a fuss."

"He's been set up to fail," Kat replied.

It was all she could do to keep from cursing. There was no shortage of people on Tyre who questioned the value of the Commonwealth itself, who worried about the effect it would have on the planetary economy . . . quite apart from the political structure. A handful of particularly talented immigrants could be assimilated quite easily—the aristocracy worked hard to ensure that their children married talented outsiders—but hundreds of millions? Some of those people even blamed the Commonwealth for the war. Would the Theocracy have attacked Tyre, they asked, if Tyre hadn't created the Commonwealth?

Even if we managed to maintain our independence when their expanding border overran us, she thought grimly, *we would still be destroyed eventually.*

She'd seen the brutality of the Theocrats personally, seen what they did to individual prisoners as well as entire populations. Tyre itself had seen just what the Theocrats were prepared to do to score a brief advantage during the opening hours of the war. Terrorist attacks, bombings and shootings . . . chaos programs loaded onto the planetary datanet, causing dozens of deaths . . . Now, with the war grinding on and no end in sight, some politicians were starting to wonder if there was a better way. Maybe, just maybe, they could come to terms with the Theocrats.

But it would be a mistake, she told herself, sternly. *You can't compromise with utter evil.*

Her father was speaking. She realized, embarrassed, that she hadn't heard a single word he'd said.

"I'm sorry," she said irked. "Can you repeat that?"

"Perhaps your ears should be cleaned," her father said. "I was saying that he might not fail."

"I wish I knew," Kat said.

She shook her head in irritation. There were plenty of *rumors* about *Uncanny*, but most of them were nothing more than tall tales from deep space. Spacers were notoriously superstitious, and Kat knew it was quite possible that a handful of incidents might have been blown out of all proportion by rumormongers. Yet she'd checked the records and one of *Uncanny's* commanding officers *had* been summarily discharged after his ship opened fire on a friendly vessel.

And since then, she's hung in lunar orbit, she thought. *She might be in worse shape than Sixth Fleet.*

The thought brought her no pleasure. Sixth Fleet had been on the border, the first target of the Theocracy when the invasion had been launched, yet the fleet's readiness had been depressingly low and her crews had been demoralized. Kat had honestly wondered if Admiral Morrison—she felt a flicker of bitter hatred at the thought—had been working for the Theocracy all along. His command had barely escaped the first engagement of the war . . .

. . . And she knew, all too well, that it *wouldn't* have escaped if she hadn't organized a number of junior officers to prepare for the inevitable attack.

"It would depend on the ship's condition," she said slowly. "And if she's spent the last six months doing nothing, with half her crew sent elsewhere . . ."

She met her father's eyes. If her former XO—her friend—had been set up to fail, there would be political repercussions. The doubters would have proof, they'd claim, that someone from off-world couldn't be trusted with a heavy cruiser and thus have an excuse to ram back integration still further. The consequences would be dire. She knew, better than many others, just how much resentment had been building up over the last two years. There simply wasn't *time* to handle the matter gently.

"We need to help him," she said.

"If he asks for our help," her father said. "And even if he does . . ."

He shook his head. "We *still* don't know who was behind Admiral Morrison."

Kat grimaced. Admiral Morrison had been incompetent, stunningly incompetent. She'd never met anyone so capable of sticking his head in the sand and ignoring reality when all the signs insisted that a full-scale war was imminent. The Theocracy had done the Commonwealth a vast favor, she was sure, by removing him from command, although by then

Cadiz couldn't be saved. Then she'd discovered him held prisoner in a Theocratic POW camp and brought him home . . .

. . . where he'd died in an accident. An accident that shouldn't have been allowed to happen.

She leaned forward. "You *still* don't have a clue?"

"Nothing," her father said. "And all we really know is that they were working for the Theocracy."

"Or expected to benefit from a Theocratic victory," Kat said. "Fools."

"It depends," her father pointed out. "We've got more industry in this system alone than the entire Theocracy. Someone could position themselves to serve the Theocracy and ensure their survival, if nothing else."

Kat shook her head. She'd seen the Theocracy at work. A handful might be ruthless pragmatics, like Admiral Junayd, but others were fanatics. They wouldn't want to leave someone, anyone, in control of Tyre and its industrial base, not when they had a holy duty to spread the faith to the entire galaxy. Besides, a person in control of Tyre could turn the planet against the occupiers once the attractions of serving as a quisling began to pall. The Theocracy was so determined to impose itself on everyone else that they hadn't even bothered to delay reshaping Cadiz—and the other occupied worlds—until they won the war. Some of the stories from behind enemy lines were truly horrific.

"They'd have to be out of their minds," she said curtly. "Father, do we have *no* clue?"

"None," her father said sharply. "Someone with vast political power, of course, but everyone with that sort of power *should* know the dangers of playing games with the Theocracy."

"True," Kat agreed. "But *someone* has clearly been playing games."

Her father cleared his throat, changing the subject.

"That may be," he said. "There is, however, another issue I wish to bring to your attention."

Kat took a guess. "We have interests in Jorlem that you don't want to see misplaced?"

"A little closer to home than that, I'm afraid," her father told her. "Have you heard from Candy?"

"I've been trying to *avoid* Candy," Kat said. Her older sister had been inviting her, time and time again, to boring parties with boring guests . . . and, given what had happened at the *last* party Kat had attended, she had no intention of going to another. "What does she want?"

Her father gave her a look that mixed understanding with irritation. "She's put one of her clients forward as your XO."

Kat needed a moment for his words to sink in. "*What?*"

"She's put one of her clients in as your XO," her father repeated. "And she didn't have any help from me."

Kat stared at him in disbelief. She'd known Candy was building up her own patronage network—establishing a set of friends and allies throughout the government—but she hadn't realized it reached so far. "She's . . . how?"

"I believe Candy spoke to two of her . . . contacts . . . in the Navy," her father said. "She was quite convincing. The Honorable Sirius Crenshaw will be serving as your XO."

"Oh," Kat said. She fought down the urge to scream in frustration. She'd already selected the officer she wanted to serve as her XO, someone with experience on *Lightning* and whose command style matched her own. To have someone else slotted in was irritating to say the least. "I've never met him."

"You've probably been at the same gatherings," her father mused. "There's a complete profile in the family processors, if you're interested."

Kat bit off a curse. She knew the Crenshaw Family—the aristocracy wasn't *that* big—but she couldn't recall meeting Sirius Crenshaw. If he was a Commander, even with such powerful connections, he had to be at least five or six years younger than she was. He would probably have grown to manhood while she'd been in Piker's Peak, embarking on her first cruise. He would have been too young to be interesting while she'd been a teenage girl. She'd spent most of those years trying to avoid aristocratic gatherings like the plague.

"And he got dumped on me," she snarled. It crossed her mind that William McElney must have felt the same way when *she'd* arrived on *Lightning*. But she'd been his commanding officer, not an XO who needed to be knocked into shape. "Why did you allow her to push his name forward?"

"I didn't have a say in the matter," her father said. "Candy has been building up her own association of friends."

"Oh," Kat said.

She shook her head in annoyance. Kat had often called her sister an airhead, but Candy was far from stupid. She *was* interested in dances and parties and countless other affairs that Kat loathed. *And* Candy had surrounded herself with a circle of people she considered interesting, including Justin Deveron, who bored Kat to tears. *But* if Candy was using her contacts to build up her own patronage network, possibly positioning herself for the dukedom after their father died, perhaps Kat should be taking more notice.

But I never wanted to build up a political network of my own, Kat thought. *I just wanted a starship.*

"I should refuse him," she said. It would cause Candy no end of problems—and a considerable amount of embarrassment—and Kat *could* refuse him. "I have no idea of his qualifications."

Her father gave her a sardonic look. "What were *your* qualifications when you took command?"

"I didn't *ask* for the command," Kat snapped. What *was* it about her father that made her act like a teenage girl? "Father, I don't *know* him!"

"Then I suggest you get to know him," Duke Falcone said. "Politics . . . Candy will never forgive you if you ruin this for her."

41

"She nearly torpedoed my career last year," Kat reminded him. "Father—"

"We need as much influence as possible," he snapped. "Kat, give him a fair shot."

Kat met his eyes. "This isn't you putting a bungee boss into the CEO's chair," she said sharply. Her father had a habit of testing his young subordinates by giving them power, just to see what they'd do with it. Some of them passed the unspoken test and remained in their new posts. Others were never trusted with power again. "This is someone in a position to make life-or-death decisions that could save or damn the entire *ship*. I won't be able to remove him from his post in the middle of a battle."

"I understand what is at stake," her father said. "Do you?"

"Politics," Kat snarled.

"Yes," her father said. "Politics."

He tapped his desk meaningfully. "The Commonwealth is under a great deal of internal strain," he said. "You know it as well as I do. The structure King Travis built was never intended to endure a long war. All our plans to gently integrate the other worlds into the whole have been tossed aside, smashed by the demands of war. The reactionaries are growing scared. What will it mean for the future?"

Kat opened her mouth, but her father held up his hand.

"If the reactionaries feel *more* threatened," he added, "they will start making demands in the Houses of Parliament. If they do, they'll bring a great many problems out into the open. Who knows what will happen then?"

He shook his head. "We need the war to end now," he warned. "But it isn't going to end in a hurry, is it?"

"No, Father," Kat said. Her mouth was suddenly very dry. She'd never seen her father look . . . *defeated* before. "We can't go on the offensive until we have a decisive superiority."

She closed her eyes for a long moment, recalling the last set of intelligence reports she'd read. A handful of additional warships had been sent behind enemy lines to disrupt the Theocracy's economy, but there weren't enough of them to make a real difference. Yet, she knew from Admiral Junayd's debriefings that the Theocracy was far more fragile than they'd dared hope. The enemy could possibly collapse under its own weight.

And if we're wrong, she told herself sharply, *we have years of fighting still to come.*

"Precisely," her father said. "And *that* is why you will be taking Mr. Crenshaw as your XO."

Kat sucked in her breath. "Father . . . how bad is the political storm likely to be?"

"I wish I knew," her father said.

He turned and rose, pacing over to look at the books lining the wall. "Tyre was founded on a powerful—and stable—economic base," he said. "Demand rose slowly, then sharply, after the Commonwealth was founded. We even embarked on a long-term investment project to uplift the economies and industries of the planets we invited to join. But we never anticipated a war on such a scale, not until we first encountered the Theocracy, and then it was far too late."

"I know that, Father," Kat said.

"Then it's time you came to grips with the consequences," he added. Duke Falcone turned to face his daughter, holding his hands behind his back. "And the ramifications. We made promises. Promises that have now, through no fault of our own, been broken and left in the dust. Our plans to absorb skilled newcomers, while creating jobs and such on their homeworlds, have fallen apart. I suspect it won't be long before there are more and more shortages on Tyre itself. How will our people cope when there are worse problems than bouts of random terrorism and sabotage? The price of just about everything is already rising. What will happen when they can no longer purchase something online and get it delivered within the hour?"

Kat snorted, rudely.

"I was at Piker's Peak," she said. The naval academy wasn't anything as bad as Marine Boot Camp, according to Patrick Davidson, but the experience had still been a shock. "I think I had worse problems than not being able to order a toy car online."

"People are going to be facing deprivation," her father said. "And that *will* have an effect on politics."

"Poor babies," Kat sneered. She knew enough about Captain McElney's homeworld, Hebrides, to feel no sympathy whatsoever. *He* knew the meaning of *deprivation*. He'd grown up with *very* limited food and drink even before the pirates had started raiding his homeworld. "Imagine how they will cope."

"It will be a shock," Kat's father agreed, seemingly unaware of her sarcasm. "And the results will be unpredictable."

He met her eyes. "Try to get on with your new XO, Kat," he added. Duke Falcone almost sounded as if he were pleading. "We can't afford another political catfight right now."

"I understand, father," Kat said. She took a breath. "But if he threatens my ship and crew, I won't hesitate to put him in the brig."

She rose, half expecting her father to call her back as she headed for the door. He very rarely let her have the last word. But he said nothing . . .

. . . and *that* frightened Kat more than she cared to admit.

CHAPTER FIVE

William had had second thoughts about holding the speech in the shuttlebay as soon as he'd seen the space—a number of components had been stripped out at some point and not replaced—but it was the largest single compartment in the entire ship. He'd put Goodrich and two of his subordinates to work, checking the bay's integrity, while he summoned the remainder of the crew to assemble at 1700. Goodrich, after being reminded that *he* would be in the shuttlebay too, had actually done a good job. William would have been pleased if the crew hadn't still been flocking into the shuttlebay at 1725.

And two crewmen had the nerve to argue that they should be excused, he thought, resisting the urge to roll his eyes. "Invitations" from a starship's commanding officer were orders, however phrased. *At least I managed to set them straight.*

He surveyed his new crew. They didn't look very professional or very military. Only an armchair admiral would expect his men to be snappy dressers at all times, but *Uncanny*'s crew looked as if they'd been on combat duty for the last two years, their uniforms filthy and ill fitting; their expressions a mixture of tiredness, bitterness, and resentfulness. William knew from his experiences that crewmembers could easily fall into the trap of blaming one's superiors for everything that went wrong. To them, he had to seem like yet another commanding officer punching his ticket while their ship decayed into uselessness. He didn't blame them for being wary.

"That's everyone, save for the watch crew," Janet said. "And those who haven't returned to the ship."

The steward sounded nervous, as if she expected him to blame her for the missing crew members. William felt a stab of irritation, which he ruthlessly suppressed. He'd already alerted the shore patrol when the missing crewmen had failed to answer the call summoning them back to the ship. They'd spend the next few days in the cells until the Admiralty decided what to do with them. Technically, they were guilty of deserting their posts, but a court-martial would be a public affair. Questions would be asked when the Opposition realized that the *Uncanny* had practically been abandoned when there was a war on.

"It doesn't matter," he told her. "The ones we have here are the ones we will have to work with."

He cleared his throat. A disciplined crew would have fallen silent at once, but the *Uncanny*'s crew took several minutes to stop muttering among themselves and start waiting for him to speak. William sighed and then gathered himself. He had to do more, it seemed, than merely introduce himself. Somehow, he had to convince them that things were going to be different in the future.

Otherwise they'll just remain in their rut, William grimly realized. He'd seen crews go bad before but never on such a big scale. An alert officer—a *strong* officer—could have stopped it, if he'd stood up and made it clear that it would not be tolerated. *And that would be the end of my command.*

"Thank you for coming," he said shortly. "For those of you who don't know me, my name is Captain Sir William McElney, and I am your new commanding officer."

He paused long enough to allow his words to sink in. It still felt odd to introduce himself as Sir William. A knighthood—a *new* knighthood—brought social cachet that an inherited title could not. They would know he'd actually done something to *earn* the title. By now, he would be surprised if some of the more enterprising members of the crew hadn't looked up his profile on the fleet's datanet. They wouldn't be able to read the classified portions, but even the unclassified sections were impressive. *He* certainly hadn't spent the last ten years manning a desk and sucking up to his superior officers.

Not that anyone would let me man a desk on Tyre, he thought wryly. *I'm too insignificant to get such a position.*

"An ordinary commanding officer would make a flowery speech at this point," William continued, when he judged the moment was ripe. "He'd tell you all what a fine bunch of fellows you are; he'd promise glory everlasting and fame eternal if you just follow him blindly. And he'd brag about his accomplishments . . ."

He paused, noting to his relief the handful of quickly hidden smiles.

"You're not going to get any of that from me. I am going to be blunt.

"This ship is a disgrace. I know, she has a bad reputation. I know, two of her commanding officers and a dozen other crewmen died in accidents. I know, she was intended as a testbed and only entered service after a dozen of her sisters. I know all that and I don't care. This ship is a disgrace! She's a threat to life and limb. Right now, she's more dangerous to her crew than she is to the enemy."

He made a visible show of getting his anger under control, silently gauging their reaction. A handful of crewmembers looked shame-faced, but others looked as if they were keeping their expressions under control. Did they think he was just another official blowhard? Or a crook? Or someone who would also be dead soon enough? He honestly didn't understand how *any* crew could have tolerated serving on such a dangerous ship. *Someone* should have contacted the IG or filed an anonymous complaint.

"This is how it's going to be," he told them.

"We have a planned departure date, one week from now," he added. He ignored the collective sharp intake of breath. A week sounded ridiculously optimistic. "By that time, I want this ship up and ready to go. I've already contacted the Admiralty and requested additional crew, both shipyard workers and starship crewmen, but *you* will be doing the majority of the work. So I have this to say to you."

He paused again. "I'm going to be working my ass off over the next week, doing everything in my power to move the work along," he warned. "I expect the same commitment from each and every one of you. This ship is going to be brought back into service as quickly as possible. If there are problems, I expect them to be brought to my attention; if you have proposed solutions, bring them to my attention too. I will not hesitate to make certain that those who work above and beyond the call of duty will be rewarded.

"Some of you are thinking that nothing is going to change. Some of you are thinking that I won't last long enough to make any real difference. Some of you are thinking that you just don't care, one way or the other. Your careers are already in the gutter and you don't have a hope in hell of getting out.

"Well, you're wrong.

"This is your last chance to be worthy of the uniforms you wear. If you forget the past and put in the effort, you'll have a clean slate and a shot at a rejuvenated career. Get rid of anything you might have that's against regulations and get to work. You have my word, as your commanding officer, that this is your second chance. Use it or leave the ship before the newcomers arrive. There will be no further warnings."

He allowed himself a moment to again survey the crowd. He knew that the crew would have a *lot* of possessions technically deemed "against regulations," from porn caches to illicit drugs. He might wink at the former, but the latter was incredibly dangerous. If there *were* any drug addicts on the *Uncanny*, they'd be wise to apply for transfer before the ship was searched from top to bottom. Tyre might have a relaxed attitude towards recreational drug use, but that attitude wasn't shared by the military. William wouldn't hesitate to throw the book at anyone caught with anything more dangerous than shipboard rotgut.

"I expect each and every one of you to remember that you are serving officers or crewmen in His Majesty's Navy," he concluded. "Like I said, I'll be working my ass off over the next week, and I expect the same commitment from you. I swear to you that any crewmember who puts in that level of commitment will have me backing him or her to the hilt. But anyone who decides to be lazy, anyone who decides to fuck around with the ship's safety . . . you'll find me your worst goddamned nightmare. And you can take that to the bank.

"I'll be in my Ready Room, putting together the intensive repair and maintenance schedule," he added. "If any of you wish to bring problems to my attention, you may visit in person or send me a message through the datanet. Until then, get some sleep. We start work in six hours, once I've finished putting the schedule together. Dismissed."

He waited, wondering just how many of the crew would remember that they were supposed to salute. A ragged wave of salutes washed through the compartment—he couldn't help thinking that his instructors would have broken down and cried—before the assembled crewmen turned and slowly filed out of the compartment. At least they weren't chatting to one another. He hoped they'd have the sense to get back to their bunks and catch some sleep before receiving their assignments. And get rid of anything that would get them in deep shit if they were caught.

It won't be that easy, he thought numbly. *An addict won't want to give up his stash, and he'll keep telling himself that he won't be caught.*

"Captain," Janet said. She held out a datapad. "I have a complete copy of the new roster for you."

William took it and ran his eyes down the list. Four of his senior officers were marked as absent, including the XO. They'd all be refused permission to return to the ship, even if the shore patrol didn't arrest them on sight. And nearly two hundred crewmen and junior officers were marked as missing. In theory, a heavy cruiser could be operated with a mere *tenth* of her seven-hundred-strong crew, but William wouldn't have cared to try it in practice. The *Uncanny*'s command data-net and automation couldn't be relied upon, at least not yet.

And if we took damage, we'd need to repair the ship, he reminded himself. *That won't be easy with a reduced crew.*

"I'll go through this in greater detail later," he said. "Put out a call for replacement crew and officers."

"Aye, sir," Janet said. She paused. "But will we get them?"

"We should," William said. *Uncanny was* due to depart in a week, after all. The personnel department wouldn't make too much of a fuss if he scooped up officers and crew, even if they *hadn't* requested to serve on *Uncanny*. Hell, he could take crewmen who were in line for other postings, citing the needs of war. "But leave the XO post to me."

"Aye, sir," Janet said.

William nodded, slowly. "Are there any other concerns?"

"The Chief Engineer needs you to sign off on an emergency request for spare parts and other supplies," Janet said before hesitating. "There's a problem with them."

"I see," William said. He looked at her. "Why am I not surprised?"

Janet flushed. "Can we discuss it . . . elsewhere?"

William made a face, but nodded and led the way back to his Ready Room. The corridors looked deserted; he hoped that meant that most of the crew were in their bunks. Yet, if Janet was fearful of being overheard . . . the sooner the command datanet was scrubbed, the better. If people had been poking into the network, they might have laid the groundwork for a systems failure at the worst possible time.

His Ready Room was a mess, much to his annoyance. Captain Abraham seemed to like clutter; he'd scattered books, paperwork, and pieces of art everywhere. And the paintings on the bulkheads were downright pornographic. William would have been embarrassed to have them hanging anywhere someone might see, if he'd been inclined to have them at all. He didn't even want to summon a team of crewmen to take them down and send them to the former captain's relatives. God alone knew what they'd think of the paintings.

He sat down on the chair and motioned for Janet to sit on the sofa. "All right," he said. "What's the problem?"

Janet met his eyes. He found it hard to read her expression. "Captain Abraham," she said finally, "was selling off military components."

William wasn't too surprised. "I see."

"He would take our regular shipments from the fleet base and have them distributed to his contacts," Janet said. "Some of the supplies would go to other warships, sir, but others were passed on to civilian ships. They were just never plugged into *Uncanny*."

"I see," William said again. He'd wondered how anyone had managed to sell components from *Uncanny*. Their buyers would wonder if they'd bring them bad luck. But if the components had never been used . . . they might just overlook their origin. "And no one ever thought to report it?"

"Captain Abraham had powerful friends," Janet said. She looked down at the deck. "And everyone who knew had an interest in keeping their mouths shut."

"Of course they did," William said. Civilian spacers would happily pay through the nose for military-grade supplies. They came with so many redundancies built in that they could last for years, particularly when installed on a civilian ship. "The whole scheme would have fallen apart eventually, would it not?"

He shook his head slowly as he spoke. Yes, it *would* have fallen apart . . . unless someone was quietly changing the records to cover their tracks. A clerk in the supply department would be more than enough to alter the files. There were so many components moving through the logistics network that any discrepancies might simply be overlooked. Captain Abraham's little scam might have gone undetected for years.

"The supply department will question our request for replacements," Janet pointed out. "And that will cause problems."

"Yes," William agreed. "It will."

"We're due to leave in a week," he reminded her. "Put in the requests anyway. I'll write a covering note. They'll have to give us the supplies if they want us heading out on time."

"They'll wonder what happened to the other supplies," Janet insisted.

"I'll leave that to the IG," William said. He rubbed his eyes in irritation. The last thing he needed, right now, was to spend the next month testifying in front of a board of inquiry, particularly when his ship was meant to depart. "Do you know who else was involved?"

"A couple of others," Janet said. She swallowed hard. "They haven't returned to the ship."

"Then pass the details on to me," William said. "The IG can handle them."

He had practically promised amnesty to any sinners on his crew, provided they put the past behind them. But the IG wouldn't be inclined to honor his promises, particularly after they discovered the scale of the deception. They'd demand heads on plates, he knew from bitter experience. And Captain Abraham, the big fish, was dead. They wouldn't have the satisfaction of having someone to put on trial if—when—the whole affair became a political football.

If they're among the deserters, he thought, *they can go straight into custody. But if they're not* . . .

He pushed the thought aside for later contemplation and leaned forward. "I have a different question for you," he said carefully. "What did you actually *do* for Captain Abraham?"

Janet flushed. "I was his . . . his *mistress*."

William groaned. Regulations flatly forbade liaisons between a commanding officer and anyone under his command, although there *was* some degree of flexibility worked into the system. It wasn't *unknown* for a captain to bring a mistress onto a ship, even though such an affair could cause a stink if something went wrong. However, Janet was a bona fide naval steward, directly under Captain Abraham's command. Their relationship was flatly illegal.

And she doesn't seem to be mourning him, he thought. *She may not have been given much choice in the matter.*

He leaned back. "How did that happen?"

Janet's flush deepened. "He talked me into it," she said. "And then . . ."

"You were committed," William said. He cocked his head. "Did you apply for a transfer?"

"He blocked the one attempt I made," Janet said. "Then I was trapped because—"

"Because you were on this ship," William finished. He met her eyes. "Rest assured, I don't want a mistress. I need a steward."

"I can do that," Janet said. She sounded relieved, her face slowly returning to normal. "Sir . . ."

"Good," William said. "I assume you know who's responsible for producing the rotgut?"

He turned to survey the compartment, not bothering to wait for her answer. Of *course* she'd know. A captain's steward should know everything she needed to know to do her job.

"Tell the producer that we're operating on the one-pint rule from now on," he added. "All the usual rules apply. I don't want a single drunken crewman on my ship while we're on active service. And if they don't feel inclined to listen to me, they're going right out the airlock."

Janet coughed. "Sir?"

"Emergency regulations," William reminded her. He wasn't *entirely* bluffing. "I can have someone put to death for sabotaging the ship and crew if necessary."

"Yes, sir," Janet said. "I'll see to it."

CHAPTER SIX

"Captain," Lieutenant Bobby Wheeler said, "Commander Sirius Crenshaw has boarded the ship."

"Thank you, Lieutenant," Kat said. "Please have him shown to my Ready Room."

She sighed as she leaned back from her desk. Two days had passed since she'd returned to *Lightning*, two days spent working her way through the files and consulting with her senior officers. Commander Crenshaw was not going to have an easy time of it. Everyone had known, even if they hadn't been *supposed* to know, that Commander Christopher John Roach, the former tactical officer, had been earmarked for the post. Having an outsider brought in didn't sit well with his friends. Kat had authorized Roach's transfer to *Uncanny* almost as soon as the request came in, trying to save herself from some trouble in the future.

It's still a problem, she thought. *Crenshaw hasn't seen any real combat service.*

The irony still didn't amuse her. She had no doubt that William had felt the same way too, when he'd discovered that his commanding officer had been promoted over his head and over the heads of countless others with more experience. He'd initially found the experience of taking orders from someone thirty-one years younger than him humiliating. Eventually he'd grown to accept her and work with her . . . she could do the same with Crenshaw. If nothing else, she reminded herself, she was his superior officer. She could beach him if necessary.

She pushed the thought aside as the hatch chimed, alerting her to Crenshaw's arrival. Keying the switch under her desk, she straightened up and watched the hatch opening, revealing a marine and a starkly handsome young man. Sirius Crenshaw looked to be in his late thirties, with bright blue eyes, blond hair, a firm jaw, and a strongly muscular body. He'd actually had his uniform tailored to show off his form, she noted; it wasn't against regulations, even though it was definitely frowned upon. He was handsome . . . and yet, there was something in the way he moved that bothered her. He wasn't quite used to his own body.

He's had his body enhanced, Kat thought as she rose to her feet. No one was *that* muscular without cheating. *And quite recently too.*

"Commander," she said. "Welcome aboard."

Commander Crenshaw saluted smartly. "Thank you, Captain," he said. He had a *very* aristocratic voice, suggesting that his experience outside Tyre and Piker's Peak had been limited. He'd certainly never learned to dampen the accent. "It is my pleasure to serve."

Kat nodded, dismissing the marine before motioning for Crenshaw to take a seat. "I'm glad to hear it," she said, once the hatch hissed closed. "I . . ."

"I must say that it is a great honor to serve with the remarkable Lady Falcone," Crenshaw added. "I was a great fan of the way you put Lord Smelly in his place."

Kat felt her mouth drop open in shock. Interrupting the captain? And Lord *Smelly*? Who the hell was he? Who the hell did Crenshaw think he was? She'd looked up his family and, while they were far from unimportant, they were hardly her social equals. Did Crenshaw honestly believe that his social rank gave him the right to talk to her as if he was her superior?

"You really taught him a lesson," Crenshaw continued. "I . . ."

"Shut up," Kat said sharply.

Crenshaw closed his mouth, his eyes going wide with astonishment. Whatever he'd expected, it wasn't *that*. Kat wondered, briefly, if she could just dismiss him right now and dispatch him back to the planet. Her superiors wouldn't be amused and her father would go ballistic, but she had a feeling the king would support her. Yet, the last thing the Commonwealth needed was another political crisis. She'd just have to do the best she could.

"You are here to serve as my XO," she said, keeping her voice level with an effort. If nothing else, he should know not to suck up to her. "I don't care about anything else, not when we're hastily prepping for deployment. If you can't do that, you can leave right now and I can put in a request for another XO."

Crenshaw stared at her. "My Lady . . ."

"That's *Captain*," Kat snapped. "This isn't the Royal Palace, Mr. XO."

She went on before he could say a word. "I understand that you served as tactical officer on HMS *Dangerous*," she continued. "Did you see action?"

"No, Captain," Crenshaw said. "We were posted to the border, not to the war front. The only real excitement we saw was a pirate ship hunting our convoy. We blew her out of space."

"I see," Kat said. "After that . . . you applied for a posting as XO?"

"Yes, Captain," Crenshaw said. "My application was fast-tracked. I received my promotion two weeks after my return to Tyre, but I wasn't posted to a ship."

Of course not, Kat thought. *Any captain worth his salt would pull out all the stops to keep an inexperienced XO from taking a post on his crew.*

"I finally had to ask my family for help," Crenshaw admitted, as casually as if he were ordering dinner. "They called in a few favors, and here I am."

"Yes, you are," Kat said. The nasty part of her mind wondered if she could arrange an accident. Or perhaps she should just send Crenshaw back to his family in the certain knowledge that she wouldn't receive reprimands until she returned from the Jorlem Sector. "I have very high expectations of my crew, Commander. I will expect no less from you."

"Of course, Captain," Crenshaw said.

"You'll formally take up the post tomorrow morning," Kat explained. "Before then, I want you—"

"Not now?" Crenshaw asked. "Captain, I . . ."

"Should not be interrupting your commanding officer! You've never served on an *Uncanny*-class cruiser before, so I *suggest*"—she hardened her voice to make it clear that it was actually an *order*— "that you spend the next few hours familiarizing yourself with the ship and crew. You'll be formally invested as XO tomorrow morning, after shift change."

Crenshaw looked irritated, but he had the wit to keep his mouth shut.

Kat gathered herself. "Make good use of the time," she ordered. "Do you have any other issues that should be brought to my attention?"

She cursed her father under her breath. It was clear that Crenshaw and she were never going to be friends. Crenshaw had been lucky— damn lucky—that *Dangerous* hadn't been posted to the war front. And so was everyone else. A failure *there* might have had disastrous consequences. Admiral Christian would not have been amused.

"I brought two servants with me," Crenshaw said. "Should I arrange for them to be assigned cabins?"

"No," Kat said. Gods! How stupid *was* this man? "You'll put them back on the shuttle and send them home."

Crenshaw gaped. "I have a right to servants . . ."

"Not on a military ship," Kat said. *She* had a steward. Everyone else had to handle their own affairs. "Did you have servants on *Dangerous*?"

"Well, *no*," Crenshaw said. "But I'm a commander now . . ."

"You still don't get servants," Kat said. Had someone set Crenshaw up for a fall? Or was he just the idiot he sounded like? "Send them back to Tyre, Commander. Then start exploring the ship. I want you aware of every last nook and cranny before we depart."

Crenshaw rose. "Yes, Captain," he said.

He saluted and then turned, striding out of the compartment as if he were on a parade ground. Kat watched him go, thinking dark thoughts about her sister. If Kat hadn't worked so hard to get Sir William a promotion . . . was someone taking an elaborate revenge? Or was she merely due for some bad luck? Perhaps the *Uncanny* curse was reaching out to strike her.

On impulse, she keyed the command datanet, ordering it to keep track of Commander Crenshaw's movements, then went back to her work. Zack Lynn, her chief engineer, had requested a multitude of spare parts from the logistics officers, but they were insisting on having the request countersigned before they produced the required items. Kat read the request, signed it, and sent it off, hoping that would be enough. *Lightning* was an important ship, but there was no hiding the fact that she wasn't on her way to the war front.

And it puts us behind ships that are going to the war, she thought, darkly.

She shook her head in annoyance. Independent command was the best post in the navy—and she was technically a squadron commander too—but it brought its own problems. *She* was expecting trouble—the reports from the Jorlem Sector had made it very clear that piracy was definitely on the rise—yet the logistics officers thought otherwise. It wasn't as if they could rely on drawing spare parts from forward bases, if necessary. There were *no* forward bases.

Messages blinked up in front of her, and she skimmed through them, wishing the ship was already underway. There was just too much crap she had to deal with, crap she would normally pass on to her XO. But she didn't know just how far Crenshaw could be trusted, particularly because he was not accustomed to the ship. The last message from William had been brief but had warned her that *Uncanny* might not be ready to depart on time. Kat had no idea how the Admiralty would react, yet she knew better than to slow her own preparations. The First Space Lord might prefer having two ships in the sector, but having one patrolling the spaceways was better than none.

Junk, she thought, crossly.

She keyed her terminal, hoping, praying, that she would find Crenshaw following orders and exploring the ship. Instead, according to the datanet, he was sitting in his cabin. She stared down at the screen for a long moment, feeling her temper rise. Unpacking his gear—how much crap had he brought?—shouldn't take long. Even if he'd brought everything he could, he certainly shouldn't be unpacking. What was he doing?

"Idiot," she said out loud.

She tapped the console. "Commander Crenshaw, report to my Ready Room," she ordered. "Now."

And if he doesn't shape up, she told herself as she waited, *I'll send him back home and to hell with the consequences.*

The hatch opened five minutes later. Kat was grimly amused. If nothing else, Crenshaw had made his way from his cabin to her Ready Room with commendable speed. He looked surprised to have been summoned back so quickly. Then it struck her, suddenly, that he didn't understand that he'd been doing the wrong thing. Clearly, no one had taken him aside and explained that this sort of behavior was unacceptable.

But I got away with a lot, Kat thought as she pointed him to a chair. On impulse, she called up his file and skimmed the reports. They were beautifully vague, but reading between the lines she saw trouble. *He probably got away with everything too.*

She kept her eyes on the terminal, forcing him to wait. It was a petty power play, something her father had taught her would only be used by a person who was unsure of herself, but she had to admit that it felt surprisingly satisfying. Perhaps Crenshaw would open his mouth, giving her an excuse to tear a strip off him . . . or perhaps he'd have the sense to keep his mouth shut and wait, *knowing* that she was putting him in his place. She was actually quite surprised, when she came to the end of the file, that he hadn't said a word. Perhaps she'd gotten through to him after all.

"I have a question," she said, "and I want a clear answer. Why were you in your cabin?"

Crenshaw looked surprised. "I was taking a rest . . ."

"I gave you specific orders to explore the ship," Kat said. "I don't recall saying that you could have a rest first."

She met his eyes. "If you have problems," she added, "you should tell me."

"I needed a rest," Crenshaw said. He didn't *look* tired. "Captain . . ."

Kat glanced back at the file. The word *lazy* didn't appear anywhere, but there was a strong suggestion that Crenshaw's work had been less than satisfactory. It didn't *look* as though there was a strong reason to bust him out of the Navy—a man with Crenshaw's connections could only be busted out if there was an ironclad case against him—yet his former CO had made no attempt to *keep* him. That, Kat suspected, was clear proof that the CO hadn't *wanted* to keep him. *She'd* certainly tried to keep good officers under her command.

"Let me tell you something bluntly," she said in a tone that *dared* Crenshaw to interrupt her. "I don't give a damn how you got this post. I don't care about your career. I don't *care* what sort of relationship you have with my sister. And I don't care how many other relatives you have that are trying to get you a post on a starship heading *far* away from Tyre. I don't give a fucking damn!"

Crenshaw flinched. "Captain . . ."

"Shut up," Kat snapped. "I don't care."

She glared at him until he leaned back in his chair. "All I care about is that you do your fucking job," she hissed. "If you can't handle it, leave now and I will happily tell our superiors that you are not qualified for anything more challenging than micromanaging a sand farm on a desert planet. If you can't handle it, and you keep *trying* to handle it, I'll kick you off the ship in disgrace. I don't *care* what happens afterwards."

"Captain . . ."

"I said *shut up*," Kat said. "This is *not* some fancy party in a fancy mansion where the only real concern is worrying about running out of fancy umbrellas for fancy drinks. This is a warship heading into a difficult situation, a sector that has good reason to dislike the Commonwealth and has the Theocracy stirring the pot. I do not have the *time* to mentor you into becoming the best XO in the Navy. I am *certainly* not going to cover for you if you're not willing to learn from your mistakes and become a better officer!"

She forced herself to calm down. "Choose now," she said. "Leave or stay."

Crenshaw flinched. Kat could practically see his mind whirring away behind his handsome, characterless face. If he left willingly, there would be little hope of another posting, even if Kat *didn't* write a scathing report on his failings. His career would go straight into the dustbin, no matter how many strings were pulled. If Kat had to kick him off the ship, it would be a great deal worse. A public court-martial for gross incompetence, dereliction of duty, disobedience to one's superiors, and whatever other charges could be thrown at him would be impossible to rig, at least not quietly. Public outrage would make sure of it.

"I'll stay," Crenshaw said.

"Then do your fucking job," Kat snapped.

She leaned back in her chair. "And one other thing? I outrank you, socially as well as professionally. I will not tolerate you trying to use your social position to push my officers and crew around. If you do, I will relieve you of duty and send you packing. If necessary, I'll stick you in the brig until we return home. Do you understand me?"

Crenshaw swallowed. "Yes."

"Yes *what*?"

"Yes, *Captain*," Crenshaw said.

Kat sighed. She'd never had *that* much respect for military protocol—she'd grown up in a mansion with far too many people bowing and scraping to her—but she couldn't overlook it if her XO didn't show her proper respect on the bridge. Or anywhere, really. Her officers would start to wonder what was going on . . .

"Good," she said tartly. "Now carry out your orders and familiarize yourself with the ship."

Crenshaw rose and saluted. "Yes, Captain."

Kat watched him leave, then glared down at her terminal. Crenshaw's file was still open, mocking her. If his previous commanding officer had filed an *honest* report, Crenshaw's career would have come to a shuddering, terminal halt long before Kat ever realized he existed. But the act probably would have cost the report writer his or her career too. Crenshaw was hardly the type to let bygones be bygones . . .

And if he didn't want to work, she thought, *why did he even join the Navy?*

She cursed under her breath. *She'd* wanted to work; she'd wanted to prove, if only to herself, that she was more than just her family name. But Crenshaw . . . he didn't seem to want to do *anything*. Had his family bullied him into joining the Navy? Or had he been more interested in fancy uniforms than doing his job? Hell, for all she knew, he'd never realized that he'd actually be expected to go to war.

Stupid thought, she told herself, as she rose. *Anyone could see that war was coming.*

But Admiral Morrison didn't, her own thoughts reminded her.

She pushed the thought aside as she headed for the hatch. There was no time to worry about her new XO, not when her ship was preparing for departure. She'd just have to keep a sharp eye on him and hope for the best.

And at least he's the XO, she told herself grimly. *I was the captain.*

CHAPTER SEVEN

"He's not really a bad captain," Crewman Roth Henderson said as he tossed a pair of gambling chips into the pot. "Is he?"

Senior Chief Joel Gibson kept his expression blank as he studied his cards. Poker games made a convenient excuse for covert meetings, all the more so as hundreds of dockyard workers and new crewmen swarmed through the ship. Whatever senior authority might say—they'd be shocked, *shocked*, to hear that gambling took place onboard the ship—it was *very* common for gaming and gambling clubs to exist at all levels. And wise officers turned a blind eye, as long as the games didn't get out of hand.

And Joel made *certain* they didn't get out of hand.

He had to admit, to his private frustration, that Henderson had a point. Captain Sir William McElney *was* a good captain. A lesser man—an aristocrat—might have exploded with rage after discovering his ship's condition, demanding miracles at one moment and threatening punishment the next. Or, if he had been a complete scumbag like Captain Abraham, he might have found a way to exploit his ship's condition if he didn't spend his days scheming to get transferred some-where, anywhere, else. But Sir William was definitely a good captain.

Too good, Joel thought as he tossed a chip of his own into the pot. *He already has enough evidence to know there's something very odd about the ship.*

"It doesn't matter," Crewwoman Jane Burnside said. "We're com-mitted anyway, aren't we?"

"Yeah," Henderson said. "But . . ."

"This isn't the time for backing out," Joel said. "We're committed, remember?"

Joel cursed to himself. Sir William, just by being a good com-manding officer, had undermined all of his careful planning. Crewmen who wouldn't think twice about mutinying against Captain Abraham and Commander Greenhill would hesitate to mutiny against Captain McElney, who clearly actually *cared* about his crew. And while he *had* banned anything illicit, he'd warned the crew in time to make sure that their illicit substances were lost long before the ship was searched from top to bottom—a practical approach, Joel had to admit, that had won Captain McElney a great many admirers.

And we might even have called off our plans, he thought, *if we weren't committed.*

"I'm out," Crewwoman Sofia Argali said. "Or should I be offering something more . . ."

"Definitely not," Joel said. Strip poker was fun, but now was not the time. "Take a seat and wait."

"Aw, come on," Henderson said. "I'd like . . ."

"Be quiet," Joel ordered. "And if you want to raise the stakes, go right ahead."

He glared at Henderson until the younger man lowered his eyes. Joel felt relieved to know that he was still feared. He didn't dare use force. Not now. Captain Abraham wouldn't have paid any attention to reports of violence on the lower decks, but Sir William would probably turn the ship upside down to identify the culprit. Giving a crewman a clout instead of writing a disciplinary report was technically illegal, and he couldn't afford to have anyone looking too closely at him. They'd wonder why his department was more organized than the rest of the ship.

But we had to keep everyone alive, he thought. *Captain Abraham would have killed us.*

Joel had no illusions about himself—he *knew* he wasn't a good person—but threatening the ship's life support was just plain stupid. Even *pirates* knew better than to leave the air scrubbers unchanged for months. The crew was lucky that Captain Abraham had died before he could sell off the *next* batch of air filters. Joel had gone to some trouble to create the *impression* of a failing life support system, but a *real* failure would have been disastrous. *Everyone* on the ship would have died.

Except Greenhill, Joel told himself. *That lazy bastard would have survived.*

"I don't know if we *can* go ahead," Crewman Thomas Rochester said. He took a pair of cards from the pile, his expression darkening as he studied them. "We've got a *smart* captain now."

Joel met his eyes. "And you'd prefer to wait and see what the IG uncovers?"

"Well, no," Thomas said, "but we're not dealing with an idiot."

"No, we're not," Joel conceded, "but this *does* work in our favor."

He took another card himself and smirked. Hopefully, they'd believe he was well on his way to winning the entire pot.

"We're due to leave in four days," he reminded them. "And we're going to be heading to the Jorlem Sector. There won't be a better opportunity to take the ship and flee."

"There'll be another cruiser right next to us," Sofia pointed out. "A cruiser commanded by a *genuine* war hero."

"A single cruiser," Joel countered. But she was right. The plan would have to be modified to deal with *Lightning*. "You want to bet that we can't blast *Lightning* from point-blank range if necessary?"

Henderson looked faintly sick. "Is that necessary?"

"They can only kill us once," Joel said reassuringly. "Why, they will have problems deciding just which one of our many crimes will be put on the death warrants."

"That isn't funny," Henderson protested.

"No, it isn't," Joel agreed. Henderson would have to be watched carefully. "There shouldn't be any need for it. I think we'll be splitting up after we reach Jorlem. We take the ship and vanish."

He smiled, as reassuringly as he could. "Look on the bright side," he added, "we won't be having to flee the entire Navy."

"We could always stage an accident," Sofia added. "No one will be surprised if *this* ship suffers a catastrophic failure in hyperspace."

"True," Joel said. The truth *would* come out, sooner or later. But by the time it did, it would be too late. "Let them list us as being lost to 'causes unknown.'"

Henderson looked relieved but kept asking questions. "What if the IG insists on us remaining here?"

"Then we slip out of the system before it's too late," Joel said patiently.

"They do keep demanding to know when we're going to leave," Sofia said. "I don't think they'll hold us here unless they realize the truth."

"And in that case, we're screwed anyway," Joel said. He considered his cards and decided that victory was probably unlikely, but put another couple of chips in the pot in the hopes that they'd think he wasn't bluffing. "All we can do is wait and bide our time."

"And see what the newcomers are like," Thomas said.

"Do *not* try to approach them," Joel warned. "Some of them may well be spies."

"They certainly won't have served on *this* ship," Henderson agreed.

Joel nodded. *Uncanny*'s crew had learned, all too well, that there was no point in reporting anything to higher authority. Captain Abraham and Commander Greenhill had set the tone for the rest of the officers, save for a couple who had been skillfully manipulated and corrupted. It was just like complaining to the teachers—tattling to the teachers—at a poorly run school. No matter what happened, he had been sure that his shipmates wouldn't go telling tales. It would only make things worse.

The newcomers, though, without that conditioning, would feel free to take their complaints to an officer who actually *listened*.

"We can deal with new crew after we take the ship," Joel said firmly. "For the moment . . . we keep an eye on them and see if we can pick out spies."

"If that's possible," Henderson said doubtfully.

Joel snorted. He'd had Julia Transom download copies of their personnel files, but he rather doubted ONI would write "spy" into a crewman's dossier. *That* would be foolish, particularly if they suspected that someone could gain access to the complete file. He'd skimmed a dozen of them himself, but there hadn't been any obvious red flags. ONI would have devised the files to pass muster, he suspected. Doing the detective work to disprove the files, perhaps by contacting eyewitnesses, would almost certainly have tipped them off.

"It doesn't matter," Joel said finally. "Once we take the ship, we can deal with the rest of the crew."

"Of course, sir," Sofia said.

Joel studied her with some interest. Sofia was strikingly beautiful, but she'd been transferred to *Uncanny* after turning down a senior officer's advances. She'd been easy to recruit once he'd convinced her of his sincerity. She was far from the only crewmember with a grudge against society. It wouldn't be hard to turn the survivors into a crew that would make any pirate proud.

But I have a far grander plan than simple piracy, he told himself, firmly.

He glanced at Henderson and Thomas, then raised the stakes again. Henderson looked back at him and then folded, tossing his cards back into the stack. Thomas frowned, clearly calculating the odds, then held up his cards. Joel allowed himself a moment of relief as his cards trumped Thomas's—it could easily have gone the other way—and then started to collect the pot. It wasn't as if the chips were worth much—he'd placed strict limits on just how much money could be gambled at any one time—but it was worth it.

"Good game," he said cheerfully. "Another?"

"I have to be on duty in twenty minutes," Sofia said, rising. "And I have to wear a proper uniform again."

"It could be worse," Joel assured her. "I'll see you tomorrow."

He watched her go, feeling a flicker of irritation. Sir William had insisted that everyone wear a proper uniform, and it was paying off. *Uncanny's* crewmembers were thinking and acting like ranked naval officers rather than a mass of discontented humanity stuck in a flying death trap. Sofia had good reason to be suspicious of officers, of course, but would she start making exceptions? Or would she remain loyal to him?

"We'd better all get back to work," Thomas said. "Sir?"

"Of course," Joel said. He waved a hand grandly. "Dismissed."

He collected the cards while brooding. His inner circle was committed—after they'd murdered Captain Abraham, the death sentence was guaranteed if caught—but there were far too many others who might think they could switch sides safely. They might be right too. The Navy wouldn't think too highly of anyone who plotted a mutiny, but any halfway competent defense lawyer would be able to point to the ship's condition and use it as a justification for almost anything. Some of his mutineers might find a soft landing on the other side.

But we have a golden opportunity, he told himself. *If we keep our nerve . . .*

Uncanny had sat in her orbital slot for over six months, her condition slowly decaying into uselessness. It had been the one weakness in his scheming, no matter what he did. He could have taken the ship and powered up the gateway generator, but it would have attracted attention from Home Fleet. Slipping into hyperspace and making their escape wouldn't be so easy if half of the Navy was in hot pursuit. He'd hoped for an enemy attack, which would have given him an excuse to take the ship out of orbit, but even *that* would have been chancy. Launching a mutiny during the chaos of a battle would have been madness.

And now, the opportunity had just landed in his lap.

Joel let out a breath as he headed for the hatch. His allies might be concerned, but it was no time to lose their nerve. They had no reason to suspect trouble, no reason to believe that they'd been detected ahead of time.

We can do this, he told himself. *And we can still win.*

"I thought you might want to see this, Captain," Commander Christopher John Roach said as he pointed to the dismantled air filter. "As you can see, the component hasn't actually decayed."

William frowned, silently grateful that Commander Roach's promotion to *Lightning*'s XO hadn't gone through. Roach was a steady man with combat experience and family connections that came in handy. He'd been supervising the repair effort for the past two days. Kat Falcone had good reason to be annoyed at losing him.

"That's odd," he said slowly. "How do you account for the smell?"

"There's some clogging in other filters," Roach told him. "But I would actually say the life support system is in good shape."

"How lucky for the crew," William said sarcastically. "Did you find anything suspicious during the sweep?"

"A lot of insect and rodent traces, sir," Roach said. "I've got the crew laying down traps now, but I'd prefer to depressurize the hull and let them all die."

"I don't think we have time," William said. He met his XO's eyes. "The Admiralty has signed off on all of our requests, Mr. XO, but they want us and *Lightning* out of here yesterday."

"They'll get their wish," Roach said. "The decay is nowhere near as bad as I was left to assume."

William nodded in grim agreement. He'd been anticipating having to explain to his superiors that *Uncanny* was in no fit state for anything other than a long stay in the shipyard, but he and his crew were actually on track to leave as planned. Yet, something was still odd. His first impression of the vessel had been of impending disaster—and the crew was still jumpy—but *Uncanny* could have been taken back into hyperspace at any moment. The more he looked at the situation, the more it puzzled him. Perhaps Captain Abraham had been a better officer than he'd assumed?

"Make sure that all the filters are replaced anyway," William ordered. The smell might have been caused by decaying animal filth, rather than too many clogged filters. "Do we have an update on the computer network?"

"They refused to sign off on a new computer core, sir," Roach said, falling into step behind him as they headed for the bridge. "But we do have a team of experts coming out tomorrow to inspect the system and make recommendations. Someone wasn't updating the programming, it seems. *Lightning* is on V.7 while *Uncanny* is still stuck on V.2."

"That could cause problems if we have to run a united datanet," William said.

"It *did* cause problems," Roach said. "The engineer believes that a mismatch in computer updates might have caused the friendly fire incident. It struck me as a little unlikely, but I don't think anyone's actually tried to put the datanet together on the fly either."

"We did have some issues when we were using the older ships for Operation Knife," William recalled. "But still . . ."

He shook his head. "Could it have been deliberate sabotage?"

"The IG went through everything after the whole incident," Roach said. "They didn't find a trace of anything remotely suspicious."

William realized the incident *could* have been an accident. God knew none of *Uncanny's* commanding officers had worried—much—about keeping their ship current. Half of the updates had never taken place, and half of the ones that *had* been installed had never been properly logged. His crew had wound up logging everything as they went along, knowing that trying to get everything logged in less than a week was asking for trouble. Yet, what choice did they have?

"We'll run a test link with *Lightning* before we depart," he said as they stepped onto the bridge. "We'll make sure to deactivate the weapons first."

"Just in case," Roach agreed.

William was relieved to see that the bridge was looking better. His crew had replaced the missing consoles, allowing him to start his officers working on simulations, drilling endlessly in anticipation of trouble. He'd visited the Jorlem Sector several times while working for ONI, but it was evident that conditions in the sector had clearly deteriorated. He knew all too well that the *Uncanny* was likely to spend most of her time escorting convoys and stalking pirates.

"I'll have to visit *Lightning* at some point in the next couple of days," he added after a moment. "Do you have any other concerns you want to raise?"

"Only that the crew doesn't trust us yet," Roach said. "And really, who can blame them?"

William nodded. "Then we keep making a good impression," he said. "I want you to make sure that *everyone's* noses are pushed to the grindstone. No one is to get away with not doing their job."

Even leaving the ship for a brief conference would be awkward, but William didn't see any other choice. Unless he wanted to invite Kat Falcone to dinner on *Uncanny . , .* he considered it for a long moment, then dismissed the thought. There were too many other matters that needed to be handled before he could hold a formal dinner. Hell, he'd been sleeping in his Ready Room because his cabin was crammed with junk.

"I understand, sir," Roach said. "How many of the newcomers are we going to keep?"

William shrugged. He'd watched a movie, once, where the hero had practically kidnapped dockyard workers to keep his ship running. But trying that in real life would be a good way to get put in front of a court-martial.

"As many as we can," he said. "But I don't know how many of them will be willing to stay."

CHAPTER EIGHT

"Captain Sir William McElney," Kat said. She gave him a genuine smile of welcome as he was shown into her Ready Room. "Welcome back."

"Thank you, Captain," William said. "It's good to *be* back."

Kat motioned for him to take a chair, then sat down on the sofa. She hadn't *seen* William for a month, but she wasn't too surprised by the change in him. He was a captain now, master of his own ship . . . she might still be his superior, yet he enjoyed an independence he had never known before. There was a new energy around him that made her smile, even though she had an apology to make. Apparently *Uncanny* wasn't wearing him down.

"Commander Crenshaw is nowhere near your equal," she said as she poured them both a cup of coffee. "He has to be pushed into doing his job."

"It's bad form to badmouth one's XO to other captains," William said mischievously. He winked. "But I saw his record. I don't understand how he got the job."

"My sister decided it was better to promote him and his career than someone who had actual experience," Kat said irked. "And I had no say in the matter."

"You probably need to push back harder," William said. "Didn't your sister get you into trouble last time too?"

"Not quite," Kat said. Her own big mouth had actually gotten her into trouble when she'd told one of society's darlings *precisely* what she thought of him, though she didn't regret it. Commanding Operation Knife had been an unexpected reward and, best of all, her enemies probably considered it punishment. "Plus, pushing back would require me to spend more time politicking at home."

She grinned. "Can we swap XOs?"

"Not on your life," William said. "I need a strong right arm on *Uncanny*."

Kat was unsurprised. "Just how bad *is* she?"

"Not as bad as the reports and my first impressions made her sound," William said. "Plenty of cosmetic damage, of course, but the remainder of the ship is in remarkably good condition. A testament to her designers, I suppose."

He shook his head. "Crew morale is still in the pits, at least among those who were stuck on the ship before I arrived," he added. "There's nothing a successful cruise won't fix."

"True," Kat agreed. "Did the IG come to any conclusions?"

"I saw their preliminary report this morning," William said. "Commander Greenhill sang like a bird. Captain Abraham was apparently the center of a criminal ring. He used a great deal of influence to ensure that his ship was effectively forgotten while he sold pieces of her off to the highest bidders. Heads are rolling, it seems. *Uncanny* wasn't heading for the scrapheap when she was recalled back to Tyre."

Kat made a face. The idea that someone could drop the ball so badly . . . it wasn't really a surprise. *Uncanny* hadn't been causing trouble, not for the last six months. She'd merely been floating in lunar orbit, out of sight and out of mind, while the IG had been more concerned about news from the war front. They'd probably been glad to forget the unlucky starship.

"I owe you an apology," she said, sitting down to face him. "My pushing for you to be given a command might just have sent you to *Uncanny*."

"It's not a problem," William assured her. "I spent enough time on *Lightning*"—he waved a hand at the nearest bulkhead—"to know *precisely* how a heavy cruiser should function. It's a remarkable challenge. I'm never bored."

"There's something to be said for boredom," Kat said dryly. She wouldn't have cared to sleep on a starship where something could go wrong at any moment. Life support failures were the source of countless horror stories, all of which had been drilled into her head at Piker's Peak. "Are you taking precautions to ensure your own safety?"

"Enough, I hope," William said. He looked hesitant for a long moment. "But I really *don't* want to suggest to the crew that I don't trust them."

Kat scowled. The idea that a crew couldn't be trusted . . . it was terrifying. She'd never served on a ship where she'd doubted the crew's loyalty. Yet, if the dregs of the service had been steadily assigned to *Uncanny*, the crew's competence, let alone their loyalty, had to be in doubt. A single bad apple could do a great deal of damage, but a whole *bunch* of bad apples could corrupt the good ones too.

"I suppose," she said doubtfully. "Did you get a response to your request for marines?"

"Not a good one," he said. "It seems I will be playing host to a company of planetary militia."

"Madness," Kat said. "They're not *trained* to serve as starship marines."

"Apparently, they've been run through a shorter version of boot camp," William assured her. "But you're right, they don't have the same training."

Kat made a mental note to find out if she could detach a platoon of marines from *Lightning* and assign them to *Uncanny*. She had nothing against the planetary militias; some of them were *very* well trained for operations on the ground, but they weren't trained for service in deep space. And yet she knew, all too well, that marines were thin on the ground. The demands of the war front came first, always.

We're supposed to be raising new regiments, she reminded herself. *But keeping standards high is a pain in the ass.*

She cleared her throat. "If you need assistance, just ask," she said. She understood how hard it would be for William to ask for help, but if he did, it would be a clear sign of trouble. "But we need to discuss our operational planning now."

William nodded, taking a sip of his coffee. "Of course."

Kat triggered her implants, sending a command to the room's processor. A holographic star chart appeared in front of them, showing the Jorlem Sector. She took a long look, silently reminding herself of the files she'd devoured over the last two days. Some of the star systems in front of her would make good Commonwealth members if they swallowed their pride long enough to apply; others would need to make significant changes to their governments and economies before they would even be *considered* for membership. But if some of the long-term projections were accurate, they'd have no choice but to make the changes sooner rather than later. The economic benefits of being part of the Commonwealth would provide more than enough incentive.

"We leave tomorrow," she said. "Can *Uncanny* depart on schedule?"

"Unless we run into unanticipated troubles, we should have no difficulty leaving with you," William assured her. "The sooner we're on the way, the sooner some of the more . . . irredeemable members of the crew get the message that things are going to be different from now on."

Kat lifted her eyebrows. "If they're that bad, do you really want to keep them?"

"Most of them have potential," William said. "I'd prefer not to dismiss them completely without due cause."

"I suppose," Kat said incredulously.

She cleared her throat. "We'll be linking up with a convoy—ten bulk freighters and a handful of smaller ships—and heading directly to Vangelis," she explained. "There may be some other ships joining us for security, but we won't have a full head count until we are actually ready to leave."

"Convoy regulations beginning to bite," William observed.

"And too many smaller operators facing ruin," Kat agreed. Her father's economists had sent her a long briefing outlining the problem. "Once we get them to Vangelis, we'll head directly to Jorlem. Apparently I'm meant to make unofficial-official contacts with the locals."

"Unofficial-official," William repeated.

"Yeah," Kat said. "Apparently, the Foreign Office believes that an *official* representative would be less . . . productive than an *unofficial* envoy."

She shook her head. Diplomacy had never been her strong suit, and she'd always found it hard to follow the tortured logic of the Foreign Office, but orders were orders. Yet, she couldn't help feeling that the strategy didn't make sense.

"It's a political thing," William said dryly.

"I don't understand it," Kat protested. "Who in their right mind would favor the Theocracy over the Commonwealth?"

William sighed. "Do you remember Cadiz?"

"Of course . . ."

"Cadiz was brought into the Commonwealth against its will," William said. "The act was the most blatant example of arm twisting by the Commonwealth, but it was hardly the only one. Traders from Tyre, and later the Commonwealth, had no scruples about abusing their commanding position, fueling local resentment. To inhabitants of Cadiz . . . the Commonwealth seemed the more immediate threat. The Theocracy was a distant nightmare hundreds of light-years away."

He met her eyes. "I suspect some of the local Jorlem governments may hope to play the Commonwealth off against the Theocracy," he added warningly. "Which is foolish, but very *human*."

"Madness," Kat said.

"Human," William said. "The situation calls for diplomacy, but any overt contacts will cause problems for local governments. Hence . . . an unofficial envoy."

"And if they prove receptive to our contacts, we can move to more formal contacts," Kat agreed.

"*Provided* that you don't set out to screw the locals, *again*," William warned. "It tends to cause long-term problems."

Kat sipped her coffee. She'd never known anything but wealth and privilege, which had eventually driven her to seek a naval career. Even in the military, she hadn't been able to get away from her name. However, William had endured a very different upbringing, which had shaped him as much as her life had shaped her, but had also given him a different perspective on the universe.

"They weren't *trying* to screw the locals," she protested. "They were just trying to establish trade links and make money."

"At Cadiz's expense," William reminded her, smiling. "And after we visit Jorlem, what next?"

"Unless we run into any real problems, I was going to suggest splitting up and showing the flag at a number of other worlds," Kat said. "There will be freighters that need escorts, which will win us some kudos from their crews and it'll give us a chance to outline what happens to infidels who try to work with the Theocracy. We may encounter other problems we can help solve. Updating the hyperspace survey charts in the region might also be useful."

William smiled. "You don't have a precise outline?"

"It depends on what we find," Kat said. "We may encounter something that forces us to throw the plan out the airlock."

She pointed to the star chart. "There are a handful of StarComs within the sector, not many, but enough for us to keep each other informed about our movements," she added, her eyes tracing out possible patrol routes. "I don't expect you to stick to a tight schedule as there's no way to know what will demand our attention. If worse comes to worst, we can hire a local courier boat to take a message to the RV point. It's not ideal, but it will have to do."

"We could use a few more bases," William observed. "And a *proper* StarCom network."

"There was a proposal to fund a network," Kat said, "but the demands of the war pushed it aside."

"And the locals probably weren't too keen on something that would give the Commonwealth much more influence in their affairs," William added. "You'd be routing every last message through Tyre."

Kat knew he had a point, though she preferred not to admit it.

"For the moment, it's just the two of us," Kat said. "Ideally, we'll spend the next six months in the sector; practically, it could be a great deal longer."

"Or shorter," William pointed out. "Has there been any progress on logistics?"

Kat grimaced. "They'll be sending a logistics ship out to meet us in a month, apparently," she said. *Lightning* and *Uncanny* were designed for long-term deployments with minimal support, but she was all too aware that they could expend most of their missile supply in a single engagement. "The demands of the war front take priority."

"That could leave us in trouble," William observed. "They're not even going to allow us to take a freighter?"

"Apparently not," Kat said. "I argued the matter with the Admiralty, but they were adamant."

"Not good for us," William said. "We might have to come home early."

Kat was in grim agreement. She had no doubt they could handle a pirate ship or a whole pirate squadron with their energy weapons alone, but a front-line warship was a very different proposition. The Theocracy *might* have decided to send a raiding squadron to Jorlem, secure in the knowledge that they'd come out ahead whatever happened. And if they did encounter a raiding squadron, Kat knew she'd have to do everything in her power to destroy it.

Assuming we even find it, she thought. *Space is vast enough to hide thousands of raiding squadrons.*

"We'll just have to make do with what we have," she said simply. "And we can head home early if we *really* run short of supplies."

She rose and walked to her desk. "This is a copy of our formal orders and my planned schedule," she said as she picked up a datachip. "It also includes some diplomatic authorization and various . . . *files* . . . you might want to read. If you *can* make contact with the locals, please do."

William grinned as she turned back to him. "And give them an honest assessment of the Commonwealth's strengths and weaknesses?"

"And tell them about the Theocracy," Kat added. She walked back to the chair and passed him the datachip. "You have authorization to share our records from Verdean and Ringer, if you like. Those should open a few eyes."

"Some of our detractors will probably claim they're faked," William warned her. "It wouldn't be difficult."

Kat scowled. It was easy to produce faked records these days. Done properly, it could be very hard to sort out truth from lies. Indeed, she'd seen a few of the more . . . *interesting* . . . fakes during her time at Piker's Peak. The fakers had done such a remarkable job that even *knowing* they were fakes, she'd found them impossible to disprove. It wasn't hard, her instructors had warned her, to put together a scenario that could confuse even a suspicious mind.

And as we would be the only source for their records, she thought darkly, *it wouldn't be hard to claim that we'd produced them from whole cloth.*

She shook her head in disbelief. The government—at the king's insistence—had released the complete and unedited footage from Verdean, showing the destroyed cities, the reeducation camps, and interviews with refugees Kat had taken from the planet before the Theocracy had arrived to regain control of the high orbitals. Their tales had been terrifying, stiffening support for the war all across the Commonwealth . . .

. . . Nonetheless, they could have been faked. And it would be very hard to prove that they had *not* been faked.

Not without access to the refugees themselves, she told herself. *And that could probably be arranged.*

She leveled her gaze at William. "Do you have any issues you wish to raise before we leave?"

"Just that I would like to carry out a multitude of exercises during the voyage," William said. "My crew has next to no experience in multiship operations."

"Good idea," Kat said. *Lightning* could do with the experience too. "Do you have a scenario worked out?"

"A couple," William said. He smiled, rather thinly. "And I asked the tactical staff to devise some more. I actually had to speak to them quite sharply for letting their imaginations run away with them."

Kat smiled back. "What was wrong with their scenarios?"

"They pitted us against a dozen enemy superdreadnoughts at once," William said. "It might work in the movies, but in real life?"

"We'd be destroyed," Kat said. A heavy cruiser couldn't survive a direct clash with a superdreadnought, not when she would be heavily outgunned. Even a truly incompetent enemy crew would have found it hard to lose. But it was good news, in a way. Sir William's tactical staff was rising to the occasion. "I trust you ordered them to come up with something a little more realistic?"

"Just a *little*," William said. "They stuck with the enhanced enemy capabilities."

Kat nodded. Tactical scenarios *always* assumed the enemy had better sensors and shields than existed in real life, as far as anyone knew. The Commonwealth was working hard to enhance their current weapons and come up with new ones, and the Theocracy was probably doing the same. If they ran into a ship with enhanced weapons . . . well, it wouldn't be a complete surprise.

Standard weapons will be easier to handle, she reminded herself. *It does make sense.*

"It's good to see you again," she said after going through the scenarios with him. If nothing else, the war had provided ample opportunities to update their tactical simulations and figure out which bright ideas were unworkable in practice. "I hope you don't run into further trouble."

"Me too," William said. He rose stoically. "I'll keep you informed."

CHAPTER NINE

Despite his brave words, William felt a flicker of nervousness as his bridge crew ran through their final checks before powering up the gateway generator. The generator was a *very* finicky piece of equipment and there were limits to how far it could be tested without actually opening a gateway. If something went wrong . . . he dismissed the thought. Losing the generator would be embarrassing, but far from fatal. It wasn't as if they were a long way from any help.

"All checks completed, Captain," Roach said. "We are ready to depart."

"Very good, Mr. XO," William said. He took a long breath as he surveyed the tactical display. Was it his imagination or were the freighters trying to keep their distance from *Uncanny*? "Communications, signal *Lightning*. Inform Commodore Falcone"—the courtesy promotion felt odd—"that we are ready to depart."

He leaned back into his command chair, trying to relax. His crew and the dockyard workers had gone through every last nook and cranny of the ship, replacing components, updating the records, and generally keeping an eye out for trouble. They'd discovered a handful of nasty surprises, yet there had been nothing dangerous enough to force him to delay their departure. Unfortunately, they had no idea who owned the drug stash the search had uncovered, but at least it had been dumped in the recycler rather than used by its owner. The medical checks he'd ordered for when the ship was underway would probably uncover the owner. William was actually looking forward to chewing the idiot out before throwing him in the brig.

In truth, he might already have left the ship, William thought as more and more updates flashed in front of him. *If he has, we'll never find him.*

"Signal from *Lightning*, sir," Lieutenant Robert Stott said. He'd been one of William's stronger supporters right from the start. William had already earmarked him for promotion if his superiors proved unsuited to their posts. "We can depart on schedule."

"Helm, bring the drive to full power," William ordered. "And then open a gateway."

"Aye, Captain," Lieutenant Cecelia Parkinson said. "Drive coming online . . . now."

William shot a fond smile at the back of Cecelia's head as a dull *thrumming* began to echo through the ship. She'd managed to get into trouble on her middy cruise, trouble that could easily have ended her career before it had fairly begun, but she'd turned into a good officer. When he'd put out a call for volunteers to transfer to *Uncanny*, Cecelia had been among the first to offer her services. It had given her a boost up the ladder, one she might not have had without the transfer, yet she could easily have avoided his ship. Thankfully, she'd ignored the rumors about *Uncanny*.

"All systems nominal," Calvin Goodrich said through the datanet. "All drive functions appear to be green."

"Good," William said.

He eyed the live stream from engineering as it appeared on his console. Goodrich had shaped up in the last week, though William found it hard to place *complete* faith in a drunkard. He had done all he could to make sure that Goodrich would have no access to alcohol, even shipboard rotgut, yet the man was an *engineer*. Building his own still wouldn't be difficult.

"Gateway generator activating . . . now," Cecelia reported. The display updated rapidly as the gateway blossomed to life in front of the ship. "Preparing to transit the gateway."

William braced himself, unsure what to expect, as *Uncanny* slid forward and into the portal. A series of shudders ran through the ship, chilling him; he braced himself before remembering that such an act was pointless. If something was wrong with the compensators, it could kill the entire crew before any of them realized that they were about to die. A queasy sensation spread through his body as the ship plunged through the gateway, then the sensation faded rapidly as the eerie lights of hyperspace surrounded them. He let out a breath he hadn't realized he'd been holding, then glanced at the status display. A handful of hyperspace nodes were marginally out of alignment. It wasn't a serious problem, but it was enough to make the crew queasy.

"Captain," Roach said, "the remainder of the convoy has followed us into hyperspace."

"Very good," William said. He'd agreed with Kat that *Uncanny* would take point, leading the way to Vangelis. "Helm, set course for Vangelis."

"Aye, Captain," Cecelia said. She keyed a series of commands into her console. "Course laid in."

"Take us out," William ordered.

He allowed himself a moment of relief as the convoy fell into formation and headed away from Tyre. The long-range sensors reported a handful of other ships entering or leaving the system, their positions obscured by hyperspace distortion, but none seemed *dangerous*. The Theocracy could possibly have a guardship covering the hyperspace routes in and out of the system, yet there was no point in the convoy trying to conceal its destination. Enough had been said about the trip on the public datanet for the Theocracy not to *need* a spy to know where the vessels were going.

They even may be grateful that we're not heading to the war front, he thought. *We've already done them a great deal of damage.*

The thought made him smile. It was hard to get any solid data, but the Commonwealth's propaganda department had been making a big deal out of the Theocracy being beaten so solidly—twice—by a mere *woman*. After Kat Falcone had bested the Theocracy at its own game, he rather doubted that anyone could continue to believe that women were fit to be nothing more than mothers, daughters, and wives. By now, according to some of the rumors he'd heard, the Theocracy had declared Kat the most loathed woman in the universe. He hated to think what enemy forces would do if they ever got their hands on her.

No doubt their population has to know they're making greater and greater sacrifices for the war, he thought darkly. *Who knows when they'll break and turn against their leaders? Or when we'll take the offensive for the final time?*

"I have a report from engineering, Captain," Roach said. "There were a handful of power fluctuations within the gateway generator. The chief engineer believes that they pose no real threat, but he would like to recalibrate the system anyway."

"Better safe than sorry," William agreed. "Were there any other problems?"

"None reported, Captain," Roach said.

But I have an appointment, William thought.

He rose. "Mr. XO, you have the bridge," he said briskly. There was no point in putting it off any longer. "Alert me if there are any problems."

"Aye, Captain," Roach said. "I have the bridge."

William took one last look at the display—*Uncanny* holding point, the freighters trailing in her wake, *Lightning* bringing up the rear—and sighed as he headed for the hatch. Piracy hadn't been reported near Tyre for years, ever since the Commonwealth had started to drive the pirates out of civilized space, but the demands of the war had allowed some of the bastards to slip back into their old habits. Thankfully, only a rare and very stupid pirate would willingly take on two heavy cruisers, yet William was uncomfortably aware that the Theocracy wouldn't care if the freighters were destroyed rather than captured. And the further the convoy headed from Tyre, the greater the chance of attracting unwelcome attention.

He stepped through the hatch and walked slowly down to Sickbay. A week of actual *work* had done wonders for his ship; the air was clear, the decks had been scrubbed, and the maintenance hatches had been slammed closed and locked. The crew looked far happier than they'd been when he'd first boarded. He couldn't help feeling pride as he opened the hatch and stepped into Sickbay. Doctor Sarah Prosser looked up at him and smiled.

"Captain," she said, "I'm surprised you came."

William resisted the temptation to roll his eyes. Doctor Prosser was yet another newcomer, a civilian doctor who'd specialized in emergency services before retraining to join the Navy after the war broke out. They were lucky to have her, he knew; the previous doctor had been unceremoniously discharged after an investigation had revealed a number of alarming discrepancies between what the ship was *supposed* to have in stock and what she *actually* had in stock. Sarah, who was around his age, had a fantastic reputation and still she'd found it hard to get a post. The Navy hadn't been sure what to make of retrained civilians.

"I have to set a good example," he said finally. "If I don't come for a checkup, no one else will want to go for a checkup either."

"And the records are crappy," Sarah agreed. "It's not so bad in your case, but everyone else . . . I don't have up-to-date records for *anyone* who served on this ship for longer than a month or two."

"You'll have them by the end of the week," William said. "Just keep an eye out for druggies and other potential problems."

Sarah looked disapproving but nodded. William understood. A civilian doctor was sworn to keep a patient's details to herself unless she had permission to share them; a military doctor had no such luxury. William could order her to open the medical files of every last member of the crew, and she would have no choice but to obey. He didn't intend to abuse his power, but if there *was* a problem . . .

He felt slightly deflated once again. Of *course* there would be problems.

"Take off your shirt," Sarah ordered. She nodded towards the nearest bed. "I'll be right with you."

William headed to the bed. Commanding officers *hated* visiting the doctor, knowing that the doctor was the only person on the ship authorized to remove them from command if they believed it necessary. It hadn't happened very often—and at least one doctor in recent memory who had deemed his captain unfit for duty had wound up facing a court-martial—but the prospect of losing their position sent shivers down the spines of commanding officers. They'd do everything in their power to remain out of sickbay as long as possible. But he had no choice. He *did* have to set a good example.

"Your records insist that you're quite healthy," Sarah said as she bustled over to the bed and stood next to him. "This really shouldn't take long."

◆　◆　◆

Joel couldn't help feeling more than a little nervous as he sat next to Julia in one of the privacy tubes. Two weeks ago, no one would have given a damn if the senior chief chose to spend his off-duty hours with a crewwoman even if it was technically against regulations, but now was a different story. A newcomer to the crew might blow the whistle, accusing him of sleeping with one of his subordinates. And while he wasn't doing anything of the sort, being caught would be disastrous.

"They missed the backdoors I worked into the datanet," Julia said quietly. The compartment was supposed to be soundproofed, but there was no point in taking chances. "I managed to download a copy of our mission orders without trouble."

"Good," Joel said. "Did you find anything else?"

"Nothing special," Julia said. "Our new captain doesn't seem to have any dark secrets stashed on the datanet."

Joel had a feeling that Julia spent too long on the datanet, forgetting that there was a real world outside her beloved computers. If Sir William had a dark secret, he'd be an utter fool to upload proof to the ship's datanet. It was supposed to record and save everything, after all. Even *classified* files could be copied and saved without warning. And besides, Sir William didn't have the *time* to be doing anything illicit. Reluctantly, Joel had to admit that the captain pushed himself harder than he pushed any of his crewmembers.

Joel took the datapad she offered him and skimmed through the orders. The Admiralty had always loved being verbose, something that even the demands of war hadn't changed. They could have boiled down their orders to three sentences, but instead they'd chosen to write a small novella. And Captain Falcone had added notes of her own. *Lightning* and *Uncanny* were to proceed to Jorlem via Vangelis, then split up and show the flag, moving from star to star before meeting up again. He had no idea just who had written the first set of orders, but the vagueness of the details suggested they'd been outlined by a uniformed bureaucrat.

Or someone who gets paid by the word, he thought as he copied the orders for his private datapad. *I could flesh out a story by a few thousand words if I had a crown for every word I used.*

"That's good to know," he said. "Did you get an updated manifest too?"

"Yeah, but it doesn't look finished," Julia warned. "In the last couple of days, we were taking on more supplies than we knew what to do with."

"As long as we have a rough idea," Joel assured her. He took the datachip she passed him and slipped it into his datapad for later contemplation. "Is there anything else in the files I ought to know about?"

"Not that I'm aware of," Julia said. "I had a look through the updated personnel files, but I didn't see any red flags. Oh . . . maybe one thing . . . Major Gareth Lupine has some family ties to the aristocracy. It might explain why he joined the planetary militia."

Joel smirked. "Trying to stay out of danger? *That* exploded in his face."

He leaned forward thoughtfully. "*Did* he volunteer for this mission or was he pushed?"

"I don't know," Julia said. "There's nothing in the files to suggest anything, one way or the other. I imagine he probably could have talked himself out of the posting if he'd wanted to."

Joel stroked his chin. "Did you pick up anything from the news?"

Julia looked at him. "What?"

"Society pages," Joel explained patiently. "Who's sleeping with whom, who cut who dead at the latest ball to support the troops, who's had a scandal they can't bury no matter how much cash they throw at it . . ."

"I didn't think to check," Julia said. She paused. "I don't know how much was archived in the datanet when we left."

Joel nodded and waited as her fingers flew over the datapad. Unfortunately, they hadn't thought to check the gossip before leaving Tyre. They *could* put in a request for information once they reached Vangelis, but if someone was monitoring StarCom traffic from *Uncanny* they'd certainly have grounds for suspicion. He wasn't sure what—if anything—it would prove, yet . . . he shook his head. It was *definitely* better not to take chances.

"Nothing too detailed," Julia said finally. She held up the datapad so he could read the articles. "Major Lupine will be taking his company of militiamen out on active service after retraining in a deep-space facility, all honor to Major Lupine, et cetera, et cetera. There's a bit of boilerplate about his family's splendid record of devotion and honesty to the crown, but nothing of any actual *use*. If there was a scandal, sir, it's been very well buried."

"There probably wasn't a scandal," Joel said thoughtfully. He would have liked a way to subvert the militiaman, but regrettably there was nothing to be done. "Has the militia done anything out of the ordinary? Anything that should worry us?"

"Not as far as I can tell," Julia assured him. "They're spending their time drilling endlessly and marching around the ship, looking tough."

"And silly," Joel added, although the drills weren't remotely funny. The militiamen were smart enough to familiarize themselves with the ship before they actually had to *fight*. He'd been relieved to hear that *Uncanny* wouldn't be receiving any marines, but the militia might make formidable opponents in their own right. "Keep an eye on them."

"Of course," Julia said.

She smirked. "Don't forget to visit the doctor for your checkup."

Joel winced. He had nothing to be afraid of, but there were several crewmen who were doing everything in their power to avoid Sickbay as long as possible. A major problem was on the horizon. God alone knew what would happen when the doctor uncovered traces of illegal drugs in their bloodstreams, but he doubted it would be pleasant. The idiots would certainly tell all they knew to avoid punishment.

Perhaps it was time to make sure his tracks were thoroughly buried.

Yet with a competent officer in command, an accident might be taken as deliberate murder, he thought. *And who knows what will happen then?*

CHAPTER TEN

"Tell me," Kat said. "What did you make of the latest exercise?"

She sat on the chair in her Ready Room, Commander Crenshaw and Major Patrick Davidson facing her on the sofa. The exercise had been fairly standard—she'd been careful not to work any particular surprises into the planning—but she was curious to know what Crenshaw had made of it. He'd been . . . odd, the past few days. She'd kept an eye on him, just to ensure he actually did his duty . . . and he had. But something was wrong. She just wasn't sure *what*.

"It was interesting," Crenshaw said. "I did wonder at *Uncanny*'s reaction speed."

"She's not taken part in exercises or real operations for months," Kat reminded him, bluntly. "Her crew needs the practice more than ours."

Not that it would keep me from drilling the crew until they can work their consoles in their sleep, she added, silently. *We're going to be very far from help.*

"That excuse won't be accepted in wartime," Crenshaw pointed out. "The enemy won't let them have an easy day because of it."

"Of course not," Kat said. "Any other thoughts?"

"We need to carry out more exercises," Crenshaw said. He paused. "There is another matter of some concern, Captain."

Kat leaned forward. "What?"

"I've been reading the crew evaluations from the last nine months," Crenshaw said. "It's hard to be sure, because *Lightning* spent the last month orbiting Tyre rather than going to war, but some disturbing patterns have begun to appear in the data. I've noticed that departments headed by foreigners or largely staffed by foreigners have poorer stats."

"I'm not sure that proves anything," Davidson said. His voice was so tightly controlled that Kat glanced at him sharply. "What are you saying?"

"They're not up to our standards," Crenshaw said. "You *must* have noticed."

Kat bit down—hard—on the comment that came to mind. Crenshaw wasn't *quite* the incompetent she'd assumed, but he *was* lazy. She'd never heard him volunteering for any duties let alone doing anything she hadn't assigned to him. But then, apparently he *had* been studying the stats. She wasn't sure if she should applaud his initiative or start worrying about what he might have in mind.

She managed a long exhale. "What are you trying to say?"

"That we have been diluting our Navy's efficiency by bringing in outsiders," Crenshaw said firmly. "And that we will pay a heavy price for it."

Davidson frowned. "I've worked with a great many non-Tyre spacers," he said. "And while most of them don't have the experience and training we try to give our officers, they learn, and learn quickly."

"And many of them have good reason to want to fight the Theocracy," Kat added.

"But they are not primarily loyal to Tyre," Crenshaw insisted. "Captain, how can we be sure they can be trusted?"

Kat rubbed her eyes, silently cursing her sister—again. She could see Crenshaw's point, but she knew better than to let him stampede her into rash action. Sir William had served in the Navy long enough to lose all the rough edges—and he wasn't the only one. The others would learn in time. Besides, the Navy was desperate for manpower. There wasn't *time* to run everyone through Piker's Peak!

"We trust them until they prove otherwise," she said. It was the Navy way. A crewman, or an officer, was considered trustworthy until they weren't. "Or do you feel we should send them all back home?"

"I think we should be concerned about their loyalties," Crenshaw said. "And how many of them have relatives behind the lines?"

That was a good point, Kat realized, better, perhaps, than Crenshaw knew. Lieutenant Aloysius Parker had betrayed Kat's squadron during her mission behind enemy lines after his captured sister had been used to blackmail him into serving the Theocracy. But Parker hadn't been a foreigner. He was born on Tyre.

"The point of the matter," she said, "is that their homeworlds have joined the Commonwealth. They have the right to join the Navy. And we are very short on manpower, so we should be glad to have them. I admit that the *planned* slow integration of foreigners into the Navy has been tossed aside by the demands of war, but . . . we must work with what we've got. I don't see any reason to mistrust them as a group, Commander, and neither do you."

Crenshaw looked alarmed. "Captain . . ."

Kat talked over him. "Or is this because you're afraid they will be competition?"

"What will happen to us," Crenshaw asked, "if we start passing command slots to outsiders?"

"By then, the outsiders will be fully integrated," Kat said. "And if they are not, they will not receive any command slots."

She sighed in irritation. She *hoped* that was true. Tyre had been founded on a very strict work ethic, one that wasn't shared by the rest of the Commonwealth. Immigrants to Tyre had to integrate or get out. But that would change, she suspected, as more and more Commonwealth worlds gained power and position. Who knew what would happen then?

"I hope you are right," Crenshaw said. He rose, then stopped. "With your permission, Captain . . ."

Kat nodded. "Dismissed, Commander," she said. "Take the conn and keep us on course."

Crenshaw turned and walked out of the Ready Room. Kat waited for the hatch to hiss closed, then turned to look at Davidson. "Is he out of his mind?"

"I think he's worried about his prospects for future promotion," Davidson said. Her lover gave her a long considering look. "And he has reason to worry."

Kat sighed. "What do you mean?"

"He's been asking a *lot* of questions," Davidson said. "I've been hearing rumors passed through the crew. Commander Crenshaw has been speaking, privately, to a number of foreign-born crewmen. Some of the rumors have been worrying."

"And of course I haven't heard a word," Kat said. She was the *captain*. There was no way she could sit down next to a junior crewman and exchange rumors. "Have you heard anything *specific*?"

"I believe he talked to a couple of my marines," Davidson said. "I'll ask them for details if you wish."

Kat rubbed her eyes, suddenly feeling very tired.

"I don't understand him," she admitted. "He's got the ability to be a good officer, but he doesn't have the motivation."

"He was probably pushed into the Navy," Davidson said. "I've met his type before."

Kat ran her fingers through her blonde hair. "What did you *do* with them?"

"A handful became good marines," Davidson said. "Those were the ones who found the grit within themselves to keep going. Others quit, eventually, or were dismissed after failing to meet the required milestones. Your XO . . . I think he's cut from the same cloth."

"I see," Kat said. "What do you think I should do with him?"

"It depends," Davidson said. "You could tell him to stop asking questions, which won't make him feel any better and will probably make it harder for him to work with you. Or you could have a quiet talk with him instead . . . or you could let him *keep* asking questions until he realizes there's nothing to be worried about."

He paused. "If indeed there *isn't* anything to be worried about."

Kat rose. "Do *you* think we should be worried?"

Davidson stood up too. "Do you remember Rose MacDonald?"

"Yes," Kat said. The political aide had sailed with *Lightning* when the ship had travelled behind enemy lines. "She was asking questions as well."

"The Commonwealth has made promises," Davidson said. "And those promises might have been made before the war, but the newcomers still expect us to keep them."

"I know that," Kat said.

"Then it's time you faced up to the implications," Davidson said. He sounded distressingly like her father. "Sir William is the *first* colonial to take command of anything heavier than a destroyer. We've been happy to accept foreigners in the lower decks, but not on the bridge. It's a point of principle with us that most if not all of our officers go through Piker's Peak, yet . . . how many colonials have been allowed to pass through her hallowed halls? I would be surprised if there wasn't some resentful muttering already."

Kat groaned. "Should we be worried about a mutiny?"

"Not yet, I think," Davidson said. "But I would be concerned about what will happen after the war."

"I already am," Kat muttered.

She led the way through the hatch and down to Officer Country, silently cursing Crenshaw, Candy, and politicians in general. There was a war on! She didn't have *time* to worry about such matters. The marine standing guard outside her cabin stepped aside, silently, as she opened the hatch and walked into the compartment. It crossed her mind, as the hatch hissed closed behind Davidson, that Crenshaw might be inclined to use their relationship against her, but she found it hard to care. She wanted, *needed*, to work off some of her frustration.

"Things will be better once we get to the sector," Davidson assured her. "And until then you can keep the crew busy by conducting endless drills."

Kat nodded in agreement as she turned to face him. The trip from Tyre to Vangelis would take at least five weeks, assuming they didn't run into hyperspace storms or anything else that would force them to change course. She wasn't anticipating trouble, but she knew, all too well, just how quickly hyperspace could turn dangerous to passing starships. And besides, Davidson was right. The drills would keep the crew—and Crenshaw—busy.

"At least *Uncanny* doesn't seem to be having any serious problems," she said softly. "That's one weight off my mind."

"And off William's," Davidson said. "She doesn't have a very good reputation, does she?"

Kat grinned, then leaned forward and kissed him, hard. It had been too long. Davidson kissed her back, one hand fumbling with her uniform clasp while the other stroked her back and buttocks. Kat gasped as his tongue slipped into her mouth, then pulled him gently towards the bedroom. She had plenty of space and she intended to make the most of it.

Afterwards, they lay together, savoring the afterglow.

"Thank you," she said softly. "I needed that."

"You're welcome," Davidson said. "I live to serve."

"I'm sure you hated every last minute of it," Kat said. She sat upright and glanced at the chronometer. She had an hour before she was supposed to be on the bridge, taking the conn and supervising the next set of exercises. "It must have been completely awful."

Davidson poked her in the chest, then sat up and gave her a long kiss. "It did have its moments," he said as she swung her legs over the side of the bed and stood. "Do you want me to join you in the shower?"

"I probably should decline," Kat said mischievously. Showering together tended to lead to more lovemaking. She turned to smile at him, then walked straight into the shower and turned on the water. "But if you want to join me, come on in."

She smiled as he followed her into the compartment and stepped under the water. "How are things in Marine Country?"

"Not that different," Davidson assured her. "We have a couple of maggots and a handful of transfers, but they're fitting in nicely. They'd like something to *do*, of course."

"We can practice boarding and counterboarding later," Kat assured him. She turned to allow him to wash her back, then returned the favor herself. "Or we might just set eyes on a pirate ship."

"If they're fool enough to come too close," Davidson pointed out. "We haven't exactly been hiding, have we?"

"We will," Kat said. The odds of running into a pirate this close to Tyre were low, but she'd privately determined to take the two cruisers into stealth a week before they reached their first destination. Ten bulk freighters, seemingly unescorted, would be a valuable prize for any pirate. "We'll see who we can lure into our web."

"They'll be calling you Lady Spider before too long," Davidson warned. "How does *that* sound?"

Kat snorted. "Compared to what the Theocracy calls me? High praise."

She stepped out of the shower and dressed hastily, then waited for Davidson to finish dressing before heading to the hatch. "Speak to your marines," she ordered as she checked her appearance in the mirror. "Let me know what they were asked, and why."

"Understood," Davidson said. Kat shook her head in quiet amusement as she turned to look at him. He looked perfect, not a single hair out of place. Kat didn't know how he did it. "I'll drop you a recording afterwards, if you like."

"Please," Kat said.

She led the way out of the hatch and headed back towards the bridge, wondering just what Crenshaw would make of their relationship. William hadn't said anything, but she'd suspected that he'd known and approved. Crenshaw . . . thanks to Candy, he probably already knew. *Candy* certainly knew Kat had been dating Davidson, on and off, for most of her career.

Which didn't stop her from trying to set me up with a bunch of weak-chinned losers, she thought with a hint of vindictiveness. Candy wasn't a bad person—Kat knew she could have had dozens of worse sisters—but they were so different that it was impossible to imagine them finding any common ground. *Did she think I'd dump him for someone with a fancy title?*

Kat pushed the thought aside as she stepped onto the bridge. Crenshaw, sitting in the command chair, hastily rose, offering her the seat with a wave of his hand. Kat nodded, then took a moment to study the status display. The convoy was proceeding normally; indeed, nothing had apparently changed in the two hours since she'd *last* looked at the display. But a series of warnings noted that the underlying ebb and flow of hyperspace was growing stronger. They might have to alter course or return to realspace soon if the threatening storm blossomed into a real danger.

"We've been monitoring the background radiation," Crenshaw said quietly. "If it continues to rise, we'll definitely have to alter course."

"And keep a sharp eye out for trouble," Kat added. Pirates liked lurking near the fringes of energy storms, knowing that any watching sensors would have trouble picking them out against the maelstrom. "Do we have anything on long-range sensors?"

"Nothing beyond a handful of random flickers," Crenshaw assured her. He gestured towards the sensor console. "There were certainly no solid returns."

How reassuringly competent, Kat thought, darkly. She couldn't help finding it a little annoying. *Why can't you be like this all the time?*

She sat down in her chair and keyed her console. "Alter course to keep some distance between us and the storm," she ordered. "And order *Uncanny* to sweep our flank."

Crenshaw glanced at her. "Captain, if there's anyone out there, they're unlikely to trouble us."

Kat was inclined to agree. There was no time to take the two cruisers into stealth, not when any watching eyes probably already had a solid lock on their relative positions.

"It's good practice," she said reassuringly. There was no substitute for real experience, even if they were jumping at shadows. "There might not be anyone there at all."

She leaned back in her command chair and watched as the convoy altered course to avoid the disturbance. Hyperspace rolled and seethed with energy, but didn't look as though it was going to blow up into a full-sized storm. Still, Kat kept a close eye on her ship's readings until the convoy had skirted the edge of the disturbance and resumed its original course.

"There *might* have been something there," Lieutenant Commander Samuel Weiberg mused thoughtfully. The tactical officer studied his readings, going over them repeatedly. "I picked up a handful of flickers that *might* have been artificial."

"*Might*," Crenshaw repeated. He didn't sound convinced. "Do you have anything *solid?*"

"Not at this distance, sir," Weiberg said. He turned to look at Kat. "We *could* reverse course and investigate."

Kat considered it, briefly. She had two ships, after all. She could detach *Uncanny* to take a look, even if there was nothing there. But time *was* pressing. The sooner they got to Vangelis, the sooner they could hand the freighters over to the locals and begin their actual mission.

Besides, she thought, *we don't know for sure there's actually something to find.*

"No," she said finally. She wondered if Crenshaw would argue with her. "We continue on our present course."

"Aye, Captain," Weiberg said.

Kat glanced at the console, checking the live feed from the long-range sensors. Was there something there? There were hints, nothing more . . . they could easily be nothing more than sensor distortions, echoes of starships that were in reality hundreds of light-years away . . .

She shook her head. She'd never know for sure. And nor would anyone else.

"We'll have plenty of time to hunt pirates later," she said finally. "But for the moment, protecting the convoy is our top priority."

CHAPTER ELEVEN

"Signal from *Lightning,* sir," Lieutenant Stott said. "We're to enter stealth mode in ten minutes."

"Acknowledge," William said. "And then alert Mr. Goodrich."

He sat back in his command chair, feeling a rush of excitement. Even with *Uncanny's* issues, the four weeks they'd spent in transit had been starting to grow tedious. But now they were crossing the border and heading straight into the Jorlem Sector. Who knew how many pirates were lying in wait?

"All systems report ready, sir," Roach reported. "And long-range sensors are clear."

"For what it's worth," William agreed. The small convoy had skirted two more hyperspace storms during the voyage, something that had probably made it harder for any prowling pirate ship to get a solid lock on their position. "Take us into stealth mode on command."

"Aye, Captain," Roach said.

William glanced down at the steady stream of reports from the ship's departments, reminding himself not to be *too* excited. Even now, ten freighters would rarely travel in convoy without an escort. The pirates might just be smart enough to give them a miss, even if they *couldn't* see any escorting warships. But then, they might also reason that the freighter crews were trying to bluff them. It was possible . . .

He checked the latest set of readiness reports. The ship's crew had shown a remarkable improvement over the last month, even if they weren't *quite* up to *Lightning's* standards. But then, *Lightning* had a decent commanding officer, a strong XO and an excellent set of senior officers. *Uncanny* had been nearing rock bottom when he'd been assigned to her. And yet she'd cleaned up nicely . . .

"Entering stealth mode," Roach reported. "The freighters can barely see us."

"Even though they know where to look," William finished. He smiled as he checked the live feed from the tactical sensors. A pirate ship would have to come very close, well within weapons range, to have a hope of picking the warships out of the background noise. "Keep a steady sensor watch at all times."

William forced himself to wait and relax as two hours passed slowly, handing the conn to Roach and walking from department to department to make sure everyone was on their toes. He trusted Roach and his other senior officers, but there was no substitute for going and checking the departments himself. And besides, it gave him a chance to impress on his officers and crew that the captain *was* paying attention to them. Too many commanding officers left such matters to their XO, in his opinion; they never bothered to press the flesh with the lower decks.

Probably because they were taught to keep a distance between themselves and the enlisted men, he thought wryly. *But it doesn't do wonders for loyalty. He'd* never been through Piker's Peak.

The crew was definitely starting to look and act more professionally, he considered, as he ended his impromptu inspection tour in sickbay. A handful of crewmen had been caught with traces of recreational drugs in their systems during their medical checks, but they'd sworn blind that they'd discarded their drugs shortly after William had taken command of the ship. William had given them a sharp lecture and a stern warning that they would be sent to a penal world if they were caught using illegal drugs while they were on the ship. He then released them for duty on the proviso that they report back to the doctor every week for a checkup. He still wasn't sure he'd done the right thing—even if they weren't addicts, they'd find it easy to justify trying to break the rules again—but as time went by without further discoveries, he decided he'd probably saved their careers.

Besides, we are short of crew, he thought, grimly. *We need to preserve as many of them as possible.*

His wristcom bleeped. "Captain to the bridge," Roach's voice said. "I say again, captain to the bridge!"

William grinned as he turned and hurried back towards the bridge. He wouldn't have been summoned unless something was happening, something *important.* Roach wouldn't want to surrender the conn any sooner than necessary . . . *he* hadn't wanted to either, back when he'd been an XO himself. Command experience *counted* when the promotions board was considering who best to promote . . .

And having the right family and planetary connections doesn't hurt either, he added mentally, feeling a trace of the old resentment.

He stepped onto the bridge. "Report!"

"Four sensor contacts, approaching us on attack vector," Roach said, rising. "They're a little hesitant, but I think that won't last very long."

William nodded, surveying the tactical display. The pirates—and they had to be pirates, because they were making no attempt to contact the convoy—were sneaking closer and closer, but they weren't committing themselves. They were probably trying to sniff out any warships while they could still break off. They'd have ample time to escape if they detected either of the cruisers before they entered attack range. But *Uncanny* and *Lightning* were in stealth. The pirates would have to be very lucky to catch a sniff of them before it was too late.

Their sensors are probably worse than ours, he thought.

"Alert *Lightning*, then take us to red alert," he ordered. "Do we have any tactical data?"

"Not as yet, sir," Lieutenant Commander Leonard Thompson said. The tactical officer was working his console with practiced skill. "They're probably destroyers, judging from the mass readings, but they *could* be using ECM to hide their true nature."

"Yes, they could," William agreed.

He contemplated the tactical situation as the newcomers came closer. A pirate ship would want to intimidate her opponents, particularly if she wanted to capture the freighters rather than destroy them. However, a Theocracy raiding squadron might want to pretend to be *weaker*, just to lull their prey into a false sense of overconfidence. In hyperspace, telltales would be hard to discern before it was too late.

But a raiding squadron would probably open fire as soon as they enter weapons range, he thought. Fighting in hyperspace could be dangerous—there was always the risk of triggering an energy storm—but raiders wouldn't care. *Unless they want to capture the freighters too.*

The thought made him smile, rather tartly. Operation Knife had taught him that the Theocracy was short on freighters. They had every reason to want to capture the convoy intact, if possible. But they had to know that *trying* would make the whole situation dangerously unpredictable. If their targets *knew* their enemy didn't want to blow them away, they'd have more room to maneuver . . .

"Establish passive tracking locks on all four ships," he ordered, "but do nothing to alert them."

"Aye, Captain," Thompson said.

"Update from *Lightning*, Captain," Stott put in. "Captain Falcone authorizes you to engage when you see fit."

"Acknowledge," William ordered, feeling a flash of pride. With *Lightning* bringing up the rear, *Uncanny* would have first shot at the pirate ships. And if they really *were* four destroyers, the other cruiser wouldn't be needed at all. "Helm, hold our course."

Roach glanced at him. "They're bound to know we've seen them."

"Yes," William said.

Hyperspace did odd things to sensors. It was possible, quite possible, that the incoming ships *hadn't* been seen. Civilian-grade sensors would have real problems picking the enemy ships out of the background noise. Most freighter crews tried to purchase military-grade sensors—some of them might have obtained gear that should have gone to *Uncanny*—but the pirates *might* have gotten lucky and stumbled over a convoy without advanced sensors. And if he knew pirates, and he did, they'd want to *believe* they'd gotten lucky.

He felt the tension on the bridge rising steadily as the pirate ships came closer, more and more details flowing into the tactical display. They *were* destroyers, four *older* destroyers; they wouldn't stand a chance, even if someone had replaced all their original fittings with modern technology. Unfortunately, *Uncanny* had yet to shake her reputation for bad luck. An incident where she'd accidentally fired on a friendly ship could not be easily dismissed. William felt something gnawing, deep in his chest, as he waited. They *needed* a victory, even an easy one.

What's more, pirates are our natural enemies, he thought, dryly. *Killing them will make us feel better about ourselves.*

"Captain," Stott said. "I'm picking up a message from the lead ship."

"Let's hear it," William said.

The transmission was badly garbled. William wasn't sure if hyperspace was playing its normal games with radio waves, even tight-beam signals, or if the pirates were trying to disguise their true origins. But it didn't matter.

". . . is the Free State of Fredrick," a harsh voice said. "You . . . ordered to stand down your . . . and prepare to be boarded. Any resistance . . . met with deadly force . . ."

William frowned. "Free State of Fredrick?"

"There's nothing in the database," Roach said after a moment. "There *is* a Fredrick, Captain, but it's right on the other side of the human sphere."

"They're faking it," Thompson muttered.

"Probably," William agreed. "They may hope we'd surrender quicker if we thought they were a legitimate force."

He had no idea what was happening on Fredrick—the files merely noted its existence, a world settled shortly before the Breakaway Wars—but he couldn't imagine it had anything to do with the Commonwealth. Fredrick was hundreds of light-years away, with the dead zone surrounding Earth and several other multi-star empires between it and Tyre.

Stott cleared his throat. "Any reply, Captain?"

"None," William said. "But order the convoy to prepare to alter course."

He forced himself to wait, knowing the pirates would have to make the next move. They'd know their bluff had failed, unless they chose to assume that the message had been garbled beyond recovery. What would they do next? They'd certainly *prefer* not to do anything that would force the squadron to scatter—chasing down ten freighters wouldn't be easy—but they'd probably want to capture three or four ships rather than lose them all . . . unless they *were* preparing to blow the convoy away and were hoping to keep the formation together until it was too late.

"They're repeating their demand," Stott informed him. "The transmission is a little clearer this time."

"Send back the convoy ID and inform them that we have clearance to proceed to Vangelis," William said. It was a gamble, but he saw no other choice. He couldn't keep pretending not to hear the transmission indefinitely. If the destroyers were a raiding squadron, he'd just told them that they were closing in on Commonwealth ships. "Then update the targeting matrix."

"Aye, Captain," Thompson said.

"Picking up a new signal, Captain," Stott said. "They're ordering us to heave to for inspection."

William nodded, feeling an odd flicker of amusement at the transparent bluff. There was no way that *anyone* from Fredrick would have a reason to inspect the convoy. The pirates—and he was sure they were pirates now—would have done better to pick a different point of origin. If they'd claimed to be from Vangelis, it would have been much easier to convince the freighters to allow themselves to be boarded. Of course, Vangelis knew better than to harass Commonwealth shipping . . .

"No response," he ordered. "But tell the convoy to alter course."

He watched as the incoming squadron picked up speed in response, closing in rapidly on the convoy. The squadron had no choice if they wanted to capture the freighters; they *had* to get into energy weapons range before it was too late. And yet . . . and yet . . . the closer they came without thinking, the easier it would be for him to target their ships. They didn't have the slightest idea *Uncanny* was there.

"Helm, bring us about," he ordered quietly. "Let them come to us."

"Aye, Captain," Cecelia said.

"Tactical, prepare to take us out of stealth mode," William added. "And then . . ."

"Missile separation," Thompson snapped. "One missile! I say again, one missile!"

"Stand by point defense," William ordered.

His heart started to pound. Had he been wrong? Had they been detected after all? No, the missile was racing past the convoy . . . a warning shot. Moments later, it detonated harmlessly. But the message was unmistakable. The convoy would be doomed if it kept trying to flee.

They must think we're idiots, William thought. *A smarter convoy CO would have ordered the ships to scatter long ago.*

"No traces of energy disturbance, Captain," Lieutenant Matthew Gross said. The navigator looked concerned. "But I don't know how long that will last."

"They're bringing active sensors online now," Thompson added. "They have solid locks on all ten bulk freighters."

"They'll pick us up soon," Roach warned. "Captain?"

"Order the convoy to heave to," William ordered. "Tactical?"

"I have locks on all four ships," Thompson reported. "All missiles armed, ready to fire; point defense grid armed, ready to fire."

"Take us out of stealth," William ordered. "Mr. Stott, demand their immediate surrender."

The pirate ships seemed to flinch as *Uncanny* dropped out of stealth mode, well within missile range of the enemy ships. William waited, wondering just what the pirates would do in response. They didn't have a hope of getting out of missile range before it was too late and they had to know it, but they also knew they weren't likely to survive *whatever* they did. Piracy carried an automatic death sentence, even in the Theocracy. A CO could offer a lesser punishment instead . . .

"Missile separation," Thompson snapped. "*Multiple* missile separation."

"Return fire," William ordered. He didn't fault the pirate commander. Firing on *Uncanny* might *just* give the pirates a chance to make their escape, particularly if they triggered an energy storm. "And inform them that we will commute their deaths to a life sentence on a penal colony if they surrender now."

He watched, grimly, as the missiles roared towards his ship. The tactical display kept updating, but he didn't need it to know that the missiles were badly outdated. It was unlikely *any* of them would get through the point defense web to slam into his shields . . . indeed, there were *civilian* freighters that wouldn't be unduly troubled. *His* missiles might as well have been made of lightning, reaching their targets before the pirate missiles even entered *Uncanny*'s point defense envelope.

"Two enemy ships have been destroyed, a third badly damaged," Thompson reported. He sounded pleased. "Their shields were definitely not up to par."

"Target the fourth ship," William ordered. The enemy ship had somehow evaded the missile aimed at its hull. "Don't give it a chance to get away."

He braced himself as the pirate missiles roared into his point defense envelope and evaporated long before they could touch his shields and detonate. Standard nukes, part of his mind noted. The pirates didn't seem to have antimatter warheads. Luckily, the odds of triggering a storm were low if the point defense took out the warheads before they could explode.

"Aye, Captain," Thompson said. William heard real enthusiasm in his tone for the first time. "Missiles locked . . . firing!"

"The third ship has lost power," Roach added. "She's spinning through space."

"Order the militia to prepare a boarding party," William said. Boarding pirate ships was always risky, but if they'd lost power and they didn't have antimatter . . . *Uncanny* might just manage to take prisoners. "Mr. XO, put together a follow-up party . . ."

"Captain, the fourth ship is trying to surrender," Stott interrupted. "She's begging for mercy."

"Order the missiles to break off and cover her," William ordered. It wasn't something he would have tried with a *real* warship—it would have given the enemy far too much time to draw a bead on the missiles as they held position—but he doubted the pirates could take advantage of it. "Are the militiamen ready to go?"

"Yes, Captain," Roach said.

William hesitated. The militiamen weren't marines, even though he had to admit that they'd been training extensively over the last month. They *weren't* prepared to board enemy warships and capture their crews. But asking Kat to send *her* marines would be a vote of no confidence in his people. Cold logic told him to make the request anyway; emotion suggested, strongly suggested, that he let the militiamen go first.

"Order the militiamen to secure the pirate ships," he ordered. "Any prisoners are to be disarmed, bound, and sent back here."

"Aye, Captain," Roach said.

"Keep our weapons locked on their hulls," William added. The pirates might have surrendered, but he knew better than to take it for granted. "If they make one false move, blast them."

"Aye, Captain," Thompson said.

William scowled as he sat back in his command chair. Boarding a pirate ship was always dangerous. The pirates had no reason to expect mercy, so they might just be waiting for their ship to be boarded before they turned off the antimatter containment chambers and vaporized both the ship and boarding party. He'd promised to accept surrender, but would the pirates believe him?

And life on a penal colony won't be fun either, he thought as the shuttles raced towards their targets. He'd read the reports. The lucky colonists lived like barbarians from a bygone age; the unlucky ones were slaves or dead. *They might see it as a fate worse than death.*

"Picking up a message from the militia, sir," Stott said ten minutes after the shuttles had docked. "Their target has been secured; the crew has been arrested and readied for transport."

"Dispatch the follow-up team, then stand down from red alert," William ordered.

He took a breath, feeling the tension fading away. "And put out a general message to all hands," he added. *Uncanny* had faced her first challenge since he'd assumed command and come through. "Well done."

CHAPTER TWELVE

The pirates, William decided as he watched from the shuttlebay control compartment, looked to be a sorry lot as the militiamen marched them into the secondary shuttlebay and ordered them to their knees. Whatever delusions they'd embraced about themselves had died with two of their ships, leaving them staring around hopelessly, knowing that they no longer had any control over their lives. A number of pirate officers had been lynched and killed, according to the militiamen. The fear they'd used to rule their crews had come to an end with their ships.

"Nine of the crew claim to have been captured and forced into service," Janet said, holding out a datapad. "Two of them are Commonwealth citizens, both listed as missing after their freighters were reported overdue. The others are from the Jorlem Sector."

William winced. "And how were they treated?"

"They were forced to serve," Janet said. "Captain, what do we *do* with them?"

"Keep them in the brig, separate from the others," William said curtly. The press-ganged crewmen would have been forced to participate in looting, raping, and murdering their way across the sector. It was a common pirate trick. They forced their new crewmen to get blood on their hands, and then told them they could never return home. "And we'll see what can be done for them later."

Janet glanced at him. "But if they were forced to serve . . .?"

"They might have picked up bad habits," William said. He was in no mood to answer questions. Bad habits could be addictive, as the crew of *Uncanny* knew all too well. "We'll hand them over to the civilian courts when we return home. They can make the final call."

He gave her a sharp glance, cutting off any other questions. "How many pirates died?"

"Seventy-three bodies were recovered from the surviving ships, according to the report," Janet said, consulting her datapad. "Nineteen were killed by their own crew; the remainder seem to have died in the general life support failure."

Her voice turned indignant. "They weren't even wearing shipsuits!"

"A useful lesson, I am sure," William said. Basic training, naval and civilian, insisted that crewmen should wear shipsuits at all times, particularly outside their quarters. "Make sure some of the videos get put on the ship's datanet. It might prevent any backsliding into bad habits."

He smiled at the thought, although he felt no real humor. The mystery of *Uncanny*'s life support problems had never been solved, not really. He would have liked to think that his crew had been maintaining their own ship, but it was hard to be sure. Why the hell would they put up with the stink? And the cruiser was so heavily overengineered that they might not have reached rock bottom by the time he'd taken command.

His wristcom bleeped. "Captain," Goodrich said. "I've completed the survey of the two pirate ships. The damaged vessel is beyond repair. It would be cheaper to construct a whole new ship rather than try to repair her. I recommend scuttling her without further delay, once the militia have finished searching her for evidence."

"Good thinking," William said. A pirate ship wasn't likely to be worth much, even if they towed her all the way to the scrapyard. Maybe she could be broken down for raw materials, but it probably wouldn't be worth the effort. "Did you recover anything from her datacore?"

"The system is badly fragmented," Goodrich said. "I don't *think* it was a deliberate self-destruct, Captain; the damage is just too erratic. My best guess is that power feedback caused most of the damage. I'd like to bring the datacore back to the ship and try to extract data, but I can't promise anything."

William nodded. "Try," he said. Smart pirates wouldn't write anything down, particularly anything that could be used against them, but it was just *possible* that Goodrich would recover something useful from the ruined datacore. "Did the militia find anything useful?"

"Nothing of great value, I believe," Goodrich said. He sounded oddly amused. "The pirates do not seem to have been well-off."

"They had four ships," William said. "That's not a small investment."

He dismissed the thought. "What about the other ship?"

"She's intact, but primitive," Goodrich said. "Her point defense system is an *original*, sir; her crew made no attempt to modify her to keep pace with the rest of the sector. I wouldn't have bet on her even if our missiles hadn't been an order of magnitude more advanced than hers. And to add insult to injury, the level of basic maintenance is *appalling*."

"*Really*," William said dryly.

"Yes, sir," Goodrich said. "Realistically, I'd recommend that she be scrapped too. Even the Theocracy would turn their noses up at her. But we might get *something* for her if we took her to Vangelis. A prize crew should have no difficulty navigating her that far."

"It might be worth trying," William agreed. "Did you pull anything useful out of her datacore?"

"Very little," Goodrich admitted. "There's no actual damage, sir, but it's clear that *this* ship wasn't allowed to store navigational data. I plan to have a crew of hackers working their way through the ship over the next few days, trying to draw the data from her systems. We might just be able to locate her base."

"If there *is* a base," William said. There were quite a few illicit pirate dens along the edge of settled space, but a skillful crew could get by with nothing more than a handful of visits to independent star systems and colonies too poor or desperate to care about where their supplies came from. It was hard to blame them too. "See what you can put together."

"Yes, sir," Goodrich said.

"And tell the crew that there will be a reward for anyone who back-tracks her course," William added. "I'll see to it personally."

He allowed himself a tight smile. There was nothing like a victory to boost morale—and morale had skyrocketed in the last hour. A little friendly competition wouldn't hurt either. He'd have to plan the reward carefully, but *that* wouldn't be difficult. A day or two of extra leave on Vangelis?

"I'll spread the word, sir," Goodrich said. "Do you want me to take command of the prize crew?"

"No, thank you," William said. There was no way he could send his chief engineer away for longer than a few hours. If *Uncanny* ran into unanticipated problems, it would cause no end of trouble. "Return to the ship once you've completed removing the damaged datacore and set the scuttling charges."

"Aye, sir," Goodrich said. He didn't *sound* disappointed. "I'll start working on the datacore as soon as I return."

William closed the connection. The surviving pirates most likely didn't know anything useful, although they *would* be interrogated over the next week. If nothing else, uncovering any fences and purveyors of stolen goods on Vangelis would make it harder for any future pirates to sell their ill-gotten treasures. Vangelis was the closest world that could actually sell the pirates what they *needed* to keep their ships going. They probably wouldn't ask too many questions, as long as the money kept flowing.

Janet cleared her throat. "Captain, who *are* you going to send to the prize crew?"

William lifted his eyebrows. "Do you want to go?"

He ignored her flush. Kat, he suspected, would want to send her XO. And he couldn't really blame her, if half of what she'd said about him was true. But the pirate ship—he wondered, suddenly, if she had a name—was *his* prize. Kat couldn't object if he gave the command to one of his officers.

But I need them all here, he thought numbly.

The thought made him scowl. Roach would want the job—command experience was not to be sniffed at, even if it was nothing more than a week of shepherding a captured pirate ship into port—but William knew he needed his XO. And yet, Roach *was* the logical candidate for the job. He'd resent *not* being sent. God knew *William* had taken command of captured vessels during his long career.

"The XO will take command," he said finally. "And he can pick his own crew."

He took one last look at the pirates, then turned on his heel and marched out of the compartment.

◆　◆　◆

"Whoever was in charge of this ship was a madman," Crewman Henderson muttered as they stood in the datacore compartment. "The whole ship's a fucking death trap."

Joel said nothing, but he was inclined to agree. The pirate ship— *Talon of Death*, according to the captured pirates—was dangerous to her crew, let alone everyone else. And she didn't even have the excuse of being hammered by a heavy cruiser! The life support system was so badly decayed that it was a miracle it hadn't failed completely, the sensors were so primitive he didn't understand how they'd managed to locate the convoy, and the weapons system could barely fart in the general direction of a target.

"And this is what we want," Henderson added, lowering his voice. "Isn't it?"

"Shut up," Joel hissed. Henderson hadn't said anything overtly, but he was clearly starting to doubt the plan. And he hadn't played any real role in Captain Abraham's death. He might think he could get out of trouble if he betrayed the other plotters to Sir William. "This isn't a safe place."

The pirate ship would in fact be an excellent place to stage an accident, *if* Joel hadn't thought it would draw attention to him. Commander Roach had brought only fifteen crewmen onto *Talon of Death*, all of whom would be interrogated closely if someone died in transit. And Sir William had the authority, if he chose to use it, to have the suspects interrogated with truth drugs or direct brain induction. Joel knew he was a strong man, but he had no illusions about his ability to conceal anything under *that* sort of treatment.

Henderson is turning into a liability, he thought. *But he has to be left alive, for now.*

He looked at Julia, instead. "Did you pull anything from the datacore?"

"Quite a bit," Julia said. "Half-assed idiots don't have the slightest idea how the system works."

Henderson frowned. "And you do?"

"Yes," Julia said simply.

She pointed a finger at the giant datacore. "You see, when a file is deleted and wiped, there are still traces of it left in the system," she added. "Most datacores, particularly civilian datacores, merely move those traces to deep storage until they actually *need* that part of their memory. And with such capacities, they rarely *do* need it. These . . . amateurs should have destroyed the datacore before surrendering. Their half-assed approach to wiping the system left plenty of traces for me to pick up."

"Good, I suppose," Joel said. "What have you found?"

"Well, they weren't fool enough to store the coordinates of their lair on the datacore," Julia told him. She flipped open her personal terminal and tapped a switch, displaying a star chart of the Jorlem Sector. "But I've been cross-referencing all the files, and I can backtrack this ship's movements over the last ten years."

Henderson snorted. "Really?"

"Oh, yes," Julia said. "It's actually an exercise they used to set us during training. They wiped all of the navigational data, of course, but you can use the remainder of the files to put together a fairly accurate picture of where the ship has been. See here . . ." She tapped a section of raw data. "The ship took ten days to move from one location to the other. There's nothing to say where it actually *was*. But here there's a reference to a hyperspace storm and another to a trio of cloudscoops. That's enough to tell me that the ship was in transit from Haverford to Vangelis."

Joel smiled. "What's at Haverford?"

"Good question," Julia said. She tapped her console. "It's a farming colony. Officially one of those petty little religious places where men are men, women know their place, and nothing more advanced than steam power is permitted."

"Sounds like paradise," Henderson said. Joel shot him a sharp warning look, but he ignored it. "The dumb fucks probably wouldn't even *notice* if the Theocracy took over."

"Quite," Julia agreed. She was speed-reading as more and more data flowed up in front of her. "Their import/export restrictions are pretty severe. They simply don't purchase very much from off-world, *officially*. Ten gets you twenty that our friends were selling the locals something they're not allowed to have."

Henderson laughed. "What *else* would they sell them?"

Joel glared at his shipmate, but he had to admit that Henderson had a point. There was no point in smuggling something, certainly not with a huge markup, unless there was no way for the buyer to purchase it legitimately. A world that banned the import of anything more advanced than hand tools would attract hundreds of smugglers, particularly when the locals discovered that life without high technology wasn't easy. And while Haverford probably couldn't offer the pirates any high tech of their own, they'd have no trouble supplying food, drink, and women.

He looked at Julia. "Do you have any idea what they were selling?"

"No," Julia said. "But I'm sure they found *something*."

"Unless they were just raiding the place," Henderson said.

Joel shrugged. The pirates had had four destroyers—primitive destroyers, to be sure, but it wouldn't take much to capture a stage-one colony. Using them to raid convoys, particularly convoys from a multi-star power with a long history of hunting down and executing pirates, struck him as showing a lack of imagination. Why do something you *knew* would eventually lead to certain death when you could use your resources to build something a little more interesting?

Savages in starships, he thought, darkly. *Not a pleasant combination.*

"There's no suggestion they fired weapons during their stay at Haverford," Julia said. "I don't think they *needed* to be unfriendly."

"Which proves nothing," Joel said. "Haverford could have been captured long ago and turned into a pirate base."

He considered the possibilities. He'd hoped to have the first look at any recovered data and, if necessary, make some of it vanish. A list of pirate contacts within the Jorlem Sector would be very helpful, although he would have been astonished if they'd actually discovered one. But now . . . if Haverford had merely been trading with the pirates, he didn't want to blow the whistle on them.

But if they've been occupied, he added mentally, *they need help.*

"Keep digging through the files," he ordered. "Let me see anything that might be useful first."

"Of course, sir," Julia said.

And hope that Commander Roach isn't expecting quick results, Joel added to himself. *If we want some of the data to vanish, we'll need to do it and then hide the evidence.*

Henderson caught his arm as he rose. "Joel . . . if we do find proof that Haverford is occupied, shouldn't we make sure Sir William knows?"

"Yeah, we probably should," Joel said, making a final decision about Henderson. "But let's see what we've caught before we decide what to do with it, shall we?"

◆　◆　◆

"I don't think they'll get much prize money out of . . . of *that*," Crenshaw said.

Kat gave him a sidelong look as they stood together on the bridge. In a way, Crenshaw was right; *Talon of Death*—and whoever had thought up *that* name was a melodramatic asshole—wasn't worth more than a few thousand crowns. Only a navy in desperate need of hulls would even *consider* purchasing her, although there were quite a few single-system navies within the Jorlem Sector who might put in a bid. But that wasn't the point.

"A few hundred crowns to the ship's crew will be appreciated," she said quietly. Crenshaw was from old money, like her. She would be surprised if he didn't have at least a million crowns in his trust fund. But that meant he had no idea of the value of money. "And it will be a promise of things to come."

"They'll spend it all on booze and strippers," Crenshaw predicted.

Kat looked at him. "So what?"

She allowed herself a smile as she looked back at the tactical display. *Talon of Death* couldn't hope to keep up with the cruisers, but as long as she could pace the convoy it probably wouldn't matter. And if she couldn't . . . having to be towed would be frustrating to her temporary CO, yet it *would* get them to Vangelis.

Then we can hand the crew over to the local authorities, she thought. The interrogations hadn't revealed anything of value. *And hope we never see them again.*

"Captain," Linda Ross said. "*Talon of Death* reports that she is ready to depart. *Uncanny* adds that the scuttling charges are primed, ready to fire."

"Very good," Kat said. She walked back to her command chair and sat down. All things considered, *Uncanny's* first true engagement had gone very well. "Order the charges detonated, and then take us back onto our planned course."

"Aye, Captain," Linda said.

The tactical display bleeped. Kat looked at it and smiled. The crippled pirate ship was now nothing more than an expanding cloud of dust. Hyperspace would eventually drag the remains into an energy storm, vaporizing the starship. If any pirates came looking, they'd never find a trace of their former comrades.

A low hum ran through the ship. "We are underway," Lieutenant Bobby Wheeler reported briskly. "Our ETA remains unchanged."

"Good," Kat said. She smiled as a thought occurred to her. "Take us back into stealth. Let's see if any other pirates come sniffing around."

CHAPTER THIRTEEN

"Captain," Lieutenant Wheeler said. "We are approaching Vangelis."

Kat had hoped to pick off a couple more pirate ships during the remainder of the cruise, but no other vessels had taken the bait. Her long-range sensors *had* reported a couple of vague contacts, yet nothing had materialized. But they might just have suspected that ten bulk freighters wouldn't be flying in convoy without an escort, even if they *looked* to be traveling alone.

"Take us out of hyperspace as planned," she ordered. "Communications, transmit our ID codes to System Command as soon as we arrive, then forward the diplomatic package to the planetary government."

"Aye, Captain," Linda said.

"Hyperspace gateway opening in five minutes," Wheeler said. "All systems reporting nominal."

Kat braced herself as the gateway flared open, allowing *Lightning* and her consorts to flow back into realspace. Normally starships would emerge from hyperspace much closer to the planet, but she didn't want to panic the planetary defenses. Vangelis was not technically involved with the war, yet her government had been buying up as many modern warships as they could get their hands on. They might even want *Talon of Death*!

She smiled at the thought, then watched grimly as the system display updated rapidly, revealing hundreds of starships and interplanetary vessels making their way around the star system. Vangelis hadn't had the vast investment that had powered the growth of Tyre—or Ahura Mazda, for that matter—but Kat had to admit that her early governments had done very well for themselves. Three cloudscoops orbited the gas giant, providing fuel for a growing system-wide industrial base. They'd already started producing their own freighter designs, she knew; it wouldn't be long before they started churning out indigenous warships of their own.

In many ways, Vangelis is the sort of member world the Commonwealth wants, Kat thought as she studied the planet itself. Tyre had more orbital activity, but Vangelis wasn't *that* far behind. Seven settled asteroids orbited the world, along with two dozen industrial nodes and several small shipyards, all protected by a swarm of Orbital Weapons Platforms. *A thriving industrial base, a growing and educated population . . . no need for any long-term investments.*

"The Theocracy will want this planet," Crenshaw muttered. "I'm surprised they haven't already tried to lay claim to Vangelis."

"They're concentrating on the war," Kat muttered back. Crenshaw had a point, but the Theocracy might have found any attempt to take and hold Vangelis incredibly costly. And much of the industry they wanted to take would be destroyed in the crossfire. "I think they'll be planning to secure Vangelis after beating us."

"Captain," Linda said. "I'm picking up a message from System Command. They're giving us an orbital slot and requesting details of our planned schedule."

Crenshaw scowled. "Is that normal?"

"It can be," Kat said. She looked at Linda. "Inform them that we will be heading to Jorlem after completing our business here. If they have any ships that want to be escorted there, they can let us know before we depart."

"Captain," Crenshaw asked, "is it *wise* to let them know our schedule?"

"It's no secret," Kat said. "And escorting a convoy from here to Jorlem might win us some additional goodwill."

She nodded to Linda, then returned her attention to the display. If the pirates were monitoring local traffic or had a source in System Command, they'd know where *Lightning* and *Uncanny* were going. But they'd *also* know that the two cruisers would be escorting freighters, ships they would otherwise have tried to take as prizes. She had no doubt that System Command would try to take advantage of the opportunity. It was what *she* would have done.

"Picking up a handful of light cruisers in high orbit," Lieutenant Commander Samuel Weiberg reported. "They're *Brandon*-class cruisers, from Tyre."

"Purchased four years ago," Kat said. The Falcone Corporation had sold them, if she recalled correctly. Her father had been hopeful that it would help strengthen ties between Vangelis and the Commonwealth— or at least the Falcone Corporation—but Vangelis had successfully maintained its political and economic independence ever since. "Are they in good condition?"

"I think so," Weiberg said. "They're not using the latest sensor gear, Captain, but there's nothing to suggest that they're not in tip-top shape. I'd have taken them for our cruisers if they didn't have the wrong IFF codes."

"We'll see if we can run an exercise while we're here," Kat said. She doubted it would be possible, for political reasons, but it was worth asking. The local navy might *want* the chance to exercise against the Commonwealth. "What's your assessment of the local defenses?"

"They look good," Weiberg said, "but they clearly haven't learned many lessons from the war. Too many of their automated fortifications are too close together. I suspect that antimatter warheads would make a mess of the datanet, whatever else they did. If the Theocracy launched an attack, just like they did during First Cadiz, they'd be able to inflict a great deal of damage quickly."

Crenshaw coughed. "Should we be pointing that out to them?"

"Perhaps," Kat said. Offhand, she couldn't recall if Vangelis had ever sent any observers to the war. It was possible, but unlikely. "We'll see how things go."

"Captain, we just received a message from the planetary government," Linda said. "They're inviting you to a meeting this evening with a high-ranking representative."

"Good," Kat said. She glanced at the details as they scrolled up on her console, reading between the lines. The words were bland, but they'd already cleared her a route through the planet's orbital space and down through the atmosphere, suggesting that she was going to meet a *very* high-ranking representative. "Tell them I'll be down ASAP."

She turned to Crenshaw. "Mr. XO, you have the bridge," she said. "Inform Captain McElney that he has command of the squadron. Now that we've reached Vangelis, the freighters can be released to their next destination."

"Yes, Captain," Crenshaw said. "And shore leave?"

Kat was privately surprised he'd thought of it. But she had to admit he'd been improving—slightly—over the last five weeks.

"We're due to remain here for two days, at least," she said. It wouldn't be very much, but after spending five weeks cooped up on a starship *everyone* would be grateful. "Organize a shore leave rota. Try and make sure that everyone gets some time on the planet."

"Aye, Captain," Crenshaw said.

Kat nodded, then returned to her cabin and changed into her dress uniform. The invitation had specified that it was a private meeting—she was surprised Crenshaw hadn't started insisting that it was a trap—which meant the local government probably wanted complete deniability. And that meant that she would be meeting either the president himself or a member of his cabinet. She checked her appearance in the mirror, her steward bustling around her until he was satisfied, then picked up her datapad and headed for the main shuttlebay. ONI's files on the planetary government were irritatingly vague—Vangelis wasn't considered *that* important—but she was fairly sure she'd be meeting one of the people on the list of major politicians. She boarded the shuttle, gave the pilot his instructions, and then settled down to read the files.

Vangelis City didn't look *that* different to Tyre, she noted, as the shuttle dropped through the atmosphere and headed towards the city. Their capital was expanding rapidly, hundreds of giant skyscrapers reaching up towards the sky, thousands of air and ground cars clearly visible as people bustled to and from their workplaces. The capital didn't seem to have any real planning, although there was no way to be sure. Kat had visited a couple of cities that had been planned out in every detail long before they'd been built; they'd all struck her as boring. The designers had had no souls.

She tugged at her uniform in irritation. *And then they went on to design the Navy's dress uniforms.*

"I'm picking up the landing beacon," the pilot said. He nodded towards a giant tower, positioned neatly at the heart of the city. "Permission to land?"

"Granted," Kat said.

She felt her heart starting to race as the shuttle touched down neatly on the landing pad, the hatch sliding open a moment later. The tower was, officially, a business headquarters, but it was close enough to Government House for a high-ranking official to make his way from one building to the other without being observed. And she was sure there was a secret tunnel or two under the streets. Tyre City was *riddled* with secret tunnels.

"Captain Falcone," a smartly dressed man said as she stepped out of the shuttle, "if you'll come with me . . ."

Kat hid her amusement as he led her down a flight of stairs and into a large, private dining room. The meeting had a complete lack of ceremony, something she knew would annoy an accredited diplomat, yet she'd never *liked* ceremony. Besides, her father had told her more than once that excessive ceremony was often used to hide weakness. It wasn't something she'd been taught to respect.

"Lady Falcone," a calm voice said. Kat straightened up as she recognized the planetary president. "That is the correct form of address, is it not?"

"Please, call me Kat or Captain Falcone," Kat said. "This is not an official meeting."

"Of course not," President Daniel Thorne said. He waved a hand at the table. "Please, take a seat and order dinner."

Kat sat, Thorne sitting down facing her. His face had been rejuvenated, giving him a strikingly youthful appearance, but she believed he wasn't any younger than her father. Clearly the fashion for mature looks hadn't yet spread to Vangelis. The files hadn't specified Thorne's age, yet they revealed that he'd been the leader of the planet's second-largest political party for five years before winning the last set of elections. He was hardly a political naïf.

"Please, order," he said, indicating the menu. "This building is often used for quiet dinners and discussions."

"Thank you, Mr. President," Kat said. She ordered roast lamb and potatoes, then settled into her chair. "And thank you for inviting me."

"I read the diplomatic package," President Thorne said. "You're an odd choice for a diplomat."

"I'm not a diplomat," Kat said honestly. There was no point in protesting otherwise. She had no idea what sort of intelligence-gathering apparatus Vangelis had in Tyre, but they wouldn't need to do anything more than ask to get her public dossier. "They sent me because I can speak bluntly and testify to the threat facing your world."

"So I hear," President Thorne said. A waiter appeared, carrying two glasses that he put down in front of the diners, and then he withdrew as quietly as he'd entered. "But I have been led to believe that the outcome of the war is inevitable."

"We would like to believe so," Kat said. She met his eyes. "But wars are often unpredictable."

"Agreed," President Thorne said.

He took a sip of his drink, then continued. "As these are *unofficial* discussions," he said, "I shall commit a terrible diplomatic blunder and be blunt. The Theocracy is a potential threat to us, despite our ongoing defensive programs, but the Commonwealth is *also* a potential threat. Our merchants are not amused at being locked out of the Free Trade Zone."

"The zone is open to Commonwealth members," Kat pointed out.

"But it also serves as a way for Tyre to dominate the Commonwealth," Thorne countered. "Even now, you are still attempting to serve the civilian market while mustering your forces for war."

"We would not want outsiders to take advantage of a war being fought on their behalf," Kat said sharply.

"Quite," President Thorne agreed. "But those outsiders would also be reluctant to surrender their independence."

"Each Commonwealth world has full self-government," Kat said. "That's a declared right, laid down in the Commonwealth Charter."

"But that isn't quite accurate," President Thorne said. "Or is it not true that all member worlds must meet certain requirements before joining?"

"Requirements that prepare them for membership," Kat explained. "It would be grossly naive to just accept *everyone*."

"Not everyone would agree," President Thorne said. "And Tyre has used its economic muscle quite extensively in this sector. If it wasn't for the war, Kat, I suspect things would be a great deal worse. For us, for the sector . . ."

He looked down at the table, idly tapping his fingers against the wood. "You promise advantages to joining the Commonwealth," he said, "but there are also disadvantages. I do not want to see our merchants locked out of markets, our industries swamped by cheap mass-produced goods from off-world, our youngsters unemployed because they do not meet the Commonwealth's educational standards . . .

"I'm sure you see our point. There are advantages to membership, but also disadvantages. I do not believe that Congress would consider membership unless they received ironclad guarantees that we would *not* be treated in such a manner."

Kat took a moment to formulate her thoughts. "First, I'm not claiming that the Commonwealth is perfect," she said. "Even if I had been inclined to believe in perfect political systems, the Commonwealth is not one of them. Its existence is a compromise between several different political imperatives, none of which work together very well."

She paused, gauging her next words carefully. "Second, there have been problems," she admitted. "There is no point in trying to deny it. But prior to the war, many of those issues were nothing more than teething problems. We always knew that investing in the new members, particularly the ones with limited industrial or educational bases of their own, would be a long-term project. Very few of our projections suggested that the whole process would be complete in less than a hundred years."

"Assuming you continued to invest in the project," President Thorne said.

"Which I believe we would have done," Kat said. "The whole system was structured to offer profit to both sides.

"But the war changed all that," she added. "And it has made . . . other matters far too complex."

She met his eyes evenly. "I'm not here to woo you to the Commonwealth," she said. "I understand that there have been problems, problems that cannot be fixed until the war is finally brought to an end. But we *do* need to discuss the war's effects in your sector."

"The war is quite some distance from us," President Throne said evenly.

He looked up as a trio of waiters arrived, each one carrying a large tray. Kat felt her mouth begin to water as they put her plate in front of her and then left the room. President Thorne smiled, motioning for her to start eating. He clearly had no trouble holding a high-level meeting over dinner.

But all of this is unofficial-official, she reminded herself.

She cleared her throat. "Yes, the war is quite some distance from you," she said. "But would that be true if the Theocracy hadn't decided to start the war? What if they'd decided to invade the Jorlem Sector instead?"

President Thorne smiled. "What if the Commonwealth hadn't uni-laterally annexed Cadiz?"

"More to the point, they are already sending advance parties into the sector and attempting to hire freighters, purchase warships, and lay the groundwork for an eventual takeover," Kat continued, ignoring the jibe. "We believe that they are sponsoring pirate outfits that are raiding your shipping . . ."

"I see," President Thorne said. "And how do you know that?"

"We interrogated the captured pirates extensively," Kat said. "They didn't tell us very much—their senior officers were killed—but they did make it clear that they were being paid for *destroyed* freight-ers, not just captured freighters. That makes no economic sense, Mr.

President. The only power that benefits from destroying freighters is the Theocracy."

"Point," President Thorne agreed.

Just for a second, she saw something hard and calculating behind his eyes. He had to understand her logic. Vangelis, or any other world within the Jorlem Sector, would have to be out of its collective mind to finance pirates, knowing that discovery would bring colossal retribution. And the pirates were definitely being funded. Only the Theocracy had the means, motive, and opportunity to provide the funding. It wasn't as if they had anything to lose by angering the Commonwealth— and everyone else—still further.

"The war is coming in your direction, whatever you have to say about it," Kat warned. "And I can *testify* that the records we have been sharing with everyone are accurate. The Theocracy will crush your entire civilization if you refuse to stand up to them."

She leaned forward. "We're not asking you to join the war," she added. "We're asking you to help secure this sector against encroachment. And yes, I am empowered to offer long-term concessions in exchange for your cooperation."

"An interesting offer," President Thorne said. "But such offers can be walked back after the war."

Kat met his eyes. "Vangelis is not a stage-one colony," she said bluntly. "You are in a good position to take full advantage of the Free Trade Zone—and Commonwealth membership. I don't believe there will be any need for long-term investment on your world, certainly not on the same scale as any of the stage-one worlds within the Commonwealth. You would certainly not have to compromise your independence. And even if you don't want to join, there is a great deal to gain by securing the sector. We would be more than happy to help."

"So you say," President Thorne said. "And I will certainly raise the issue with my cabinet."

He paused. "I understand you will be leaving the system in two days?"

"Depending," Kat said. "We've offered to escort a convoy to Jorlem. We may end up leaving later, once System Command works out a schedule."

"I'll speak to you before then," President Thorne said. He indicated their meal. "And now, let us talk of something else."

CHAPTER FOURTEEN

"They don't look too happy," Roach observed as they watched the scruffy pirates being herded into the shuttles. "Anyone would think they were going to their execution."

"They probably are," William said. Vangelis wasn't particularly corrupt, unlike a couple of other worlds he could mention. The pirates would spend the next couple of months in a holding camp until they were finally dispatched to the penal world, instead of bribing their way to freedom as soon as *Lightning* and *Uncanny* were safely gone. "Vangelis isn't a safe place for them."

"But a profitable one for us," Roach said. "The crew is very happy."

William smiled. *Talon of Death* had been sold to a local government-approved broker for five hundred thousand chips, roughly seven thousand crowns. There would be a ruinous rate of exchange, he was sure, if any of the crew wanted to take their prize money home with them, but he'd been assured that five hundred chips were more than enough for a blowout in Spaceport Row. It would definitely do wonders for morale.

He turned to look at his XO. "The shore leave schedule is worked out?"

"I had to do some bickering with Mr. Crenshaw, but I think we sorted it out," Roach said. "I managed to convince him that our crew deserved the first set of leave slots, even though they're only six hours apiece. Thankfully, they're not going to be going very far."

William nodded. Shore leave could be a sore point, at times; it was counted from the moment the crewman stepped off the shuttle, not when he reached his final destination. It wasn't uncommon for a large part of a crewman's shore leave to be taken up by travel, getting to his destination and then heading back. It was a constant niggle.

"Take care of it," he ordered, dismissing the thought. "I'll be in my Ready Room if you need me."

He took one last look at the pirates—it was unfortunate that their interrogations had revealed so little—then turned and made his way through the hatch. A pair of crewmen saluted as he passed, their faces showing genuine enthusiasm. There was *definitely* nothing like a victory, even an easy victory, to boost morale. The prospect of shore leave didn't hurt either.

And they're heading to the privacy tubes, he thought, concealing his amusement as he hurried down the corridor. It had been easy to tell, although he could never have put the reason into words. There had been something . . . *furtive* about their behavior, yet no real guilt. He didn't care, as long as their relationship didn't breach regulations. *That will probably boost their morale too.*

He stepped through the hatch into his Ready Room, then poured himself a cup of coffee and sat down at the desk. The latest set of intelligence reports from Vangelis's navy were already on the terminal, informing him that ONI's estimate of shipping losses within the sector had been, at best, understatements. *Dozens* of vessels had been reported missing, ranging from outdated bulk freighters that simply weren't competitive anywhere else to modern starships from Vangelis or the Commonwealth. No interstellar power was capable of providing regular patrols and convoy escorts. No wonder over fifty freighters had requested permission to travel with the two cruisers to Jorlem.

It's a mess, he thought. *And it's only going to get worse.*

His terminal bleeped. "Captain Falcone is calling, sir."

"Put her through," William ordered.

Kat's image materialized in front of him. "Captain," she said. "I trust you had a moment to read my report?"

"I skimmed it," William said. He'd planned to go back and reread the report in greater detail, but he'd had too many other duties to attend to first. "Do you think Vangelis is interested?"

"It's hard to be sure," Kat admitted. "I think I made some pretty good points, but the local political situation isn't entirely in our favor."

"Of course not," William said. He had to smile at her droll expression. Kat Falcone was better than most, but too many naval officers suffered from myopia where other planets and multi-star powers were concerned. "They're worried about opening the door for Commonwealth expansion."

"It isn't as if they have much to fear," Kat objected, crossly.

"They don't see it that way," William reminded her. "But Vangelis will probably come around, if you give them time."

Kat nodded, ruefully. "We'll be here for four more days instead of two," she said, changing the subject. "System Command wants to gather a dozen additional freighters for our makeshift convoy. I've actually requested that the local navy assign a couple of destroyers to provide additional protection, but they haven't gotten back to me yet."

"I hope they don't expect two cruisers to cover over sixty ships," William said. He'd thought *fifty* was quite bad enough. A single Theocracy raider could pop off a spread of antimatter warheads, triggering a massive energy storm that would do a great deal of damage. "It will be a minor nightmare."

"I hope so too," Kat said. "But they don't have any experience in large-scale deployments."

William couldn't disagree. Tyre had been building up its navy for decades, slowly developing both the fleet and the infrastructure to support it. He knew, from his long experience, just how many lessons had been learned and relearned as the navy swept Commonwealth space clear of pirates and raiders. But Vangelis had only just begun to build up its navy. By his estimate, it would be at least ten years before they were ready to start producing superdreadnoughts, if they ever did.

"We can see what they say," William said. "We *are* providing a service here, after all."

Kat smiled rather tiredly. "We also have to decide what we're doing after we reach Jorlem," she said. "The interrogations didn't *suggest* that Haverford had been occupied."

"No, they didn't," William agreed. His hackers had pulled a considerable amount of data out of *Talon of Death's* datacore, but most of the intelligence was fragmented in one way or another. They apparently wouldn't be led straight to a pirate base. "I don't think they managed to conceal anything from us."

"But they probably wouldn't have much to say," Kat mused. "Pirate crews are often kept in ignorance."

She cleared her throat. "But we should probably drop in anyway," she added. "*Someone* has to tell them off for purchasing supplies from pirates."

"That might be a bad idea," William said. "Kat, we know nothing about local conditions. If the settlers are desperate, they're not going to care about where their supplies come from."

"That's no excuse for trading with pirates," Kat pointed out. "They wouldn't be raiding ships for supplies if they didn't have a ready market."

"And what will the pirates do," William asked, "if Haverford starts refusing to buy?"

Kat grimaced. "You think the pirates would turn nasty?"

"There's no law and order in this sector, outside of a few places like Vangelis," William reminded her. "Yes, I *do* think the pirates will turn nasty."

He scowled. Kat wasn't stupid, but she'd never been truly *helpless*. She'd never had to watch as pirates threatened her homeworld, demanding supplies and women in exchange for *not* bombarding the planet's cities from orbit. There was no way she could understand just how it felt to have to compromise one's principles, time and time again; there was no way she could grasp how ashamed the weak felt, even as they bent their knees.

"Perhaps we should have sold *Talon of Death* to them instead," Kat mused. "That *would* give them a few more options, wouldn't it?"

William rather doubted it. *Talon of Death* was primitive compared to *Uncanny* or *Lightning*, but she would still need a crew who understood *how* to maintain her. Haverford most likely couldn't produce such a crew, not when the files had made clear that her founders had deliberately set out to create a no-technology culture. Still such a stance probably wouldn't last more than a generation or two. Whatever pressures had convinced the original founders to ban technology would crumble as later generations asked why and discovered that their elders had no good answers.

"In any case, we should make a point of calling on Haverford," Kat added. "It might convince the pirates that the system is being watched."

"A sweep through the system might even go unnoticed," William agreed. "They don't have any orbital installations, according to the files."

Kat nodded. "But for the moment, we'll head directly to Jorlem," she mused. "Do you have any other issues you want to raise?"

"Not at the moment, I think," William said. "But if you can find a way to convince the planetary government to send a few escort ships with the convoy, it would be good."

"I know," Kat said. She sounded frustrated. "I hadn't realized just how many ships would take advantage of our offer."

William smiled. "We're offering to escort them through the most dangerous region of space, short of the war front itself," he said. "Offering to stay long enough to let System Command round up more potential travelers *might* have been a mistake."

Kat smiled back. "It might have been," she agreed. "I'll speak to you nearer our departure, ideally with a handful of Vangelis starships in our party. But if none accompany us, we'll just have to make the best of it."

"You might want to think about what will happen once we reach Jorlem and the freighters want to go farther," William added. "Escorting them will probably do more to win us goodwill than talking to the planetary governments."

"We'll just have to see," Kat said. "I'll speak to you soon."

Her image vanished. William allowed himself an amused smile, then returned to the latest set of reports from his crew. Roach was handling his duties well—better than William himself, at that age—but there was no excuse for William not keeping as close an eye on things as possible. Who knew *what* surprises were lurking below decks?

A few more victories will change that, he told himself. *The crew will no longer fear a curse.*

It was unusual, Kat knew, for the senior chief to request an interview. Personnel matters were normally handled below decks or by the XO if it was a matter that didn't have to be brought before the starship's captain. But Senior Chief Alex Houghton had sent a message requesting a private interview. She puzzled over it for a long moment—there was something oddly mealymouthed about the way he'd worded the request—then sent back a short reply, inviting him to meet her in an hour. Perhaps it was something that couldn't wait for the XO to return from his brief shore leave.

But it's hard to imagine what, Kat thought, as she returned to her notes. She'd already written out a short report for her father, but she needed to write her impressions before they faded from her mind. *What could have happened that requires immediate attention?*

An hour later, the hatch chimed. She opened the door and lifted her eyebrows, in surprise, as the senior chief escorted a young midshipwoman into the Ready Room. Kat recalled meeting her briefly during her introduction to the ship, but she couldn't say she'd seen much of the younger girl since then. The woman was strikingly young, almost certainly on her first cruise. Her dark hair was cut close to her scalp, her almond eyes peering from tinted skin, darting around as if she expected a blow at any moment. She wore the uniform well, but there was an odd hint of vulnerability that worried Kat more than she cared to say. Had she been molested by one of her crewmates? The senior chief would have taken care of that, surely?

"Captain," Houghton said. He looked older, somehow. "Midshipwoman Tasha Reynolds has a report for you."

Kat blinked, feeling apprehensive. This wasn't going to be good.

"Captain," Tasha said. She swallowed, hard. Kat couldn't help thinking that she looked like a very small girl who had been called before the headmistress. "Captain . . . is there a chance of promotion for me?"

Kat hadn't been sure what to expect, but she honestly hadn't expected *that*. A midshipwoman on her first cruise would be lucky to see promotion in less than a year, unless she did something very heroic to prove she deserved it. And even if she did, she could expect trouble from her next set of superior officers, officers who would suspect she'd been promoted well ahead of her competency. Even Kat had taken a year and a half to get promoted to lieutenant, despite her family connections. Tasha certainly didn't have *those*.

"An interesting question," she said finally. She hadn't heard anything *bad* about Tasha, which suggested she hadn't screwed up *too* badly. The

XO normally handled all matters relating to the midshipmen. "Why do you ask?"

Tasha made a visible attempt to screw up her courage. "The XO asked me a number of questions, Captain," she admitted. "And he said I'd be lucky to get promoted."

Because she's not from Tyre, Kat finished. Tasha might not have had anything to unlearn, as she was too young to have served in any other navy, but her accent marked her out as a foreigner. *What did he say to her?*

"What . . . exactly . . . did he say? Did you record the conversation?"

"No," Tasha said. "Captain . . . *should* I have recorded the conversation?"

Kat grimaced. Implants, even civilian-grade implants, could record a person's entire life, but recording another person without their permission was considered bad manners. And recording a superior officer's words without permission was against regulations, although she knew a number of officers who did it anyway. It was useful, sometimes, to have a recording of what was actually said. But Tasha, a midshipwoman who hadn't been born on Tyre, had no leeway at all.

"Probably not," she said finally. "What did he say to you?"

She listened, feeling her temper start to flare, as Tasha stumbled through the entire conversation. Crenshaw had asked her about her homeworld, about her early life . . . and then questioned her loyalty to the Commonwealth. He'd asked her where she would stand if there was a major disagreement between Tyre and the rest of the Commonwealth; he'd openly accused her of bringing foreign attitudes into the Navy. And, in the end, he'd simply dismissed her, leaving Tasha with the impression that her career was doomed. She'd confided in the senior chief, and *he'd* insisted on going to the ship's captain.

"One moment," Kat said when Tasha had finished. "I need to review some files."

She tapped her console, bringing up Tasha's file: born on New Petrograd, a stage-three colony that had joined the Commonwealth during the early years; passed the entry exams for Piker's Peak at seventeen; entered the academy itself at eighteen. She hadn't taken any honors, Kat noted, but that proved very little. No one passed through four years at Piker's Peak without being head and shoulders above their civilian counterparts, even if they didn't have strong family connections. She didn't have any pre-academy experience, yet that was hardly uncommon.

Crenshaw had done a good job in keeping the files updated, she admitted, as she skimmed through Tasha's service record. No major problems, thankfully. The young woman *had* committed the usual string of errors committed by any newly minted ensign, but none of them were particularly career ending. Tasha might not have been marked out for greatness, either through skill or connections, yet she hadn't blotted her copybook either. She should have a promising career ahead of her.

Kat looked up. "This happened two days ago, right?"

"Yes, Captain," the senior chief said. He didn't make any attempt to sound apologetic. "I felt it best to wait until the XO was off the ship."

So I didn't send them back to talk to the XO, Kat thought.

She shook her head in bitter frustration. Crenshaw hadn't written any negative comments into Tasha's file . . . but if he wanted to ruin her career, there were ways to do it without writing anything blatantly untruthful. What was he *thinking*? Kat could have crushed him for sexual harassment or molesting a junior officer, but this was different. Crenshaw might well be able to justify his conduct before a court-martial board.

"Thank you for bringing this to my attention," she said. She glanced at the senior chief. "Is there any other reason for concern?"

Tasha shifted from side to side, nervously. Kat looked at her. "What?"

The young woman cringed but held her ground. "I may be being paranoid . . ."

"Spit it out," Kat ordered, sharply.

"We're assigned to different departments by the XO," Tasha said. "Neither I nor Midshipman Collins have been assigned to either tactical or the helm. I've spent time in life support and engineering . . ."

Kat resisted, barely, the urge to groan. Unless she missed her guess, Collins would be another foreigner. And Crenshaw had found a subtle way to hamper their careers. Tasha had entered command track at Piker's Peak, but she wouldn't have any hope of promotion unless she spent time in the tactical and helm departments.

"Thank you for bringing this to my attention," she said finally. "I'll deal with it."

Although, she admitted to herself as Houghton showed Tasha out of her office, she didn't have the slightest idea how to proceed.

CHAPTER FIFTEEN

"That's *Lightning*'s XO over there," Henderson muttered. "Lucky bastard has two women on his knee."

Joel concealed his amusement with an effort. The bar was dark—the only illumination came from flashing spotlights that flickered on and off at random—but there was no point in taking chances. If Commander Crenshaw realized they were laughing at him, or even talking about him, the consequences could be disastrous. He wanted—he needed—to remain unremarked.

He took a sip of his drink, leaning back in his chair. The bar could easily have passed for a spaceport bar on Tyre: cheap booze, flashing lights, loud music, scantily clad girls, pools of darkness to conceal the dubious stains on the fittings . . . very much like home. And the space was crammed with hundreds of spacers, frittering away their bonuses before returning to their ships for the next voyage to some godforsaken destination. He'd already had to squash one fight between a handful of his crewmen and a couple of civilian spacers. The civilians had been moaning and whining about having their shore leave cut short because their commanders wanted to join the planned convoy.

Idiots, he thought. *You'd think they'd be grateful to have a better than even chance of reaching their damn destinations.*

"Now *there's* something interesting," Henderson muttered as he took a bite from his sandwich and washed it down with a swig of his beer. "Look at the girls."

Joel followed his gaze, watching as the five girls stepped onto the stage. There was nothing remotely sophisticated about their appearance, but the crowd wasn't very sophisticated. The only thing keeping their outfits on were the prying eyes of every man in the room. He rolled his eyes as the music changed and the girls began to dance, thrusting out their chests and shaking their bottoms while the crowd hooted, hollered, and threw credit chips towards the stage.

Henderson elbowed him. "Wouldn't you like to get your hands on one of them?"

"Everyone else will have had a go at them," Joel pointed out. "Or doesn't that bother you?"

He grimaced at the thought. Most spaceport brothels were owned and operated by the local authorities, ensuring that the prostitutes were clean, the spacers were not charged through the nose, and anyone who caused trouble was hastily evicted. The amateur establishments, on the other hand, were often a different story. They could be cheaper—and they took immense risks—but they were also filthier.

"Pussy is pussy," Henderson said. The dance came to an end. The girls removed their costumes, then started to dance again as the music changed. "Or would you rather a man?"

Joel kept his face impassive. Henderson was already well on his way to drunkenness or he would never have dared poke Joel like that. But it hardly mattered. He watched Henderson as the crewman stared at the dancers, his tongue practically hanging out of his mouth as the girls went through a dizzying series of motions. By the time the dancing was finished, Joel knew the local prostitutes waiting outside would have plenty of clients.

He caught Henderson's hand as another dance came to an end. "I know somewhere where we can get cheap and clean women," he said with a leer. "Shall we go?"

Henderson laughed, emptying his latest mug of beer. "You always know the best places to go."

Joel smirked as Henderson rose to his feet, his legs wobbling dangerously. The booze might be cheap, but Henderson had drunk enough to put a serious dent in his wallet. Joel followed him out the door and onto the darkened street, ignoring the handful of women waiting outside. None of the local prostitutes looked very good, at least not to him. But he rather doubted Henderson would care.

"Just like home," Henderson said as they stumbled down the street. "Where is this brothel?"

"Follow me," Joel said.

He covertly checked their surroundings as they walked, glancing around to make sure no one was paying attention to them. The street was lined with bars, brothels, and a handful of stores designed to separate the spacers from their pay. The crowds of drunken spacers making their way back to the spaceport didn't seem to notice their presence. Joel spotted a couple of young women pickpocketing drunken spacers while clinging to their arms, luring them into alleyways for quick trysts. Such acts wouldn't be tolerated outside the wire, he suspected, but that hardly mattered. Spaceports had always been a law unto themselves . . .

. . . and besides, spacers spending cash freely was good for the local economy.

"Shouldn't walk too far," Henderson said. He giggled, as if he were too drunk to laugh properly. "I have a baseball bat in my pants."

"You'll be doing some battering in the future," Joel said, mimicking his tone. "The girls will love you."

He kept his face impassive with an effort. Henderson simply didn't have any common sense, did he? A few more drinks and he'd probably be bragging about their plan—or as much as he knew of it—to the next pretty girl who crossed their path.

"Of course they will," Henderson said. He hiccupped loudly. "I'm rich."

Not as rich as you were, Joel thought. *How many drinks did you buy?*

He smiled darkly as he pulled Henderson into a dark, shadowy alleyway that was a shortcut to the next set of brothels according to the map he'd downloaded from the local processor. A handful of cats scurried out of waste bins as they passed; he glanced around, half expecting to see a dozen prostitutes servicing their clients in the darkness. But the smell was probably enough to drive them away. No one wanted to lower their pants when the air smelled worse than a pirate ship.

"I saw a pussy," Henderson said. He snickered as he glanced around. "But it's the wrong kind of pussy."

"Very funny," Joel said.

He allowed Henderson to slip ahead of him, then slipped the improvised cosh out of his pocket and cracked it into the back of Henderson's neck. The big man crumbled to the ground. Joel slipped on a pair of gloves before searching his body, carefully removing his wallet and anything else a thief might take. As soon as he was sure he'd taken everything, Joel hefted up the body and dumped it into a giant trashcan half-filled with foul-smelling liquid. If he was lucky, the body would never be found; the trashcan would be shipped out of the spaceport and its contents fed into a processor long before someone realized that Henderson was missing. But even if they *did* find the body, they'd probably think it was a mugging gone bad. There was enough alcohol in Henderson's bloodstream to prove he'd been drunk when he'd died.

Idiot, he thought. Henderson had been committed even if he hadn't realized it. A good commanding officer made no difference. Plotting a mutiny was one thing, particularly if they never went through with it, but murdering their former commanding officer was quite another story. Sooner or later, *someone* would have put the pieces together. *And now he's dead.*

He hurried to the edge of the alleyway, wondering just how long it would take for someone to move the trashcan. If someone thought to look inside before sending it out of the spaceport . . . he dismissed the thought as he stripped off his gloves, dumping them and the cosh into a plastic bag. There were ways to dispose of almost anything within a spaceport; he knew from long experience. No one would think twice about a spacer dumping a bag in the recycler.

And even if they did, he thought, *they would have no way to connect it to Henderson's death.*

Shaking his head, he slipped back onto the main road and hurried down toward the nearest brothel. Joel had been careful to make sure that he and Henderson had been some distance from the rest of the crew—spotting Crenshaw had worried him, although he suspected that Crenshaw didn't know him from Adam—and no one knew the two had been together. If anyone asked, Joel could swear blind that he'd been in one of the brothels. He certainly had enough money to pay for several hours of frolicking with a couple of girls.

He sighed as he joined the line of spacers outside the building. Killing Henderson was a risk, even though an accident on Vangelis would be far more convincing than anything on the ship. But he'd had no choice. Henderson had been wavering to the point where he might have started to doubt the goal. And a single word from him would have been more than enough to tear the whole plan wide open.

Good riddance, Joel thought. *Rot in hell.*

◆ ◆ ◆

Janet, at William's request, had cleared his cabin of Captain Abraham's possessions, but William still preferred to sleep on an uncomfortable sofa in his Ready Room so that he remained closer to the bridge. If nothing else, he'd told himself, he could respond quickly to any problems before they managed to get out of hand.

He was half-asleep when his wristcom buzzed. "Captain, this is Richmond," Janet's voice said. "We have a missing crewman."

William sat upright, rubbing his eyes. "Details?"

"Crewman Roth Henderson was due to report back to the ship thirty minutes ago," Janet reported. "He didn't return to the shuttle for uplift. I tried to contact his wristcom, but apparently he didn't take it with him."

Fuck, William thought. Regulations were clear. Spacers on short-term shore leave were to carry their wristcoms with them at all times. There was no way to know when they might need to be recalled to the ship. *A deserter . . . or something worse?*

He sat upright. He'd stayed up late reading the reports and only had a little sleep before Janet had woken him. He was used to getting by on very little sleep, but he had the nasty feeling that age was slowly catching up with him. His body didn't have the genetic enhancements that Kat Falcone and her family took for granted, merely a handful of improvements spliced into his DNA over the years. He felt old.

"Contact the local authorities," he ordered as he stood. He'd take a quick shower and shave while waiting for updates. "Ask them to put out an alert for him, then make inquiries among the crewmen who went down with him. See if they can tell you where he was last seen."

"Aye, Captain," Janet said.

"Alert Major Lupine too," William added. "His men might be needed for the search."

He closed the channel, then stumbled into the small washroom for a shower. It was possible, he had to admit, that Crewman Henderson might have merely managed to forget when he had to return to the ship. He'd hardly be the first crewman to lose track of time while enjoying himself with local women. There had been times, before the war, when William had had to speak quite sharply to a number of spacers who hadn't taken the matter quite as seriously as they should. And a couple of them had ended up on report . . .

But there were other possibilities. Henderson could have deserted, or he could have been kidnapped. Vangelis wasn't exactly a pro-Commonwealth world. Someone could have seen Henderson and decided to use him as a bargaining chip. William had no idea why they'd take the risk, but he had to admit it was a possibility. Or he could have picked a fight with someone bigger than him and wound up in the hospital. There was no way to know.

He washed quickly while considering the possibilities. Vangelis was hardly an under-populated world. If Henderson had decided to desert, he would have no trouble hiding within the mass of immigrants and finding work somewhere on the surface. Politicians might cheerfully talk of searching entire planets, but anyone with a gram of sense would know that searching even a single *city* was a nightmare. Even if the local authorities cooperated, finding Henderson would be tricky. And if they refused to help, William knew that matters would get sticky.

His wristcom buzzed as he stepped out of the shower. "Captain," Major Lupine said, "I checked with the spaceport sickbay. None of our crew have been admitted. I asked them to run a check against the DNA and biometric records and nothing showed up."

William nodded, unsurprised. Henderson might have left his wristcom behind, but he wouldn't have forgotten his ID card, which served as a bank card as well as a number of other things. And even if *that* had been stolen, the sickbay would have logged his DNA as a matter of course. There was no chance he'd been admitted as a John Doe patient. And if he'd been killed, the local sickbay would have had first look at the body.

"Check with security," he ordered. "See if he made his way through the wire."

"Aye, Captain," Lupine said. "They might not have logged his passage, though."

"Check anyway," William said.

He sighed. By long custom and interstellar agreements, spaceports and their surrounding red light districts were not behind a customs and immigration barrier. Spacers could go for shore leave without having to pass through any security checks. But leaving the spaceport for a visit to the planet beyond was a very different matter. In theory, no one could leave the spaceport without passing through the security gates.

But if he found someone willing to help him, he thought, *they might have been able to get him through without being checked.*

There was a pause. "There's no record of his passage," Lupine reported. "But they don't sound very worried."

"They probably wouldn't be." William sighed. "Ask them to keep an eye out for him."

He sighed again as he closed the connection. A single missing spacer, a foreign spacer at that, was hardly an emergency. The locals would be more concerned about asserting their independence from the Commonwealth than finding a missing man. But it was a problem for him. They were due to depart in three days. If Henderson didn't show up by then, he'd have to leave the matter with the local authorities and hope for the best.

And if he has deserted, he thought sourly, *he will have made a clean getaway.*

William ordered coffee, then sat down at his desk and skimmed through Henderson's file. There wasn't anything special, as far as he could tell; Henderson had been born on Epsilon Cool, joined the Royal Navy as a crewman at twenty, and served for nearly nine years before his assignment to *Uncanny*. There were no major red flags in his file, but his superiors had noted several times that Henderson had a nasty habit of drinking himself into a stupor. That was probably why he'd been assigned to *Uncanny*, William decided. There wasn't enough cause to arrange for a dismissal, particularly when the Navy was desperate for manpower, but too much to allow him to serve on a ship that might actually go to war.

And he's not from Tyre, William thought. *That's not going to look good.*

Janet buzzed him a moment later. "Captain, the local authorities have put out an alert for our man," she said. "They seem confident they'll find him."

"They probably are," William said. "But keep checking with the rest of the crew anyway."

He keyed his terminal, then wrote out a brief report for Kat. There was no need to declare a full-scale emergency, not yet, but she might have to contact President Thorne if the local authorities started stonewalling. And William had to admit that they might well stonewall, particularly if Henderson wasn't located quickly, wanting to keep their reputation as pristine as possible.

The cat's already out of the bag, he thought, morbidly. *And if Henderson has been kidnapped . . .*

He paced his Ready Room, too distracted to concentrate on reading reports or intelligence bulletins from the planetary government. He'd seen crewmen die before, but this was the first time he was in command. He was the master of his ship, the person with sole responsibility for his crew . . . if one had gone missing, the responsibility lay with him. And even if Henderson turned up alive and well, there would still be trouble . . .

His wristcom bleeped. "Captain," Janet said. She sounded shaken and crestfallen. "They found a body."

William cursed. "Henderson?"

"It looks like it, sir," Janet said. "The DNA definitely matches. They're inviting us to send a party down to the surface to join the investigation."

And if the DNA matches, it is him, William thought, dryly. In theory, one could force-grow a full-body clone to serve as a decoy, but he'd never heard of that being done outside bad police procedurals. It struck him as a great deal of effort to hide one lowly deserter. *Shit.*

He cleared his throat. "I'll go down to the surface myself," he said. "Ask Doctor Prosser and Major Lupine to join me in the shuttlebay."

"Aye, Captain," Janet said. "Should we cancel the remaining shore leaves?"

William scowled. The crew wouldn't like it. They'd been cooped up on *Uncanny* for over five weeks, but better safe than sorry.

"Yes," he said. "And make sure *Lightning* is updated too."

CHAPTER SIXTEEN

"Captain McElney," a man said as William was shown into the spaceport's sickbay. "I'm Doctor Rogers, Senior Medical Officer, and this is Commander Garial, Planetary Police."

William nodded, glancing from one to the other. Rogers looked young and reassuringly competent, wearing a white doctor's overcoat rather than a uniform, while Garial wore a black uniform and looked nervous. William couldn't help feeling a flicker of sympathy for the young woman despite the seriousness of the situation. Normally, a case with interstellar implications would be handled by a far more senior officer. Her superiors probably intended to blame any diplomatic issues on her if necessary.

"Thank you for inviting us," he said. He looked directly at Garial. "Where and how did you find the body?"

"We put out an alert as soon as your crewman was reported missing," Garial said. "The usual haunts were checked at once, of course; we found nothing. It wasn't until the garbage men arrived to remove the trashcans that the body was discovered. Someone dumped it into a trashcan by the edge of the spaceport zone."

"I see," William said. He caught himself before he could begin to berate the younger woman for ignorance. The investigation had barely begun. "Please show us the body."

Rogers nodded and beckoned them through a solid metal hatch. William shivered, despite the heating elements in his uniform, as they entered the morgue. He'd seen too many dead bodies in his life. Crewman Henderson lay facedown on a table, a nasty wound clearly visible on the back of his head. William was no expert, but he was fairly sure that there was no hope of reviving the corpse. Even modern medical technology had its limits.

He wrinkled his nose at the stench. The body had clearly been suspended in liquid—he didn't want to *think* about what had been *in* the liquid—and the uniform was completely ruined. He checked, as best as he could, but he didn't see any other wounds. As far as he could tell, there had only been one blow. But it had been enough to kill Henderson . . .

"That was inflicted by a cosh, or I'm a fool," Lupine muttered. "And whoever wielded it knew *precisely* what they were doing."

"We took a brief look at the body," Garial confirmed. "That *was* the cause of death."

William forced himself to breathe through his mouth as Doctor Prosser went to work on the corpse. "Did you recover any of his possessions?"

"No, Captain," Garial said. "He was stripped of everything save for his ID card. That's bagged up on the table over there."

"It would be useless to a thief," William agreed. There *were* ways to fool a spaceport cash machine, but they required expensive implants. Anyone capable of purchasing them wouldn't *need* to wallop spacers on the head to steal their money. "I assume the murderer stole his cash. Can you trace it?"

Garial looked as though she had bitten into a lemon. "I don't think so, Captain," she said. "If your man was using paper and metal currency, it's largely untraceable. We might get lucky, but I doubt it."

William quickly considered it. Purely electronic currencies had never really caught on, certainly not outside the most advanced worlds. No one really wanted to be traced, even when they were merely going to brothels instead of engaging in criminal activity. Henderson *could* have used his ID card to purchase something—it would have to be checked—but he doubted it. There was no way to know where Henderson had gone between leaving the shuttle and dying in an alleyway.

"See what you can do," he said gently. "Do you have any preliminary conclusions?"

"It looks like a mugging," Garial said. "We can carry out a full autopsy if you wish, but there's no reason to assume anything worse. The killer may not even have *intended* to kill his victim. There's no way to know."

Lupine turned to look at her. "You can't check the cameras?"

"There are very few cameras in this part of the spaceport," Garial said. "Our guests demand privacy."

"They would," William observed. "Doctor?"

Sarah looked up. "I can confirm the cause of death," she said. "Blood alcohol levels are quite high. I'd say he was well beyond tipsy, definitely drunk. I wouldn't expect him to be able to find his way back to the shuttle without help."

"He might just have wandered down the alleyway and gotten mugged," Lupine put in. "Are there traces of any other pieces of DNA?"

"Not that I can find," Sarah said. "I can take the body back to the ship and run through a proper autopsy, but I suspect there won't be any. Dumping the body into stagnant water alone will have blurred the trail."

"I can have the body prepped for transport," Rogers said. "You'll just have to sign for it."

William looked at Garial. "Your superiors don't want it?"

"My superiors would probably be happy to merely hand it over to you," Garial said. She looked coldly furious. "Captain, the blunt truth is that we have no real leads. We'll be checking everything we can, but unless we get a lucky break the case may never be solved."

Lupine frowned. "Is this the first mugging and murder you've had?"

"We get a handful of muggings and quite a few more pickpockets, but murders are very rare," Garial confessed. "They don't always get solved."

"I see," William said. He would have liked to have the murderer's head on a platter, after interrogating him to find out if it was a mugging gone wrong or something far more sinister—but it looked as though he was going to be disappointed. "If we turn up any traces of DNA on the corpse, we'll let you know."

"Thank you, Captain," Garial said.

She didn't look pleased, William noted. Her superiors were probably torn between urging her to solve the murder and hoping the whole affair would just go away. There was no way to avoid a minor diplomatic spat, even if the murderer was caught within a day; the planetary government would want to prove it could catch the killer, but at the same time it would want to prove it wasn't the Commonwealth's lapdog. It was one hell of a mess.

At least it won't cause a major crisis, he thought. *And maybe they will be encouraged to tighten up their security.*

He turned back to look at the corpse, watching as the two doctors turned Henderson over so they could slide his body into a stasis tube. Henderson didn't look surprised, William noted; he didn't look as if he'd known he was in trouble. Had he been too drunk to realize the looming danger? Or had he *known* his killer? It was a worrying thought, but there was no proof of anything beyond a simple mugging. He had a nasty feeling that the case would never be solved.

"My superiors wish me to convey their profound regrets, Captain," Garial said, once the body was secured within the stasis field. "I have been ordered"—her mouth twisted—"to keep you apprised of our progress."

"We will be departing shortly," William said. He doubted Kat would agree to stay longer, not when there were now *seventy* freighters to escort. "I thank you for your assistance."

"Thank you, sir," Garial said. "Please accept my regrets too."

William nodded, then watched as the stasis tube was carried out the door to the waiting shuttlecraft. He and his accompanying shipmates would be back in orbit soon. William would have to read Henderson's will to determine what he wanted done with his body . . . *after* the doctor had carried out a full autopsy to see if there were *any* traces of the killer left. Henderson had been a crewman, sleeping in a compartment that held five *other* crewmen. There would be too many false trails for William to be sure of a quick solution to the mystery.

William scowled as he followed Lupine through the door, silently bidding farewell to Garial and Rogers. They'd been helpful, but their superiors *definitely* wanted them to bury the whole affair as quickly as possible.

"The security situation seems unchanged," Lupine said once they were on the shuttle and heading back to orbit. "But this is quite a rough area."

William blinked at him, then remembered that the planetary militia wasn't charged with policing Tyre's spaceports. The shore patrol handled that, with backup from the marines if necessary. To Lupine, the local spaceport had to look like a wretched hive of scum and villainy. And it was, to some extent, but it was also supposed to be reasonably safe. A spacer might lose his money to rigged gambling games or overpriced prostitutes, but he wasn't supposed to lose his *life*!

"I'll discuss the matter with Captain Falcone," William said. He had no doubt that the planetary government would prefer to have the whole matter settled as quickly as possible—the incident was going to cost them dearly, even if the Commonwealth didn't start demanding compensation—but he was reluctant to risk any more of his crew. "She can make the final call."

He glanced at Sarah as the shuttle docked. "Do the autopsy now," he ordered. "And then let me know what you find."

"Of course, sir," Sarah said.

William nodded. "And keep checking with the others who went on shore leave," he said, addressing Lupine. "If they know where Henderson went, we might be able to solve the mystery."

"Yes, sir," Lupine said.

◆ ◆ ◆

"I thank you for your consideration," Kat said. "And three destroyers will be very helpful."

"It's the least we can do," President Thorne said. His holographic image was seated, facing Kat. "You *are* escorting seventy-two freighters to Jorlem."

Kat smiled rather wanly. She rather doubted that *all* of those freighters would be going to Jorlem, but she couldn't blame their commanders for wanting an escort for some of the trip, even if they were going farther into the sector. They'd have a chance to *continue* in convoy as well, if there wasn't a more pressing concern at Jorlem. Kat hadn't made any promises, but escorting freighters was a good use of her time.

"I don't think we can escort any more ships," she said warningly. "We simply don't have the numbers."

"I understand," President Thorne said. "But I can't spare more ships."

He leaned forward. "And I am truly sorry about the recent . . . incident."

"Me too," Kat said. So far, no one had found a shred of evidence that pointed to the murderer. The local authorities seemed to believe that it was an opportunistic mugging . . . and there was nothing to suggest otherwise. But Kat's instincts told her it was something more. "If you discover any further leads . . ."

"I'll be sure to have you informed," President Thorne said.

Kat kept her true feelings from showing. Henderson's murder *could* have been a deadly mugging, but it could also have been a kidnapping gone wrong. God knew there were parties on Vangelis with good reason to hate the Commonwealth. Or the Theocracy could have attempted to kidnap Henderson with dire intent. If they'd held him long enough, they could have reconditioned him into a spy—or an assassin—and then sent him back. Henderson would have been unaware of what had been done to him until he heard the command words. After all, there wasn't a strong Theocratic presence on Vangelis, was there?

Moreover, I should know better than to see them lurking behind every bush, she told herself sharply.

"I have discussed the issue with my cabinet and a number of other leading politicians," President Thorne said. "We will probably not be joining the Commonwealth until we see clear proof of your bona fides. But we are open to discussing an alliance and closer relationships as well as limited military cooperation. I believe, if an *official* representative were to be dispatched, he would find us most welcoming."

"Thank you, Mr. President," Kat said.

"We would want concessions, of course," President Thorne added.

"Such matters can be settled by an accredited envoy," Kat said firmly. There were clear limits on her powers to negotiate, and he knew it. She wasn't sure if Thorne was teasing her or attempting to secure concessions she had no right to offer, but she'd be damned if she was going to fall into a trap. "My government will be happy to dispatch someone, or open discussions via StarCom."

"Of course," President Thorne said. "I wouldn't want to suggest otherwise."

He smiled at her. "If nothing else, please know that you have my thanks for escorting the freighters," he added. "And I hope to see you again soon."

His image vanished. Kat stared at where it had been for a long moment, then glanced at the files she'd been sent. Three destroyers—*Hawthorne*, *Rosebud*, and *Lily*—had been attached to her command, although they had strict orders to return to Vangelis a week after they arrived at Jorlem, with or without additional freighters. The solution wasn't ideal, but three additional destroyers would make it easier to protect the convoy.

As long as the merchant skippers obey orders, she thought darkly. *Admittedly, they're not very good at obeying orders.*

She scowled at the thought. Her inbox had already started to fill with complaints, ranging from protests about flying in formation to sharply worded demands to leave immediately without waiting for anyone else. She didn't blame the freighter crews for worrying—they were losing money every day they waited around at Vangelis—but there was no way she could leave at once. If nothing else, she needed to take the time to make sure that everyone, military or civilian, knew what to do in an emergency.

Her hatch buzzed. "Come!"

Crenshaw stepped into the Ready Room, looking surprisingly relaxed for someone who'd had his shore leave cut short by a murderer. Kat rather suspected he hadn't enjoyed his leave very much—his file stated that he'd never been outside the Commonwealth—even though Davidson had told her there weren't many differences between the spaceports on Tyre and Vangelis. Nonetheless, to Crenshaw, being on a foreign world had probably been enough to give him hives.

Or perhaps I'm just being mean, she thought, as she nodded to him. *Perhaps he's just trying to look after the Commonwealth's interests.*

"You wanted to see me, Captain?"

"I did," Kat confirmed. "Have a seat, Commander."

She allowed her voice to harden as Crenshaw sat down. "It has been brought to my attention," she said, "that you have been questioning members of the crew about their loyalties."

Crenshaw looked surprised, but he didn't look guilty. Kat wasn't sure if that was a good thing or not. He clearly didn't *think* he'd been doing anything wrong. Indeed, there were people who would argue, she was sure, that it *wasn't* a bad thing.

But it is, she thought. *It's bad for crew morale.*

"I have been doing my duty to the Navy," Crenshaw said finally. "It is important to know where their loyalties lie."

"It is also important not to damage crew morale," Kat snapped. "Or to introduce divisions where there were none."

She scowled at him. Maybe there were good reasons to question Sir William's position, certainly for anyone who hadn't *met* him, but Tasha had been through Piker's Peak. And she was hardly the first foreign officer to go through the academy. To suggest that she had divided loyalties would undermine the Navy—an utter disaster during wartime.

"It is my duty," Crenshaw said stubbornly.

"Only if you have a reason to be concerned," Kat said. "*Do* you have a reason to be concerned?"

"A person raised on Tyre is heir to our traditions," Crenshaw said. "They understand, at an instinctive level, how our society works. Outsiders . . . do not. How can they? They look at how you were raised to command and see nepotism. They don't see the underlying reality of building a patronage network."

"Of *course* they see nepotism," Kat said. Tyre had often claimed to be a meritocracy, but outsiders had good reason to argue that the planetary system was nothing of the sort. "What do you think they see when they hear that *you* were promoted?"

"Nor do they see how talented outsiders are absorbed into the aristocracy," Crenshaw added, seriously. It wasn't a real answer. "Or how untalented aristocrats are quietly shuffled aside."

He had a point, Kat silently conceded. She knew that her father would want his children to succeed him . . . but a continuing dynasty wasn't guaranteed. There would be a major struggle over the dukedom when her father died, even though Peter Falcone had largely taken over his father's duties when Duke Falcone had become the Minister for War Production. And while Kat's brother would have an advantage, it would hardly be decisive. The rest of the family would want a say too.

Meanwhile true incompetents are shifted elsewhere, she thought, *because if they were promoted into high places, such moves would reflect badly on their patrons.*

"You may be right," she said. "But I cannot allow you to continue to disrupt the crew."

Crenshaw leaned forward. "Captain?"

"You are to confine yourself to the regular duties of an XO," Kat added. "That is an order, *Commander*, which you can have in writing if you wish."

"That won't be necessary, Captain," Crenshaw said.

"Glad to hear it," Kat said. She glanced at her terminal, then back at him. "We've finalized the departure date. Make sure that all the freighters are ready to leave without delay."

"Aye, Captain," Crenshaw said.

CHAPTER SEVENTEEN

Joel stood in the observation blister, staring out into the eerie lights of hyperspace.

No one had realized that Henderson's murderer was on *Uncanny*. Julia had hacked sickbay's computer files, allowing Joel to read the autopsy report. There had been nothing to suggest that Henderson had been the victim of anything but a random mugging gone wrong. Doctor Prosser certainly hadn't found any traces that might lead her to Joel.

Unless they're concealing something, Joel reminded himself. He knew that wasn't particularly likely. They were on a warship, in a time of war. Sir William had more than enough authority to order an interrogation if he had *any* reason to suspect Joel of anything remotely criminal. *No, they don't know anything.*

He clasped his hands behind his back, contemplating the affair. Joel had felt no remorse for Captain Abraham's death. The man had been an unimaginative criminal, too stupid or too arrogant to realize that, eventually, someone would put the pieces together. Captain Abraham believed that his aristocratic connections were enough to save him from the hangman. And he might have been right. Joel suspected he *had* been right. But he'd been too stupid to consider the possibilities . . .

Henderson had been different. He'd been an ally right from the start. Joel had thought he could be trusted, that all the little resentments souring the crew would be more than enough to keep him onside. Furthermore, Joel had had plans for him, once upon a time. Yet Henderson had been too easily led to be left alive. The man had genuinely *admired* Sir William. He hadn't truly comprehended that he was already too deeply implicated to back out.

He had to die, Joel told himself.

Nevertheless, he still felt regret. Henderson's death looked like an accident—as far as he knew, none of the other plotters believed it to have been anything else—but it was still dangerous. There was no honor among thieves, no shared loyalty to a greater cause . . . if his other allies came to believe that Joel considered them expendable, they would try to kill him or betray him. They wouldn't have any other choice.

In addition, we now need a replacement for Henderson, he thought. *Finding one won't be easy.*

Joel was frustrated. He was a *senior chief*. He had *years* of experience in reading people, from greenie lieutenants issuing hundreds of orders to cover up their inexperience to surly crewmen bitter and resentful because they were constantly passed over for promotion. He was a past master at sounding out potential allies without revealing too much, at least until they were committed. And he had to admit, despite himself, that Sir William had done an excellent job of draining the lake dry. Too many of the newcomers were true believers in the Navy, convinced of its essential benevolence. Approaching even one of them might be far too revealing if the person he chose took his concerns to his superiors.

He gritted his teeth in annoyance as his wristcom bleeped. The original plan would need to be modified before Sir William managed to turn too many members of the crew into loyalists. And he *would*. Joel had met dozens of commanding officers in his career, but none of them had shown the same willingness to get his hands dirty as Sir William. *He'd* worked as hard on *Uncanny* as the remainder of the crew. He'd won respect and admiration from his subordinates . . . hell, *Joel* would have admired him if he hadn't known it was a trap.

Shaking his head, Joel turned and strode towards the hatch. The remembrance ceremony was due to take place in ten minutes. Even *that* was frustrating. Captain Abraham wouldn't have bothered with a ceremony for a murdered crewman, not when he could be scheming to find a way to take advantage of the man's death. But Sir William had decided to hold one as soon as the massive convoy slipped back into hyperspace. And nearly two-thirds of the crew would attend, even if they hadn't known Henderson personally. He'd still been one of them, after all.

On top of that, we'll soon be at Jorlem, Joel thought, *where* Lightning *and* Uncanny *will go their separate ways.*

Joel scowled as he walked through the hatch. The original plan was still workable, with a few covert modifications. But it would be chancy. He considered, briefly, deserting at Jorlem. Fleeing wouldn't be hard. Jorlem had a fair claim to being the most corrupt planet outside Theocratic space. He had enough money, in three different currencies, stashed away to purchase everything he'd need to remain unnoticed, even after Sir William sounded the alert. A few weeks in an underground hospital would be long enough to warp his DNA out of all recognition, then he could obtain papers that would get him a berth on a freighter heading farther from the Commonwealth. Still, deserting would mean giving up.

All my dreams would be torn asunder, he told himself. *Better to dare greatness than live a life in the shadows . . . never knowing when I might have to start running again.*

Julia nodded to Joel as he entered the shuttlebay. A quarter of the mourners were already there, standing in front of the coffin and remembering Henderson. If they *could* remember Henderson, Joel thought, cynically. He doubted that many outside Henderson's compartment really knew him. But that wasn't the point. Henderson had been a member of the crew. He had to be given a proper good-bye.

He took his place next to Julia and waited.

◆ ◆ ◆

William felt tired and frustrated as he stood in front of the sealed casket—no one had been allowed to see the body after the doctor had finished her autopsy—and worked his way through the remembrance service. Henderson had expressed a wish to be buried in hyperspace, like so many other spacers; he hadn't requested a particular service or even to have his body shipped home. It was all too clear, in so many ways, that Henderson hadn't had any other home. His will stipulated that his possessions were to be divided among his bunkmates while his salary was to be added to the shore leave fund. It was the mark of a man who had no life outside *Uncanny*.

Poor bastard, William thought. William had had no life outside the Navy, but then he'd never really wanted to go home. Perhaps Henderson had felt the same way. *Plus, he died so far from his friends.*

"Crewman Henderson requested to be buried in hyperspace," he said as he finished the ceremony. "His body will be launched into space this afternoon, after final farewells."

He closed his eyes for a long moment, then opened them. "Dismissed."

The shuttlebay emptied rapidly, the crewmen and officers who hadn't known Henderson heading back to their bunks while the ones who had known him gathered in front of the casket to say a final good-bye. William didn't blame the ones who had left, although he saw a few nasty looks aimed at their backs by the ones who remained. Even if they *had* known Henderson, they needed to catch up on their sleep before they returned to duty. The body wouldn't be launched into space for a few hours, even though the ceremony had been completed. Everyone had to have a fair chance to say good-bye.

He waited until the last of the mourners had left the shuttlebay, then walked over to the casket and peered down at the synthetic wood. There was no way to see the body, but he'd read the doctor's report and seen the images. He could imagine what lurked within the box. The doctor had practically broken the body down, piece by piece, but she'd found no clues leading to the murderer.

"He was definitely drunk," she'd said. "There was enough alcohol in his body to ensure that he was practically helpless when attacked. But there's no suggestion he was in a brothel or even having a quickie on the streets."

William's lips thinned in disapproval. He *hated* mysteries. Henderson was the first crewman to die under his sole command, and his death might never be explained. And yet, it was *possible* it was nothing more than a tragic accident. A mugging gone wrong . . . knocking out the victim *would* be the safest way to mug them. The body then may have been concealed after the killer had realized what he'd done. God knew the planetary authorities wouldn't hesitate to hand the killer over to the Commonwealth if they caught him. They wouldn't dare risk *that* sort of diplomatic incident.

Poor bastard, he thought again. *What happened to you down there?*

He cursed under his breath. Save for the blow that actually killed Henderson, there was no evidence of trauma. There was nothing to suggest that the original theory was wrong, yet it nagged at his mind. Bad luck . . . or an incident someone had tried to make look like an accident? Still, the simplest theory was often the right one. Henderson had been so drunk that a half-witted mugger would have had no difficulty spotting the mark, and then sneaking up from behind.

"I'm sorry," he said, addressing the casket. "I wish I'd known you better."

William was always good at remembering the people under his command, even after he'd become an officer and started the long climb towards a captaincy of his own. Just remembering a man's name and a few facts about him went a long way towards earning loyalty. He remembered Henderson, a crewman who'd been on *Uncanny* for over a year before William had assumed command. But nothing made him stand out. No prospects for quick promotion, no black marks that would have damned him on any other ship . . . the man had been an average crewman. And now he was dead.

I do wish I'd known you better, he thought bitterly.

Perhaps the aristocrats are luckier, he told himself as he turned to walk back to his Ready Room. They rarely spent time on the lower decks before being promoted. Kat cared about her crew, he knew, but she didn't feel it the same way he did. How could she? She'd been trained to be an officer right from the start rather than starting her career among enlisted men. She hadn't been taught to see them as *people*. She'd even been warned that getting too close could make it harder to send them to their deaths.

But I wouldn't give it up for the world, he thought. He stepped into his Ready Room and silently blessed Janet when he saw a pot of coffee on his desk. *They're just too detached from the crewmen under their command.*

He sat down and poured himself a mug of coffee, then pulled up Henderson's file, searching for his next of kin. Like William himself, Henderson didn't seem to have any particularly close relatives on his homeworld. His sole listed family member was a sister, one he probably hadn't seen in years. William couldn't help thinking that he and Henderson had a great deal in common, even if Henderson hadn't possessed the drive to better himself by trying to become a mustang. But then, life could be hard for mustangs. William knew it all too well.

Opening his drawer, he pulled out a sheet of paper and a pen. Tradition demanded a physical letter, even though his sister would be informed of her brother's death almost as soon as the StarCom message reached her homeworld. The Navy worked hard to make sure that the next of kin were notified first before the news outlets learned of the deaths . . . although William found it hard to believe that any of the big media corporations would care. Henderson simply wasn't famous and his death wasn't particularly glorious.

He felt like a fraud as he jotted down a few lines. There was no way he could say very much, certainly nothing *sincere*. None of Henderson's supervisors had had very much to say about him, positive or negative. William had been taught to keep the letter positive, but what could he *say*?

Shaking his head, William started to write. He owed it to Henderson, who'd died under his command; he owed it to the Navy, in whose service Henderson had died. But he couldn't help feeling as though he was lying to the poor woman. How long had it been since she'd heard from her brother?

Perhaps years. The thought caught at William's heart. *If he was anything like me . . .*

◆ ◆ ◆

"Taking so many ships was a huge risk, Captain," Crenshaw said.

Kat resisted the urge to ask if he'd worked that out by himself or had a five-year-old point it out to him. Taking so many freighters *was* a huge risk; in hindsight, she should have placed a limit on how many ships could be escorted at any one time. But she hadn't realized just how many freighters would want to go to Jorlem . . .

. . . and just how many others would plan to make the trip with a guaranteed escort?

"Risk is our business," she said. Her response was unsatisfactory, but as one of the Navy's unofficial mottos, it was unanswerable. "But you're right, it *is* risky."

She looked up at the holographic display, cursing under her breath. Thankfully, most of the merchant skippers had enough sense to maintain formation, but she'd had to herd a couple of the more imprudent ships back into line. She'd ringed the convoy with sensor and ECM drones in hopes of spotting trouble, yet she was grimly aware that a handful of antimatter warheads could scatter the entire convoy. In an attempt to keep pirates from preying on the convoy, she'd offered the Theocracy a target it couldn't miss.

Unless they don't know we're here, she reminded herself. *And they shouldn't.*

She scowled at the thought. She'd filed a flight plan with Vangelis's System Command, then unilaterally changed it as soon as the convoy had entered hyperspace. If they were lucky, any leakers within System Command would have passed the wrong flight plan to pirates champing at the bit to attack. But if there *had* been an enemy spy watching the convoy's departure, he might just have been able to see them change course.

They shouldn't have time to move their ships, if they were planning an ambush, she thought. *But we won't ever know for sure.*

"We could send half of the freighters off on their own," Crenshaw said. "Or we could leave them waiting in interstellar space."

Kat considered the suggestion for a long moment. If they were lucky, and the odds *would* be massively in their favor, they *could* hide half the convoy somewhere in the depths of interstellar space where the pirates wouldn't have a hope of finding them. But they simply didn't have time to play games. According to reports, pirate activity, and raider activity perhaps, was on the rise. She needed to start patrolling the sector as quickly as possible.

"It's a good idea," she said. "But we don't have the time."

Crenshaw beamed. Kat wondered idly if he was pleased at the acknowledgement or being in a position to blame her if something went wrong. She was surprised he hadn't asked for his doubts to be noted in the log. But then, if everything went *right*, his doubts would make him look like an idiot. Part of the XO's job was to bring concerns to his commanding officer, but there were limits.

She looked up at him. "How did the crew cope with having their shore leave curtailed?"

"No trouble," Crenshaw assured her. He sounded surprisingly confident. "They understood the dangers."

Kat lifted her eyebrows. She had no doubt that her crew *did* understand the dangers, but she would have been surprised if there hadn't been any grumbling. *Lightning* was hardly a tiny gunboat, yet her crew had been cooped up in her hull for the past six weeks. They'd *want* to get out of the ship for a few hours, despite the risks.

"They do have some reason to look forward to shore leave on Jorlem," Crenshaw added after a moment. "There are plenty of stories about that world."

"Few of them good," Kat said. Vangelis was relatively decent; Jorlem, if half the reports were to be believed, was staggeringly corrupt. The planet was nothing more than a dictatorship held together by overwhelming force. "But we should be able to get some shore leave."

"I'm sure they will be pleased to hear that," Crenshaw said.

Kat tended to agree. "As long as they don't leave the spaceport zone," she added. Some members of her crew would want to go elsewhere. "I can't guarantee their safety outside it."

CHAPTER EIGHTEEN

Somewhat to Kat's surprise, the two-week journey to Jorlem passed without even catching a sniff of a pirate vessel, let alone an enemy raider. It was possible, she concluded as the convoy made its final approach, that her deception plan might have sent the pirates in the wrong direction, but it was *also* possible that they'd been fooled into believing that the escorts were waiting for them. Hyperspace played enough odd tricks on sensors to make it difficult for the pirates to sort out the *real* warships from the drones.

"Captain, we are approaching the planned emergence zone," Lieutenant Wheeler said. "I estimate that we can open the gateway in five minutes."

"See to it," Kat ordered. She'd been careful not to give Jorlem the correct emergence zone coordinates either. Ships usually didn't fly out of hyperspace right into the face of enemy fire, but if the pirates knew *precisely* where she was going to arrive . . . she pushed the idea aside and took one last look at the fleet display. "Take us out as planned."

She leaned back in her command chair as the final few seconds ticked down to zero. They'd succeeded, despite the risks. They'd escorted a vast number of freighters to Jorlem, something that would do wonders for the sector's economy *and* the Commonwealth's reputation. Kat knew all too well that some of the freighters would probably be caught when they went on to their next destinations, but it didn't detract from their current achievement . . .

"Gateway opening now," Wheeler reported. "We're going through."

"The freighters are following us," Crenshaw added. "They're falling into the post-emergence formation."

"Tactical scan," Kat snapped.

"Working, Captain," Weiberg said. "No immediate threats; I say again, no immediate threats."

Kat relaxed, just a little. The odds had been in their favor, but still . . . They'd made it out of hyperspace without incident.

"Continue scan," she ordered. "I want a full accounting of everything within the system."

"Aye, Captain," Weiberg said.

"*Uncanny* has exited the gateway," Linda reported.

"Good," Kat said. She watched the tactical display as it updated rapidly. Jorlem had been settled for longer than Vangelis, but had only around half as much interplanetary traffic making its way through the system. And there was . . . *something* . . . about the world that suggested that the local government didn't have complete authority outside its atmosphere. There was something haphazard about the cloudscoops, asteroid bases, and freighters that reminded her of the early days of space travel. Kat couldn't escape the impression that there was no rhyme or reason to the settlement . . .

The display flashed red. "Captain," Weiberg snapped as alarms began to howl. "I'm picking up a Theocratic starship orbiting Jorlem!"

"Red alert," Kat ordered. The alarms grew louder. "Order the convoy to prepare to reenter hyperspace on my command."

She thought rapidly as the display updated. The enemy ship was clearly visible, making no attempt to hide. The local government had to be aware of its existence, which meant . . . what? Had Jorlem surrendered to the Theocracy? But none of the scans suggested that there had been a recent battle. The planetary defenses, such as they were, seemed to be intact. So were the handful of destroyers and gunboats operated by the planetary navy.

They might have sold out, Kat thought. It wouldn't be the first time, according to ONI, that the Theocracy had found willing allies among a planetary government. *Or they might have been bribed into compliance.*

"Tactical report," Crenshaw said. "What *is* that ship?"

"It looks like an overcompensating battlecruiser," Weiberg said. Kat would have smiled if the situation hadn't been so dire. "I would have said she was actually closer to a battleship, but her power curves are definitely lighter than any battleship on record . . ."

Kat was no expert on starship design, but it *did* look as though the vessel's designers had been trying to crossbreed a battlecruiser with a battleship, combining the former's speed with the latter's armor. The Commonwealth had tried to build heavier battlecruisers, if she recalled correctly, yet the designers had run into problems balancing the two aspects. Had the Theocracy solved a problem that had plagued the Royal Navy for years? Or had they merely put together a testbed starship and then pressed her into service?

She glanced at Weiberg. "Is she hostile?"

Weiberg frowned down at his console. "I'm not sure, Captain," he said. "She's running a standard tactical scan and her shields are up, but she hasn't targeted us."

"That means nothing," Crenshaw said sharply.

Kat nodded. The convoy hadn't been trying to hide. She would have been surprised if the enemy ship *hadn't* managed to get a passive lock on her hull without using anything that would alert her crew. ONI believed that the Theocracy's sensors were poor, but not *that* poor. And yet . . .

She scowled. Two heavy cruisers *might* be able to take the battle-ship-battlecruiser, even if the Vangelis ships avoided action. And she had authority to engage the Theocracy wherever she found it. But she could be certain of taking heavy casualties, perhaps losing one or both of her ships . . .

"Captain, I'm picking up a message from System Command," Linda said. "They're ordering us to stand down and take up orbital positions on the other side of the planet."

Crenshaw snorted. "They're ordering *us* to stand down?"

Kat silenced him with a glare. "Ask them what's going on," she ordered. Had the planet been threatened into submission? Or were they silently hoping that Kat and her tiny squadron could drive the enemy ship away? "And request updated shipping slots for the freighters."

She waited, bracing herself as the convoy neared the planet. The enemy ship hadn't moved, nor had it done anything to suggest that it was preparing to attack. Kat puzzled over the scenario as more and more data flowed into the display, telling her things she didn't want to know about the battleship-battlecruiser's known and presumed abilities. More missile tubes and energy weapons than a standard battlecruiser, estimated drive curves only barely below a heavy cruiser's . . . none of the reports made reassuring reading. She could evade the ship with ease if she wanted to avoid engagement, but beating her would be a different story.

Linda made a choking noise. "They're claiming that the Theocracy has sent a diplomatic mission to Jorlem," she said. "And they're *insisting* that we do nothing hostile within their space."

Kat blinked in surprise. A diplomatic mission? In her experience, the Theocracy didn't *do* diplomacy. The ambassadors they'd sent to Tyre had been spies, rather than genuine diplomats. And *that* had been to a major power. The Theocracy's approach to minor planets was nothing more than intimidation backed by brute force, a "submit or die" strategy.

She thought rapidly. Her orders authorized her to engage the Theocracy . . . but picking a fight in someone else's space would cause a diplomatic nightmare, even if she won without causing any damage to the local infrastructure. She had no great regard for the local government, but the rest of the sector would be unamused. All the goodwill she'd won by escorting the freighters would be lost. And yet, a ship of that size and power could not be allowed to fly around the sector without hindrance.

It's an odd choice, she thought. The battleship-battlecruiser was intimidating, at least to anyone who didn't have a superdreadnought or two to defend their world, but it wasn't designed to raid shipping. It was just like swatting flies with a sledgehammer. *They'd have done better to flood the sector with light units.*

"Inform them that we recognize their right to control their space," she said. "But we will defend ourselves if attacked."

"Aye, Captain," Linda said.

Crenshaw gave her an incredulous look, but she ignored him. The enemy ship *had* to have arrived within the last two weeks, after the convoy had left Vangelis. There would have been an alert, she was sure, if it had arrived sooner. The StarCom orbiting Jorlem certainly *looked* intact. And even if it wasn't, a freighter crew would have spread the word . . .

"And request a priority message slot from the StarCom," she added. "Send the alert to Tyre."

She leaned back in her command chair and watched as the convoy neared the planet. The locals were smart to insist on keeping the planet's bulk between the two warring sides, although only a few minutes were needed for one force to alter position and bring the other under fire. And the Theocracy would have no qualms about launching antimatter warheads in planetary orbit. It wasn't as if more enemies would make any difference to the war.

"Captain," Crenshaw said. "I really must protest . . ."

Kat looked at him. "Do you have a better idea?"

She glanced down at her terminal, hastily reviewing the regulations concerning enemy ships in neutral systems. Technically, she was supposed to demand that the battleship-battlecruiser be told to leave, but Jorlem didn't have the firepower to enforce its will. If the planetary government requested that *she* leave instead . . . she'd have to do as she was told. And if the Theocracy starship really *was* on a diplomatic mission, ordering them out would be a bad move.

At least we know where the battleship is, she thought morbidly.

"We could engage her," Crenshaw said. "She's a long way from home."

That was true, Kat had to admit. But it was also true of her ships. Crippling the enemy ship would probably strand her in the Jorlem Sector, yet if it cost Kat one or both of her cruisers . . .

"If she's genuinely on a diplomatic mission," she said, "we have no legal right to engage her."

She cursed under her breath. The Theocracy wasn't a signatory to the Diplomacy Treaty, but the Commonwealth *was*. Interfering with a diplomatic mission from one state to another would be a breach in the treaty . . . and while the Commonwealth and the Theocracy were already at war, it would bring protests from most of the other interstellar powers. The Commonwealth would have to punish Kat for breaking the treaty, even if her superiors understood what she'd done.

And it won't be a slap on the wrist this time, she thought, savagely.

The rules were clear. She could engage the enemy ship in interstellar space without consequences, but she couldn't pick a fight near Jorlem unless the enemy fired first. And if the Theocracy was playing it smart, they *wouldn't* fire first. They'd want to do something to undermine the Commonwealth's position, perhaps by manipulating matters until *Kat* fired first . . .

"Entering orbit," Wheeler reported. "They've cleared an orbital slot for us."

Putting the ships on opposite sides of the planet was pointless, Kat knew. Given the speed and power of modern weapons, they might as well have been two gunfighters standing right next to each other when they started shooting. But she suspected she understood the real point. The local government was terrified. Three powerful starships in orbit, each one capable of trashing their defenses in an hour of hard fighting . . . and two sides, caught in a war that would only end when one of them was crushed. And Jorlem, not the most powerful system in the sector, would be crushed between them if the two sides started shooting.

"Very good," she said. She looked at Crenshaw. "All shore leave is cancelled until we have a better idea of what's going on here."

"Yes, Captain," Crenshaw said.

"We will remain at red alert, with shields and weapons charged at all times," Kat added. It would put immense wear and tear on both cruisers—and she knew the supply department back home would be furious—but it couldn't be helped. They were far too close to the enemy ship. The situation could turn nasty in seconds, too quickly for her to bring up her shields from a standing start. "And keep a very close sensor watch. If that blasted ship so much as twitches, I want to know about it."

"Yes, Captain," Crenshaw said.

He paused. "We *could* plan a preemptive strike."

Kat shook her head. She had no doubt that the enemy ship was watching her too. Her shields were already up. By the time *Lightning* and *Uncanny* unleashed hell, the enemy ship would be ready to meet them. And a fight in high orbit would devastate the surrounding infra-structure even if the planet itself remained unscathed.

"We can wait," she said. "In the meantime, start detaching the freighters from the convoy. If any of them want to go onwards, tell them we don't know where we're going yet."

She rose. "Communications, send a copy of the diplomatic package to the planetary government. Inform me if there is a response."

"Aye, Captain," Linda said.

Kat nodded to Crenshaw. "I'll be in my Ready Room," she said. "Call me if anything changes."

She stepped through the hatch and sat down at her desk, then keyed her terminal, calling William. They needed to chat privately.

"Kat," William said as his image appeared in front of her. "We are in an interesting pickle."

"That's an understatement," Kat said. She brought up the latest set of analysis reports from the tactical department and skimmed them rapidly. The analysts thought that the battleship-battlecruiser design had a number of potential flaws, but Kat doubted that any of them would be fatal. "We can't fight her here, and we can't wait for her to leave."

"Particularly not as she will be expecting us to follow her," William agreed. "She might even have diplomatic credentials from right across the sector."

Kat scowled. Jumping the enemy ship in hyperspace *might* not be a breach of the treaty, but it would certainly make the Commonwealth look very bad. Even with a clear reason to attack the ship, such action could still be turned against them. Any evidence she cared to submit to the other interstellar powers could easily be branded fake. And yet, very few of the powers would *care* to side with the Theocracy . . .

It's the principle of the thing, she thought darkly. *Blowing up their diplomats would set an awkward precedent.*

"The other alternative is to ignore her," William offered. "We came here to win goodwill, Kat."

"And to destroy raiders," Kat said.

"That ship isn't a raider," William pointed out.

Kat nodded in agreement. She'd had the same thought. But still . . . it was an odd ship to send on a diplomatic mission. She would have thought that the Theocracy was too desperate for hulls to send such a ship so far from the front lines. Unless they were trying to suggest that they had starships to spare . . .

She rubbed her forehead. She *hated* diplomacy.

"We'll stay here until we learn what the planetary government has to say," she said reluctantly. "And then we'll decide what to do next."

"They may have good reason for siding with the Theocracy," William warned. "It isn't as if the Commonwealth will give their dictatorship the time of day."

"Point," Kat agreed. "But they won't last forever if the Theocracy wins the war."

Unless they're gambling on the Theocracy losing, her thoughts added. *They might be planning to take all they can get, then hope we win before the bills come due.*

William cleared his throat. "There's another approach we could take," he offered. He sounded as though he was checking his words very carefully. "Some of my . . . contacts . . . might be present on Jorlem. I was here back before Operation Knife. If we could get some information from them . . ."

Kat frowned. "Will they talk to you?"

"It's worth a try," William said. "If I make the approach, they'll certainly check with their superiors before making any commitments. And even if they refuse to help directly, they can probably put us in touch with information brokers."

"For which we will have to pay," Kat observed darkly.

She shook her head. "If you think it's worth it, do so," she ordered. "I leave that in your hands."

"Thank you, Captain," William said.

It galled Kat to rely on smugglers and information brokers, even if one of the smugglers was William's brother, but she suspected they would be more reliable than anything she heard from the planetary government. Information brokers in high society as well as low would rapidly lose clients if they provided false information, intentionally or otherwise. And there were too many ships coming and going from

Jorlem for her to believe that the local government could control everything.

Her intercom bleeped. "Captain, we received a message from the planetary government," Linda said. "They're inviting you to a meeting on the surface."

"It might be a trap," William warned. "I could go in your place."

"That would be a sign of weakness," Kat said. She understood his concerns, but she knew she couldn't give in to them. "I have to go."

"Then take a dozen marines," William urged. "If there's anyone the Theocracy would want to capture, Kat, it's you."

"The planetary government won't take the risk," Kat said, wishing she felt confident. A dictatorship wouldn't survive if the Commonwealth expanded into the sector. "And I'll have Pat with me."

"One marine?" William pressed. "This is madness."

"Perhaps," Kat said. Dictators were dangerously unpredictable. "But I have to go anyway."

CHAPTER NINETEEN

"This place reminds me of Cadiz," Davidson muttered as they drove from the spaceport towards Jorlem City. "And not in a good way."

Kat bowed her head in quiet agreement. Jorlem City was a brooding oppressive mass, giant apartment blocks placed so close together that the streets were shrouded in perpetual semidarkness. Hundreds of security guards were visible everywhere, keeping an eye on a population that seemed driven by sullen anger. The scent of revolution, of a powder keg ready to explode at the slightest spark, hung in the air. She could see dozens of teenage boys loitering at street corners, their expressions bitter and resentful, but she could only see a handful of women, all older. That wasn't a good sign.

She gritted her teeth as they passed yet another looming statue of Ruthven Alexis, the third planetary dictator. He'd taken power in a military coup, according to the files, when the previous dictator had grown a little careless. Kat had read enough about force-based societies to know, all too well, that carelessness meant death. No dictator could ever give up power, not when his enemies would move in for the kill. He'd stay in office until he died, or he was overthrown, or an outside force removed him. With proper medical care, a dictator could remain alive and healthy for decades.

A waster, Kat thought angrily.

She felt a stab of sympathy for the planet's population, trapped in an iron cage. She was used to power, she'd been *born* to power, but her family believed that power should be put to good use. Alexis, on the other hand, seemed only interested in self-glorification. She'd counted dozens of statues and hundreds of posters, all showing his face. And the buildings were monstrous pieces of Gothic design, a repulsive historical nightmare. Alexis could have built his system up to rival Vangelis if he hadn't wasted so much of his resources on his capital. Instead . . .

Davidson shot her a sharp look as the car turned the corner and drove towards the palace, a giant and utterly tasteless structure looming over the square. Hundreds of soldiers, wearing uniforms that made Kat's dress uniform look comfortable, were stationed in front of the palace, so still and unmoving that she honestly wondered, just for a moment, if they were statues or holograms. But in a dictatorship, they'd probably been taught to stand perfectly still for hours. She couldn't help wondering if the rifles they were carrying were actually loaded.

The car came to a halt. A uniformed flunky appeared from nowhere—his uniform made him look like an admiral—and opened the car door, inviting Kat and Davidson to climb out. Kat did so, feeling as if she had stepped into a trap as she was led up the stairs and into the palace. Her implants reported a whole series of security scans, one after the other, poking and prying at her body. She wondered, absently, if Alexis was so paranoid he'd insist on a strip search, then decided it was unlikely. It would be an insult to the whole Commonwealth.

She kept her face impassive as they strode down a marble corridor large enough to hold a full-sized tank. The designers seemed to have scaled everything up, as if citizens on Jorlem were two or three times the size of citizens elsewhere. They'd covered the floors in stone and the walls in a greenish marble, leaving them completely bare. The audience chamber was so massive she almost laughed out loud when they were shown through the giant doors. The space was easily larger than the throne room on Tyre, yet it was completely empty, save for a single table in the exact center of the room. Her footsteps echoed on the stone floor as she approached the triangular table. Three people were seated, waiting for her.

"His Grace Alexis, President of Jorlem," the flunky announced. "I present Captain Katherine Falcone and Major Patrick Davidson."

Kat was almost disappointed when President Alexis—she reminded herself, sharply, to call him Mr. President—rose to his feet. He looked nothing like his statues, although the malice in his eyes was enough to worry her. He could have rejuvenated himself into a god, but instead he was grossly overweight and going bald. And his grip, when she shook his hand, felt clammy.

"Welcome," Alexis said. He looked her up and down, his gaze lingering on her breasts for just a moment longer than necessary. Kat suspected it was a deliberate attempt to make her uncomfortable, and it would have worked if she hadn't served as a midshipwoman. "My new friends"—he waved a hand towards the table—"were just telling me all about you."

Kat looked past him and frowned. The two Theocrats—they couldn't be anyone else—were eying her with undisguised hostility. She stared back at them calmly, her face emotionless. They were both bearded, wearing long red robes, but one of them was clearly much younger than the other, perhaps the same age as Kat herself. The older one looked disdainful as well as hostile, while the other showed naked hatred and rage. Did he have something personal against her? She might well have killed one of his relatives during the war.

"This . . . this *woman* . . . is a murderess," the younger one snarled. "You shouldn't trust anything she says."

"These . . . *people* . . . are monsters," Kat countered. "They'll use you, and then they'll dispose of you."

The older Theocrat cleared his throat. "I believe we were discussing options for providing security to your sector, Most Honored President," he said. He had an oozing voice that made Kat distrust him immediately. In some ways, she would have preferred his partner. "Our offer is quite sincere."

"And what offer is that?" Kat said.

"We would hate to discuss such matters with you," the Theocrat said. "Most Honored President . . ."

"She can hear your offer," Alexis said casually. "The Commonwealth may want to better it."

The Theocrat's expression didn't change. Kat couldn't help feeling that he was *pleased* at this development, although his younger companion looked furious.

"We are prepared to offer convoy escorts and various military supplies to Jorlem, in exchange for basing rights and allowing missionaries to move freely among your population," the Theocrat said. "Our ships will be more than capable of protecting your shipping from the raiders."

Kat kept her expression blank with an effort. What sort of idiot would *accept* such an offer?

Her mind raced. She rather doubted the Theocracy could spare enough ships to make a dent in the pirate populations . . . but if they were *controlling* the pirates, all they'd have to do was call the bastards off. And basing rights at Jorlem would cause a whole series of problems for the Commonwealth. The Commonwealth would either have to attack Jorlem, opening a new front in the war, or let them get away with terrorizing an entire sector. Such an endeavor wouldn't last, but they could do a great deal of damage before they were stopped.

She looked at the older Theocrat. "How many ships can you spare?"

The Theocrat ignored her. "We would not be making any political demands," he added, addressing Alexis. "You would be free to run your planet however you wish."

"Until the war is over," Kat said, "and too many of your people have embraced the faith."

"Enough," the younger Theocrat exploded. "I must *insist* that this . . . this *girl* . . . be removed from the room."

His elder shot him an angry look. "I apologize for my companion, Most Honored President," he said. "He is as yet unused to the requirements of diplomacy."

"And unaware of how to behave," Davidson rumbled.

Kat kept her expression blank, even though she knew the enemy had scored an own goal. Alexis most likely didn't give a damn about her being a woman, but trying to order the dictator around in his own palace would worry him. He'd have to wonder, deep inside, if it was a harbinger of what was to come, if the Theocracy won the war.

"The Theocracy has taken heavy losses in the war," she added, pouring fuel on the fire. "I doubt they could supply enough ships to make a difference."

"Your ignorance of our fleet numbers is our strength," the older Theocrat said. "We can and we will meet our commitments."

"One would hope so," Alexis murmured.

"And we would not be making political demands," the older Theocrat repeated. He nodded towards Davidson. "The *Commonwealth* would be making political demands."

Kat felt her expression tighten. The Commonwealth believed in equal opportunities, if not equal outcomes. A governing system that made it hard for newcomers to enter, thus ensuring that those who *did* enter were the best of the best, was one thing, but a system that was nothing more than a dictatorship held together by naked force was beyond the pale. Jorlem would never be allowed to join the Commonwealth until it carried out some much-needed political reforms, reforms that would cost Alexis his position and quite probably his life.

And that gives him a reason to favor the Theocracy, she thought. *It might prove just as fatal, in the long run, but they wouldn't be undermining him in the short term.*

"There is room to maneuver," Kat said. She wondered just how carefully Alexis had read the diplomatic package. Kat *did* have some authority to negotiate, but not enough to leave the dictator in place. "And you might remain in control as your planet began to reform."

"Doubtful," the younger Theocrat said. He sneered rudely. "How like a *girl* to think that such an absurd claim would be believable."

Kat studied him, thoughtfully. Her first impression had been that he'd been given the job because of connections, rather than any actual skill, but she was starting to wonder if that was actually true. His interjections had been quite successful in undermining her positions. Hell, Alexis might even find them *amusing*. Watching the Commonwealth representative being put in her place would please him even if he took Kat's words to heart.

"You could also leave your planet and live on Tyre," Kat added. "It *has* happened before."

Alexis didn't look pleased. It *had* happened before—the Commonwealth had offered asylum to various unsavory individuals to get them out of the way—but such an act would mean giving up his power. *Undoubtedly*, he would never be allowed to leave his gilded cage on Tyre. Perhaps he would take the offer if a mob was storming his palace, but by then it would be far too late.

Kat forced herself to lean back as the discussion raged on. Alexis was trying to play the Theocracy off against the Commonwealth, striving to see who would give him the better bargain, but he had to know that both powers would eventually prove fatal to his dreams of independence. Kat listened as the Theocracy made a number of promises she doubted they could keep, then offered a handful of smaller concessions of her own. But, in the end, she suspected that neither side had actually *won*.

"It has been an interesting discussion," Alexis said, resting one hand on the table. He nodded politely to the Theocrats. "But now I must ask Lady Katherine to speak to me in private."

Davidson looked alarmed, but Kat nodded. The thought of being alone with Alexis wasn't remotely pleasant, but he would be out of his mind to try to molest or capture her. Two heavy cruisers could make short work of his planet's defenses, even with the battleship-battlecruiser orbiting Jorlem. And no one in the Commonwealth would think twice about it.

"You'll need to be careful," the younger Theocrat spat. "This one"— he jabbed a finger at Kat as he rose to his feet—"has a habit of fucking her way into high places."

Kat kept her expression blank. She'd been right. The younger Theocrat wasn't an idiot, even though he looked like one. He'd picked his words carefully to undermine her positions. And he might well have sowed doubt in Alexis's mind, although she knew that Alexis would most likely never side completely with the Commonwealth. She waited, watching calmly, until the Theocrats and Davidson were escorted out of the room, then turned to look at the planetary dictator. She felt as if she'd been left alone with a poisonous snake.

"They have made many claims and promises," Alexis mused, almost as if he were speaking to himself. "But can they be trusted?"

"No, Mr. President," Kat said. "Jorlem will merely be the next world to be hollowed out from within if they gain a toehold."

Alexis looked at her coldly. "But can *you* be trusted?"

Kat studied him, thoughtfully. He'd probably like flattery, yet unless she missed her guess, he had his ego stroked every day. No one but a narcissist of towering proportions would have built so many wasteful statues to himself. Perhaps he'd respond better to bluntness.

"It is true that worlds are not allowed to enter the Free Trade Zone, let alone the Commonwealth, until they meet certain criteria," Kat said. There was no point in trying to hide it. "But it is *also* true that the Commonwealth does not attempt to subvert or invade worlds that might make good members."

"Except Cadiz," Alexis said.

"Cadiz was a special case," Kat said. It wasn't entirely true, but it had to be said. "There were strong factions on the surface in favor of annexation."

"And the planet sat along the shortest route from the Commonwealth to the Theocracy," Alexis pointed out.

No fool, Kat reminded herself. "That may be true," she said. It *was* true, but she suspected there was nothing to be gained by admitting it. "Is that true of Jorlem?"

She met his eyes evenly. "There's nothing here to attract us," she added bluntly. "You have cloudscoops and a growing asteroid industry, but so do several other worlds within the sector. As long as you do nothing to draw our attention, like signing a treaty with the Theocracy, we will leave you alone."

"But your traders will force their way into our markets," Alexis said.

"Not unless you have something to attract us," Kat said. "The truth is that you have nothing unique."

"An interesting thought," Alexis said. "Then, why did you come here?"

"I have orders to provide security for the sector," Kat said. "We'll decide on our next destination, then see how many freighters wish to accompany us. If you want to send a warship or two of your own along to provide additional security, we will be happy . . ."

"Out of the question," Alexis said flatly. "But I will tolerate you inviting freighters to join you, if you wish."

He paused. "And while we are prepared to allow your people to take leave on our planet, they may not leave the spaceport zone."

Kat nodded, unsurprised. Jorlem wasn't *that* closed a society, but she doubted the government would *want* its people meeting outsiders in uncontrolled circumstances. ONI had insisted that the dictatorship censored everything, even the datanet. Who knew what would happen if the population realized that the outside universe didn't have evil designs on their world?

"It would depend on certain matters," she said. Her crew *would* want to take shore leave, even if it was in just another grubby little spaceport, but she wasn't keen on allowing *anyone* off the ship while an enemy warship was in orbit. Theocratic forces might do something drastic if they believed they were on the verge of losing *all* of their influence. "But we will certainly let you know."

"I would advise your people to pay attention to the import restrictions," Alexis added. His face twisted, as if a nasty thought had just occurred to him. "A night in the cells will not be a pleasant experience."

"It rarely is," Kat said.

Alexis smiled. "There is one other matter," he warned. "I'm sure you were surprised when you discovered *Glory of God* in orbit."

"Yes," Kat said. There was no point in trying to hide that too. "We were surprised."

"Jorlem is officially neutral in your war," Alexis said. "Anyone can enter orbit and trade with *anyone*, as long as they behave themselves. Ambassador Lord Cleric Abdullah respects your right to enter orbit. Please respect his right to do the same."

Ambassador Lord Cleric Abdullah, Kat thought. The name meant nothing to her, but she could send a note back to Tyre to see if Admiral Junayd knew him. *Is he the older one or the younger one?*

She pushed the question aside for later contemplation. "We will certainly try not to start anything," she said warningly. "But if they start something, we will certainly do our best to finish it."

"That is understandable," Alexis said. He knew, he *had* to know, that he couldn't *force Glory of God* to leave. Or *Lightning* and *Uncanny*, for that matter. "I thank you for coming, Captain Falcone. My people will give you a tour of the city before you return to your ship."

"That would be very nice," Kat lied. She would sooner return to orbit, but a tour, even a sanitized one, would tell her more about the city than any number of files. If the area felt close to exploding, the Commonwealth might have a chance to make inroads with the new government. "I'm sure I will enjoy it."

"I'm sure you will too," Alexis said. He gave her a genial smile that still managed to look sinister. "And I will speak to you soon."

CHAPTER TWENTY

"That *bitch*," Inquisitor Bin Zaid spat as soon as they were back on the shuttle. "Did you see her . . . ?"

"I saw," Ambassador Lord Cleric Abdullah said calmly. He picked up a datapad and started to read through the reports from orbit. "It isn't a serious problem."

"She's undermined us with the *president*," Bin Zaid said. "He won't believe us now!"

Ambassador Lord Cleric Abdullah turned to look at him. "President Alexis is not a fool," he said flatly. "Sinner he may be, but he is no fool. He knows that we are deadly to him. But he also knows that the *Commonwealth* is deadly to him. The trick lies in convincing him that we may be *less* deadly in the short run."

"Assuming the infidel gives much of a damn about anything beyond himself," Bin Zaid snarled.

Abdullah didn't look concerned. "Such a mind will always associate the good of his planet with the good of himself," he said. "Whatever he does will be done with an eye towards keeping and securing his position."

"And that *woman*," Bin Zaid yelled. "Do you know who she is?"

"An odd choice," Abdullah said. "I would have expected her to be sent back to the war front."

Bin Zaid ground his teeth in helpless fury. There was something profoundly *unnatural* about a woman who carried herself like a man, who wore a uniform like a man, who commanded *men* in combat. What weaklings her crewmen must be! How could they *possibly* take orders from a woman? And yet, her reputation had spread through the Theocracy, despite the best efforts of the Inquisition. Bin Zaid knew better than to believe that a woman could actually best a man in combat— his wives never beat him at chess—but it seemed to have an effect on the lower classes.

They want to believe it, he thought. *If we can be beaten by a woman, it makes us look weak.*

"They probably thought she would be exposed as a fraud," he said finally. "She's not a . . ."

"She's not stupid either," Abdullah said sharply.

"She's a man who became a woman," Bin Zaid snarled. Sex change operations were forbidden in the Theocracy, but he knew they were theoretically possible. "A perverted . . ."

"No, she isn't," Abdullah corrected.

The elder of the two sighed loudly. "Picking her for this mission may not have been a bad choice," he added thoughtfully. "She has a strong reputation, excellent connections with Tyre's ruling class and her mere existence gets under our skin. They may be hoping that we will do something . . . intemperate."

"She's under sentence of death," Bin Zaid reminded him.

"And we will do *nothing*," Abdullah told him firmly. "We are diplomats. Act diplomatic."

He turned to peer out of the porthole as the shuttle started to pass through the upper atmosphere. Bin Zaid glared at his back, silently cursing the older man. Abdullah might be a Lord Cleric and thus deserving of unquestioning obedience, but he'd spent too long among the infidels. No one who had spent *any* time among the infidels could be trusted fully, not when the infidels were too good at seducing Believers from the path of righteousness. Bin Zaid had heard too many whispered stories of rebel cells in the Theocracy itself to believe that anyone, even himself, was truly safe from being seduced. Being *here*, among a group of infidels barely worth his attention, was galling. He should be back with his comrades, rooting out heresy before it brought the Theocracy crashing down.

No, he told himself firmly, *before it taints too many of the Believers.*

The thought made him shiver. He'd heard dark rumors about the situation along the front, even though the official news bulletins made it clear that the Theocracy was winning the war easily. Of *course* the Theocracy was winning the war. The Commonwealth was soft, weakened by its hedonism, and had no hope of standing up to the True Believers, to the men who were prepared to die in defense of their religion. And God had truly blinded their enemies. No matter how desperately the infidels struggled, the noose was slowly tightening around their necks . . .

. . . and yet, there were too many rumors.

He'd reported the defeatists, of course. He *was* an Inquisitor. Rooting out everything from idle grumbling to outright heresy was his *job*. However, no one had been able to track down the source of the rumors, let alone counter them. They just seemed to spring up from nowhere, whispered from person to person . . . and no matter what the government said, they never quite seemed to fade. There were times, when he was lying in the darkness, that Bin Zaid wondered if the rumors were actually true. It had led to too many sleepless nights.

Of course they're not true, he told himself savagely. *The enemy within cannot beat us by force, so they strive to subvert us instead.*

He tensed as the shuttle docked with *Glory of God*, remembering yet another rumor about airlocks that had failed at the worst possible moment. A low hiss ran through the cabin as the hatches mated and opened; he felt a flicker of panic he struggled to dismiss, muttering prayers under his breath. Space travel was supposed to be *safe*! Still, the rumors just kept spreading. The sooner Tyre was scorched from orbit, the better. Mass slaughter was sinful—countless potential Believers would be killed along with the irredeemable infidels—but he found it hard to care. He just wanted the war to end.

"We will monitor her operations," Abdullah said. He rose and led the way into the battleship, a handful of crewmen falling to the deck in prostration as the Lord Cleric passed. "And if there is an opportunity to do her harm, we will take it."

"We could take her little ships," Bin Zaid said. The crewmen, rising to their feet, refused to meet his eyes. Normally, he would have enjoyed their fear—it kept them honest—but right now he was too angry to care. "*Glory of God* can smash them both with ease."

"It would be unwise to count on that," Abdullah said. "Besides, that's Captain Samuel's decision."

Bin Zaid glared at his back. "You have the authority to overrule him."

"Yes, but I will not use it unless strictly necessary," Abdullah said. "We have time to consider how we will turn this situation to our advantage. And we will."

He turned to give Bin Zaid a reassuring smile, then led the way into the intership car. Bin Zaid ground his teeth in silent frustration. Every instinct he had told him that they needed to strike and strike now, before the infidels had time to summon reinforcements from their homeworld. But Abdullah was the one in command, for the moment. And *he* wasn't doing his damn job.

Patience, he told himself firmly. *Abdullah will not stay in command forever.*

"So that's the situation," Kat said after she'd shared the recordings she'd taken during the meeting. "President Alexis appears to be trying to play us off against the Theocracy."

"And the Theocracy has an immensely powerful battleship in orbit," Crenshaw mused. "The President may have been threatened into compliance."

"That ship isn't as powerful as it looks," William's holographic image said. "My analysts think that she's got a whole series of crippling design flaws."

"Which won't make much of a difference if we face her at close range," Crenshaw countered, grimly. "Our simulations suggest that taking her will be costly. We could lose both ships."

"That's always a risk," Kat pointed out. "And we've beaten long odds before."

Roach cleared his throat. "We could simply try to outbid the Theocracy," he pointed out carefully. He was the youngest officer in the conference. "I don't think they could offer much, if anything, in the way of payment for services rendered."

"The problem is that the planetary government doesn't trust us," Davidson reminded him dryly. "And, of course, there's an extremely large warship orbiting their world."

They must feel the same way about us, Kat thought.

She cleared her throat. "The Admiralty has been alerted to her presence," she said, nodding towards the tactical display. The red icon representing *Glory of God* glowed balefully on the other side of the planet. "They may have new orders for us soon enough."

"They may expect us to breach Jorlem's neutrality and attack that damned ship," Crenshaw commented.

"That would be bad," William pointed out. "There are interstellar treaties . . ."

"We *can* demand that Jorlem orders them to leave," Crenshaw said.

"Which they can't enforce," Davidson reminded him. "That . . . that *ship* can smash their entire defense force in an hour."

"Less than an hour," Roach injected.

"And then it can turn their planet into a wasteland," Davidson continued. "I don't think they'll want to push the matter."

"Probably not," Kat agreed.

She tapped the table, meaningfully. "We'll remain here for the next two days, in any case," she added. "We'll remain at full tactical alert, shields and weapons at standby. If they so much as blink, I want to be ready to fight before they get into attack position. After that . . . we may have to split up and escort the next set of freighters to their destinations."

"Captain," Crenshaw said, "splitting up now strikes me as risky."

"It is," Kat agreed. She hated to admit it, but she *was* tempted to keep the two cruisers together. Neither *Lightning* nor *Uncanny* could reasonably hope to take *Glory of God* in a fair fight, not alone. "But we have too much to do in too little time."

"And that ship isn't causing any actual *trouble*," William said.

"She doesn't have to," Davidson said. "As long as we know she's there, she's a looming threat over the entire sector. We have to keep one eye on her at all times."

"Which we will," Kat said.

She glanced from face to face. "We'll allow a handful of our crew to take shore leave," she said after a moment. She wasn't keen on the idea, not with an enemy ship lurking high overhead, but after much consideration she'd decided that the granting of leave would show the locals that she wasn't intimidated. "But make sure they are warned to take every precaution, and that they are *not* to leave the spaceport zone."

"I don't think they can," William said. "The briefing papers said that leaving the spaceport requires special permission from the planetary authorities."

199

"Probably in triplicate," Davidson commented.

"And countersigned by at least two officials," William agreed seriously. "Judging from the *unofficial* reports, hardly any freighter crews seek liberty on Jorlem."

"The President said as much," Kat agreed. In addition to keeping locals from interacting with outsiders and their brazen ideas, the planetary government could also make a great deal of money for itself in a restricted zone simply by offering everything from cheap booze to cheaper prostitutes. "It doesn't sound like a good place to take leave."

In addition, everything is probably taxed heavily, she thought cynically. *They'll want to extort as much off-world currency as possible.*

"There *is* a security issue," Crenshaw pointed out. "The Theocracy will have their own crewmen running around on shore leave."

Davidson snorted. "I doubt it," he said. "Their crews *never* take shore leave."

"Too much prospect of them deserting, I expect," Kat said.

"They might also try to kidnap or kill some of our crewmembers," Crenshaw pointed out grimly. "It's a risk!"

"I know," Kat said. "But it is one we have to take."

She took one last look at the tactical display. "Take the bridge," she ordered. "Sir William, Major Davidson, remain behind."

Crenshaw nodded and rose, heading out of the compartment. Roach's image vanished a second later. Kat cursed the enemy ship under her breath. Davidson had been right. Just by existing, *Glory of God* was disrupting her plans. Using a battleship-battlecruiser to smash freighters was overkill, but Kat was all too aware that the enemy ship could take out any convoy escorts she might reasonably expect to encounter in the sector.

"I found a potential contact," William said quietly. "But I'll have to go down to the planet to speak to him personally."

"See to it," Kat said. "But watch your back."

"Take a couple of marines along," Davidson offered.

"They won't talk to me if I have escorts," William said bluntly. "Making contact alone will be tricky. Even with my . . . *relations* . . . it won't be easy to convince anyone to talk to me. I might have to shell out a great deal of untraceable cash."

"We can afford it," Kat told him. She understood his concerns—he'd grown up on a poor world—but she would sooner spend money than her crew's lives. "We need whatever advantages we can get."

"The local criminal fraternity must be worried," Davidson said. "If the Theocracy takes over . . ."

"They'll probably wait and see what happens," William said. "Some of them probably think they can make a deal with the Theocracy."

"And they might be right," Kat agreed.

She shook her head in frustration. "Do we have a set of potential freighters to escort?"

"Four possible destinations, so far," William said. "If we split up, we'll each have around ten freighters to escort."

"We'll work it out when we're ready to leave," Kat said. "This time, we'll have to limit the number of ships that can join the convoys."

"Particularly with *Glory of God* watching us," William agreed. "*They* won't care about triggering an energy storm."

Kat scowled. Tracking a starship in hyperspace wasn't easy, particularly if the starship had a solid lead, but the enemy would have no doubt of their destination. They *had* to tell the freighter crews where they were going, after all. She would be surprised if the Theocracy didn't know almost as soon as she made the announcement.

It can't be helped, she told herself. *All we can do is stay off the regular shipping routes as much as possible.*

"The Admiralty may expect us to deal with her," Kat said quietly. "Until then . . ."

She looked at William. "Good luck," she added. "Dismissed."

"You took a hell of a risk," Davidson said as soon as William's image had vanished from the compartment. "President Alexis might have meant you harm."

"He's not suicidal," Kat said stiffly. "Kidnapping or killing a commanding officer would be a declaration of war and he knows it."

"He might have expected *Glory of God* to back him up," Davidson pointed out.

"Jorlem would still be screwed," Kat countered. "They might win the first engagement, Pat, but the Admiralty would send a full battle squadron to demand redress."

"Unless the demands of the war prevented a full response," Davidson replied.

Kat nodded towards the tactical display. "A couple of battlecruisers would be more than sufficient," she reminded him. She looked up, meeting his eyes. "I knew there was a risk, but I judged it manageable."

"I know," Davidson said.

"We're on a warship, in the middle of a war," Kat said. "There's no way to escape *risk*."

She gave her lover a reassuring but weary look. Davidson wasn't as insanely overprotective as her father's security officers back during her childhood, but she knew he worried about her. The dynamic was frustrating at times, a droll reminder why relationships like theirs were regarded as dubious when they weren't outright forbidden. And yet she appreciated him caring about *her*. Too many others saw nothing more than the Falcone name.

"All we can do now is wait," she added quietly. "And see what happens."

"They may do something hasty," Davidson warned. "I don't think they hate anyone more than they hate you."

Kat nodded, grimly. "If they do, we'll deal with it," she said. "That ship has to be on its own, doesn't it? They can't have any backup."

"Not unless they've decided they can spare a few more ships," Davidson said.

"I doubt it," Kat said. She hadn't had a chance to read the latest set of analysis reports, but she was fairly certain that the battleship-battlecruiser had no place in a line of battle. *Glory of God* had been kept from the front because she had no real role there. "I don't think they could spare a handful of freighters for logistics, let alone a handful of additional warships."

She grinned at the thought. If she was right, the enemy ship couldn't hope to replenish any missiles it fired. Or anything else, for that matter. *She* wasn't in a better position, she had to admit, but *her* supply dumps were closer. And the Admiralty might send her a few more ships once they understood the need.

Davidson gazed at his captain. "Are you planning something?"

"We might be able to jump her," Kat said. Two could play games with energy storms in hyperspace. "If we caught her by surprise and crippled her, she'd have no way home."

"But that wouldn't matter so much as long as she was *here*," Davidson warned.

"I know," Kat said. "Even if she can't open a gateway, she can still dominate Jorlem until we get enough ships out here to deal with her."

If we can, she added silently. There were too many demands on the Navy's limited number of ships. *Jorlem is simply not as important as Vangelis.*

She tossed the ideas around in her head for a long moment, then put them aside. There were too many other things to do. She hated the idea of just leaving an enemy warship alone, but she might have no choice. The Theocracy, deliberately or otherwise, had created a nasty headache for the Commonwealth. Almost anything she did would reflect badly on her superiors.

And as long as the Theocracy doesn't start anything, she thought sourly, *we can't start anything either.*

"We shall wait," Kat said. "It's all we can do."

CHAPTER TWENTY-ONE

Jorlem's spaceport zone, William discovered as he strode down the main street, was essentially identical to a hundred other such spaceports he'd seen in his long career. The streets were lined with bars and brothels, loud music echoing through the air as streams of spacers made their way from their shuttlecrafts into the nearest bars. A cluster of young women in skimpy dresses waved at him as he passed, clearly taking him for yet another spacer out for a good time. William ignored them as he kept moving, following the map he'd loaded into his implants. His destination was right on the edge of the zone.

And Henderson died somewhere like this, he reminded himself. *I need to stay alert.*

The building looked more like a prison than a bar, he noted, as he approached a surrounding fence. The official maps didn't show any of the security precautions, but orbital observations confirmed the existence of a kill zone surrounding the spaceport, a zone where escaping spacers could be spotted and shot without hesitation. President Alexis would have to be insane to risk shooting spacers on shore leave, William thought, but it was clear he didn't want to risk contamination. Who knew *what* ideas foreign spacers might introduce to his people.

The bar loomed up in front of him, utterly unremarkable, making little attempt to attract customers. William wasn't surprised. The people who had business at the bar would know about it. Anyone else would be quietly told to move on as quickly as possible. William pushed the door open and stepped into the lobby. A bouncer, his enhanced muscles clearly visible even through the nice suit he wore, glared at him suspiciously. William gazed back evenly.

"I'm expected," he said simply.

The bouncer checked his ID, then scanned his body with a hand-held sensor. William suspected the gesture was pointless—he would be astonished if the local security service didn't know about the bar's *true* line of work—but he had a feeling it helped reassure some of the customers. They would prefer to hold their discussions well away from the prying eyes and ears of the planetary government.

And everyone else too, William thought as he was shown into the bar. *Jorlem is a haven for spies.*

He smiled in genuine amusement as he heard soft music playing. The bar looked like a high-class officer's joint rather than the cruder places reserved for merchant spacers and ordinary crewmen. Instead of dancing girls, the space offered a handful of privacy booths and a number of waitresses dressed in elegant uniforms. One of them bowed politely to William, then led him towards the nearest booth. His implants reported a number of security fields blinking into existence as he sat down, making it hard to record anything. The technology wasn't quite on par with that of the Commonwealth, he noted, but it was good enough to disrupt anything short of his implants. Even *their* readings would be very limited.

"Mr. Abramson will be down in a few moments," the waitress said. "Can I fetch you anything?"

"Fresh orange and lemonade," William said. "Just bring it over here when he arrives."

William settled into the comfortable chair and waited. He'd sent the message, using some of his brother's codes, knowing it would either open doors or slam them shut. The reply had told him to come to the hidden bar . . . but nothing else. There was no way to know just what was waiting for him. He doubted it was a trap—the spaceport zone was meant to be neutral —but it could easily be a waste of time.

"Captain Sir William McElney," a quiet voice said. "Welcome to Jorlem."

William looked up. An elderly man was standing in front of him, his unkempt white hair reminding William of a grandfather he'd known and loved as a child. Mr. Abramson didn't *look* like a criminal, William had to admit as the man sat down, but that was an advantage in his line of work. An information broker who acquired a reputation for being untrustworthy wouldn't remain alive for long.

"Thank you," William said. "Mr. Abramson, I presume?"

"Your brother was quite keen that I should be of service," Mr. Abramson said. "But I should tell you upfront that I *do* have operating costs."

"I understand," William said. His brother's contacts had their limits. "I am authorized to pay for services rendered."

"Of course, of course," Mr. Abramson said. He smiled cheerfully. "And what sort of services would you like?"

William leaned forward. "Information on Theocratic and pirate activity within the sector," he said slowly. "And information on what governments have made contact with the Theocracy."

Mr. Abramson cocked his head. "And what will you do with the pirates?"

"Hunt them down and kill them," William said. There was no point in trying to hide his intentions. Mr. Abramson didn't need to be an information broker to know the Navy's standing orders concerning pirates. "Do you have a problem with that?"

"Perhaps . . ." Mr. Abramson said. He shrugged. "I will give you one piece of information for free and another for ten thousand crowns. *Untraceable* crowns."

William worked to keep his face impassive. His expense account could cover it, but he knew from bitter experience it was better to haggle. A negotiator who didn't get beaten down would suspect, perhaps rightly, that they could have held out for more. And yet William couldn't help feeling that time was pressing.

"It depends," he said. "What piece of information is worth so much money?"

"The location of a pirate base," Mr. Abramson said.

William sucked in his breath sharply. A base . . . Mr. Abramson was right. A pirate base was worth a great deal of money. But was it worth ten thousand crowns?

"We'll give you two thousand now and three thousand if it checks out," he said after a moment. "Is that suitable?"

"Five thousand now and three thousand afterwards," Mr. Abramson said. They haggled backwards and forwards until they settled on a price. "And the piece of information I'm giving you for free is a location under pirate control."

William frowned. "A location?"

"A cloudscoop, to be precise," Mr. Abramson added. "It's proving quite a nuisance."

"It would," William agreed. There weren't *that* many cloudscoops in the sector, and most of them were in systems that could fend off any number of pirate ships. He was surprised he hadn't heard about a captured cloudscoop from Jorlem or Vangelis, although the planetary authorities might not have known. A pirate who seized a cloudscoop would have every incentive to keep it quiet. "And you want them removed?"

"They're bad for business," Mr. Abramson said.

William understood. Pirates, smugglers, and information brokers were often interlinked, but the more extreme pirates were *very* bad for the other two. He could understand Mr. Abramson wanting to get rid of them, even if the only way to do it was to tip off the Royal Navy. And if the pirates were a real problem, the broker would be happy to sell them down the river for free.

The base he betrayed might belong to a set of really nasty pirates, he thought.

"We'll be happy to deal with them," William said. "What else can you offer?"

"Very little about pirates," Mr. Abramson said, "however, I *can* tell you that seven governments have been contacted by the Theocracy. They've all been given the same offer—allow missionaries to enter their society in exchange for protection."

William shook his head in disbelief. "And they actually think the Theocracy will honor its promises?"

"I don't believe so," Mr. Abramson said. "But there are . . . factions . . . within several of the governments that will be quite keen on accepting outside assistance, without caring about the price."

"Of course," William agreed dryly.

"I've been monitoring the situation closely," Mr. Abramson added. "You can have a complete copy of my findings for five thousand crowns."

"One thousand," William countered. They haggled again until they agreed on a price. "Is President Alexis likely to make an alliance with the Theocracy?"

"He's holding out for a number of weapons and warships," Mr. Abramson said. He smiled rather thinly. "Despite his best efforts, discontent is growing on Jorlem. He's purged a number of officials already for ideas above their station and installed a whole new layer of spies within the security forces, but . . . it's not working. He thinks the Theocracy can give him the tools to keep his population under control."

"They're not going to be able to supply warships," William said.

"Probably not," Mr. Abramson said. "They *have* been purchasing every ship they can get, though. Prices have been going up all over the sector because their agents have been outbidding everyone else. It's actually having an effect on shipping prices too."

"How the hell are they *paying* for it?"

"Good question," Mr. Abramson said. "And no, I don't have an answer."

"Oh," William said.

He contemplated the problem for a long moment. The Theocracy wasn't exactly poor, but their currency wasn't accepted outside the Theocracy itself. They had very little to sell, beyond warships . . . and they wouldn't *want* to sell warships. They *did* have access to dozens of asteroid belts, he supposed, but so did countless other star systems. There was nothing they could offer that couldn't be matched or exceeded by the Commonwealth . . .

Maybe they just took out loans, he mused. *Or . . .*

He leaned forward. "Are they forging the payments somehow?"

"I doubt it," Mr. Abramson said. "We're not talking about a handful of crowns, not here."

William nodded, ruefully. A handful of crowns might be passed, unchecked, but anything over a couple of thousand—far less than anyone would need to purchase a warship—would be checked via StarCom before the transaction was made. Conning the system repeatedly would be difficult, perhaps impossible. It *might* be possible, as a one-off, but doing it repeatedly would be noticeable. Too many people would have to be involved . . .

"If you figure out the answer," he said, "we'd like to know."

"I'm sure you would," Mr. Abramson said. "So . . . do you have anything else you want to know?"

William nodded. "Is the Theocracy working with pirates and smugglers?"

"I believe so," Mr. Abramson said. "I don't have any direct proof, but bounties have been offered on all starships, either captured or destroyed. Quite a number of pirate outfits have benefited from the situation. Smugglers . . . rather less so."

"Because they don't care *who* gets attacked," William said.

"Quite. I believe they *are* establishing connections, but . . . I don't have any direct proof. Most of the smugglers have good reason to remain quiet about such matters."

"Of course," William agreed dryly.

He met Mr. Abramson's eyes. "One final question," he said. "Is there anyone on the planet who might overthrow the government?"

"I couldn't point to a specific figure," Mr. Abramson said. "Everyone I might have suspected has already been purged."

He paused. "So, do you want the datachips sent directly to your starship or would you like them handed to you now?"

"Now," William said. He removed the credit chip from his pocket and held it out. "You can take the first part of the payment too."

"Thank you," Mr. Abramson said. He rose. "I'll be back in a moment."

William nodded shortly.

◆ ◆ ◆

"This isn't good news," Kat said an hour later.

"No," William agreed. His analysts had checked and rechecked the datachips carefully before copying their contents onto the ship's datanet. "On one hand, we have a captured cloudscoop; on the other, we have a genuine pirate base."

"That cloudscoop is the immediate problem," Kat mused. "We need to liberate it before too many unsuspecting ships can dock."

"But we also need to destroy that base," William said. "We don't know how long they'll remain there."

Kat threw him a sharp look. "I thought exclusivity was part of the deal."

"It is," William confirmed. "But smart pirates won't stay in the same place too long if they can help it."

"True," Kat agreed. She studied the star chart for a long moment. "The cloudscoop is in the Generis System. We were planning to take a convoy of freighters to Aston Villa, which is only a handful of light-years from Generis. If I escort the freighters there, in *Lightning*, you can take others to Potsdam and then proceed to the pirate base. Capture or destroy the base."

"Of course, Captain," William said. He wondered, absently, which one of them had the better mission. Liberating the cloudscoop would be a good deed, but capturing the pirate base and their ships might lead to a great deal of prize money. "The report *did* say that the cloudscoop crew were being kept prisoner."

"We'll have to try to free them too," Kat said slowly. "If it's a family business . . . Was there any information on the base?"

"It's a converted asteroid, apparently," William said. "But there wasn't much else."

He sighed. He'd have to sit down with his senior officers and plan the operation, although he had a nasty feeling they'd be making most of it up as they went along. Mr. Abramson hadn't possessed enough information to allow for detailed planning. Firing a spread of antimatter-armed missiles at the asteroid would be more than enough to take it out, but that would kill any prisoners as well as the pirates themselves. And there *would* be prisoners.

Sex slaves, if nothing else, he thought sourly.

"I leave that part of the operation in your hands," Kat told him. "Do what you can to collect intelligence, but if you have to destroy the asteroid . . . I'll understand."

"ONI won't," William said. "They always have unrealistic expectations of what we can do."

Kat's face tightened. "I'll make sure they understand," she said. "But I don't think anyone will be too upset if the pirate base is destroyed. Organize a pair of convoys too, but no more than ten ships each," she added. "I don't want to have to ride herd on too many ships this time."

"Understood," William said. He paused. "If you announced your intention to head onwards, perhaps to Ayton, you'd have a few more ships requesting escort. And then you could leave them at Aston Villa."

"I could also take a couple of ships to Generis," Kat mused. "But would that be too revealing?"

"I don't know," William said.

He scowled. The pirates hadn't destroyed the cloudscoop, which suggested they were more interested in exploiting it than anything else. But if they thought they were doomed, they'd be quite happy to take the cloudscoop and its crew down with them. And losing a cloudscoop would drive the price of fuel up all over the sector.

"You might have to dicker with them," he said.

"That would be bad," Kat said. "ONI will make an even *bigger* fuss over that."

William nodded in grim agreement. It seemed to be a universal law that the people who weren't actually on the spot *thought* they knew better than the people who were. Making a deal with the pirates—ransoming the cloudscoop and her crew—might be the best solution, the only way to end the problem, but the REMFs back home wouldn't see it that way. They would come up with an idealized solution that wouldn't have had a hope of working in the real world, then complain loudly about Kat's failure to come up with such a brilliant scheme.

"Good luck," he said.

"We did get a message back from the Admiralty," Kat said. "They want us to—and I quote—'monitor the situation.'"

"At least they don't want us to breach Jorlem's neutrality," William observed. "I'm surprised they didn't ask one of us to remain here until *Glory of God* departs."

"We don't have enough ships," Kat said. "There wasn't a mention of reinforcements."

"Ouch," William said.

The ships they'd borrowed from Vangelis had returned home, escorting a handful of freighters from Jorlem. He doubted the local defense force would join the engagement, even if they'd had enough firepower to make a difference. *Glory of God* would have to be practically dead in space before the locals dared take her on. Even complete surprise wouldn't tip the odds in their favor.

"We'll depart tomorrow," Kat said. "Keep in touch through the StarCom network. We'll try to meet up back here in a month, assuming nothing else gets in our way."

"Of course, Captain," William said. He paused. "Did the Admiralty have anything to say about Jorlem's flirting with the Theocracy?"

"Nothing," Kat said. "Right now, I suspect they think there's nothing they can do."

"And that the Theocracy won't be able to keep its promises," William added. "Perhaps we should be trying to outbid them. If we were the ones buying ships instead . . ."

"I'll have to suggest that," Kat said. "But would the sellers know they were selling to the Theocracy?"

William didn't know. It wasn't easy to follow the money in the Commonwealth, let alone the Jorlem Sector. The purchasing agents might have no idea where the ships were going . . . hell, they might assume they were purchasing ships for pirates. And outbidding everyone would have awkward long-term effects.

"Perhaps if we just outbid everyone for warships," he mused slowly. "We could then loan them to Vangelis and every other world willing to assist in convoy protection."

"Good idea," Kat said. She smiled. "And I'll make sure to suggest it to the Admiralty."

"They might take it more seriously if it came from you," William countered.

"It involves spending money," Kat said. Her smile widened. "They'll hate it on principle."

She shook her head. "I'll see you in a month, all being well," she added. "Keep me informed."

"Of course, Kat," William said.

CHAPTER TWENTY-TWO

"We really need more data," Roach said grimly.

William nodded in agreement. The convoy was two days out of Jorlem, heading to Potsdam on a course that, William hoped, would make life difficult for anyone shadowing their passage through hyperspace. William had taken the opportunity to sit down in his Ready Room with his XO and do some planning before starting more departmental inspections.

"All we really know about the pirate base is that it's an asteroid," Roach added, "but what *sort* of asteroid?"

"We'll sneak into the system and find out," William said. Mr. Abramson's datachip *had* shown a precise location for the pirate base. "And then we'll plan our operation."

He clicked off the tactical display. "How's crew morale?"

"Improving, sir," Roach said. "Some grumbles about limited shore leave on Jorlem, but Henderson's death put a damper on them. The crew probably does need some proper leave sooner rather than later."

"There may be opportunities at Potsdam," William said. "It doesn't *seem* to be a security nightmare."

"No, sir," Roach said.

He pulled his datapad off his belt and glanced at the latest reports. "Overall, shipboard efficiency is as good as can be expected," he added. "The old hands seem to have lost most of their bad habits, thankfully. None of the officers have reported any major problems. Indeed, I think a number of crewmen could be put down for promotion right now. There are still a number of gambling rings, apparently, but none of them seem to be getting out of hand."

"Good," William said. "I trust you have been monitoring the crew's spending patterns?"

"Yes, sir," Roach said.

He sounded unhappy. William didn't blame him. There was no way that *any* of the crew could be mistaken for a child, a child whose parents needed to keep an eye on his spending. Also, privacy was *important* on Tyre. Covertly monitoring a grown man's spending went against the grain.

"It has to be done," William said. "It's better to nip any gambling problems in the bud."

"Yes, sir," Roach said. "But they might be gambling other things."

William took a deep breath. In his experience, young crewmembers could get into trouble with depressing ease. Gambling . . . drugs . . . women . . . men . . . there were just too many temptations for a young serviceperson leaving his or her homeworld for the first time. And older crewmembers, the ones who would probably never be considered for a promotion, didn't help. He still shuddered at the thought of *just* how much alcohol he'd been talked into consuming during his first period of shore leave many, many years ago. The whole experience was a blurry memory.

"Yes, they could be," he said. "That's why it's better to leave them an outlet for their mischievous sides. There's always *someone* who will try to push the limits."

"Yes, sir," Roach said.

He paused. "Maintenance schedules are being kept," he continued. "We're actually using more spare parts than predicted, but we should have enough to keep us going until we return to the Commonwealth. If worse comes to worst, we can borrow additional spares from *Lightning* or refurbish some of the older components. They're designed to be refurbished on the fly, if necessary."

"But only as a last resort," William said. He'd had too much experience on ships held together by spit and baling wire. "Continue to monitor the situation."

"Yes, sir," Roach said. "The bean counters will not be pleased."

"Fuck them," William said curtly. He had yet to see a projection from the bean counters that wasn't a gross underestimate. "Keeping the crew alive is more important than satisfying their figures."

"Yes, sir," Roach said. "I—"

He broke off as the alarms howled. The intercom squawked a moment later. "Captain to the bridge! I say again, captain to the bridge!"

William rose, leading the way through the hatch and onto the bridge. "Report!"

"Two contacts approaching on attack vector," Lieutenant Commander Thompson said, rising from the command chair. "They're coming directly for us."

"They must have been shadowing us for some time," Roach muttered.

William sat down and studied the tactical display. The two contacts were approaching from the rear, bearing down on the last couple of ships in the convoy. They didn't seem to be making any attempt to hide; hell, there wasn't even enough nearby hyperspace distortion to make it hard to see them. Either they were the most careless pirates in existence or they *wanted* to be seen. And that meant . . .

"Order the convoy to alter course," he said, keying his console. If the pirates were trying to distract him, chances were that at least one more pirate ship was lurking along the convoy's projected course. "And launch two probes ahead of us."

"Aye, Captain," Thompson said.

"They both read out as destroyers," Roach commented. "Flag unknown."

William frowned. *Theocracy?*

He shook his head. ONI had amassed extensive files on starships from all over the human sphere, but it was quite possible that *something* had slipped through the net. It was also possible that the *Uncanny* was merely facing ships that had been modified so extensively that they were now unrecognizable.

"Get your best guesses up on the tactical display," he ordered. "And ready firing solutions."

"Aye, Captain," Roach said.

The enemy ships drew closer. The probes hadn't detected anything lying in wait, which meant . . . what? Were the pirates incompetent? William had no respect for pirates, most of whom treated their ships so badly it was a miracle they didn't suffocate, but very few pirates were stupid enough to play games with a heavy cruiser. The two destroyers were doomed if they kept closing on his position, and they had to know it. Unless . . .

"Order the convoy to pick up speed," he said. The tactical display was still clear, save for the two enemy ships. "And warn them to be ready for a crash-transit back into realspace."

"Aye, Captain," Lieutenant Stott said.

Roach glanced at him. "You think they'll try to trigger an energy storm?"

"If they just want to destroy the ships," William commented, "it's their best chance."

"Shit," Roach breathed.

William nodded. It was rare for major fleet engagements to take place in hyperspace, if only because no one knew *precisely* what it would take to set off an energy storm. A couple of antimatter detonations would be more than enough. And if the approaching ships were armed with antimatter warheads, they'd cause a storm even if his point defense managed to pick them off in time.

"We could drop back into realspace now, sir," Roach suggested.

"I considered it," William said. "But they'll just wait for us in hyperspace."

He looked at Thompson. "Are there no other enemy ships within sensor range?"

"No, sir," Thompson said. "I'm only picking up two ships."

And there isn't enough distortion to cause too many sensor problems, William thought. A stealthed ship might be hiding in front of them, but their course change would have thrown it off. Unless the enemy had guessed their new vector ahead of time . . . No, that was unlikely. He'd picked the vector randomly. *They want to set off a storm.*

"Helm, bring us around," he ordered. "Tactical, prepare to engage as soon as the enemy ships are within weapons range."

"Aye, Captain," Cecelia said.

"Weapons ready, Captain," Thompson agreed. "Warhead loads?"

"Standard nukes," William ordered. There was no way to be sure, but that option *should* minimize the chances of their setting off a storm themselves. "Fire on my command."

He tensed as the three ships converged rapidly. Moving away from the convoy was a risk, even though it would give the freighters a better chance at opening a gateway and returning to realspace if a storm *did* blow up. If there *was* another watching ship lurking in the shadows, the freighters would have to face it alone. But it was the only way to keep the enemy ships away from the convoy.

"Weapons range in twenty seconds, Captain," Thompson reported. "Targets locked. I . . ."

He paused as an alert sounded. "Missile separation! I say again, missile separation!"

William swore. Unless there was something *very* odd about that missile, the pirates didn't have a hope of actually *hitting* them. But it didn't matter. A handful of antimatter warheads would be more than enough to set off an energy storm.

"Evasive action," he ordered. "Helm, ready the gateway generator . . ."

"*Detonation*," Thompson snapped. "Antimatter warhead! I say again, antimatter warhead!"

"Take us back to the convoy," William ordered.

He braced himself as a dull shuddering ran through the ship. The energy surge wasn't going away. A storm was already forming, waves of energy flaring out of nowhere and blurring together into a wall of unimaginable power. The enemy ships, trapped on the other side of the wall, vanished into nothingness. He hoped, absently, that they'd been swallowed by the monster they'd unleashed, but there was no way to know. All he could think about was getting out of the storm before it surged towards them. *Uncanny* was far too close to the energy nexus for comfort.

"Captain, the storm is building rapidly," Lieutenant Gross reported.

"Keep us moving," William ordered. They *could* try to return to realspace, but he had a nasty feeling that they were too close to the energy storm to open a gateway safely. "Alert the convoy. Order them to head away from the storm."

"Aye, Captain," Stott said.

The shaking grew stronger, sending chills down his spine. *Uncanny* was terrifyingly powerful compared to the ships of the Breakaway Wars, but she was still a toy compared to the raw power of hyperspace. No one could plunge into an energy storm and live. Skirting the edge of the storm alone was supremely risky . . .

William gripped his command chair, keeping his face impassive. He'd been through worse during their mission into enemy territory, back before the start of the war. The Seven Sisters had been far worse than a simple energy storm. But it was hard to keep focused, even though he needed to present a calm face to the crew. There was something deeply *primal* about the terror unleashed by the storm.

Uncanny shook one final time, then leveled out. William allowed himself a moment of sheer relief as he glanced at the display, watching as the storm slowly started to fade back into the ether. There was no sign of either of the enemy ships. But that proved nothing. The enemy might have jumped back into realspace or turned and fled the moment their warhead detonated. There was no way to be sure.

"The storm is fading," Gross reported. "But I'm picking up a great deal of additional distortion."

William sucked in his breath. "Take us back to the convoy, then alter course to keep us as far from the storm as possible."

"Aye, Captain," Cecelia said.

"No major damage reported, Captain," Roach said when William glanced at him. "The shaking might have knocked a few components loose, though."

"We'll have to check," William said. It could have been worse. It could have been a great deal worse. "Injuries?"

"None reported, as yet," Roach said.

William nodded, studying the display as *Uncanny* caught up with the convoy. The storm would make life harder for the pirates if they wanted to keep tracking the convoy, although the bastards knew precisely where they were going. They'd have ample opportunity to stake out Potsdam before the convoy arrived, if they headed there directly. He considered, briefly, triggering another set of storms before dismissing the thought. Energy storms were dangerously unpredictable. Even the Theocracy hesitated before setting one off.

"Launch a shell of recon probes to watch the approaches," he ordered. He keyed a vector into his console. "And then alter course as directed."

"Aye, Captain," Cecelia said.

William watched her work for a long moment, then ran through a set of calculations in his head. Assuming they didn't run into any further trouble, the course change would add an extra couple of days to their flight time. He doubted the merchant skippers would be too unhappy, although he had a feeling that their superiors would bitch and moan about the delay. *They* weren't the ones facing pirates and energy storms on a daily basis.

We never gave a guaranteed ETA, he told himself firmly. *If they want to complain, they can take it to the local counsel.*

"I have the final set of reports, Captain," Roach said. "The chief engineer reports that there was a set of unusual power fluctuations in Fusion Two and Drive Nodes Three through Seven, probably caused by close proximity to the storm. He'd like to shut them down for a few hours to run inspections."

William made a face. Losing one of the ship's fusion plants would be bad enough, but losing a drive node would be worse. Replacing one in the middle of hyperspace would be an absolute nightmare. But shutting the nodes down long enough for an inspection would be problematic. If the pirates showed up again, *Uncanny* wouldn't be able to go to full power until the drive nodes were restored.

"Tell him to hold off for twenty minutes," he said finally. Power fluctuations weren't *uncommon*. It was certainly *possible* that they were nothing more than random flickers within the drive field. But there was no point in taking chances. "If the enemy ships don't reappear, we can take the nodes offline for inspection."

"Aye, Captain," Roach said. He sounded relieved. "A handful of bumps and bruises have been reported, but nothing serious. We survived the storm intact."

"Thank God," William said. "Tactical, do you have an analysis of the enemy ships?"

Thompson looked up. "Nothing conclusive, Captain," he said. "Their drive fields were modern, but their missile was crude . . . nothing more than a containment field mounted on a primitive missile drive. We didn't see any other systems during the brief engagement."

Roach scowled. "They may have been trying for the destruction bounty," he said. "They weren't even *planning* to try to capture the ships."

"It certainly looks that way," William agreed. He couldn't think of any other explanation for the whole affair. "Unless they just wanted to annoy us."

He rose. "Continue on our current heading," he ordered. "Mr. Roach, you have the conn. Inform me the moment you detect any other starships."

"Aye, Captain," Roach said.

William stepped through the hatch and headed down to the inter-ship car. He hadn't inspected Main Engineering in several weeks, even though Roach had been keeping a sharp eye on the chief engineer. And watching the engineers as they deactivated and inspected the drive nodes would tell him more about their skills than any number of reports.

It will help to make sure Goodrich is not falling back into bad habits, as well, he thought. *The last thing we need is him crawling back into the bottle.*

◆ ◆ ◆

"That was quite an adventure," Joel said cheerfully. "I trust you weren't *too* badly hurt."

Crewman Robin Selfridge scowled angrily. He'd somehow managed to sleep through the alarms, much to Joel's amusement, only to roll out of his bunk and fall to the deck when the ship began to shake. He hadn't been injured, thankfully. Selfridge's bunkmates, once they'd reassured themselves that he *wasn't* injured, had promptly begun pretending to treat him as an invalid. Being told, for the fifth time, that he wasn't to exert himself had to be maddening.

"I wasn't hurt at all, Chief," Selfridge growled. His tone was thoroughly insubordinate, but Joel ignored it. "I just landed on my ass."

Joel laughed. "I assure you that there are people who would pay good money for that," he said. "And to think you got it for free!"

"Fuck it," Selfridge said. "How long will it be before they shut up about it?"

"Not long," Joel assured him. "Something else will happen, I'm sure. Until then, don't rise to the bait. The more they think they've found a chink in your armor, the more they will exploit it to get a rise out of you."

He paused, studying the younger man carefully. Selfridge was a newcomer to the crew, but he had reason to be resentful . . . didn't he? He *was* a colonial . . . Chances were his dreams of becoming a mustang were so much hot air. Yet, Sir William *had* become an officer. His achievements made it harder to convince the newer crewmembers that they didn't have hope of advancement if they stayed in the Navy.

"Thank you, Chief," Selfridge said. "I won't let it get to me."

Joel concealed his irritation as he dismissed Selfridge from his workspace. Approaching him—even while maintaining deniability—was too risky. The younger man was *too* enthusiastic, too new at his job to have any real resentments Joel could exploit. And he probably admired Sir William, just like so many of the other crewmembers. He might not be *too* loyal to the Navy, but he'd be loyal to his commanding officer.

It was frustrating, Joel admitted to himself. His plans had assumed an incompetent commander and a bunch of senior officers who didn't give a damn, save for the one he'd already subverted. Now he had a competent commanding officer with a dedicated command team, a CO who was impressing his crewmen . . . it was *truly* frustrating.

In addition, if someone works out what happened to Captain Abraham or Henderson, he thought, *I'm dead.*

Desertion was a possibility, he had to admit. He was no naive innocent. It wouldn't be hard to jump ship on Vangelis or even Potsdam. But he was damned if he was giving up so quickly. He had a dream . . .

. . . Nonetheless, without the ship, his dream would never come true.

CHAPTER TWENTY-THREE

"It's morning," a voice whispered in Kat's ear.

She shivered with anticipation as she felt warm lips kissing the back of her neck. Kat shifted automatically as the kisses grew more passionate, opening her legs to allow him to slip into her. His hands reached underneath her back and stroked her breasts as he began to move inside, pumping faster as their passion grew. And then she gasped in pleasure as they came together . . .

Afterwards, Kat allowed herself to enjoy the stillness before remembering her duty. "What time is it?

"You should have been on the bridge ten minutes ago," Davidson said.

Kat swore, sitting upright and reaching desperately for her wristcom. She was the captain—she could remove herself from the watch roster if necessary—but not showing up for duty would make her look bad. Crenshaw would probably find a way to use her tardiness against her. She glanced at the wristcom, then gave Davidson an evil look. She wasn't due on the bridge for another full hour.

"Gotcha," Davidson said.

"You bastard," Kat said. She picked up the pillow and clobbered him with it. "You . . ."

She shook her head as she swung her legs over the side of the bed and stood. "I really need to learn some new swearwords. I don't know anything vile enough for you."

"Me neither," Davidson said. He aimed a slap at her rump, which she dodged with ease. "It did get you out of bed."

"I hope that's not the way you get your marines out of their bunks," Kat said severely. "I'd bet good money you'd have a mutiny on your hands if you tried."

"Probably," Davidson said. "But my first drill instructor was fond of bellowing for us to get out of our bunks and threatening push-ups for the last ten recruits to stagger onto the field."

"He made a man out of you," Kat said dryly. Her academy instructors had been *marginally* politer. "Coming into the shower?"

"Just a moment," Davidson said.

Kat stepped into the compartment and turned on the running water. One definite advantage of being captain was having a compartment large enough for two—although, after spending years as a cadet and then a midshipwoman, she was quite happy merely to have a private compartment of her own. Bracing herself, she stepped under the water and washed the sweat and grime from her body. Davidson might not be too concerned about being unclean—he'd spent weeks on deployment where even body wipes were a luxury—but *she* was. She'd always hated feeling dirty.

She considered her ship's current status as she washed herself. She'd expected the convoy to come under attack as it made its slow way to Aston Villa, but nothing had materialized. No other starships had been detected, not even in passing. She'd instead run inspections and put the crew through countless exercises, but it wasn't quite the same. She felt almost frustrated.

Be grateful, she told herself as Davidson slipped into the shower. *The objective is to get the convoy to its destination, not merely to kill pirates.*

"I put the coffee on," Davidson said. "It'll be ready when we come out."

"Thanks," Kat said. She had always felt a little embarrassed asking for java from her steward when Davidson was sharing the cabin. "I think we both need it."

"I need to be down in Marine Country in thirty minutes," Davidson added as he took the shower head and washed himself. "We're running through yet another boarding exercise."

"Good luck," Kat said. "Have you cracked it yet?"

"Getting onto the cloudscoop is easy," Davidson said ruefully. "But they'll still have plenty of time to blow the installation before we kill them all and take possession."

Kat had watched the exercises, then read the postmortems. There were just too many variables for her to feel comfortable gambling with the lives of Davidson and his men. And it wasn't just the marines who were at risk. According to the files, the cloudscoop was owned by a large family, including a number of young children. All of them might be killed in the crossfire, even if the pirates didn't manage to destroy the station.

"You can't guarantee saving the hostages," she queried.

"No, we can't," Davidson agreed. "We were always taught to expect a certain number of civilian casualties if we had to rescue hostages."

"I know," Kat said.

She gave him a tight hug, suddenly wishing that they were back on shore leave. Neither of them had a high threshold for boredom, but sharing her bedroom on Tyre had allowed them to relax and spend the entire morning in bed if they wished.

Duty called.

She kissed him on the lips, then stepped out of the shower and hastily dressed. Davidson followed her a moment later, dressing so rapidly that his hands seemed to blur. But then he'd been taught to get dressed in less than a minute.

"Don't forget your coffee," Davidson said.

Kat drank the warm brew while she glanced at the status report, then her inbox. Crenshaw would have called her directly if there was anything urgent, she was sure, but it never hurt to double-check. There was nothing, save for a brief report of an odd hyperspatial power surge several hundred thousand kilometers off the port bow. The surge hadn't posed any immediate threat—Crenshaw hadn't needed to order a course change—but the navigation department was keeping an eye on it anyway. Hyperspace in the Jorlem Sector wasn't as closely monitored as hyperspace back home.

We need to get them sharing weather reports out here, Kat thought, as she finished her coffee. *It would do wonders for interplanetary cooperation.*

"I'll see you afterwards," Davidson promised. He winked at her. "Let me know if you're going down to the surface."

"I will," Kat said. She had no idea if the planetary government would request a meeting after she sent them her papers, but she'd make sure to take him with her if they did. "Good luck."

Davidson gave her a warning look. "Don't count on the simulations, Kat," he said. "You *know* the dangers."

Kat pursed her lips in acknowledgment. She'd run through countless simulations from the day she'd joined the Navy, going through them again and again until she was perfect. Real life didn't come with a reset switch, though. There would only be one chance to liberate the cloudscoop . . . and a single mistake, something as simple as a bulkhead being out of place, would be enough to doom the entire mission. They had copies of the cloudscoop's original plans—a standard design, one dating all the way back to the Breakaway Wars—but the whole structure was designed to be altered to fit local requirements. There was no way to know what the interior was like until the marines crashed through the airlocks . . .

. . . By then, it might be too late.

She watched him go, wondering idly what his junior officers thought of the whole affair. Pat had no way to hide that he wasn't sleeping in Marine Country, not when he wasn't on watch; she would have been very surprised if they *didn't* know he was sleeping with her. Marines had few secrets from one another. But they wouldn't care as long as the romance didn't affect Pat's duties. Marines were also remorselessly practical. She would have joined if she hadn't disliked the idea of crawling through mud. Besides, she knew how to fight, but she didn't like it.

Kat took one last look at her terminal and then headed for the hatch, walking up through Officer Country to the bridge. The marine on duty outside the bridge hatch saluted smartly, then stepped aside as Kat entered the compartment. Crenshaw, sitting in her command chair, rose at once, nodding toward the status display. It was clear.

"I have the bridge," Kat said, sitting down.

"You have the bridge," Crenshaw confirmed. "We are due to emerge from hyperspace at Aston Villa in two hours, thirty-seven minutes."

"Very good," Kat said. "I'll see you on the bridge when we arrive."

Crenshaw left the bridge. He seemed to have been doing a good job over the last ten days, or at least Kat hadn't heard any complaints. She ruefully admitted that he was improving as an XO. But she still worried that she was missing something. Did people really change that rapidly?

Maybe, she thought. *Or maybe the penny is just waiting to drop.*

She read her way through a number of reports as the hours passed slowly and the convoy made its way towards Aston Villa. The merchant skippers didn't seem to have any complaints either, although *that* wasn't a surprise. Being escorted, even for part of their trip, had to be better than traveling alone. She reminded herself, once again, that getting the freighters to their destination was more important than anything else. Keeping interstellar trade alive was a priority.

"Captain," Wheeler said, "we are approaching the designated emergence point."

"Stand by to return to realspace," Kat ordered. She heard the hatch hiss open behind her and knew that Crenshaw had returned to the bridge. "And take us out when we arrive."

"Aye, Captain," Wheeler said.

"Go to yellow alert," Kat added sharply. A low drumbeat began to echo through the ship. "If there's anything waiting for us, I want to be ready."

She braced herself as the gateway blossomed to life in front of her ship, the entire hull shuddering slightly as *Lightning* led the way back into normal space. The tactical display began to update itself at once, reporting a handful of interplanetary transports and a couple of installations scattered across the star system. It felt oddly disappointing, but she hadn't expected much more. Aston Villa was a stage-three colony, barely beginning the long process of exploiting the resources of an entire system. Compared to Jorlem or Vangelis, the planet wasn't *remotely* developed.

"All freighters have returned to normal space," Lieutenant Ross reported. "I'm picking up a challenge from the planetary defenses."

"Such as they are," Crenshaw commented.

Kat was tempted to agree. There were seven automated weapons platforms and a couple of primitive gunboats holding station over Aston Villa, barely enough to stand off a pirate attack. A destroyer from the Breakaway Wars could have trashed everything in orbit within ten minutes, perhaps less; *Glory of God* could simply ignore the defenses while she hammered the planet below into submission. Aston Villa was caught between the devil and the deep blue sea, wealthy enough to offer rich pickings for anyone willing to simply take them, too poor to afford the sort of planetary defenses they needed. Kat wondered if Jorlem might be considering a little local imperialism if the Theocracy ever supplied the warships they promised. A vest-pocket empire would give President Alexis a great deal more clout.

"Send them our ID and the diplomatic paperwork," she ordered curtly. Aston Villa hadn't *quite* completed the transition from a ruling corporation to an elected government, according to the files. Historically, such periods were almost always rough for both the founding corporation and the new government. "And then release the freighters from our control."

"Aye, Captain," Linda said.

Crenshaw glanced at her. "Captain, three of the freighters requested escort to Sullivan."

Kat thought quickly. She *could* take the freighters to Generis with her and *then* head to Sullivan, only adding three or four days to *Lightning*'s journey, but such a move would complicate matters. And yet she didn't want to allow the freighters to proceed unescorted if possible. Very few pirates would be reluctant to take on a lone freighter, even if the thought of encountering a heavy cruiser made them wet their pants in fear.

"Tell them to hold position for the moment," she ordered. "We'll have to take them to Generis first."

Crenshaw nodded. "Aye, Captain."

Linda glanced up, sharply. "Captain, we're picking up a signal from the surface," she said. "Governor Hemphill is requesting a private discussion."

"I'll take it in my Ready Room," Kat said, rising. "Mr. Crenshaw, you have the bridge."

Kat deliberated further as she walked into the Ready Room, the hatch hissing closed behind her. Governor Hemphill was supposed to be the *last* governor, according to the files; technically, his position was meant to be largely ceremonial as real power was transferred to an elected government. But matters were rarely that simple. A capable founding corporation would maintain a dominant role in the planet's economy for years to come. Was trouble brewing on Aston Villa?

The Falcone Corporation might have some shares in the founding corporation, she thought, sitting down in front of her terminal. *They're always solid investments.*

She pushed the thought aside as a dark-skinned man appeared in front of her. His age was indeterminate, as always, but she knew from his file that he was in his late fifties. He wasn't *quite* a corporate drone—his position called for diplomacy as well as merely issuing orders—but he would be considered reliable by his superiors. They wouldn't want someone siding with the settlers if something went wrong.

"Captain Falcone," Governor Hemphill said. His accent suggested a Terra Nova background. "A pleasure to meet you."

"Likewise, Your Excellency," Kat said. She couldn't help immediately warming to the older man. There was something dignified about him that reminded her of her father. "It is a pleasure to be here."

"I read your diplomatic notes and discussed them with my successor, President Coalman," Governor Hemphill continued. "Is the Commonwealth serious about establishing stronger ties with the sector?"

"Yes, Your Excellency," Kat assured him.

"Then we need to ask for your help," Governor Hemphill said. "Aston Villa would like to join the Commonwealth."

Kat blinked. She hadn't expected *that*.

"There *is* a formal procedure for applying for membership," she said slowly. Just *who* was actually asking? And why? Did Aston Villa *really* want to join the Commonwealth or was it just a small party? Cadiz had been a disaster, at least in part, because only a tiny minority of its inhabitants had genuinely wanted to join. "I can forward you the papers, if you wish."

Governor Hemphill leaned forward. "Is there a way to fast-track the process?"

"It would depend," Kat said. Politics, *again.* There was no StarCom in the system, so she'd have to handle the request herself without referencing her superiors. "First, you would have to meet the minimum requirements; second, you would need to hold a referendum to ensure that your population *wants* to join; third, the Commonwealth Chamber would need to vote to accept you. I don't see it happening in less than five years."

She sucked in her breath. "Why do you want to join so quickly?"

"The sector is growing more and more unstable by the day," Governor Hemphill said. "We're not *that* isolated from the mainstream. It's only a matter of time before *someone* decides he wants our world for himself. Joining the Commonwealth may be the only way to gain protection *and* yet retain a degree of freedom."

Not everyone would agree, Kat thought, *but the Commonwealth will certainly be less dangerous in the long run.*

There were other advantages, she knew. If Aston Villa started down the path to Commonwealth membership, investment would flow into the system. She'd have a good chance to race forward and overtake many of the other worlds in the sector, even though Jorlem and Vangelis had a good head start. If most of the other worlds tried to stay *out* of the Commonwealth, Aston Villa would benefit hugely from free trade.

Turning the planet into a naval base would be a blessing, she considered. *A couple of starships on permanent station here would deter just about everyone from attacking the system.*

"An application for membership is somewhat outside my purview," Kat said, finally. "And I have to take the ship to Generis. But I can take a request for membership back to the Commonwealth, if you wish."

"I understand," Governor Hemphill said. He smiled warmly. "I wouldn't expect you to rubber-stamp our membership."

Kat had to smile as well. "My superiors would not be amused," she said. "But I think they'll be pleased to receive your formal application."

They'll still have to determine who has the right to speak for your world, she added silently.

"That's all we can ask," Governor Hemphill said. He bowed his head. "I hope to see you down on the surface when you return."

"I certainly hope so too," Kat agreed. "And I look forward to meeting both you and the president."

"Of course," Governor Hemphill said. "And thank you."

Governor Hemphill's face vanished from the terminal, but Kat continued to stare at it in amused disbelief. A planet that was actually *eager* to sign up with the Commonwealth? It was unexpected, although Gamma Orion and the other early members had also been eager. Hemphill's request was refreshing but also worrying. Who *did* have the authority to speak for Aston Villa? She would have to find out before the process could be started in earnest.

And I'll have to file a report, she thought sourly. The Admiralty and the Foreign Office would want her impressions, which would be tricky. She just didn't have the time to go down to the surface and chat to the population. *There are too many other things to do.*

She keyed her console. "Mr. Crenshaw, inform the freighters that we will be departing to Sullivan via Generis two hours from now," she said. "If they still want to travel with us, they can do so."

"Aye, Captain," Crenshaw said.

"And then lay in a course for Generis," Kat added. "Time is not on our side."

CHAPTER TWENTY-FOUR

"There isn't very much here, Captain," Lieutenant Commander Samuel Weiberg said thoughtfully. "There certainly isn't a habitable *planet*."

"But enough asteroids to keep a small civilization going for quite some time," Crenshaw pointed out. "There's a *lot* of asteroids."

Kat agreed. Generis had no Earth-compatible world, merely a couple of dead planets that would require a long-term terraforming program to turn them into places humans could live. But there *was* a large gas giant and a *colossal* asteroid belt, the latter housing a growing settlement. Given time, Generis might become very important indeed. Asteroid settlers made the best industrial workers in the galaxy.

"Keep us under cloak, but take us towards the cloudscoop," she ordered quietly. There would be time to make contact with the settlement later. She had no idea if the pirates had taken the asteroid colonies too, although the report suggested they hadn't. "Are you picking up any transmissions from the settlements?"

"Just standard emissions," Linda noted. "I suspect they're using lasers for direct communications."

Kat forced herself to wait as *Lightning* made her way towards the gas giant. Generis-III was huge, only slightly smaller than Jupiter. The planet reminded her, vaguely, of a proposal she'd once read to turn a gas giant into a second sun. There *were* five moons orbiting the gas giant that might become habitable, if the planet *could* become a star, but she knew such a feat wasn't possible yet. Even her father had regarded the whole scheme as a dubious investment.

"I'm picking up the cloudscoop," Weiberg reported twenty minutes later. "She's right where the report said she'd be."

Good, Kat thought.

The cloudscoop came into view on the display. It was surprisingly simple for such an important piece of technology: a long tube reaching down into the gas giant's atmosphere with a large cluster of processing and habitation modules—and docking struts—at the top. The setup looked remarkably fragile, but she knew from her research that cloudscoops were surprisingly strong. And if conditions on the planet below grew too intense, the scoop could be retracted until the weather calmed down.

Crenshaw coughed. "Any starships?"

"One ship docked at her lower strut," Weiberg said. "I think she's a corvette, judging by her mass readings. She doesn't seem to be running any active sensor scans."

Kat sucked in her breath. *What were the pirates doing?* If they snatched every ship that docked, the remainder of the settlements would *know* that something was wrong. And yet, if they allowed ships to buy fuel freely . . . maybe they were just jacking up the price as much as possible. *And* perhaps selling fuel to pirate ships too.

They'll be holding the entire system hostage too, she thought, grimly. *If their supplies of HE3 get cut off, their economy will suffer until they can replace the cloudscoop.*

She keyed her console. "Major, your opinion?"

"We could make a covert transit," Davidson said through the intercom. "But they'd know the moment we landed on the hull."

"And then they'd have an opportunity to do something about it," Kat mused.

Kat had ordered the freighters to return to realspace on the edge of the system and go dark, shutting down all unnecessary systems to ensure that they weren't detected. If she called one of them in and used it as a Trojan horse . . . they might *just* be able to sneak the marines up to the cloudscoop without being detected. But there would still be too much risk of being detected before they were in position to take the station.

Besides, none of the skippers signed up to play hero, Kat thought. *They might not want to put their ships at risk.*

"Captain," Wheeler said. "How close do you want us to go?"

Kat gritted her teeth. The cloudscoop wasn't operating active sensors. She was fairly sure *Lightning* would remain undetected for some time as long as she didn't use her own active sensors, but Kat couldn't just lurk in the system and keep an eye on the cloudscoop. She had to recover the station before the pirates could destroy it.

Crenshaw leaned toward her. "We don't *know* the station has actually been taken."

"There's a corvette parked below her," Kat pointed out. "She wouldn't be there if she wasn't a pirate ship."

She thought quickly. Assuming the corvette's life support was maxed out, there could be over fifty pirates on the station. The station itself was over-engineered, designed to comfortably support at least a hundred inhabitants. She doubted the pirates would have turned the cloudscoop into a base, but they *could* be holding their prisoners there as well as the hostages. The Commonwealth officially disapproved of paying ransoms, yet Kat knew that there was a standing offer to ransom any merchant crewman who fell into pirate hands—often the only thing standing between the captured crewmen and a horrible death.

"There's no way we can sneak the marines onboard," she added. "Major?"

"I suspect you're right, Captain," Davidson said. "There's too much electromagnetic distortion in the surrounding space to guarantee an undetected crossing."

"Then we have to try to talk them into leaving peacefully," Kat said reluctantly. She didn't like the idea—allowing pirates to escape scot-free was a loathsome thought—but she saw no alternative. "They can depart in their ship and we'll recover the cloudscoop."

Crenshaw looked doubtful. "It will take them at least twenty minutes to put enough distance between themselves and the gravity well to open a gateway and jump out," he said. "They'll be exposed to our fire all the way. They'll never go for it."

"I have to agree," Davidson said. "Captain, they'll insist on taking a few hostages with them."

Kat saw the wisdom of Pat's words. A family with youngsters had too many potential hostages. She refused to knowingly fire on *children*. And once the pirates slipped into hyperspace, they could either keep the hostages or simply space them.

They won't believe a complete concession, she thought. *I'll have to let them talk me into doing what I want to do.*

"I have a plan," she said, the idea gelling in her head. "Helm, take us to an overwatch position. I want to be ready to intercept anything leaving the station."

"Aye, Captain," Wheeler said.

"Major Davidson," Kat added, "prepare a platoon of marines for a stealth insertion."

"Aye, Captain," Davidson said.

Kat forced herself to wait as *Lightning* moved closer to her target. There were just too many variables for her to feel remotely comfortable, even though she had a plan. If she'd misjudged the pirates—or she accidentally panicked them—the plan was going to fail spectacularly before it had even begun. She didn't dare give the pirates too much time to think, yet—at the same time—she knew there was too much they could do to frustrate her . . .

Once we reveal ourselves, we are committed, she thought grimly.

She looked at the tactical console. "Do we have a threat analysis for the corvette?"

"No, Captain," Weiberg said. "She's largely powered down. Analysis thinks she'll need at least ten minutes to bring all her systems online."

Catching an enemy warship unawares was every tactical officer's dream. No hull material ever produced could stand up to antimatter warheads slamming into unprotected metal. Kat would give her right arm to catch *Glory of God* in such a vulnerable pose. But there was no way she could take advantage of the scenario, not now. The pirates *needed* to think they had a way out.

"We could take her out with a single missile," Crenshaw pointed out.

"She's too close to the station," Kat explained. "The explosion would take out the cloudscoop as well."

She gritted her teeth. No matter what she did, there were *far* too many variables.

"Captain," Wheeler said. "We are in position."

"There's no hint they've detected us," Weiberg added.

Kat's lips twitched. The electromagnetic distortion around the gas giant made the cruiser's cloaking device somewhat unreliable. An alert sensor crew, even relying on their passive sensors alone, might well have been able to detect *Lightning*'s presence. But the pirates didn't seem to care about watching nearby space for intruders. Had they cowed the rest of the system? Or did they merely think no one would give a damn about the cloudscoop?

It isn't as if Jorlem or Vangelis dispatched a ship to deal with the problem, Kat thought. *If they knew, they just ignored it.*

"On my command, drop the cloak and go to full tactical alert," she ordered. "Sweep the station and the surrounding area of space with passive sensors, then open hailing frequencies."

"Aye, Captain," Weiberg said.

Kat braced herself. As soon as they dropped the cloak, they'd be committed.

"Drop the cloak," she ordered.

She allowed herself a moment to imagine the enemy reaction as *Lightning* appeared out of nowhere. Pirates were scumbags, but they were *spacers*. They knew, on intuitive levels groundhogs never grasped, the realities of interstellar travel. The iron laws of science guaranteed they were doomed. Kat didn't need to throw anything more complex than a handful of KEWs, nothing more than rocky projectiles, to smash the cloudscoop into rubble. A single hit would be enough to render the entire structure unusable.

They can't run, she thought. *They have to feel trapped.*

"Picking up emissions from the corvette," Weiberg reported. The display updated, showing the enemy ship bringing up its systems. "They're powering up the drive."

Kat smirked. They didn't have a hope of getting the corvette ready to fight in time.

"Captain, they haven't responded," Linda reported.

"Signal them again," Kat ordered. Pirates were cowards at heart. The simple fact that she hadn't blown the cloudscoop into falling debris would give them a *little* hope. But they *had* to make sure she knew they had hostages, if they wanted to get any use out of them. "Keep repeating the signal."

"Aye, Captain," Linda said.

Kat felt something coiling in her gut. The plan was dangerous enough . . . but what if she was wrong? What if she'd misjudged the pirates? A group of utter madmen might just dare her to storm the station . . . and if they did, she'd already given up the advantage of surprise. The bastards would have ample time to prepare to blow up the station and kill everyone.

"Picking up a response," Linda said. "Audio only."

"Put it through," Kat ordered.

". . . off, bitch," a voice said, harsh, defiant . . . But Kat could hear fear underlying the pirate's words. "Back off or we'll kill the girls."

"This is Captain Katherine Falcone of HMS *Lightning*," Kat said, keeping her voice even. She had to seem calm. They had to think she was in control. "To whom do I have the pleasure of speaking?"

"Fuck off," the voice spat. "You're dead, cunt!"

Kat ignored the insults. She'd heard worse. "Let me outline your position," she said, briskly. "You are well within missile range. Your point defense is puny, and all I have to do is throw rocks to eventually destroy the station. There is no way you can power your ship up in time to fight, let alone make your escape. There is no way out."

"We can kill the bitches," the voice snarled. "Do you want to watch as we tear them apart?"

"If you surrender peacefully and hand over the hostages," Kat added, "we'll ship you to a penal colony instead of tossing you out an airlock. You'll remain alive . . ."

"And doomed," the voice snapped.

Kat shrugged, even though she knew the pirate couldn't see her. "You're also doomed if you stay there," she pointed out, dryly. "I can't leave you in possession of the cloudscoop."

"So we're dead anyway," the voice said. His tone carried a hint of hysteria. "Come and take us, if you dare!"

"Let me propose a compromise," Kat said, after a moment. The pirates would be desperate, she was sure, but she didn't dare let them think too much. They had to take the bait she offered without thinking. "You hand the hostages over, and we'll allow you to leave freely."

"And then you gun us down when we leave," the voice said. Kat heard, just for a second, angry muttering behind the speaker. His comrades might be determined to take the offer, no matter what their leader said. The pirate would be lucky if he wasn't knifed in the back. "I don't think so!"

He paused. "We take some of the bitches with us!"

"Unacceptable," Kat said coolly. "We want them alive."

There was more angry muttering. "We can put them in an escape pod once we reach a safe distance," the pirate voice said. Kat could hear a stronger undercurrent of fear as he spoke. "You can pick them up once we're gone."

"Also unacceptable," Kat said. The plan would have been workable *if* she'd trusted the pirates to keep their word. "There would be nothing stopping you from just keeping them."

She grimaced at the thought. She'd spent too long cleaning up after pirate raids during her term on HMS *Thomas*. She knew what fate awaited prisoners, male and female, young and old, when they outlived their usefulness. There were ways she could offer ransoms, she supposed, but making the trade would be difficult. There would be no way to guarantee that the pirates would keep their side of the bargain.

"You don't have any other choice," the pirate said. His voice rose. "You either take our bargain or watch as the bitches die."

"Let me propose a compromise," Kat said. "How many hostages do you have? Men and women who are not members of your crew?"

A pause. "Fifty-seven," the pirate said. "Men, women, and children."

Kat frowned. That couldn't be just the station's crew, then. The pirates had to have taken other prisoners, starship crews, or hostages from the rest of the system . . . Fifty-seven hostages were a manageable number. Her team could handle it.

"I will fly a shuttle over to the station," Kat said. She ignored the rustle that ran around the bridge at her words. "A large one, easily capable of carrying fifty-seven people. She can take the hostages back to *Lightning* while I remain with you. You can drop me off in a lifeboat before you leave the system."

She kept her expression under tight control as she waited for the response. The offer *had* to be tempting. If they had the slightest idea who she was—and she *was* famous—they *had* to know she'd be worth a king's ransom. The idea of keeping her prisoner had to be astonishingly tempting. Her father would pay billions of crowns for her safe return.

Take the bait, she thought, grimly. *Please.*

"You fly the shuttle alone," the pirate said after a long delay. "One of our . . . guests . . . can fly her back to the ship."

"She can fly on automatic," Kat assured him blithely. They'd swallowed the bait! Even if the pirate leader suspected a trap, his crew wouldn't let him say no. "I just need to set the autopilot before leaving the craft."

"And then your ship moves away," the pirate said. His voice hardened. "I want her out of weapons range."

"And *I* want to be sure that I'm your *only* hostage," Kat countered. "*Lightning* will monitor the exchange, then withdraw once the shuttle has returned to the ship. They will not fire on your ship as long as I am with you."

There was yet more angry muttering from the speaker, too quiet for her to make out the words, but she could guess. The pirates *knew* they were screwed, and Kat had offered them a way out. She wondered, absently, if their leader was about to be brutally killed by his own people.

"Very well," the pirate said. "You fly the shuttle over here now while we power up the ship. Then you'll be our guest until we reach hyperspace."

Probably a great deal longer, Kat thought. She'd tempted them with something they didn't have a hope of resisting. *Or so you think.*

"I'll be over in fifteen minutes," she said. "Be seeing you."

She tapped her console, closing the connection. "Have a shuttle prepared . . ."

"Captain," Crenshaw interrupted. "I really must protest! This is madness!"

"No, it isn't," Kat said. She rose. "You have the bridge. Hold our current position and wait."

"Captain," Crenshaw said. His voice was almost pleading. "You *can't* offer yourself as a hostage."

"I agree," Davidson said through the intercom. His voice was flat, so flat she *knew* he was screaming inside. She wondered if he was seriously considering handcuffing her to the command chair. "They won't let you go."

Kat understood the dangers. Her father's security team had briefed her when she'd turned twelve, old enough to understand the dark underside of the life she led. A kidnap attempt was a real possibility. Her father would receive a demand, then another demand, then another demand . . . while she'd be kept prisoner, raped and tortured . . . perhaps the security team had exaggerated some of the dangers, but she knew what pirates could and would do. They wouldn't give up such a valuable prize so easily.

"I know," she said. "Which is why we're not going to let them have me." She took a breath. "This is what we're going to do."

CHAPTER TWENTY-FIVE

Kat had never felt so alone.

She knew, deep inside, that she was physically brave. She'd passed through Piker's Peak, then served on three starships before being promoted to command rank. She'd fought in a dozen combat actions before and during the war. And yet she'd never felt so exposed as she did now, piloting a shuttlecraft toward the cloudscoop. She felt naked and vulnerable and very, *very*, alone.

It had seemed a simple plan when she'd devised it on the bridge. But now, sitting alone in the shuttle's cockpit, she knew she might have made a fatal mistake. If she'd miscalculated, if the pirates managed to take her prisoner, she was in deep shit.

If I ever get home, she thought morbidly, *I'll probably be put in front of a court-martial for putting my life at risk.*

Davidson had told her that the plan was utter madness. Even after she'd told him what she really had in mind, he'd still been reluctant to go through with it. Kat *was* his commanding officer as well as his lover. It was his *job* to keep her alive, even at the cost of his own life. But there was no other bait they could use. The pirates had to be offered a decent chance to not only escape but come out ahead.

He's going to be furious afterwards, Kat thought. *The Admiralty will be horrified.*

Kat forced herself to remain calm as she guided the shuttle towards its destination. Up close, the modular station looked crude, the modules patched time and time again until there was very little of the original material clearly visible. That was par for the course so far from heavily industrialized planets like Vangelis and Tyre. The current owners would know every last square inch of their facility intimately; they'd know *precisely* how to refurbish most of the components or produce new ones from scratch. There was very little about the structure that was *advanced.*

Certainly nothing irreplaceable, she thought. *But replacing a cloud-scoop so far from the Commonwealth would be a very low priority.*

The radio buzzed. "Dock at the upper airlock," a voice ordered. A radio beacon came on, guiding her to her destination. "And then remain seated."

"Of course," Kat said, feeling her heartbeat starting to race. "I should be docked in two minutes."

Sweat trickled down her back as she pulled the shuttle up and made contact with the station, a dull thump running through the craft as the airlocks mated. She glanced at the telltales, then swung the chair around and waited as the pirates fumbled with the hatches. They took longer than she'd expected to open the hatch, even though it was a standardized design. Even the *Theocracy* used the same basic design. And then there was a hiss as the hatch opened, allowing the pirates to step into the shuttle.

Kat kept her face expressionless as they turned to face her. They wore basic shipsuits, torn and stained so badly that any protective qualities were long gone. She doubted they would survive a sudden depressurization, even if they *did* manage to get their masks on before they ran out of air. Their faces were unshaven, their eyes wild and dangerous. She cursed mentally, wondering if she'd made a deadly mistake. Far too many pirate crewmen were drugged out of their minds when they weren't on duty.

If they didn't start out as monsters, she thought, keeping herself still by force of will, *they're soon made into monsters.*

The lead pirate pointed a gun at her forehead. His hand shook so badly that Kat couldn't help wondering if he'd pull the trigger by accident. He looked her up and down, his eyes leaving trails of slime over her body; his companion, more interested in the shuttle, seemed to pay little attention to her. But that, Kat reminded herself, meant nothing. The best security officers were often the ones who seemed to be doing nothing.

"Get up," the pirate growled. "Keep your hands where I can see them."

Kat obeyed, silently considering his accent, which reminded her a little of President Alexis's voice, although she knew that meant nothing. Plenty of spacers, including pirates, passed through Jorlem, probably spending a great deal of time with prostitutes while selling their wares and waiting for the next job.

The pirate took a step forward, inching towards her as if he feared she'd turn into a whirling blur of hands and fists at any moment. She would have smiled at the thought, if she hadn't been so tense. *That* sort of thing only happened in bad movies. Kat clenched her jaw as he removed a pair of metal handcuffs from his pocket, then motioned for her to turn around. She'd anticipated it, but it was still awkward. She swallowed, hard, as she felt cold metal around her wrists.

"Spread your legs," the pirate ordered harshly, an unholy hint of gloating anticipation in his voice. "And then stay still."

Kat nodded, not trusting herself to say a word as he ran his hands over her body, groping her breasts, caressing her buttocks and rubbing between her legs with a sickening eagerness that chilled her to the bone. She'd been careful not to carry anything that could be used as a weapon, knowing she'd be searched when she arrived, but still . . . she fought to show no reaction at all as his hands started to pull at her uniform's fastenings, threatening to strip her bare. There was no way she could convince herself that someone else was touching her.

"You really don't have time," she said as evenly as she could. "Your boss will want to get the hostages onto the shuttle and out of here before it's too late."

The pirate turned Kat around and leered. "There's always time for fun."

Kat made a show of shrugging. "Your boss may not agree," she said. "There's time for fun later."

She kept her face expressionless, refusing to let him see just how much his touch bothered her. She'd met too many sadists who found excitement in tormenting others. They didn't *want* submission to be offered willingly, she knew all too well; they wanted to wrest control. They wanted their victim to *hurt*.

She promised herself, silently, that the pirate wouldn't survive the day, no matter what else happened.

"You might have something up your ass," the pirate said. "Perhaps I should check."

"And then the captain will ram a bullet up *your* ass," the second pirate said. He caught hold of Kat's arm and pulled her towards the hatch, ignoring his comrade's squawk of protest. "If we don't get out of here soon, we're dead."

The pirates frog-marched Kat through the hatch and into the station. The air tasted musty, as if the filters hadn't been replaced for weeks, although she *did* have to admit that it smelled better than the average pirate ship. A line of hostages, their hands secured behind their backs with plastic ties, was already forming outside the hatch, guarded by three heavily armed pirates. She felt sick as she looked at the hostages, realizing that too many of them had been molested—or worse—in the last few minutes. Clothes mussed and torn, nasty bruises on their faces . . . They looked as if all hope had long since gone.

"Get them onto the ship, then secure them to the chairs," the second pirate ordered. "Make damn sure none of you are onboard when the autopilot comes online."

Kat glanced at him. "You have to issue such an order?"

The first pirate reached around and pinched her nipple, hard. "Shut up," he said as she winced in pain. "Or I will teach you respect."

"Behave yourself," the second pirate ordered.

Kat quietly studied the station as they made their way through a twisting maze of compartments. It looked very much like a family-run business. The bulkheads were decorated with children's paintings and a handful of photographs. A pair of teaching machines were parked in the lounge . . . A family had hoped, once upon a time, to turn the station into a home as well as a business. She hoped, prayed, that the owners had survived long enough to be rescued . . .

The interior doesn't quite match the plans, she thought as her implants silently ran a comparison. *If we'd stormed the station, we'd be operating at a disadvantage.*

She braced herself as she was pushed into the control room. Five men—three calculating, two wild-eyed—looked at her. They seemed surprised to *see* her, as if they hadn't really expected the captain to keep her side of the bargain. Kat glanced from face to face, silently picking out the leader. A pirate leader couldn't call on a chain of command to back him up if he ran into trouble with his crew. He'd be the roughest and toughest of them all.

"My Lady," the leader said. The voice was familiar. "Welcome to hell."

Kat scrutinized him for a long moment. He was heavily muscled, so heavily muscled that she was sure he'd had some bootleg enhancement as well as adaptations and improvements spliced into his genetic code. His face was hard, his eyes cold, dark . . . This wasn't a man, she realized, who gave much of a damn for anyone apart from himself. The only thing that had kept him at bay was the threat of being blown away along with the station. He wore an armored ship-suit and carried a belt crammed with weapons, trying to make himself look as intimidating as possible.

"Thank you," she said sarcastically. "Move the hostages to the shuttle, and then they can fly back to the ship, and we can head out past the gravity well."

The pirate tilted his head. "And what is to stop us from keeping the hostages, and you?"

"*Lightning* will blow the station away if the shuttle isn't sent back," Kat said. "And if you try to keep the hostages, they'll blow the station away too."

"You'll die," the pirate snarled.

"Of course," Kat agreed. "And so will you."

She saw a flicker of pure rage cross the pirate's face and inwardly shuddered. The man was psychopathic. Being humiliated so badly, being threatened by his own crew . . . The pirate would take his rage out on Kat if he made it away from the system. She'd be lucky to last long enough for the ransom demand to reach her father . . .

. . . and she would be astonished if she was ever returned.

"There's no point in trying to alter the deal now," she added, allowing her voice to lighten submissively. Let him think she'd bend the knee. "Let the hostages go, then we can depart the station and make our way beyond the gravity well."

"Of course, *Captain*," the pirate sneered.

She read her fate in his voice and shuddered. The only thing keeping him from rubbing her nose in it was the awareness that she might be able to use her implants to call for help, if, of course, he'd considered her implants. No, he had everything to gain by playing along . . . for the moment. He'd alter the deal when he thought he could get away with it.

The pirate glanced at one of his officers. "Make sure all the bitches and the rest of the unwilling are on the shuttle," he ordered. "And then key the autopilot to take them home."

"Sir," the pirate said.

Kat braced herself as the pirate leader turned his attention back to her. "We have prepared a lifeboat just for you," he said nastily. "I'm sure you'll enjoy your time in space."

"I can catch up on my sleep," Kat said, trying to inject humor into her voice. Let him think she believed him, for the moment. "Commanding a starship is *very* tiring."

The pirate laughed. "It is *very* tiring," he agreed. He jabbed a finger at her. "Sit against the bulkhead and wait."

Kat did as she was told, cursing the handcuffs under her breath. They were too tight, cutting off her circulation. Her hands were going numb. The pirates hurried around the complex, doing their work as the shuttle was slowly loaded with hostages, yet they kept glancing at Kat, cold anticipation in their eyes. They knew what was awaiting her too.

"The shuttle is packed," a pirate eventually reported. "They're ready to go."

The leader looked at Kat. "They'll be on their way in a moment," he said. "And then we'll be on our way."

He looked back at his subordinate. "Send them on their way."

"Yes, My Lord," the pirate said.

Kat forced herself to wait, calmly, as the shuttle detached itself from the station and headed back towards *Lightning*. The hostages would be out of the firing line, if nothing else; the only people on the station, save for herself, were the pirates. And she was ready to die, if necessary, to stop them.

"Get up," the leader said. He watched as Kat made a show of struggling to rise, then reached down and yanked Kat to her feet. "It's time to go."

Kat braced herself as the pirates thrust her out of the hatch and down the corridor. The lights seemed dimmer, somehow. She wondered if the pirates had deactivated the fusion core during their mad scramble to leave. The batteries would eventually run down, leaving the entire station dead in space. She couldn't help wondering, as she was pushed through a series of hatches, if something had gone badly wrong. If the plan had failed . . .

"Our ship," the leader sneered. He nodded towards the airlock. "I'm sure you'll enjoy your stay."

"Of course," Kat said. The hatch began to open. Had something gone *really* badly wrong? If the plan failed, she'd have no choice but to use her implants to kill herself. "Perhaps we could play a round or two of cards while we crawl out of the gravity well."

The leader shoved her into the bulkhead. Kat grunted in pain as she felt her nose break, warm liquid flowing down to stain her uniform. She'd pushed him too far. She felt more than heard the pirate drawing a knife from his belt . . .

"My ship has kept me alive for years," the leader snarled. "And you . . ."

The lights went out. Kat reacted instinctively and dropped to the deck, trying to crawl away. A weight landed on her back—she gasped as the breath was knocked out of her—a second before she heard a dull thud. Someone started shooting, bullets ripping into the compartment, only to be silenced a moment later.

"Bitch," the leader growled. Kat felt his fist slamming into her back. "What have you—?"

He was yanked away, hard. Kat allowed herself a moment of relief a second before the lights came back on. The pirates were lying on the deck, dead or unconscious; marines were standing over them, wearing black armor. One of them stamped over to Kat and helped her back to her feet. His helmet snapped open a moment later, revealing Davidson's face.

"Kat," he said. "I . . ."

He caught himself. "Let me remove those cuffs, Captain," he said. "And then you're going to see the medic."

Kat sighed in relief as the metal cuffs were cut away from her skin. "You managed to gain control of the station?"

"Slipped into their ship as soon as you docked," Davidson said. The pirates had *known* she was coming in a shuttle, but it had never occurred to them that an entire platoon of Marines might be clinging to the hull. "We now have complete control of their vessel as well as the station itself. No surprises as far as we can see."

"We'll have to do a thorough search," Kat said. She'd done her best to arrange things to make sure that the pirates would have limited time for mischief, but they'd probably had enough time to rig a destruct charge. "Did Crenshaw pick up the hostages?"

"He did," Davidson confirmed. "They're in sickbay now."

Kat rubbed her nose, then forced herself to stand still as the Marine medic poked and prodded at the wound. The pain was already fading. She'd be left with a throbbing sensation she knew would be gone in time and a story she suspected would grow in the telling until everyone believed she'd stormed the station stark naked and killed everyone with her bare hands.

"The nose will need some work, but it's OK for now," the medic said. "You'll be fine."

"Not such a pretty face any longer," Kat said, ruefully.

"You'll be back to normal tomorrow," Davidson assured her. He motioned for the medic to leave the compartment, then lowered his voice. "That was immensely brave . . ."

He gazed at Kat and gently touched her shoulder. "Do you know how many things could have gone wrong?"

"Yes," Kat said. "But I didn't see any other choice."

She rubbed her wrists absently. Her entire body wanted to shake, and shake badly. Indeed, she knew just how many things could have gone wrong. And the pirate's touch had left her feeling filthy . . .

But I won, she thought, looking at the bodies. The pirate who'd groped her was among the dead. *I fucking won*!

CHAPTER TWENTY-SIX

"I don't know how we can ever thank you," Manager James Hammond said.

Kat smiled at him as reassuringly as she could. The poor man was twitching backwards and forwards, as if he expected a blow to fall at any moment. His family—six adults, twelve children—hadn't been physically harmed, but they *had* been traumatized. They'd known what would happen when the pirates no longer needed them. And even now, onboard a heavy warship with freedom restored, Hammond still feared the worst. Kat had a nasty feeling he and his family would be heading back to the core worlds soon.

"Just tell everyone what we did," she said. It was simply too good a story *not* to tell. And the trick wouldn't work twice. "Make sure they know the Commonwealth came to the rescue."

"I will," Hammond promised. "And thank you for taking care of my family."

"You're welcome," Kat said. She cocked her head slightly. "Do you intend to return to the cloudscoop?"

"I don't know," Hammond admitted. "Are you planning to remain here permanently?"

Kat shook her head ruefully. The pirates had apparently threatened the remainder of the system's settlements into sullen submission once the settlements had realized that something was wrong on the cloud-scoop. Even now, the locals didn't have the firepower to fend off another pirate attack once *Lightning* departed. Unless . . .

"I think we'll be staying here for a couple of days," she said. The freighter crews wouldn't be pleased, but they'd have to live with it. "After that . . . I don't know."

"I'll have to discuss future plans with my family," Hammond said. "Staying here . . . I thought it would be a good way to get in on the ground floor. But instead . . ."

"Let me know what you decide," Kat said. She touched her nose self-consciously. The doctor had fixed the damage—no one would be able to tell Kat's nose had been broken—but she still felt a dull ache that wouldn't fade for a few more days. "If you wish, I can transport you to Jorlem or Vangelis."

"Thank you. I will let you know," Hammond promised.

Kat was struck by a wave of sympathy as the older man was escorted out of her Ready Room. His family had been brave to set up a home so far from civilized space . . . and the move had cost them badly. She would understand if he wanted to go back to the core worlds, or even just set up shop at Vangelis. His nerves might have been shot to hell for good.

Her door chimed. "Come."

Crenshaw stepped into the Ready Room, the hatch shutting behind him. "Captain," he said. "I have the latest report from the away team. The cloudscoop is in good working order, *despite* the marines subverting its command software. The enemy ship is in . . . *rough*, but acceptable condition."

Kat lifted her eyebrows as she motioned him to a chair. "Rough, but acceptable?"

"She's not going to kill her crew tomorrow," Crenshaw said. His voice was crisp, yet sounded as if he was distracted by an even weightier matter. "In the long term, she'll need a great deal of work, but she's not an immediate problem. Her missile bays are well-stocked too. We could probably reconfigure them to launch from our tubes."

"I was thinking we might leave her here," Kat mused. "How big a crew does she need?"

"Ten would be sufficient, for the moment," Crenshaw said. "But ideally she'd need at least thirty experienced spacers for long-term operations."

He paused. "You don't plan to sell her?"

"The cloudscoop is vitally important," Kat reminded him. "Losing it will drive prices up all over the sector and heighten dependence on the more developed worlds. If we left the corvette with the locals, they'd have a better chance at defending themselves against any future attacks."

"Not against *Glory of God*," Crenshaw pointed out.

"No, but few pirates would dare to take on a warship even when the odds were in their favor," Kat said. "And, realistically speaking, having a star system out here that owes us something might be better for us, in the long run, than a few thousand additional crowns."

"I suspect the crew might disagree," Crenshaw said dryly.

"They'll have to live with it," Kat countered. "And we can definitely make sure there's something nice in their pay packets for when they take shore leave."

"Yes, Captain," Crenshaw said.

Kat took a breath. "Open discussions with the settlers," she ordered. "Offer them the corvette in exchange for intelligence sharing, nothing else."

"They don't have much else to offer," Crenshaw said.

"Yeah," Kat agreed.

She looked at Crenshaw for a long moment. He *still* seemed distracted. Kat waited, wondering if he was going to come right out and say what was on his mind. But the XO said nothing.

Her patience snapped. "Was there something else?"

"Yes, Captain," Crenshaw said. He looked almost relieved. "Permission to speak freely?"

Kat hesitated, then nodded. "Granted."

"What you did was absolutely *insane*," Crenshaw said. "Do you know what could have happened to you?"

He went on before she had a chance to answer.

"They could have smuggled you out of the system," he added, his voice rising sharply. "They could have raped and murdered you, or sent pieces of your body to your family, or even handed you over to the Theocracy! You could have been killed out of hand . . ."

"I was aware of the dangers," Kat said stiffly.

"I couldn't have fired on a ship carrying you," Crenshaw insisted. "They could have waltzed out of the system with you and we could have done nothing! It could have gone horrendously wrong!"

"Yes, it could," Kat agreed. "But it didn't."

"You're not *meant* to put your life at risk," Crenshaw said. "*I* should have gone."

"You're not so valuable," Kat pointed out. She doubted the pirates would have known who Crenshaw was if she'd offered him as a hostage. "I had to offer them a prize worth the risk of playing along with me."

"You could have been killed," Crenshaw repeated.

Kat took a long breath. "Thank you for your commentary," she said coldly. She resisted the urge to rise to her feet. "Do I get to make a response?"

Crenshaw met her eyes with a stubborn gaze.

"I am a serving officer in the Navy," Kat said. "Risk is part of my life, and it is part of yours. We do what we can to *minimize* risk, but we cannot eliminate it altogether. If I had wanted to stay safe, I would have stayed at home."

She looked back at him, wondering just how much of his concern was for her instead of for his own career. If he'd gone back home, having watched helplessly as his commanding officer was kidnapped or killed . . . his career would have been blown out of the water. Candy wouldn't help him find another posting if her sister had died on his watch. And the Admiralty would have grave doubts about any officer who *allowed* his CO to set out on a suicidal solo mission.

I couldn't think of an alternative, she told herself, numbly. *Nothing that minimized the risk to others . . .*

She shook her head. "This uniform charges us with the protection of innocent civilians," she reminded him. "It is our *job* to put ourselves between them and harm. My life is far less important than theirs."

"With all due respect, Captain . . ."

Kat spoke over him. "Which one of the hostages would you like to sentence to death, in my place? The nine-year-old girl? The sixteen-month-old baby boy? Or the thirteen-year-old girl, just old enough to understand the threat looming over her . . .

"Which one would you ask to die in my place?"

"I wouldn't," Crenshaw said. "But I wouldn't want you to die either."

"Over thirty thousand military personnel have died in the war so far," Kat reminded him. "I have no idea how many *civilians* have died, or how many Theocrats have died. This isn't a movie and I don't have a patriotic scriptwriter . . ."

She stopped and took a breath. "I understand your concerns. And if you want to write them into the log, you may do so. I don't believe the Admiralty will be too concerned. All's well that ends well. But if you feel otherwise . . ."

"I don't like it," Crenshaw said. "You shouldn't have taken such a risk."

"I saw no choice," Kat said.

She met his eyes. "I have no doubt that *someone* will come up with the perfect solution to the whole problem," she added. "Some smartass in a rear office who's never set foot on a starship in his entire career. He'll say I should have done *this*, or *that*, or . . . *whatever*. I had to come up with a plan on the fly, and it *worked*."

"Barely," Crenshaw said.

"We got the hostages out, we liberated the cloudscoop, and we killed or captured a bunch of pirates," Kat reminded him. "I'd say it was a good day's work."

She allowed her voice to harden. "Like I said, if you want to write your concerns into the log you may do so," she said with a new edge in her voice. "For the moment, however, go open discussions with the locals."

"Aye, Captain," Crenshaw said, stiffly.

He rose and saluted, then headed for the hatch. Kat watched him go, feeling oddly discontented. Sir William wouldn't have been happy either, she knew, but he would have understood. And he would have *known*, on an instinctive level, that she *had* to do whatever it took to liberate the hostages. Crenshaw, on the other hand . . .

She sighed. He'd make himself look a fool if he wrote his concerns into the log *now*, but the Admiralty might still take note. She'd taken a terrifying risk . . .

Her intercom bleeped. "Captain, this is Davidson," he said. "My team has completed the interrogations."

"Come up here," Kat ordered, feeling exhausted. "We may as well go through them together."

She opened her terminal as she waited for him to reach the Ready Room and glanced through the first set of reports. A couple of pirates had died under interrogation, their implants detecting the mind probes and self-destructing, but the others had talked freely. Their cooperation wouldn't make any difference to their final fate, she knew. They'd had their chance to surrender and declined.

The hatch opened. Davidson stepped into the Ready Room.

"I was just looking at the reports," Kat said as she rose and strode over to the sofa. "They don't have *that* much to say."

"There's a bit," Davidson said. He sat next to her and held out a datapad. "There's a long list of contacts on several worlds, including Jorlem."

Kat frowned. "Brilliant," she said sarcastically. "President Alexis will be getting *plenty* of kickbacks."

"Probably," Davidson agreed. He didn't look concerned. "Although we might be doing him an injustice, Kat. The contacts seem involved in smuggling out spare parts and crewmen as well as fencing their ill-gotten gains. I doubt the planetary government will take that lightly."

"Perhaps," Kat said. It was yet another political hot potato. If President Alexis *wasn't* involved, asking him to round up the pirate contacts would be easy. But if he *was* involved, making the request would be enough to tip the pirates off. They'd go underground before Kat could find another way to get to them. "I'll have to discuss it with the Foreign Office."

She shook her head in frustration. Pirates were an interstellar menace. *No one* would do more than file an ineffective complaint if she blockaded Jorlem until the pirates and their supporters were handed over to her, but *Glory of God* made that impossible. If the ship's commander chose to fight in defense of the planet . . . Hell, for all she knew, the Theocracy was involved in smuggling weapons and supplies to the pirates.

"Maybe they'll send us some reinforcements," Davidson said.

Kat doubted it. *Lightning* would have been sent on her own if *Uncanny* hadn't had such a bad reputation. Besides, she'd need a couple of superdreadnoughts to handle *Glory of God*, and it was unlikely the Admiralty would send them away from the front lines. There was no way they could be recalled in less than a couple of months, whatever happened. And battles had been won or lost before on the presence or absence of a single ship.

She looked up at Davidson. "Did they have anything to say about the Theocracy?"

"Nothing," Davidson said. "Of course, they might not know who they're dealing with."

"Of course," Kat agreed tartly.

She looked down at the datapad for a long moment. They'd done well, she knew; they'd uncovered the existence of an entire pirate support network threaded throughout the sector. A *competent* investigation would be more than enough to root out the remainder of the ring and eliminate them. But Jorlem . . . it was all too possible that the pirates would be warned before they could be arrested. The only advantage she could hope to gain was disrupting the network for a few months, perhaps a year . . .

"I think we drained them dry," Davidson said finally. "Do you want to keep them alive?"

Kat shook her head. "They didn't surrender," she said. Her skin crawled as she remembered the pirate running his hands over her body. "And they have done too much to be left alive."

She keyed the datapad, bringing up the death warrants and ticking them off, one by one. The pirates would be marched to the nearest airlock and launched into space on a trajectory that would eventually send their bodies plunging down into the gas giant's atmosphere. By then, they'd be long dead. She wondered, idly, if she should order them shot first, then dismissed the thought. The horror of their death might just dissuade others from following the same course.

They deserve it, she thought, looking down at the reports. The pirates had gleefully confessed to a whole string of crimes as they ravaged their way across the sector. She had very few qualms about sentencing them to death. *They are monsters.*

"Put them out the airlock in an hour," she ordered, passing the datapad back to him. "I'll be there to watch."

Davidson *looked* at her. "Is that wise?"

"I owe it to my conscience," Kat said. "I need to be there."

Kat would shed no tears for pirate scum, but she wanted—*needed*—to watch them die. And yet, death was so *impersonal* in the middle of an interstellar war. She'd seen hundreds, if not thousands, of people die when their starships were blown out of space, but she'd never quite comprehended it.

"As you wish," Davidson said.

Kat looked intently at Davidson. "Crenshaw was saying that I took a terrible risk," she said. "And . . ."

"He was right," Davidson told her.

"Yeah," Kat agreed humorlessly. "I could have blown his career out of the water along with my life."

Davidson gave her a reproving look. "I wouldn't care to be the XO who lost a captain," he said. "Certainly not like *that*."

"I couldn't do anything else," Kat said. "If I'd done nothing . . ."

"I know," Davidson said. He leaned in to kiss her forehead. "And I love you for it."

Kat smiled wanly. "I hear a *but* coming."

"*But . . .*" Davidson said.

He kissed her again, gently. "*But* you took a terrible risk," he added. "And now that the affair is over, just how *big* a risk is sinking in."

"I know," Kat said.

"And not just for you," Davidson said. "For me, for Crenshaw . . . for anyone who would have wound up in deep shit if this had gone horribly wrong. Putting my life, or his life, at risk is one thing. But putting your own on the line . . ."

"I can't ask anyone to do something I wouldn't do myself," Kat said, stiffly. She knew he had a point, but she *still* saw no alternative. "And who else could have been sent?"

"I know that," Davidson said. "And I imagine Crenshaw knows it too. But that doesn't make it any easier."

He gave her a tight hug and then settled back. "Are you feeling all right?"

Kat gave the question serious consideration. "I had a shower after the doctor saw me," she said. "I probably need a few hours of sleep, but other than that I'm fine."

"Make sure you do," Davidson warned. "And we should spend more time practicing unarmed combat."

"You just want an excuse to kick my ass around the mat," Kat teased. She knew she was no match for him hand to hand. "Don't you?"

"It does have its moments," Davidson agreed. "And I should probably teach you how to get out of handcuffs too."

"I suppose that explains the complaints from the Shore Patrol," Kat said. There *had* been an odd report about two half-drunk spacers who'd escaped their handcuffs and vanished when the patrolman's back had been turned. "Were they marines in spacer uniforms?"

Davidson laughed. "Ask me no questions and I'll tell you no lies," he said. "But I'll tell you one thing . . ."

He paused, teasing her. "You earned a lot of respect from my men," he added. His voice was even. "They'll follow you anywhere now."

Kat flushed. She *knew* what marines went through to wear their uniforms. There was no way she met even the *basic* requirements for boot camp. To win the respect of some of the bravest and most dangerous soldiers in the galaxy . . .

"Thanks," she said, feeling an odd lump in her throat. "That means a lot to me."

Davidson kissed her once more. "It should," he said. "They'll never doubt you again."

CHAPTER TWENTY-SEVEN

The pirate system was a desolate wasteland circling a dull red star.

William sat in his command chair and watched as the tactical display slowly updated as more and more information flowed into the sensors. Very little in the system—it hadn't a proper name, merely a catalogue number—would attract attention. A handful of asteroids, a number of floating comets and parsecs upon parsecs of empty space . . . and nothing else. He doubted that anyone, save for settlers who wanted complete isolation, would take any real interest in the system. And establishing an isolated colony would be a serious technological challenge.

"There's no sign we were detected," Lieutenant Commander Thompson said. "But they might have established a whole network of passive sensor arrays."

"They're *pirates*," Roach pointed out. "This isn't *Tyre*, Commander."

True, William thought.

He'd still taken the precaution of coming out of hyperspace on the other side of the red dwarf, just to minimize the chances of being detected, but it was unlikely there was any real risk. Vast sensor arrays that could detect a gateway opening within a light-year of the planet were staggeringly expensive, so expensive that only Tyre and a handful of other stage-five worlds *could* afford them. No pirate group in existence could hope to monitor local space so thoroughly.

"Best not to get complacent," William said. There *had* been a vague report of a handful of recon ships being lost near Ahura Mazda. The Theocracy might have vast sensor arrays of its own. "Tactical report?"

"No active emissions, Captain," Thompson said. "But I don't think they need them."

"And it would alert any passing patrol ship that there was *something* in this system," William said. "Cloak us, then take us closer."

He felt the tension rising on the bridge as *Uncanny* picked up speed. The pirate base, according to the report, was one of a number of rocky asteroids orbiting in a loose cluster around the star. There was no way to know, yet, just what *sort* of settlement it was . . . he reminded himself, firmly, that any real planning would have to wait until they knew just what they were facing. He leaned back in his command chair and concentrated on projecting confidence, waiting patiently as the minutes slowly turned into hours . . .

"Contact," Thompson hissed, as a red icon blinked into existence on the display. "A starship just dropped out of hyperspace."

"Stay calm," William ordered dryly. The newcomer was well out of weapons range. Even if she'd seen *Uncanny* and turned to face her, they'd have plenty of time to prepare for an engagement. "Tactical report?"

"I'm not sure, Captain," Thompson said, after a moment. "She reads out as a scaled-up destroyer, perhaps a frigate. Warbook says she's built off a UN-designed Type-98 hull."

"One that can be reconfigured extensively," Roach commented. "The bastards did good design work."

"Starships were less powerful in those days," William reminded him. Putting *Uncanny*'s drives in a Type-98 hull would be enough to rip the ship apart, if they were ramped up to full power. "Threat analysis?"

"Unknown," Thompson said. "Her tactical sensors are in stepped-down mode."

He paused. "She's heading right towards the base."

"Keep sneaking up on them," William ordered. "And stand by to launch stealthed probes."

He forced himself to watch calmly, despite the growing anger in his heart. The pirate ship—and it *had* to be a pirate ship—was returning to its base, carrying loot from countless raids right across the sector. There would be prisoners onboard—hostages held for ransom, young women for the slave market—and he could do nothing, not yet. He clenched his fists in frustration, silently promising himself that the pirate base wouldn't last the week. Blowing it up would be easy . . .

. . . And if there was no other option, it was precisely what he would do.

"I think they just hollowed out an asteroid and installed gravity generators," Thompson said, as they closed in on the pirate base. "They don't seem to have made any attempt to spin the asteroid to produce gravity. I guess they're not intent on settling permanently."

"Probably not," William agreed, thoughtfully. It was rare for pirates to set up their bases from scratch, but the asteroid might have been settled by an isolationist group who'd then lost it to the pirates. God knew they'd done it before. "Can you pick up any defenses?"

"None," Thompson said. "But they could have a couple of weapons platforms on permanent standby."

"They'd need time to power them up," Roach offered. "I think they have no defenses at all."

William was inclined to agree. Defending such a settlement against determined attack would be pretty much impossible. A single antimatter warhead—perhaps even a nuke—would turn the entire asteroid into rubble. The asteroid's only real defense was obscurity—and it had lost that, the moment its location had been discovered. There could be any number of unwilling guests on the asteroid, from conscripted workers to slaves and hostages. The pirates could—probably would—use them as human shields.

We can't risk giving them time to set up a defense, he thought grimly. On the display, the frigate had slipped into the giant asteroid. *Still, we can't simply blow the base into rubble.*

He scowled as he contemplated possibilities. Mr. Abramson had included a couple of ID codes they could use to gain access to the base, but no one could possibly mistake a heavy cruiser for a destroyer or a captured freighter. Even if he'd thought it was workable, he wouldn't have risked taking *Uncanny* so close. He *could* decloak and demand surrender, offering to let the pirates live if they surrendered at once . . .

But that would give them time to turn off the antimatter containment chambers, he thought, sourly. *If they have antimatter . . .*

"Helm, pull us back to ten light seconds," he ordered, finally. "Tactical, continue deploying stealth probes."

"Aye, Captain," Cecilia said.

"This isn't going to be easy," Roach commented. "If we *knew* what was in there . . ."

He paused. "We could send in a shuttle, using the ID codes."

"That's a pirate base, not a smuggler base or a black colony," William pointed out. ID codes or no ID codes, he couldn't imagine the pirates not asking a few questions when a strange ship—or shuttle—arrived. They'd *certainly* want to know how the shuttle had reached the system in the first place. "We could try to capture one of their ships and then sneak through the defenses . . ."

His voice trailed off. Perhaps, if they took one of the freighters, they could claim she was a prize. They'd definitely let her dock if the manifest claimed she was carrying all sorts of useful things. And then he'd have an assault team on the base. But it was really far too risky, far too likely to make the pirates panic. Unless they thought they were beaten . . .

. . . And that there was a way to keep their miserable lives.

He keyed his console. "Major Lupine, report to my Ready Room," he said. "We have an operation to plan."

"Aye, sir," Lupine said.

William rose. "Mr. XO, you're with me," he said. "Mr. Thompson, you have the conn."

"Aye, sir," Thompson said.

"Make sure they don't even catch a *whiff* of us," William added. "If they do, the game is up."

He strode into his Ready Room, nodding to Lupine as he entered through the other hatch. The lack of Marines was going to cost them, he suspected. Lupine's men weren't bad—he'd watched their drills—but they hadn't been put through hell during basic training. And yet, he was short of options. They *had* to force the pirates to surrender themselves as quickly as possible.

"Captain," Lupine said.

William nodded for him to take a seat. "You've seen the sensor reports," he said, as he put the live feed up in front of them. "What do you think?"

"It's going to be a bitch," Lupine said bluntly. "Getting onto the asteroid won't be that hard—we know where the main doors are—but we know fuck all about the interior. We might wind up running around in circles while the pirates muster a counterattack."

"We could try to sneak a team through on a freighter," William said.

"I wouldn't want to try, if it could be avoided," Lupine said. He nodded to the display. "It could go badly wrong. Forcing our way through the main doors might be easier."

"Particularly if I was blotting out the airwaves with demands for surrender," William said.

"Yeah," Lupine said. "We'd take shuttles and drift up to the asteroid, only going active once we were close enough to get into the main doors . . . we *could* try to burn through the rock, but without knowing anything about the interior, I wouldn't care to take the risk."

William nodded. There was no way to know *what* the boarding party might encounter. A mile of solid rock, a pressured chamber . . . or the pirate fuel dump. Boarding an asteroid was always nightmarish. They had no choice.

"Organize the mission," he ordered. "If we demand surrender at the same time you reveal yourselves, we might just cow them into submission."

"Of course, sir," Lupine said. "Stun bolts only?"

"We want to take prisoners, if possible," William said. He wanted—needed—to interrogate the pirates, even if they were due to be executed afterwards. "And the pirates may not be the only people on the asteroid."

Lupine nodded. "Stun them all, and ask questions later."

"Yes," William said. "How long will it take you to prepare?"

"I'd like to borrow the remainder of the shuttles," Lupine said. "And crews. If I ask for volunteers and then brief them . . . I'd say it'll take around half an hour to prepare, then another half hour to get into position."

"See to it," William said. Marines would be quicker. But he had none. "And make sure the volunteers know the dangers."

"Of course, sir," Lupine said.

He rose and headed for the hatch. William sat back in his chair, feeling uneasy. They were committed now . . . unless he wanted to simply decloak and threaten the pirates with a missile barrage. That would give the pirates too much time to think. They'd *have* to know he'd be reluctant to risk civilian lives.

They won't trust us to keep our promises either, he thought. *And even if we did, sending them to a penal colony is like sending them to hell.*

◆ ◆ ◆

"The mission is simple," Major Lupine said. "You will take the shuttles along the preset course"—he nodded to the display—"and go active once we're close to the asteroid, half of you landing on the rock and the other half taking your craft directly into their landing chamber. At that point, my men will deploy into the asteroid; you crewmembers will remain in your crafts, ready to transport wounded or prisoners as necessary."

Joel sucked in his breath. He hadn't expected the summons as it had been quite some time since he'd flown a shuttlecraft, at least outside the simulator he'd used to keep his skills honed. He was tempted not to volunteer. The mission struck him as the sort of fancy half-assed scheme that looked good on paper but was disastrous in real life. Yet, if Sir William had authorized the deployment, perhaps the endeavor wasn't so farfetched . . .

You're starting to admire him too, Joel told himself crossly.

He pushed the thought aside as he studied the mission plan. It looked workable, on paper; he knew he could learn a great deal from watching the militiamen in action. Still, his death would mean the end of the plan. He would be astonished if the pirates didn't have a few basic defenses on their base, even if it was just a simple point defense system. No threat at all to *Uncanny,* of course, but easily capable of blowing a defenseless shuttle into atoms. It was no consolation to know that his death would be avenged. Everything he'd worked for would die with him . . .

Even with the threat of death, though, Joel knew that *refusing* the mission would also be held against him.

Oh, it wouldn't be *official*. Sir William wasn't the sort of person to hold a grudge. However, he wouldn't consider Joel for any commendations either. Joel would be classed as someone unwilling to put his life on the line when needed. He might not be officially marked down, but he wouldn't be raised up either. He didn't *need* that sort of attention from the ship's commanding officer, not now. Running rings around a genuinely *competent* commanding officer—one who knew the *Uncanny*-class inside-out—was a great deal harder than fooling an incompetent and crooked aristocrat.

Besides, he thought, *it will help get rid of the competition.*

He strode forward. A couple of volunteers were already standing in front of Major Lupine, looking disturbingly eager. They probably saw the whole stunt as a way to gain a bigger share of the prize money . . . if, indeed, there *was* prize money. The pirates might blow the entire base into atoms, leaving *Uncanny* with nothing to show for her efforts. And if Joel was unlucky, the blast would take out the shuttles as well.

"Chief," Major Lupine said, "you can fly a shuttle?"

"A lot of us were cross-trained," Joel said, striving to keep the irritation off his face. What sort of idiot would claim to be able to fly a shuttle if he couldn't? "You can download my certification from the datanet if you wish."

He supposed he should be grateful that some idiot in the Admiralty had thought that assigning militiamen to starships was a good idea, but it was *stupid*. The militia and the planetary armies didn't need to cross-train as extensively as starship crewmen or the marines. *Uncanny* had nearly twice the number of crewmen she needed during routine operations, but her operations wouldn't *stay* routine. Having excess crewmen came in handy.

"Very well," Major Lupine said. He didn't seem inclined to check Joel's certification. Joel silently marked him down another point or two. "You'll fly Shuttle Four, carrying a platoon of militia and several boxes of supplies. Remember to stay ballistic until you receive the alert signal."

"Of course," Joel said, biting down the urge to make sarcastic remarks about teaching spacers to keep their facemasks within reach. The pirates might not be operating any active sensors, but they wouldn't need them to see a wave of assault shuttles screaming towards their base on full thrust. "I'll see you in the bay."

He saluted, then hurried down to the shuttlebay. The crews were already running through preflight checks, the militia donning their armor as they readied themselves for the coming engagement. They looked efficient, Joel decided, although he knew from bitter experience that that didn't always mean they actually were. Captain Abraham had been fond of wearing full dress uniform at all times, and he'd been a crook.

Joel nodded to the LT in charge, then hurried into the shuttle and took the helm. The course was already programmed into the flight computer, as if the craft didn't need a human pilot at all.

Except a computer couldn't handle a surprise, he thought as he ran through his own set of preflight checks. He trusted the shuttlebay crew, but this was *Uncanny*. Even a minor power surge at the wrong time could prove disastrous, if only by revealing the vessel's position to any watching sensors. *We might have to take evasive action at a moment's notice.*

Joel glanced back at the ten-man platoon as they took their seats in the shuttle, and then powered the shuttle up as soon as the order arrived from the bridge. It wouldn't have been hard to fit more militiamen into the shuttle, but he suspected that Major Lupine was trying to minimize his exposure. Losing the shuttle would mean losing the platoon as well. A moment later, a dull shaking echoed through the craft as tractor fields picked her up and propelled her towards the hatch.

They should let us make our own way out of the bay, he thought as the gravity field shivered slightly. *It isn't as if it would make a difference. Uncanny is cloaked.*

"We're on our way," he said as he triggered the gas jets. They were laughably weak compared to a standard drive field, but they *did* have the advantage of being almost completely undetectable. "Are you ready?"

"Yes, Chief," the LT said. "Ready to move when necessary."

The inky darkness of space enveloped the shuttle. It was going to be a long flight to their destination . . .

And we could be detected at any time, Joel reminded himself. He couldn't help feeling vulnerable. The shuttle was fast but required time to bring up the main drives if detected. Joel might have no time to take evasive action. *And that will be the end.*

CHAPTER TWENTY-EIGHT

William had to force himself to remain calm.

He was no stranger to danger, but there was no way he could take command of the mission himself. The captain *shouldn't* leave the bridge during combat operations. And *that* meant he had to watch Major Lupine and his men go into harm's way while he was completely out of danger. It didn't sit well with him and he hoped it never would.

"Twenty minutes to contact, Captain," Thompson reported. "No sign they've been detected."

William wasn't reassured. The pirates would be fools to run any sort of active sensor sweep, even in an otherwise deserted system. A single stray signal might bring a warship down on their heads. But he still worried. A passive sensor array *might* pick up *something* in time to make a difference.

"Keep us crawling in after them," he ordered. The asteroid was unlikely to have any weapons that could threaten *Uncanny*, but he didn't want to give the pirates a chance to prove him wrong. "Is the message recorded?"

"Aye, Captain," Stott said. "We can transmit on your command."

William glanced at the timer. He was too used to space combat moving swiftly, he suspected; he'd never had to wait so long before jumping into action. But the militia needed to be in place before he made his move.

If we bugger this up, he thought, *nearly fifty militiamen and twenty of my crew are going to die.*

"Captain," Thompson said, after fifteen minutes. It had felt like hours. "The shuttles are almost in position."

"Prepare to drop the cloak," William ordered. "And stand by all weapons."

"Aye, Captain," Thompson said. "The shuttles are in position . . . *now!*"

"Drop the cloak," William snapped. "Transmit the signal."

"Aye, Captain," Thompson said. "The shuttles are going active. No defensive fire detected."

Yet, William thought.

"No response," Stott said. "We're transmitting on all channels. They're *bound* to hear it."

William nodded. The pirates were in deep shit. Their starships, however many they had, were trapped *inside* the asteroid. Trying to open a gateway inside the asteroid would prove disastrous, the gravity flux tearing the mass apart and sucking the debris into hyperspace while simultaneously crushing their starships' hulls. They had to know there was no way out, but surrender . . .

. . . and if they felt pressured both inside and outside the asteroid, they might surrender without further ado.

◆ ◆ ◆

"Picking up targeting sensors," Joel snapped as an alarm sounded. "Hold on!"

He threw the shuttle into an evasive loop, silently grateful that he'd had time to power up the drive nodes before the pirates got over their shock and reacted. The point defense weapon, nothing more than a plasma cannon, fired wildly, missing the shuttle by several miles. He threw a counter-missile back at the cannon then steered the shuttle towards the asteroid's giant hatch, watching as two penetrator missiles slammed into the hatch and blew it wide open.

"Shit," the LT breathed.

Joel allowed himself a tight smile. The interior cavern was *huge*, easily large enough to take an entire squadron of superdreadnoughts. A cluster of smaller starships hung in the air, hanging over a landing field so vast that he could almost believe that it was on the surface of a planet. Someone had been playing games with the gravity field, he noted, as he guided the shuttle towards the hatches that led into the base. The ground was low-gee, presumably to make unloading shuttlecraft easier, but there was no gravity field threatening to tug the starships down to the surface. The installation was clearly designed by someone who lived and breathed space.

"The CO's deploying scout bugs now," one of the militiamen said. "And . . ."

Joel cursed as an alarm sounded. "The bastards just vented the chamber," he said. It was also equally possible that one of his missiles had taken out a force-field generator as well as the doors, but he preferred to blame the enemy. "Keep your masks on."

The shuttle grounded, hitting the deck hard enough to shake the entire craft. Joel glanced at his sensors then opened the hatches. The militiamen didn't hesitate. They rose and jogged out of the craft, holding their weapons at the ready. There didn't seem to be any organized resistance. Other shuttles were buzzing around the starships, force-docking with their airlocks and boarding them. The pirates had to know they had very little chance of escape.

Unless some idiot decides to try to open a gateway, he thought. *This chamber is large enough to convince someone that it might be possible.*

He kept a wary eye on the enemy starships as more and more reports flowed into the communications network. The pirates *definitely* hadn't had time to organize a resistance, certainly not at one of the chokepoints that would have doomed the entire mission. If Joel had designed the asteroid, he would have made sure there were only two connections maximum between the depressurized starship chamber and the remainder of the habitat. A staunch defense, with the intention of holding that section as long as possible, might have given the pirates time to either start bargaining or take more drastic measures.

Now all I can do is wait, he thought, feeling the pistol on his hip. He'd been told to stay out of the firing line, though he had one of the best shooting records on *Uncanny.* Besides, he wasn't a militiaman, and he certainly hadn't trained with them. *Wait and pray the pirates don't blow the entire asteroid.*

◆ ◆ ◆

William felt sweat pouring down his back as the stream of reports flowed into the command network. The pirates had been taken completely by surprise—the microscopic recon drones were already mapping out the asteroid's interior—and their starships had been captured with remarkable speed, but their resistance was stiffening as the militia pushed their way towards the asteroid's command network. Dozens of pirates had already been stunned, along with a number of sex slaves they'd tried to use as human shields, but others were fighting back with surprising effectiveness. And there had been no response to the message.

"Signal from the boarding parties," Stott commented. "They're requesting permission to power up the captured ships and start moving them out of the chamber."

"Granted," William said. He had no idea how long it would take to get the ships out, but the pirates would *have* to despair when they saw their starships flying away. "Order them to hold position as soon as they're clear of the asteroid cluster."

He sucked in his breath as he studied the latest set of reports. The pirate base was a warren; they'd simply tunneled into the rock like rabbits. Still, the passage to the enemy command center was heavily blocked. Worse, the enemy had finally started deploying counter-drones of their own. The growing diagram of the interior had some gaping holes.

"Keep repeating the signal," William ordered.

He thought hard, wondering just what was going on. How long would it take the pirates to see reason? Or were they trying desperately to detonate a nuclear warhead? Setting off an antimatter warhead was easy—one just turned off the containment chambers—but it was a great deal harder to trigger a nuke. It was quite possible that they were having problems overriding the safety protocols. Missile warheads weren't *designed* to be triggered inside their launch tubes.

"Captain," Stott said, "I'm picking up a response. Audio only."

Of course, William thought. In his experience, pirates never sent visual images if they could avoid it. *What will they have to say?*

"Put it through," he ordered.

"Prepare to die," a frantic voice said. "I'm going to blow the entire base!"

"Yet you could live," William said, concentrating on projecting as much reassurance as he could into his tone. The speaker sounded young . . . too young? William knew how to handle nervous young officers who were nominally in charge. "The offer to take you to a penal colony is genuine."

"I'd rather die," the speaker insisted. "Do you know what they *do* there?"

Better than you, I suspect, William thought.

He kept that thought to himself. "If you blow up the asteroid, you'll kill everyone on the rock; your people, my people . . . everyone," he said. "But if you surrender, you get to live."

"On a penal colony," the speaker seethed.

"If you surrender now, I can arrange for you to be transported to a stage-one colony to serve as conscripted immigrants," William offered. "It won't be an easy life, but you'll have a chance to make something of it. I'm sure some of you have skills you can parlay into a better position there."

A long pause followed. "How do we know you'll keep your word?"

"You don't," William said. "Right now, you have the choice between killing yourself or seeing what awaits you if you surrender."

He wondered just who he was actually talking to. The speaker didn't *sound* like a hard-boiled pirate. If he hadn't seen footage of sex slaves and piles of stolen goods as the drones swept the asteroid, he would have wondered if he and his crew had made a terrible mistake. Perhaps he was dealing with someone who'd been left behind because of a lack of nerve . . .

Any smart pirate would have spaced him, William reminded himself. *A subordinate unwilling to compromise himself is a dangerous subordinate.*

He glanced at the latest set of reports. Major Lupine was readying his men to punch through the defenses, abandoning the attempt to stun rather than kill the defenders, but that might panic the base commander. Maybe he'd just had delusions of grandeur. William had met far too many people who lied to themselves, constantly, just to feel good about themselves. It was easy to feel like a brave freedom fighter, rather than a terrorist, when everyone was too scared to stand up to you.

Hardly anyone dares resist the pirates, William thought. There was something in human nature that made resistance hard, even though resisting could hardly make matters worse. It wasn't as if the pirates could be dissuaded by spurious claims of being orphans. *It must come as a shock to be attacked on their home ground.*

"This applies to all of us?" the pirate asked, carefully. "Each and every last one of us?"

William slightly regretted his promise. Chances were that there were a few monsters among the stunned, men and maybe even women whose mere existence made the galaxy a little fouler. To let them live, even if they *were* dispatched to a penal colony, went against the grain. But he needed the pirates to surrender . . .

"You all get to live," he said carefully. "And those of you who cooperate will be offered the chance to go to a stage-one colony."

He waited, wondering just what the pirate would say. A stage-one colony wouldn't be *comfortable*, certainly not for a conscripted immigrant, but it *would* offer the pirates a chance at redemption. On the other hand, they might also see it as another kind of slavery . . .

"We accept," the pirate said, finally. "What do we do?"

William had a moment of relief. "Order your men to stop shooting and put down their weapons," he said. "My men will take them into custody. As long as they behave themselves, they will be left unharmed. Your prisoners will be released and transported to safety."

There was a long pause. "We understand."

"Good," William said. He keyed his console. "Major Lupine, the pirates have surrendered to us. Take them into custody as planned."

"Yes, sir," Lupine said.

William watched as the militiamen moved forward, weapons at the ready. It wasn't over yet. A single idiot unwilling to surrender after his superiors had ordered him to put his weapon down could get a lot of people killed . . .

One by one, the pirates were disarmed, secured, and then pushed against the bulkhead to await their fate. The remainder of the militia kept advancing up into the control compartment, surrounded by a swarm of drones.

"We have the base secure, sir," Lupine said finally. "The computer network is under our control."

"Very good," William said. "How many prisoners and slaves are we looking at?"

"At least three to four hundred," Lupine said. "Processing them all is going to take time."

"Of course," William said.

An alarm sounded. "Captain," Thompson said. "A gateway is opening . . ."

William turned just in time to see a pair of mid-sized destroyers flying out of hyperspace on a direct course for the base. There were no IFF signals, nothing to suggest they might be from Jorlem or Vangelis or anyone else who might have an interest in suppressing pirate activity. And the odd power fluctuations surrounding them suggested they were not in good condition.

"One of the destroyers is a known pirate ship, Captain" Thompson reported. "She was noted and logged during a brief engagement seven months ago. Her drive field matches the record perfectly. The other is unknown."

"Helm, bring us around to face them," William ordered. If the pirates chose to launch a spread of missiles at their former base, there was too great a chance of them scoring a hit and killing everyone on the asteroid. "Communications, demand their immediate surrender."

"Aye, Captain," Stott said.

The pirate ships altered course sharply, having seen the uncloaked, unstealthed *Uncanny* almost as soon as they exited hyperspace. There hadn't been any time to cloak the ship or even slip into stealth mode. And now the pirates were running . . .

Any hope of luring more bastards into our clutches is now gone, William thought glumly. *They'll tell everyone that the base has fallen.*

"Captain, they're powering up their gateway generators," Thompson reported. "They're still well out of missile range."

"Understood," William said. A moment later, two gateways opened and the pirate ships vanished into hyperspace. He balled his fists in frustration as the gateways closed. A clean getaway. There wasn't a hope in hell of catching even one of the pirate ships. "Take us back to the asteroid."

"Aye, Captain," Cecelia said.

All twelve of the captured ships had been maneuvered out of the asteroid and were now holding station on the edge of the cluster. Six were candidates for the scrapyard judging by their fluctuating drive fields, but the remainder would probably bring in a great deal of money. The ships would have to be sold carefully, he knew; they'd have to go to someone who wouldn't sell them back to the pirates. His crew had good reason to be pleased, though. *Everyone* would be due another share of the prize money.

"Update from the asteroid, sir," Stott said. "There are roughly four hundred prisoners, ranging from sex slaves and prostitutes to enslaved workers and hostages. There are also five hundred and seventy pirates and their hangers-on. The former are currently being prepped for the move back to *Uncanny*."

"We're going to have problems taking four hundred people on the ship," Roach warned. "I'm not sure I'd trust the life support to handle so many additional passengers."

"I know," William said. He would have been reluctant to take the risk regardless of *Uncanny*'s reputation. "Some of them will have to be transported in the captured vessels."

He sighed. Space and life support weren't the only problems. Some of the prisoners would have been slaves so long that Stockholm syndrome was a real possibility. They might do something stupid or desperate once they were on his ship, convinced they were helping their masters. Others might be fearful of what would happen when—if—they returned home. They might have been forced to get their hands dirty merely to stay alive.

Getting the pirates to their final destination might be tricky too, he thought. *We can't take so many potential troublemakers onto one ship.*

"Detach additional engineering teams to the captured vessels," he ordered. "If they can be made safe, then we'll use them for transport. Then see if engineering can blow up a few life support bubbles. The pirates can stay there until we can transport them to the nearest stage-one colony."

Roach frowned. "Will the settlers *want* them?"

"Depends how much they need manpower," William said. It was quite possible that the settlers would demand that the pirates were taken elsewhere. "But we'll make sure to interrogate the pirates first. They'll probably know a great deal we need to know."

"Yes, sir," Roach said.

"And see if you can do a preliminary valuation of everything we've captured," William added. He had no way to be *sure*, but he suspected they were looking at around a million or more crowns. "We might as well share the good news."

His crew's morale was about to skyrocket. Destroying a pirate base was a good deed in and of itself, but capturing one was even better. The starships could be put to good use, the pirates would be interrogated so that their recruitment agents and fences could be rounded up, the prisoners and hostages would be returned to their homeworlds . . . not a bad day's work. If he and his crew were *very* lucky, they might find clues that would lead them to another pirate base.

If Kat had just as much success herself, he thought, *we will have put a major dent in pirate operations. That will do wonders for our reputation out here.*

CHAPTER TWENTY-NINE

"Two to three *million* crowns?"

"It looks that way," Julia said. She knelt beside the pirate computer, her face calm and composed. "Or at least that's the valuation report our beloved XO put on the datanet."

Joel sucked in his breath sharply. He and a good third of the crew had spent the last two days supervising prisoners, assisting the former hostages, and searching the pirate base with a fine-tooth comb. It had been an interesting experience, he had to admit, but not one he was inclined to repeat. Whoever had originally designed the asteroid settlement had done a good job, yet the pirates had mistreated the habitat so badly that their life support was permanently on the edge of collapse. The few maintenance workers on hand were unequal to the task.

Now a whole new problem had blown up.

"Are you sure?"

"I can read," Julia said testily. "The ships themselves aren't worth more than a million, at best, but there are *tons* of supplies and various pieces of equipment stored in the base. Some of them will probably be returned to their owners; the remainder will be sold onwards, reaping the ship a great deal of money."

Joel had done his best to spread discontent among the newer crew members, but results had been minimal even before this windfall. Even a million crowns, shared among the crew, would boost morale into the stratosphere. There wouldn't be any more grumbling about limited shore leave, or constant inspections, or endless series of drills. Hell, if he *hadn't* been plotting to take the ship, Joel would have found the bonus very satisfying. Some careful investment would have made him a moderately rich man if he ever returned to Tyre.

"Assuming they manage to sell the ships," he mused slowly, but he knew it was wishful thinking. There was such a high demand for warships in the sector that *all* of the pirate ships could be sold with minimal effort. The dangerous ones could be cannibalized, if nothing else. "And what about the supplies?"

"Enough to keep a small fleet going for a few months," Julia said. She tapped the datapad meaningfully. "Plus a staggering amount of data."

The pirate networks were in deep shit. A whole web of fences, recruiting agents, and other scumbags was on the verge of being obliterated. There would be others, of course, as the pirates were hardly a unified organization, but losing so many illicit agents would deal a body blow to countless operations. If, of course, the planetary governments could be induced to cooperate.

Sir William can simply threaten them into submission, if they're unwilling to make even a token effort to round the bastards up, he thought. *No one would say a word in complaint.*

Joel gave Julia a long look. "Can you hide the data?"

"Not without being too revealing," she said. "They'll have already copied the entire database into a secure core. If they find *too* many discrepancies . . ."

"They'll know someone was playing games," Joel said. "Time isn't on our side."

"No," Julia agreed.

Joel rubbed his forehead in frustration. He'd planned to simply take weapons from the marine lockers and use them to seize control of the ship. Now that was impossible. The militiamen had taken over Marine Country and sealed the hatches. They didn't expect trouble, Joel thought, but they'd neatly blocked his route to the lockers. Getting into the section would attract attention.

Was there a way to take the pirate weapons? They'd had countless armaments stockpiled, ranging from crap that wouldn't have been out of place on pre-space Earth to advanced core-world artillery. But the weapons had been secured by the militiamen to keep them away from the pirates' former hostages. Who knew just *how* tainted the hostages had become?

"Make a copy of the data," he ordered. "We might be able to find a use for it."

"Yes, sir," Julia said.

Joel rose and paced the compartment. It *was* frustrating. His inner circle was as hopelessly compromised as himself, but everyone else . . . they could just swear blind that they hadn't the slightest idea of what he'd been doing. It wouldn't last, of course, and a person with even moderate intelligence would have to know it, yet . . . he couldn't deny that hope sprang eternal.

I told them that the Navy didn't give a shit about them, Joel thought. *I was right. The captain was a crook, the first officer was an asshole, the engineer was a drunkard, a quarter of the crew were either gamblers or druggies . . . the ship was falling apart. They knew I was right.*

He shook his head. It had been easy to build on such resentments, easy to convince his handpicked men that there was a greater destiny out there. It wasn't as if the crew didn't have *cause* for resentments. Now . . . whatever doubts the crew had had about their new commanding officer would fade, completely, once the prize money landed in their bank accounts. Even the youngest and most junior of crewmen would be looking at a cool ten thousand crowns. It would buy Sir William one hell of a lot of loyalty.

"Done," Julia said. "Shall we go?"

Perhaps we are done, Joel thought. He watched absently as Julia cleaned up all evidence of their presence. *If we were to leave the ship on Jorlem . . .*

He scowled at the thought. It would be easy to desert—he'd been putting together plans to do just that over the last few weeks—but it would mean abandoning the plan. *And* the remainder of his inner circle. They all had skills he could use, skills that would allow them to make a decent living, but would they stay with him afterwards? It wasn't as if there was anything binding them to him.

Furthermore, a whole party of deserters will be easier to track down than one or two, he reminded himself. *But if we don't go as a group, someone will betray us.*

He opened the hatch as soon as Julia was finished scrubbing their presence from the scene and led the way out into the corridor. The air was foul, far worse than anything on *Uncanny*. He couldn't help thinking, as he walked down to the giant hangar, that there was something oddly eerie about the pirate base, as if someone or something was about to tap him on the shoulder at any moment. It could just be his sense of how poorly maintained the place was.

They'll probably vent the entire asteroid, once everything has been removed, he thought. *It can't make the problem any worse.*

◆ ◆ ◆

"Thirty-seven of the former prisoners are in a pretty bad state," Doctor Prosser said, "and require more . . . concentrated medical attention than we are able to provide. I've put them into stasis tubes for the moment, but they'll have to be offloaded at Vangelis."

"Understood," William said. He rubbed his heavy eyes. "And the remainder?"

"Minor problems, ranging from malnutrition to various injuries," Sarah said. "I've already started treatment programs for them, although it is pushing our resources to the limit."

She paused. "It's the mental problems that bother me," she added. "Many of the former hostages are traumatized, even the ones who weren't physically harmed. The slaves . . . it may be a long time before they're ready to reenter society, if they ever do. Such treatment always leaves a mark."

Roach leaned forward. "Should we consider putting them *all* into stasis?"

"We don't even *begin* to have enough stasis tubes," Sarah said. "Frankly, sir, I would advise heading straight back to Jorlem and borrowing a colonist-carrier. They come with enough tubes to put everyone on ice until we can get them somewhere safe."

"Jorlem wouldn't be good enough, of course," William growled.

"I wouldn't count on it, no," Sarah agreed. "However, we probably will need to beg medical supplies from them."

She sighed. "For the moment, I think most of the former hostages will just have to remain on the captured ships until we reach Jorlem," she added. "I've detached medical teams to provide support to the crews."

Detaching more than a third of their medical personnel was against regulations, but William had no choice. If there *was* a medical emergency on one of the captured ships there would be no time to transport the doctor over from *Uncanny*. Really, he wasn't too keen on detaching so many other crewmen from his ship either. *Uncanny could* be operated with only a tenth of her crew, but such reductions weren't something he wanted to try during war.

"Very good," he said. "Major?"

"We've got the prisoners into inflated life support bubbles," Lupine said. He sounded pleased. His men had handled their first test well. "Most of them were happy to start blabbering as soon as they realized they weren't going to be shot out of hand. My people recorded some of the more . . . interesting stories."

He paused. "We *did* find some evidence that the Theocracy is involved," he added. "It's nothing *entirely* conclusive, but apparently the pirates were told that taking captured ships to an RV point along the border of Theocratic space would garner twice the starship's market value. I suspect they were meeting up with a shipping agent there and making the exchange."

Roach grinned. "Perhaps *we* should go there," he said. "How far is it from here?"

"Nearly four weeks," Lupine said. "The pirates might well have found a shipping agent closer to their base."

William was inclined to agree. An eight-week round-trip would be frustrating for anyone, particularly pirates in dangerously unsafe ships. They *might* take a few prizes along the way or they might not. Then they'd be gambling that they *could* sell the ships. The Theocracy was desperate, but even *they* would have their doubts about some of the older freighters that might be passed in their direction. If the pirates earned nothing from the voyage, they wouldn't want to make it again.

"The potential interception would take us away from the sector," William said. *Uncanny* could make the cruise with ease—there would be something hugely satisfying in blowing away whatever enemy ship came to collect the captured freighters—but their first priority was to patrol the sector and suppress pirate activity. "We'll forward the details to the Admiralty when we return to Jorlem."

Roach looked at him. "We're going straight back there?"

"We need to start rounding up the pirate contacts before they vanish," William said. He had a nasty feeling they'd dawdled too long already, as the two ships that had escaped had probably gone to warn their comrades, but there hadn't been a choice. Leaving the prisoners behind would have been dangerous no matter how many precautions they took. "And we should link up with *Lightning* again."

"Yes, sir," Roach said.

"Check and double-check that the pirates are going to be fine, for the moment," William ordered. "Then we can drag the bubble a few light-minutes from their former base."

"Aye, sir," Major Lupine said.

Sarah cleared her throat in evident disapproval. "Captain, I really must protest," she said, stiffly. "Leaving so many . . . *people* . . . in inflatable bubbles. The risk . . ."

William shrugged, dismissively. He wouldn't have treated Theocratic POWs in such a manner, but pirates had no rights. They'd *survive* in the bubbles, at least until the squadron could return with a prisoner transport to ship them to their new home. He had a nasty feeling that discipline would break down quickly, that the pirates would tear each other apart, but that was their problem. He'd seen the medical reports; he knew what they'd done to their helpless victims. It was hard to feel sympathy for pirates who'd looted, raped, and destroyed their way across an entire sector.

"The risk is tolerable," he said. The only *real* danger, as far as he was concerned, was the pirates being rescued by some of their comrades. One of the fleeing ships could have managed to sneak back into the system without being detected. He'd had an antimatter mine rigged, just in case. "If the pirates survive long enough to be recovered and sent to their new home, well and good. If not . . ."

He turned away. "I'm not going to shed any tears over them."

"As you wish, *Captain*," Sarah said. She sniffed, then rose. "With your permission, I will attend to my other patients."

"Of course," William said. He understood her reason for being irked. "We'll discuss them later."

He watched her leave the room, then looked at Major Lupine. "Your men did very well."

"Thank you, sir," Lupine said. "We'll be conducting post-battle assessments as soon as we depart the system."

"Let me know what conclusions you draw," William said. He had a feeling that Major Davidson would be impressed even though the marines could probably have taken the base quicker. "What did you make of the base itself?"

"A poor design in many ways," Major Lupine said. "Our best guess is that it was originally an unregistered black colony, but the pirates put a stop to that. None of the captured pirates seem to know anything about whoever actually built it."

William sighed. "But probably not the Theocracy."

"I doubt it," Major Lupine said. He nodded towards the display. "Dating scans tell us that the base is at least forty years old, predating the Theocracy's rise to power. I suspect the poor bastards who built it were simply killed or enslaved when the pirates arrived. There's nothing to suggest they had any real defenses."

"They might have wanted to limit their exposure to high tech," Roach added.

"Idiots," William said. One could survive in space on a low level of technology, assuming you could *get* to space, but it struck him as insane. Technology made life so much better that he found it hard to imagine why anyone would want to leave it behind. "We'll see what, if anything, we can dig up in the records on Jorlem."

"Yes, sir," Roach said.

"We can sell the ships too," William added. Taking them away from the pirates was one thing, but putting them to use would do wonders for the Commonwealth's reputation. "A dedicated patrol vessel in each system would be more than enough to put a damper on pirate activity."

"Maybe we can pay the bastards to go after the Theocracy," Lupine suggested.

William had been privy to rumors that Operation Knife had merely been the first of a series of raids into enemy space. While he'd heard nothing *official*, he had reason to believe that was actually true. The more effort the Theocracy was forced to expend on defending its convoys, the less effort they could put into hammering the Commonwealth's defenses. Sending the pirates into enemy space might well be overkill.

Either they hurt the enemy or they get wiped out, he thought. It sounded perfectly satisfactory, even though the thought of *paying* pirates was anathema. *Either way, we win.*

He tapped the table, meaningfully. "Mr. XO, slave the captured vessels to our command datanet, and then prepare them for the trip to Jorlem," he ordered. "We'll try to depart within the hour, once the base has been secured and locked down."

"Aye, sir," Roach said.

"Major Lupine, make sure the base is rigged to blow if someone tries to board it," William added. "We don't want to lose the captured supplies to the enemy."

"Aye, sir," Major Lupine said. "There's no need to use an antimatter mine. A standard nuke should suffice."

"Good," William said. Anyone stupid enough to disregard the warning signal wouldn't live to regret it. "Any other issues?"

"Goodrich was talking about trying to refurbish some of the captured starship components for our use," Roach said. "We should take what we need before we go."

William frowned. "Is he sure he can integrate them into our systems?"

"Some of the basics would be very useful, he thinks," Roach said. "But they'll all need to be checked carefully."

"Yeah," William mused. "Let him take some of the supplies, but make sure they get checked and rechecked thoroughly before we try to integrate them."

"Yes, sir," Roach said. "Goodrich is well aware of the dangers, sir. Everything will be checked completely before it's even brought onboard."

He beamed. "Shore leave on Jorlem is going to be a blast," he added. "The crew is already looking forward to its bonus."

"Remind them we have to sell the ships first," William said. The Admiralty would pay a bonus if the ships couldn't be sold, but it would take time to get it through the system. "Also, that it will take time to get back there."

"Aye, sir," Roach said.

"But on the whole, they did well," William added. The crew had in fact done *very* well. They deserved a few days of shore leave. "Perhaps we've broken the *Uncanny* curse."

"Or perhaps there's worse to come," Lupine said.

William gave him a nasty look. "You're not allowed to talk anymore."

CHAPTER THIRTY

"Captain," Weiberg said as *Lightning* slid back into realspace, "*Glory of God* is still holding position over Jorlem."

Kat had expected as much, but she'd hoped otherwise. "Tactical analysis?"

"Her shields are at standby; her weapons and drives seem to be largely powered down," Weiberg said. "But she'll probably be able to bring herself to full alert before we enter weapons range."

"Understood," Kat said. "Communications, raise System Command. Request an orbital slot on the other side of the planet from *Glory of God.*"

"Aye, Captain," Linda said.

Kat settled back into her command chair, studying the display. *Glory of God* didn't *seem* to be doing anything hostile, but she couldn't help wondering if her CO would be tempted to pick a fight now that *Uncanny* was gone. *She* would certainly have considered an attack herself if she'd been in a similar position. The prospects for victory against one heavy cruiser would be far better than the prospects for fighting *two*.

"Contact the StarCom," she added as the ship approached the planet. "See if there are any messages waiting for us."

"Aye, Captain," Linda said.

Pity we never tried to duplicate the mobile StarCom, Kat thought. The Theocracy had designed one, but it had been a grossly inefficient model. *It would have come in handy right now.*

"We have several message packets waiting for us, Captain," Linda reported. "None of them are from *Uncanny*."

Kat cursed under her breath. There was no way to know what had happened to Sir William and *his* ship until he either returned to Jorlem or visited a system with a StarCom. She found it hard to imagine a pirate base capable of standing off a heavy cruiser, but she knew from bitter experience just how much could go wrong. They *were* due to meet back at Jorlem now, yet there was no way anyone could guarantee a timetable.

"Download them to my console," she ordered. "And then send a message to the planet requesting a *private* meeting with the president."

"Aye, Captain," Linda said.

Kat keyed her console, opening the first set of messages from the Admiralty. She'd half hoped and feared for orders to engage *Glory of God*, but the Admiralty had merely dumped the whole question in her lap. There was something wishy-washy about the response that made her suspect that it had actually been written by the Foreign Office. Destroying *Glory of God* was important, apparently, but so was respecting Jorlem's neutrality. The planet was to be considered a neutral power until her government signed a treaty with the Theocracy.

So we cannot pick a fight with Glory *in-system*, Kat thought. *And as long as she stays here, she can intimidate the locals into submission.*

Kat glanced through the remainder of the message packet but saw nothing of immediate importance. An update from the war front, a set of intelligence updates that would have to be studied later . . . nothing that had any real bearing on her situation. There wasn't even an assessment of the battleship-battlecruiser's capabilities. She felt as if she'd been left to handle the problem on her own.

But that's what they pay me for, she thought. *I wanted to sit in the command chair.*

"Picking up a signal from the planet, Captain," Linda said. "The president invites you to dinner, this evening."

"Thank him for me," Kat said. "And inform him I will gratefully attend."

Me, alone, she thought as she scanned the message. *He doesn't want witnesses.*

Davidson was going to be worried, but Kat forwarded the message to him anyway. She *had* asked to meet the president alone, after all; he'd taken her at her word.

"Compile the list of pirate contacts," she ordered. "Mr. XO, you have the conn. I'll be in my Ready Room."

Crenshaw gave her a faintly horrified look as she rose and headed for the hatch. He'd written a formal complaint into the log, listing his concerns about Kat using herself as live bait. She suspected he'd be just as concerned about her going down to Jorlem without an armed escort, although President Alexis would have to be out of his mind to try to kidnap her. There was no way he would be allowed to escape punishment, even if the Commonwealth had to detach an entire battle squadron to administer it. His own people would probably hand him over rather than face the Commonwealth's wrath.

Five minutes later, Davidson stepped into the compartment.

"It is my duty to point out," he said stiffly, "that going down to the surface alone is extremely risky."

"Not as risky as setting foot on a pirate base," Kat said. She was worried about *Uncanny*, although she had complete faith in Sir William. "The president may mock and belittle me, Pat, but he won't threaten my life."

"All that's really needed is a kill-team to either snatch or assassinate you," Davidson warned. "I don't think the Theocracy is *that* willing to coddle President Alexis."

"No, but any kidnapping would happen on his watch," Kat said. "He has every reason to make sure nothing happens to me."

Davidson didn't seem impressed. "I can't talk you out of this, can I?"

"No."

"Then I'll have the entire company ready to perform a combat jump," he told her. "If you run into trouble, we'll be ready to jump in and save you."

Kat lifted her eyebrows. "You do remember how many soldiers we saw around the presidential palace?"

Davidson snorted. "Jorlem isn't a democratic society," he reminded her. "I'd be surprised if the president hasn't worked hard to coup-proof his regime. Reacting to any sudden crisis will probably be beyond them. It's not impossible"—he smiled, rather darkly—"that most of his people will sit on their hands when the balloon goes up out of fear of being branded potential rebels. It's happened before."

"Still," Kat said. "And don't forget *Glory of God.*"

"She'll have to drop her janissaries if she wants to take part," Davidson assured her. "Unless she *wants* to start dropping KEWs into a boiling multisided faction fight."

Kat sighed. "I'll be fine," she said. "Don't worry about me."

She finished reading the intelligence briefing and interrogation summaries, then headed back to her cabin to shower and change into her dress uniform. She had a feeling that President Alexis wouldn't care what she wore, but not turning up in full formals could be used to spark a minor diplomatic incident. It would be a petty and pointless strategy, yet it would give the locals time to bury any connections they might have to the pirates.

Bastards, she thought.

She checked her appearance in the mirror and then headed for the shuttlebay. Her personal shuttlecraft was ready to depart.

"We've been given a landing coordinate right next to the palace," her pilot said as he took the craft through the hatch and out into space. "They're warning us not to deviate from the flight path they've provided."

Kat's lips twitched. "Better do as they say," she said. "We don't want to make them jumpy."

She kept a wary eye on the sensors as the shuttle entered the atmosphere and headed towards the capital. The air was surprisingly clear; the constant stream of shuttles entering or exiting the atmosphere were steered around the city. Kat noticed very few aircraft in the air, none flying over the city itself. Kat wouldn't have been surprised to discover that the city was ringed by ground-based antiaircraft defenses, ready to shoot down any aircraft flying towards the palace. She couldn't blame the locals for being paranoid. A single rogue pilot could decapitate the regime in a single blow.

"We'll be on the ground in a moment," the pilot said. "I'll just wait here?"

"Please," Kat said.

She braced herself as the shuttle touched down neatly; then she rose and walked to the hatch. It hissed open in front of her, allowing her to step into the cold evening air. It felt later than it actually was, despite her implants. Starship lag was taking its toll

Kat ignored her tiredness as she followed a gaudily dressed flunky through a maze of passageways and into a small dining room. The chamber was surprisingly Spartan compared to some of the other rooms of the palace. Yet the table was groaning with enough food to feed an entire platoon of marines.

"Ah, Katherine," President Alexis said. He rose and bowed to her. "Can I call you Katherine?"

"If you wish," Kat said, silently thanking her mother for all the etiquette lessons. As hard as it was to believe, she'd met worse people at family dinners. The best way to deal with the assholes was simply to ignore them. "Thank you for meeting me."

"It's always a pleasure to introduce someone to my planet's cuisine," President Alexis said as he motioned for her to sit down. "Please, take what you like. I'm sure you'll enjoy it. We can discuss matters of state after the repast."

Kat sat impatiently and filled her plate. Jorlem apparently placed a high value on spicy meats, cooked vegetables, and several different wines. The president took open delight in pointing to the different jugs of gravy and explaining how each of them complemented the meat, describing in loving detail precisely how they were made. Kat couldn't help wondering if he cooked himself as she took a bite of the dish. The meat was surprisingly good, leaving a pleasant aftertaste lingering in her mouth. The wine accented the meal perfectly.

"Your cook should open a restaurant on Tyre," she said after sampling all of the different meats. "We're always looking for new cuisines."

"Tyre is so much more cosmopolitan than many other worlds," President Alexis said. "Can you believe that the Theocracy's ambassadors refused to eat with me?"

"They're not supposed to eat with unbelievers," Kat said. "They hold everyone who isn't one of them in absolute contempt."

"Theirs is a joyless religion," President Alexis agreed. He speared a piece of chicken with a fork and munched it thoughtfully. "Their bid to establish missionaries in missionary positions"—he snickered rudely—"will fail. Why would anyone want to join?"

Kat tensed. "You allowed them to send missionaries into your society?"

"No one will join," President Alexis assured her.

"Don't be too sure," Kat said. "There are *always* people willing to join."

She remembered just how many problems the missionaries had caused on Tyre. The Commonwealth had freedom of religion, but did that include tolerance of a religion that was also a disguised political movement? Should the converts be rounded up and expelled, as some had argued, or tolerated, even though a handful posed a threat to the planet itself? If nothing else, the war had made dealing with the issue a great deal simpler—the converts had been interned—but she knew there would be trouble in the aftermath.

Once the Theocracy controls the high orbitals, she thought grimly, *they just enforce their will on the population.*

"We shall see," President Alexis said.

A team of maids appeared and cleared the table, working with practiced, silent efficiency. Kat felt uncomfortably full, having eaten more than she should. She promised herself a long session in the exercise compartment when she returned to the ship. She straightened up, signaling her desire to speak of different concerns. The food might have put President Alexis in a good mood, but what she was about to tell him would probably ruin it.

"So," President Alexis said. "What do you want to talk about?"

Kat reached into her belt and removed a datachip. "We liberated a cloudscoop that had been captured and occupied by pirates," she said. "In the course of their . . . *interrogation* . . . we discovered a number of contacts on Jorlem, ranging from a trio of fences to a number of recruiting agents. I am obliged to inform you, under the various anti-piracy treaties, that your government is responsible for rounding these individuals up and arresting them."

The president's eyes narrowed. "I cannot arrest my citizens merely on your say-so," he growled. "Do you have any proof?"

"You may read the interrogation transcripts if you wish," Kat said. She passed him the datachip. He took it automatically. "We were not gentle, Mr. President. They were interrogated using standard mind probes."

"We would need to see the prisoners ourselves." President Alexis temporized.

"They're currently floating in space, dead," Kat said flatly. "As you are aware, starship commanders have wide latitude to deal with pirates as they see fit."

She took a breath. "Mr. President, I have no wish to step on your toes. But if these . . . these *vermin* are on your planet, you have an obligation to deal with them. They need to be rounded up before more of your young men are seduced into working for the pirates."

"We have no control over matters off-world," President Alexis said sharply.

"No," Kat agreed, "but you *do* have control over your surface. We are looking to you to deal with the problem."

She met his eyes. "It isn't just the recruiting agents, Mr. President," she said. "The fences are the ones who pay the pirates for their ill-gotten gains. They're the ones who make crime pay. By allowing them to exist, you are covertly supporting the pirates preying on local shipping—including yours. How many freighters have you lost in the last year or so? Your economy is being damaged by these people. Are you going to tolerate it?

"I am aware of your political weakness," she added. Let him think she understood his problems, if necessary. "That's why I chose to seek a private meeting rather than issue demands that might be overheard by your political enemies. But this is not a situation I can allow to get any farther out of hand."

The president glowered at her for a long moment. "I cannot be seen to bend to off-world pressure."

"There will be no open demands or threats if you cooperate," Kat promised him. "I gave you the details. Round up the bastards and have them interrogated, then arrest any others you happen to find. You can claim full credit for smashing a pirate ring wide open. I'll even see to it that plaudits flow in from the rest of the galaxy."

"That and a coronet will buy me a cup of coffee," President Alexis said. His eyes went very cold for a long chilling moment. "And if I choose to deny your . . . request?"

Kat peered at the dictator evenly. For all of his geniality, she had no illusions about just how far President Alexis was prepared to go to maintain his power. He'd happily purge and execute members of his own family just to keep his planet under control. Countless civilians would wind up dead, if he wished. Kat had a dark suspicion that some of the pirate slaves had actually been arrested on Jorlem and sold to the pirates. If he'd been able to kill *her*, she knew Alexis would have done it in a heartbeat.

"The Commonwealth will have no choice but to take steps," Kat told him. "Jorlem will be blacklisted. Interstellar trade will trail off and come to an end. You will be denied access to interstellar banking or any other form of interstellar support. And if that fails to force you to take the matter seriously, the Commonwealth will have to take more . . . *direct* . . . action."

The president's face turned impassive. "The Theocracy will not be impressed by your blacklist."

"No, it won't," Kat agreed. She leaned forward warningly. "The Theocracy is in no state to guarantee your security. They are losing their war. There is no way they can spare enough ships to protect you when the Commonwealth sends a battle squadron to make its feelings clear. Even if they did . . . we might greet it with unreserved delight. It would just make it easier to drive on their homeworld and end the war."

She rose, wondering if he would try to detain her. Davidson's mad plan to drop an entire company of marines on the palace might be necessary after all. Although it would be absolutely insane . . .

"I am quite happy to let you handle the matter and take credit for it," she finished. "However, it needs to be done, and the sooner the better. If we don't see any solid action being taken in the next few days, Mr. President, we will take steps ourselves."

She turned and stalked out of the room, feeling an unpleasant prickling sensation between her shoulder blades. If looks could kill . . . she pushed the morbid thought aside as a flunky appeared out of nowhere to guide her back to the shuttlepad; his face torn between blank servitude and surprise. No one had ever walked out on the president before, she guessed, a rude gesture by almost any standards.

It had to be done, she thought. *If he doesn't take action, those bastards are likely to get away with their crimes.*

"Captain," the pilot said as she stepped into the shuttle, "we have a flight path back to orbit."

"Good," Kat said. She took her seat and checked the display. The stealth drones she'd slipped into orbit at Davidson's suggestion weren't reporting any unexpected military moves, while *Glory of God* was still silent. "Any problems?"

"None," the pilot said. "They did offer to refuel the shuttle, but I turned them down."

He paused dramatically. "And *Uncanny* has arrived," he added "She's not alone."

Kat blinked. "Not alone?"

"She captured a dozen pirate ships," the pilot said. He sounded almost gleeful. "And an entire base."

"Good," Kat said. Sir William had done *very* well. "Take us back to orbit."

CHAPTER THIRTY-ONE

"There's going to be a blarney soon," Senior Chief Houghton cautioned.

Joel was inclined to agree. *Lightning*'s crew hadn't done *too* badly, but *Uncanny*'s crew had hit the jackpot. Two days after the ship had returned to Jorlem, nine of the pirate ships had been sold after a brief, frantic bidding war. Now *Uncanny*'s crew was celebrating in the bars and buying drinks for their comrades from *Lightning*, making snide remarks all the time about how unlucky *Lightning* had been to choose the wrong mission.

It would be very useful, he thought, *if I had been plotting to take* Lightning.

"I'll take four of the worst drunks out of here," Joel said. "You can deal with the others."

He yanked the loudest drunk to his feet and pointed him towards the exit, then motioned for three more to follow him. The third lunged forward, ready to fight; Joel stepped to one side, stuck out a foot, and watched the drunkard topple to the floor. Joel caught him before he could roll over and get back up, half carrying him to the door. The man started to sober up as soon as the cold night air struck his face. It felt very much as though it was going to rain.

"Idiot," Joel muttered.

Word had spread rapidly, he discovered, as he marched the four drunkards back to the nearest shuttle. Hundreds of prostitutes and salesmen had descended on the bars where *Uncanny's* crew were drinking, trying to claim a share of the wealth. The prostitutes were probably going to be working double shifts, Joel thought; he doubted the salesmen would do so well. Or perhaps they would. Prize money was tax free by long tradition. The spacers could blow it all on wine, women, and song and no one would care.

They'd still have to get it to orbit, he thought. He still smiled whenever he thought of the spacer who'd bought a used aircar on shore leave and then discovered he couldn't get it back to the ship. *Better to spend the money on beer and prostitutes.*

He sobered as he handed the drunkards over to the militiamen on duty outside the shuttles, then turned and walked back down the street. A pair of missionaries stood in front of a bar, telling everyone who passed about the glory of the One True God and His True Faith. They didn't look to be having any luck at winning converts, but Joel had a suspicion that that wasn't the point. The missionaries were the Theocracy's key to Jorlem, having already established a major temple on the surface.

It will serve as more than just an embassy, he thought. He looked down at the wristcom on his wrist. *They'll be running their spies out of their base.*

Crewman Thomas Rochester met him, as planned, outside an expensive bar. The prostitutes outside looked higher class than the ones outside the other venues, their fees probably a great deal higher too. Joel passed Rochester his wristcom, reminding him to stay in the bar and out of sight. He had a portable com with him too, in case of emergencies, but as far as the ship's sensors were concerned, Joel, or at least his wristcom, would be in the bar too.

"I'll take care of it for you," Rochester promised. "Good luck with the supplier."

Joel nodded, and then turned and hurried towards the temple. The rest of his inner circle thought he was going to find a supplier, but Joel already knew it would be pointless. They needed more specialized help, and he could only think of one group who could provide it. Yet, it was risky as hell . . .

They can only shoot me once, he thought, as he stepped through the doors. His implants reported a whole series of privacy fields, far more than he would have expected in a House of God. *They'd probably consider me a traitor anyway.*

A man stepped out of the shadows wearing a monkish robe and cowl that kept his face concealed. "My Brother," he said in a whispery voice. "Have you come to hear of the True Faith?"

"I have come to speak to one of your intelligence officers," Joel said. "We don't have time for games."

The Theocrat hesitated for a second. "Very well," he said. "Follow me."

He led the way through a door and down a long corridor into a secure room. Joel's implants reported more privacy fields, including one that would have jammed his wristcom if he'd kept it with him. He couldn't have the device tattling on him. A single man, wearing a long red robe, sat behind a solid metal desk. His face was so bland that he could have passed unnoticed almost anywhere, even on a planet like Jorlem.

"I need to talk to someone who can make decisions," Joel said. He shivered in fear. Red robes meant an Inquisitor, he thought. "Can *you* make decisions?"

"I can," the Theocrat said. His voice was surprisingly warm. "And I have no time for games either."

Joel nodded as he sat down and studied the Theocrat. He'd spent hours trying to decide how best to approach them. Should he claim to be a convert? Or should he tell them the truth, or as much of it as they needed to know? It was unlikely they'd betray him, but they might not be willing to help. And he desperately needed help. He was running out of time.

"I am a crewman from *Uncanny*," he said. "We have been planning to stage a mutiny and take command of the vessel."

The Theocrat rocked back in surprise. "May I ask why?"

"Money," Joel said. It was a believable motive. More to the point, it was one the Theocracy would accept without question. "We were planning to sell *Uncanny* to the highest bidder."

"We would be the highest bidder," the Theocrat said. "But you don't have the ship, do you?"

"Not yet," Joel said. "We need your help."

The Theocrat cocked his head. "And you think we would just accept you, no questions asked?"

"No," Joel said. He removed a datachip from his pocket and dropped it on the table. "I believe you will find that information to be a sufficient down payment."

◆ ◆ ◆

Inquisitor Bin Zaid hadn't expected much from his assignment to Jorlem's newly converted and consecrated temple. Indeed, he had a private suspicion that Senior Cleric Abdullah had ordered him to take the job merely to get Bin Zaid out of his hair. Whatever else could be said about the spaceport, it just wasn't the kind of place anyone would expect to find converts. In addition, far too many shipping agents had been rounded up or simply gone underground in the last two days.

But this . . .

He stared at the infidel, fighting to keep the scorn and disbelief off his face. He'd had dozens of visitors offering to sell him information, most of which was valueless, but *no one* had come to him and offered an entire heavy cruiser. And a top-of-the-line Commonwealth heavy cruiser at that! The opportunity was literally priceless. Taking the ship home would *guarantee* him promotion. Was the offer too good to be true?

"Check the datachip," the infidel said. "You'll find it quite interesting."

Bin Zaid gave him a sharp look, then pulled out his datapad and inserted the chip into the reader, a universal design. The menu popped up at once, showing a list of classified naval documents, ranging from shipping line schematics to maintenance and repair manuals. He knew there were designers, back in the Theocracy, who would give their right arms for such information. Unless it was all faked. He wouldn't put it past the Commonwealth to tempt him with such a staggering piece of bait.

What if it was real, though?

"This will all have to be analyzed, of course," Bin Zaid said. He heard his voice quiver and cursed under his breath. "How do you believe we can be of service?"

"We need weapons and some other supplies," the infidel said. "If we take the ship, we'll hand her over to you shortly afterwards. You can pay us each a billion crowns for our work and give us transport somewhere a long way from the Commonwealth. That's around fifty billion crowns in total."

Bin Zaid swallowed, hard. *Fifty* billion crowns was *well* out of his budget. He knew precisely what his superiors would say if he requested so much money. If the infidel was a fraud, he was a bold one. Still, the heavy cruiser was worth . . . he didn't even want to *think* about how much it might be worth. Fifty billion crowns might be cheap if the entire ship fell into their hands.

We don't have to pay them, he thought. He licked his lips nervously. *We can immediately execute them after they hand over the ship.*

"Fifty billion crowns," he said. He shook his head slowly. There was no point in trying to bargain. "If you hand over the cruiser, with her computer files intact, we will happily pay you for her."

"Of course," the infidel said. "Give us the weapons now, and we will bring you the ship."

Bin Zaid nodded. "Once you have the ship, bring her to the border," he said carefully. "We'll make the swap there."

"We would prefer to make the swap here," the infidel said. "It would be safer for all concerned."

Safer for you, Bin Zaid thought. *It would be harder to cheat you in a system we don't control.*

Yet, he would have been suspicious if the infidel had agreed *too* quickly. Doing the swap at Jorlem made perfect sense, where the banking transfer could be arranged before the command codes were handed over. Perhaps they'd have to pay up after all . . .

"I'll have your datachip reviewed," Bin Zaid said, summoning one of his assistants. "If it checks out, we'll provide the weapons you requested."

He waited, studying the infidel as his assistant took the datachip for inspection. A competent intelligence service would have no trouble coming up with a piece of data that would pass a cursory inspection, he knew, but what would be the point? The Theocracy wasn't going to rush out and start building a carbon copy of *Uncanny* and her sisters. And the mere presence of the weapons wouldn't prove anything. Commonwealth forces already knew that *Glory of God* was orbiting Jorlem, and they already knew the Theocracy was active on the planet's surface. They didn't really need any more proof of *anything.*

"You are betraying your planet," he observed. "Why?"

The infidel made a throwaway gesture. "I want to be rich."

Bin Zaid felt a flicker of sharp contempt. The infidels had no loyalty to anything greater than themselves, no concept of stern obedience to a single will. He doubted the man in front of him had suffered for anything, let alone submitted himself to the question so that every last flicker of doubt or unbelief was flushed out of his system. Inquisitor Bin Zaid and his brothers had put themselves through fire just to prepare themselves for their roles. The infidels might be powerful, but they lacked the inner strength they needed to take the entire universe and bend it to their will.

"And you'll be very rich afterwards," Bin Zaid said.

His assistant returned, looking surprised. "The data checks out, Your Holiness," he said. "I think it's genuine."

"Good," Bin Zaid said.

He smiled coldly. There was no point in informing his superior, not yet. Either the milksop would refuse to work with the infidels or steal the credit for himself. Bin Zaid could arrange for the weapons to be handed over on his own, without permission. By the time his superiors found out, they would be unable to steal the credit. He'd have to tell them, sooner rather than later, but no one would ever be able to take it from him.

"It seems to be fine," he said, addressing the infidel. God had truly weakened those who chose not to embrace the faith. "And how do you want the weapons delivered to you?"

◆ ◆ ◆

Joel kept his face impassive through force of habit even though he felt almost lightheaded with relief. They'd bought it! The files he'd given them were genuine—he couldn't risk the Theocracy discovering a fake—but asking them for weapons might have been a step too far. He'd offered them something beyond price, yet they might have asked— quite reasonably—if the whole deal weren't too good to be true.

"I have ways to slip a crate or two up to the ship," he said. His people were in the right positions. They were already taking on some supplies at Jorlem. Adding a couple of additional shipping crates wouldn't be a problem. "You slip them into the warehouse nearest the spaceport, and I'll see to it they get picked up."

"Very clever," the Theocrat said. He couldn't hide the eagerness in his tone. "And then you bring the ship here."

"Of course," Joel said. If he *had* intended to hand *Uncanny* over to them, Jorlem was the logical place. They'd have very little opportunity to screw them. "I'll even throw the remainder of the crew to you as well."

The Theocrat's eyes gleamed. "It will be our pleasure to do business with you."

Joel nodded in agreement. The Theocrat was planning *something*, he was sure. It hardly mattered. *Uncanny* wouldn't be returning to Jorlem, whatever happened. They'd just have to make do with a datachip full of outdated manuals. Joel suspected the enemy intelligence service might already have copies of some of them. Not that it mattered, in any case.

"The weapons will be available tomorrow morning," the Theocrat added. "And may God go with you."

I rather doubt He wants anything to do with me, Joel thought. He was an oath breaker by any reasonable definition of the word, and now a traitor too. *Whatever happens, we are committed.*

He nodded shortly, then rose to his feet to head for the door. The hooded man appeared, leading him back to the exit. Joel allowed himself a moment of relief when he saw that the rain had finally started, pelting down so hard that even the hardened prostitutes had been driven indoors. He could hear thunder grumbling high overhead as he hurried across the street and into the bar. Rochester was sitting at a side table, a topless girl sitting on his lap.

"Hey, boss," he said. "Did it go well?"

Joel shot him a meaningful look as he sat down next to the crewman and recovered his wristcom. A brown-haired girl wearing a long dress materialized from nowhere, her eyes nervous even as she tried her hardest to look seductive. Probably not a professional then, Joel decided as he studied her. More likely someone who'd bribed her way into the spaceport for a day in the hopes of making some money.

He grinned, rather toothily. "First time?"

The girl flushed. "N-no," she stammered. "I've been here before."

Joel rolled his eyes. He'd heard a great many tall stories before, normally told by spacers trying to avoid a chewing out for something; he was *good* at sniffing out a lie. If the girl had ever set foot in the spaceport before, he would have been astonished. He doubted she was a virgin, but it was probably her first time doing it for cash.

"I'm sure," he said.

"The girls here are hot," Rochester said. The blonde on his lap giggled, pressing her breasts into his face. "Come on, Chief. Live a little."

"I have a room upstairs," the girl said. "Are you . . .?"

"Why not?" Joel asked. He snapped his wristcom back on his wrist, then rose. "Lead on, my dear."

The girl took his arm, pulling him towards a stairwell. Joel shook his head as he followed her. She was nineteen, perhaps twenty, but she probably had no hope of a decent career on her homeworld. Even if she did, she could lose it all in an instant if she offended the wrong man. He couldn't help feeling a stab of sympathy. The girl—he didn't even know her name—would ply her trade here until she grew too old, unless she was robbed or raped or mutilated by one of her customers. No one would give a damn about an inexpensive prostitute. There were plenty more where she came from.

We make it worse, he thought tightly. Brothels on Tyre were closely regulated; Jorlem was far less controlled. *Spacers like us, eager for a quick fuck.*

He pushed the thought aside as he followed her into the bedroom and closed the door. There was no point in worrying about it. Instead, he watched as she fumbled with her dress and let it fall to the floor. Underneath, she was naked. He took a long moment to look her up and down, her face reddening as he inspected her, and then he reached for the girl.

I need to relax, he told himself as her fingers fumbled with his uniform buttons. An experienced prostitute would have been able to strip him in seconds. *She needs to earn the money.*

Afterwards, feeling an odd sensation he didn't want to admit to, he left a dozen crowns on the dresser for her.

Even so, he knew it wouldn't be enough to make a difference.

CHAPTER THIRTY-TWO

"He seems to have rounded up a few dozen of the pirate contacts," Kat said as she poured them both a drink. President Alexis had sent a few bottles of his favorite wines to her as a gift. "But I don't know how far the purge goes."

William nodded. "As long as the pirates and their allies are ducking for cover," he said, "it'll make it harder for them to continue recruiting newcomers, as well as fencing loot."

"It depends," Kat said. "How many of them will be quietly released from jail and allowed to leave the planet after we leave?"

"The president has good reason to *appear* to cooperate, even if his cooperation has its limits," William reassured her. "And we have access to the interrogation records. If we recapture any of the bastards, we'll know they were allowed to escape."

Kat sipped her wine. She'd sent copies of the records to Vangelis and every other world with a StarCom. Not *everyone* checked the crews of arriving freighters, even when they landed on the surface, but now former pirates had a good chance of being caught if they passed through planetary immigration. If it was shown that Alexis had let pirates escape, all hell would break loose.

They'll have to have their DNA reconfigured if they want to escape detection, she thought wryly. *The technology to do so probably doesn't exist in this sector.*

"President Alexis wasn't happy about me sharing the records," she said thoughtfully. "He seemed to feel it will reflect badly on his planet."

"It probably will," William said. "And if someone managed to trace looted supplies to Jorlem, there would be a case against the planetary government. A merchant in the Commonwealth might even try to bring suit against Jorlem."

"Which would be a diplomatic headache," Kat said. "As well as making Jorlem look bad."

She took another sip of her wine before moving on. It was the first chance they'd had for a private chat since *Uncanny* had returned to Jorlem. There was no point in wasting it brooding over President Alexis and his deeply corrupt government. They had too many other matters to discuss.

"Good work on the pirate base," she said. "It should definitely put a crimp in their activities."

"One would hope so," William said. "I just hope we haven't accidentally sold the ships right back to their former owners."

"I don't think so," Kat said. "We checked the buyers extensively. They're all legit shipping agents. We'll have someone to blame if the ships go back into pirate hands."

She smiled. Selling the starships to various planetary governments had been a good idea—she'd even accepted a handful of lower bids to make sure they went to places where they could do the most good—but she didn't know if the new owners could handle the ships. They *were* simple, nothing remotely as advanced as *Lightning* or *Uncanny*, yet most stage-two colony worlds would struggle to recruit trained spacers. Some former hostages were willing to stay on the ships and work for their new owners, but they wouldn't be enough. The new crews would have to learn on the job.

Even a small ship will be enough to deter pirates, she thought. *Doubtless, selling them at such low prices will win us some goodwill.*

She shook her head as she looked up at the display. They'd checked, as best as they could, but they didn't *know.* It wouldn't be hard for a greedy little toad on a stage-two world to resell the starship as soon as it arrived, then vanish out-system before anyone realized what he'd done. He probably wouldn't survive—pirates hated to leave loose ends—but the prospect of being brutally murdered hadn't stopped hundreds of idiots in the past. And he'd leave his homeworld with a serious problem. *They* would get the blame for anyone that ship killed.

"That always helps," William said. "Just running patrols and making it clear that there *will* be accountability will encourage good behavior."

"I hope so," Kat said. She grinned at him. "Did you get your crewmen out of the brig?"

William looked embarrassed. A number of his crewmen had not only drunk themselves silly on Jorlem, they'd also taken a number of recreational drugs and gotten high. By the time the shore patrol had finally responded, the entire quadrant had been in chaos. The locals had stunned a number of crewmen and carted them off to the local jail, keeping them there to cool off. Kat had received a number of painfully polite communications from the planetary government about the whole affair.

Because they wanted to distract me from watching how they deal with the pirates, she thought. *It isn't as if spacers haven't gotten drunk or high before.*

"I did, eventually," William said. "A couple of them will need long-term medical attention. They took enough crap to do permanent damage."

Kat winced. She'd never understood why anyone took recreational drugs, particularly when direct brain stimulation was far less risky. Medical science could fix anything that didn't kill the user, but it was far harder to overcome the cravings for bigger and bigger highs. Drug use onboard starships was a constant headache, even though it was more than enough to end a crewman's career. Kat hated to think what her first CO would have said if he'd caught her with drugs. The old man would have pitched her out the airlock without a second thought.

"Take care of them," she said.

"I intend to," William said. "There'll be punishment duties for everyone involved."

Kat didn't blame him. Bar fights weren't exactly uncommon—there had been a whole *string* of fights between their respective crews as *Uncanny's* inhabitants flaunted their new wealth—but they *were* embarrassing. She had no doubt the spaceport authorities would try to ramp up their claim for compensation as much as possible, knowing the Commonwealth would probably prefer to pay just to make the whole problem go away. She knew she didn't have time to argue over each and every item on their list.

Bar stools, a million crowns each, she thought sarcastically. *And a whore's broken nose, ten thousand crowns, plus medical treatment.*

She shook her head. If anyone had actually been injured during the whole affair, she rather doubted they would see any actual compensation. Whatever money Kat paid would go straight into an off-world bank account and vanish. The higher-ups would take the cash, their subordinates would get . . . nothing. She would be surprised if *any* of it was used to repair the damage and renovate the spaceport.

Which won't stop them from trying to demand enough cash to build a whole new spaceport, she thought.

She pushed the thought aside. "We've secured the services of a colonist-carrier," Kat said. The deal had been surprisingly cheap. There just wasn't much call for such a vessel's services in the Jorlem Sector. "I want you to escort that ship back to the pirate base, pick up the prisoners, and ship them to Haverford. We'll meet you there."

William nodded. "You intend to go directly to Haverford?"

"The pirates have been showing too much interest in that world," Kat said. She'd meant to visit earlier, but liberating the cloudscoop and destroying the pirate base had taken priority. "It's a stage-one, William. I don't think they're *willingly* supporting the pirates."

"Which means they're probably under occupation," William agreed.

"Yes," Kat said.

It was a worrying thought. There was no way anyone could get away with simply taking over a stage-one colony world within the Commonwealth, yet someone could have done just that on Haverford. Very few starships visited a colony that had so little to offer save food and women. A careful pirate leadership could have kept their takeover secret for years with minimal precautions. And even if she was wrong and Haverford wasn't under occupation, the pirates could have bribed or threatened the planetary authorities into compliance.

"I'll go straight there and find out," she said. Haverford *would* have a use for a few hundred unwilling colonists, even former pirates. Stage-one colonists took a remorselessly practical view of the universe. The pirates could work or starve. "If they are under occupation, I'll deal with it. If not . . . I'll play it by ear."

William studied the display for a moment. "If we fly straight to the pirate base, we can link up with you in two weeks, more or less," he said. "Is that enough time to handle the planet?"

"I hope so," Kat said. "If it isn't . . ."

She shook her head. It was unlikely the pirates had enough weapons to stop *Lightning*. If worse came to worst, she could merely pick off their positions from orbit, dropping KEWs until the pirates surrendered or were wiped out. If they were holding an entire population hostage, she might have to dicker again and allow the pirates to trade their lives for the safety of the population. A single nuke in the right place would drive the death toll into the stratosphere.

"We'll see you there," she finished. "Do you have any other concerns?"

"We could do with some supply dumps, the sooner the better," William said. "And ideally a little closer than Vangelis."

"Aston Villa was talking about joining the Commonwealth," Kat said. "They might agree to host a supply dump."

"If they could protect it," William said. "Your report suggests they want our protection."

"They do," Kat confirmed. "But I don't know what, if anything, the Admiralty can spare."

"A couple of dozen gunboats and a converted freighter would be more than enough," William said. "And we have a surfeit of gunboats."

"And all we need are the assault carriers to take them to war," Kat said. Gunboats were easy to produce. Tyre had been grinding out thousands every month. "And then we can kick the enemy's ass."

She paused. "But you're right," she added. "A couple of squadrons of gunboats would definitely make a commitment."

"And prove we will send more ships, if necessary," William agreed.

Kat nodded. "While you're gone, try and think of a way of luring *Glory of God* out for a fight," she concluded. Her latest set of orders was unsatisfactory. "The Admiralty wants her destroyed, but not anywhere near Jorlem."

"She'll leave eventually," William pointed out. "We can strike then."

"Sure," Kat said, "*if* we're in position to follow her."

◆ ◆ ◆

"That's the last of the crates," the loader said. "Good luck!"

Joel waved good-bye as he turned and headed towards the shuttle's cockpit. If there was one advantage to the whole disgraceful affair on the planet's surface, it was that it had made it easy for him to ensure that *his* crates were only handled by his people. They had already been scanned and secured—or at least the records *claimed* that they had been scanned and

321

secured—but he didn't want to take the chance of someone deciding to open up one of the crates and taking a peek inside. It was too great a risk.

Despite regulations, *Uncanny*'s crew had a nasty habit of opening crates whenever they arrived. Joel was unwilling to count on Sir William having managed to break his crew of *that* particular habit, not when far too much of his future was at stake. If the wrong person discovered a crate of weapons, particularly when the manifest stated hydroponics equipment, it would be catastrophic.

"Take us up to orbit," he ordered as he sat down behind the pilot. "There's no need to break records getting there either."

"Yes, Chief," the pilot said.

The shuttle came to life. Joel had found it easy to get himself tasked with supervising the loading—as senior chief, it was his job to make sure everything was properly loaded and secured—but he still felt tense. He was now committed to his plan in a different way. Now there was no hope of taking his money and vanishing into the planet's population. He would take the ship . . .

And it isn't just Uncanny *now*, he thought. *There's* Lightning *out here too.*

He winced inwardly as he realized just how many things had gone wrong with the original plan. It would be easy just to take the ship—and perhaps even hand her over to the Theocracy—but that wouldn't be anywhere near as satisfying as what he had planned. No, the original plan was still workable . . . if they managed to do something about *Lightning*. To be sure, *Lightning* had a competent commanding officer and a very experienced crew. She wouldn't be taken easily.

I can't give up now, he thought. *Not after I've done so much.*

"We'll be docked in ten minutes," the pilot said. "Just sit back and enjoy the ride."

Joel chuckled, keying the console to bring up the orbital display. Jorlem's orbital space wasn't particularly crowded, not now. A surprising number of freighters, he'd been told, had departed mere hours after

Lightning had arrived, heading out without taking on cargos or filing flight plans. Pirates or smugglers, he suspected; men who had reason to fear that they would be rounded up once the arrested fences on the planet started to talk. The only threatening sign was the looming bulk of *Glory of God*, holding position on the other side of the planet. Jorlem's underground economy was in deep trouble . . .

. . . and yet, the system had a striking amount of potential.

Government made the difference, Joel knew. Tyre's government had focused on long-term investment rather than trying to turn a quick profit. The original development corporation had folded into the monarchy rather than surrender control to an elected government . . . precisely as planned. But Jorlem? The planet had embraced democracy too quickly without all the underlying institutions that made democracy work. Hastiness had ensured the eventual *destruction* of democracy. And yet, the potential for a greater world was still there. Someone with *vision* needed to take control.

He deactivated the display and rose as the shuttle made its way through the hatch and landed neatly in the lower shuttlebay. His teams were already there, ready and waiting to move the crates into the holds. The pilot opened the hatches, the low hum of the drive fading away as the shuttle powered down. Joel stepped through the hatch, keeping his face under tight control. They were *definitely* committed now.

"We're departing in two hours," Crewman Thomas Rochester said quietly. "We're heading straight back to the pirate base, then to Haverford."

Joel wasn't too unhappy. Haverford would make an ideal place to dump anyone who didn't want to cooperate after they took the ship. He still had no idea what the pirates had been doing there—it was clear they'd failed to deter Sir William from investigating—but it hardly mattered. So few starships visited Haverford that no one would notice a settlement on the other side of the planet. Taking the supplies from the pirate base would be *very* helpful.

We can throw most of the pirates into space as well, he thought. He had no particular inclination to keep Sir William's agreement with the bastards. *That will put an end to any threat they pose.*

He checked off the crates as they were moved into the hold, the three from the Theocracy steered into a side compartment and isolated. He opened one of the crates himself, once the loading was completed and the crews were dismissed, and checked the contents. The Theocracy had done a very good job. Stunners, assault rifles, grenades . . . anyone would think they'd *expected* to supply him with weapons.

They're probably planning to supply terrorist cells with weapons, he thought morbidly. It had worked across the Commonwealth, although most of the terrorist cells had been rapidly rounded up after they'd reared their ugly heads. They'd caused a great deal of disruption, but very little significant damage. *Subverting the entire sector might work in their favor, even if they lost the war. Their faith would live on.*

"Chief," Julia said as he left and sealed the compartment, "we're going back to the pirate base."

"I heard," Joel said. He took a long moment to think. They needed to move *after* the pirate base but before reaching Haverford. "We'll keep our heads down until after we strip the base bare."

Julia nodded. "You still intend to move?"

"There's no choice," Joel said. "Either we move or we die."

He glanced at his wristcom as a low rumble echoed through the ship. Sir William wasn't wasting time. They'd be on their way shortly, with a cargo he *knew* he didn't dare let anyone see. And then . . . victory or death. He had no illusions about their fate if they lost. Mutiny was a capital offense.

Perhaps it was a mistake not to desert when I had the chance, he thought. *I could have vanished with ease. It's far too late to contemplate that now.*

He smiled humorlessly. *Victory or death indeed.*

CHAPTER THIRTY-THREE

"Captain," Stott said, "our automated monitoring systems on the bubble report that a third of the pirates are dead."

William let out a long breath as *Uncanny* decelerated towards the former pirate base. POWs were meant to maintain *some* discipline, but pirates hadn't often had *any* discipline in the first place. Hell, he'd seen captured *Theocrats* break down into chaos after discovering just how willing their officers were to screw them. Nonetheless, losing a third of the prisoners was an embarrassment.

Not that many people will care, he thought.

"Order Major Lupine to start transferring the remainder of the prisoners to the colonist-carrier," William ordered as he checked the feed from the pirate base. It didn't look as though anyone had bothered to attempt to rescue the pirates, not entirely to his surprise. Pirates weren't known for loyalty to their own kind. "Mr. XO, prepare to supervise the . . . *stripping* of the pirate base."

"Aye, Captain," Roach said.

The voyage had been uneventful. With only one ship to protect, *Uncanny* could have taken the gloves off if *anyone* had dared to attack her. The only real excitement for William, however, had come from chewing out the crewmen involved in the riot and monitoring their medical treatment, making sure that they received the best possible care.

"Once the base is stripped, destroy it," William added. None of the records he'd checked on Jorlem or Vangelis, via StarCom, had pointed to the original owners. The founders had covered their tracks well. They could have remained hidden forever if the pirates hadn't stumbled across them. "We don't want to linger."

"Aye, Captain," Roach said.

William sighed as the hours started to tick by. Goodrich had come up with a wish list of supplies from the pirate base—and a list of components that could probably be sold, even if they couldn't be refurbished to naval standards—but William honestly wasn't sure if it was worth the effort. Yet, it did serve a purpose. The devil made work for idle crew—he knew from bitter experience. Giving the crew something to do, even if it was just make-work, would keep them out of trouble.

We did sell those ships on, he thought. *Their new owners will want some of the supplies.*

William glanced at the timer, then pulled up the latest set of reports. The Theocracy's latest thrust into Commonwealth space had been stopped dead, according to one set of reports; the analysts had concluded that the Theocracy was likely reaching the limits of its strength. Even the most optimistic projections insisted that the Theocracy couldn't have produced more than two or three squadrons of superdreadnoughts since the war began. And *that* meant that the Commonwealth would soon have a decisive advantage.

If we don't have one already, William thought.

Every instinct in William called for liberating his homeworld as soon as possible, before the Theocracy could shatter what remained of its society beyond repair. Yet he knew the importance of building up the Navy into a force of overwhelming power. The Theocracy could explain away tactical defeats if it wanted, but not several hundred superdreadnoughts bearing down on its homeworld. And that would destroy the Theocracy's faith in itself.

"Captain," Stott said, "Major Lupine reports that the remaining prisoners have been transferred safely. The bubble is being deflated now."

"Good," William said. "Do we have a progress report from the XO?"

"Yes, sir," Stott said. "He's just finishing up."

William rather suspected that they were wasting time. The pirates *knew* their base had been compromised. Soon enough, they'd know it had been destroyed too. They wouldn't dare return to the unnamed star system. *Uncanny* needed to be patrolling the shipping lanes or escorting convoys, not hanging around in a useless system. They'd made an impact already, but he knew just how easily pirates could creep back into the system.

"As soon as he's back, lay in a course for Haverford," William ordered, anxious to begin the four-day trip. "Ready a couple of drones to pose as freighters."

"Aye, Captain," Thompson said. "Do you want to try to lure the pirates into our web?"

He looked surprisingly jumpy, as if his thoughts were elsewhere. William made a mental note to have a word with him if he didn't improve.

"Ideally," William said.

His console bleeped. "Captain, this is Roach," the XO said. "The base has been stripped bare of everything usable, and I've brought the crews back to the ship. I can detonate the nuke on your command."

"Very good," William said. He checked the tactical display, then nodded. "Push the button."

"Aye, Captain," Roach said.

The tactical display flashed as the asteroid shattered into a million fragments, the debris rocketing out in all directions. Some of it would eventually plunge into the dull red star, he knew; the remainder would drift through space forever excepting an encounter with another star system or collision with a starship. The odds against such an impact were staggering.

"Captain," Thompson said, formally. "The asteroid has been destroyed."

"Communications, order the colonist-carrier to accompany us," William ordered. "Helm, open a gateway and take us out of here."

"Aye, Captain," Cecelia said. "Straight-line course for Haverford."

The gateway opened, the ship shuddering slightly as she made her way into hyperspace. Whatever was wrong at Haverford, Kat would have dealt with it by now. *Uncanny* could offload the prisoners as soon as they arrived, then head straight back out on patrol.

Then we can get on with some real work, he thought morbidly. *Taking out as many pirates as we can before we are called back to the war.*

♦ ♦ ♦

"We move in two days," Joel said. He addressed a small group of fourteen supporters, handing out weapons as he spoke. "We use stunners at first, as long as we can. Only switch to lethal weapons if you have no choice."

He took a moment to gauge their reaction. He'd spent months sounding them out, back when it had seemed that *Uncanny* would never leave orbit, but that had been before they'd been graced with a competent commanding officer. They'd had great plans—what little he'd chosen to share—yet now . . . some of them might think they could back out. If they went straight to the captain, any hope of a peaceful takeover would vanish like snow in hell.

"We don't want to kill anyone," he added. "Many will join us, if they are given the opportunity."

There was another reason, he knew. Not *everyone* was enthusiastic about killing their fellow crew, the men and women they'd worked beside for the past three months. He knew better than to push them too hard. The prospect of dumping the undecided, those unwilling to side with a mutiny, on Haverford would calm their consciences. A stage-one colony might be a boring and hard place to live, but it wasn't a death sentence.

"We move when the captain is off the bridge," he added. "His movements are already being monitored, correct?"

"Correct," Julia said. "I *own* the datanet now. We can track him even if he takes his wristcom off."

Joel smiled. It was polite to pretend that the datanet tracked crewmen through their wristcoms, but it wasn't true onboard ship. There were several other tracking systems worked into the datanet, allowing the computers to locate anyone almost at once. A civilian would be horrified to know just how extensively military personnel were watched, but to the military, such scrutiny was a fact of life. Privacy was nonexistent in the wardrooms.

If one happens to know how the surveillance is conducted, Joel thought, *it's actually quite easy to evade it.*

"I'll deal with the captain personally," he said. The last thing he wanted was someone else getting cold feet. Sir William could *not* be given a chance to purge the datanet, let alone fight back against the mutiny. "Team One will take the bridge, with a little help from our friend; Team Two will take Main Engineering; Team Three will take life support. As soon as we have control, we run a formal lockdown drill. No one will think anything of it."

"Apart from the militia," Crewman Hanson warned. "They'd be alarmed."

"They'll go into lockdown too," Joel said. Sir William's insistence on repeated emergency drills, everything from combat alerts to repelling borders, had paid off. No one would realize that there was a *real* emergency until it was far too late. "And once they're sealed in Marine Country, we *keep* them sealed in."

"The whole section is designed to be isolated," Rochester agreed. "Bit of a mistake on their part, right?"

Joel had no intention of looking a gift horse in the mouth. The marines were responsible for internal security as well as providing troops for boarding pirate vessels and storming targets on the ground. He still found it hard to believe *just* what they—and Kat Falcone—had done to the cloudscoop pirates. The militia on board *Uncanny* had been spared that responsibility. They'd done well in their training, he had to admit, yet they weren't marines. They'd be caught and trapped before they realized what had happened to them.

Their life support will run out, he thought coldly. The militiamen couldn't be allowed to live. They were just too dangerous. *Some* bright spark might manage to blast their way out of Marine Country if they were left alone long enough. *That will be the end of them.*

"We'll keep the rest of the ship in lockdown," he added. Better not to mention the next part of the plan. "We can take out a couple of crewmen at a time, giving us a chance to see if they want to join us. If they don't, we'll hold them until they can be dropped off somewhere harmless."

He paused. "Are there any questions?"

Rochester frowned. "What if someone stumbles across some of our weapons?"

"We move ahead of time," Joel said. He tapped his wristcom. "Julia worked hard to give us a private frequency, so don't waste it. If you get the alert, stun everyone in sight who isn't already one of us and then move."

If they *did* have to move ahead of time, everything was going to become *very* chancy. There was no reason to think the captain *knew* there was trouble brewing—he didn't seem to have been unduly alarmed by Henderson's death—but that would change very quickly if someone discovered a stash of illicit weapons. Joel didn't know if the captain had contingency plans when it came to mutiny, yet he knew what *he* would do if he had reason to suspect trouble. Arm the militia, lock down the ship, and head straight for *Lightning*.

Then use her marines to search Uncanny *from top to bottom*, Joel thought. His throat was dry. *That would be the end.*

Hanson swallowed. "Chief . . . do we really *need* to move?"

Joel felt a shiver run down his spine. "What do you mean?"

"We planned this whole affair because no one gave a damn about us," Hanson said. "We're *colonials*, most of us; we didn't have a hope of escaping *Unlucky* or rising in the ranks. We owed no loyalty to a Navy that wasn't loyal to us. No one batted an eyelid when Captain Abraham started to sell off the supplies that kept us alive or did anything when the life support system began to fail. Why the hell *would* we be loyal?"

He took a breath. "But Sir William is different," he added. "He *does* give a damn about us!"

Joel met his eyes. "Do you expect his behavior to be anything more than an act?"

"He's a *colonial* himself," Hanson pointed out. "And now he's the captain . . ."

"He's a lone *colonial* in command rank," Joel snapped. "And they gave him *Unlucky!*"

"They might have expected him to fail," Rochester offered.

"They probably did," Joel said. He fought to keep his voice flat. "If the ship had been in as bad a state as they assumed, he probably *would* have failed."

"He's one of us," Hanson said. "He isn't a toff with his nose in the air . . ."

"He was promoted because he kissed a Falcone's ass," Joel said angrily. He'd been covertly spreading that rumor and many others. "His hand is so far up inside her that it's coming out of her mouth!"

"He turned this ship around," Hanson said. "And if he can reach command rank, we can rise too."

Joel carefully reached for the stunner he'd concealed in his uniform jacket. Hanson *might* be able to escape the death sentence for his part in the conspiracy, but he was deluding himself if he thought he could escape punishment entirely.

"Do you really think," Joel asked, "that we can just . . . abandon the plan and get away with it?"

He took a breath. "We killed a commanding officer," he added sharply. "Captain Abraham was a complete waste of space, but he was still a commanding officer. And we killed him!"

"He deserved it," Hanson said.

Captain Abraham had received a cleaner death than he deserved, Joel considered, but there was no point in worrying about it now.

"Yes, he did," Joel said. "How long will it be before someone realizes he was murdered?"

"This ship has a reputation for being unlucky," Hanson said pleadingly.

"And any *competent* officer will eventually realize that the ship *wasn't* on the verge of falling apart at the seams," Joel said quietly. "Then he will start wondering just why the shuttle had a catastrophic failure at the worst possible moment."

He met Hanson's eyes. "We can't back out now," he said. "Are you with us or not?"

Hanson hesitated, a fraction of a second too long. Joel pulled the stunner out of his pocket and shot him. His body crumpled to the deck.

"We'll dump him off with the remainder of the crew," Joel said, bracing himself. If Hanson wasn't the only one to have doubts . . . he waited, but no one moved. "If there's anyone else who wishes to quit, just bear in mind that you are thoroughly implicated."

He sucked in his breath. Hiding Hanson for a couple of days would be easy enough. He wouldn't be reported missing. The asshole could be tied up and sedated, then left in a tube until the ship reached

Haverford. And if something went badly wrong and the mutiny failed, he probably wouldn't be found until after he starved to death. Joel allowed his voice to harden.

"You all know what to do with your teams," he told them. "Remember, do *nothing* suspicious until I give the signal. Julia?"

"Yes, Chief?"

"Did you alter the rosters as I suggested?"

"Yes, Chief," Julia said. She held out a datapad. "We'll all be off duty at zero hour, save for our friend on the bridge."

"I'll speak to him directly," Joel said. Only a handful of people knew he'd subverted a bridge officer. "He'll have to sneak a weapon onto the bridge once his shift begins."

He made a show of looking at his wristcom. "And now some of us have to go on duty, so I declare this meeting at an end."

He nodded for Rochester to stay behind as he removed a roll of duct tape from his belt and used it to secure Hanson. There were a few things Joel could do to make Hanson's death seem like another tragic accident—a drug overdose would be easy to fake—but he didn't dare do anything that might attract attention. Better to maintain the illusion that Hanson was still alive and doing his job than try to explain his death.

Besides, if I kill Hanson, someone else with doubts might take them straight to the captain, he thought. *And that would doom the entire plan.*

"Help me get him into the crate," Joel ordered as soon as Hanson was tied and gagged. "We can get him down to the hold and seal it there before anyone thinks to look."

"Of course, Chief," Rochester said. He picked up Hanson without apparent effort and dropped him into the crate. Joel banged the lid down and secured it with more tape. If Hanson suffocated . . . well, he wasn't going to care. "What a louse. Didn't he *know* he was committed?"

Joel showed no reaction, but he was annoyed. A *competent* commanding officer could earn staunch loyalty. A captain might be a tyrant, but as long as he showed he cared about his crew, he would earn their respect. No one had mourned Captain Abraham . . .

. . . But Sir William was a very different story.

Was, Joel thought. He scowled. Sir William had messed up all his plans without even knowing it. *Yet, soon it won't matter at all.*

CHAPTER THIRTY-FOUR

William hated to admit it, but he was bored.

Boredom was something every military officer learned to appreciate. Boredom meant that no one was trying to kill you. But the boredom William experienced as *Uncanny* made her steady way towards Haverford was deadening. The pirates hadn't taken the bait he'd dangled in hyperspace. He'd been hoping to lure one or two ships into weapons range. He honestly didn't know if they'd even *seen* the bait or not. The *Uncanny* wasn't on any of the regular shipping lanes. There was certainly no reason to *assume* that the pirates might be watching them.

They might have seen us leave their base, if they were, he thought sourly. *They know we don't have a cluster of freighters with us.*

He sat in his cabin and worked his way through an endless series of updates the Admiralty appeared to believe that every commanding officer should know. William had no idea who had compiled the bundle, but he would have bet good money that he'd never been in command of a starship. Shipping movements were of interest—particularly when focused on the Jorlem Sector—and intelligence updates were always important, yet why was he supposed to care about recruitment policies all over the Commonwealth? And just what idiot thought it was a good idea to send out an all-ships alert for a crate of spare parts that had gone missing on the other side of the Commonwealth?

We only just started our first real war, he told himself. *The time servers and bureaucrats haven't been weeded out yet.*

William turned his attention to the reports from his departmental heads. A number of crewmen had been marked down for promotions, which he would have to authorize and then have confirmed by the personnel department back on Tyre. The process was annoying as anyone who had served on *Uncanny* was automatically considered a failure, but it would have to be endured. Besides they *had* maintained a very successful cruise so far. The stigma would have faded, even if it hadn't been washed away completely. Soon it would be gone for good.

He rubbed his eyes as he glanced through the files. A number of crewmen had also been recommended for special commendations—they'd flown the shuttles into the pirate base—and he had no doubt those would be authorized by Tyre. The others . . . he might have to fight to get them their promotions. But he would. Crewmen moving up the ladder would do wonders for morale.

His intercom buzzed. "Captain, do you want more coffee?"

William smiled. He'd never gotten used to having a steward, and he'd largely banned Janet from his quarters unless he needed coffee. It wasn't as if he *needed* someone to take care of his clothes. He had only brought a handful of uniforms and a single set of civilian clothes with him when he'd boarded *Uncanny*. Janet had very little to do, beyond keeping the coffeepot filled.

"No, thank you," William said. He'd drunk so much that he'd probably slosh around when he went to bed. "Get some rest if you want."

"Aye, Captain," Janet said.

William felt his smile fade as she closed the connection. Captain Abraham had compromised her career beyond all hope of repair unless she was *very* lucky. The Captain's Whore, they called her . . . she would be lucky to get promoted even if she *did* pass her exams. William intended to sponsor her if she completed the pre-academy training modules before *Uncanny* returned home, but she would have a difficult time. Still, her future path looked brighter than if she'd stayed with Captain Abraham.

William rose. Roach could handle the ship for a few more hours. He and his XO had already agreed to give some of the other junior officers some additional command experience. He could get a few hours of sleep himself and then start studying the shipping routes. If *Uncanny* picked up a few more freighters at Jorlem, she could head deeper into the sector and dare the pirates to come after her . . .

The doorbell chimed. William frowned. It was unusual for anyone to visit the captain when he was in his cabin. He keyed the switch. The hatch hissed open a moment later, revealing the senior chief. Why would *he* visit without calling ahead?

"Chief," William said, turning to face him. "What . . .?"

The senior chief lifted his hand. William barely had a second to register the weapon's presence . . .

. . . a moment before the world went away in a flare of blue-white light.

◆　◆　◆

Joel watched, feeling an odd mixture of emotions as Sir William collapsed to the deck. The captain was still dangerous. He should be killed. Joel *knew* he should cut the man's throat before he could recover. But he needed the command codes locked in the captain's brain. Sir William would have to be forced to surrender them willingly.

Joel looked around the cabin and then removed a roll of duct tape from his pocket. He wrapped a strip around the captain's hands, binding them behind his back. Another strip was wrapped tightly around his ankles, rendering him immobile. Joel sat back and checked his work and then glanced into the remainder of the suite. He'd slipped in and out of Captain Abraham's cabin before with its embarrassing decadence, but it seemed that Sir William preferred a more Spartan appearance. The bling that had dominated Captain Abraham's living space was gone. Joel wondered absently if his family had even dared claim it.

Shaking his head, he peered into the bedroom. The frilly bed was gone, replaced by a simple bed that had clearly been taken from the ship's stores. He recalled a handful of pornographic paintings hanging from the bulkheads, but they were gone too. Instead, the bulkheads were barren save for a handful of photographs placed in a neat row above the bed. He recognized Kat Falcone, wearing her naval uniform, but the others were strangers. Joel considered them for a long moment, then walked back to check the bathroom. It was easily twice as large as a wardroom, but again, all of the bling had been removed. Joel felt a pang of a familiar . . . *something* . . . as he stepped back into the main compartment.

If things had been different, he and Sir William could have been friends.

This is no time for sentimentality, he told himself sharply. He dared not allow himself to forget. *You were committed from the moment you murdered Captain Abraham.*

He keyed his wristcom. "Report," he ordered.

"The bridge is secure," Rochester reported. "Life support is also secure. There was a fight in Main Engineering, but we locked down the datanet before they could summon help."

Joel rubbed his forehead. Who would have thought that *Goodrich*, of all people, would become a competent engineer? The man had crawled into a bottle and stayed there . . . until Sir William came along. Somehow, the captain had given Goodrich back his pride. Joel had a handful of engineering crewmen under his banner, but could they be trusted if their superior was actually worthy of respect?

"Very good," he said. Soon, their opinions wouldn't matter any longer. "Put the entire ship into lockdown."

"Of course, Chief," Rochester said. "Or should I call you *Captain?*"

". . . Maybe later," Joel said.

The alert tone started to howl. Lockdowns were rare, but thankfully, Sir William had run through the drill during the long voyage from Tyre to Vangelis. All nonessential crewmen had ten minutes to get back to their wardrooms; all essential crewmen had strict orders to remain on duty without leaving their compartments. The militiamen, already inside Marine Country, would be trapped. By the time they realized it wasn't a drill, their life support would be deactivated completely.

He took one last look at Sir William, feeling an odd twinge of guilt. Joel would have enjoyed strangling Captain Abraham with his bare hands, but Sir William . . . Shaking his head, he walked out of the cabin and locked the hatch behind him. Julia had already scrambled the entry system, but there was no point in taking chances. Anyone who wanted to launch a counterattack would have to get through the solid hatch to rescue the captain.

They'd have to realize that something was up first, Joel told himself as he walked towards the bridge. *As long as they think there's a drill underway, they won't realize that something else is badly wrong.*

He paused outside the hatch, bracing himself. The militiaman who should have been on duty was lying on the ground, stunned. Judging from the drool dripping down from his mouth, he'd been stunned repeatedly. The prospects for long-term damages, as if it mattered in the slightest, were very high.

"Captain," Rochester said as Joel stepped onto the bridge, "the ship is yours."

Joel took a moment to savor the statement. This was it! This was what he'd wanted and been denied ever since he'd joined the Navy. Command of a starship, Master under God . . . it did not matter, not at all, that no one had *given* him the ship, that he'd mutinied against her legitimate commanding officer. All that mattered was that *he* was in command.

He swept his gaze around the compartment. A dozen stunned officers lay on the deck, their hands bound firmly behind their backs with duct tape. Most wouldn't join, Joel knew; the ones who had followed Sir William from his former posting would be *very* loyal. They'd have to be dumped on Haverford with the remainder of the crew unless they switched allegiance. And yet, would it be wise to trust them if they did?

"Mr. Thompson," Joel said as he sat down in the command chair. The tactical specialist was the lone officer left in the compartment. "Ship's status?"

"We are currently in lockdown, as ordered," Thompson said carefully. He licked his lips nervously. Joel had enough blackmail information to send him to the hangman, and both of them knew it. If anything had been *proved*, back on his old ship, he would have been executed rather than being dumped on *Uncanny*. "So far, there haven't been any requests for clarification from any of the departments, but that will change."

"Of course," Joel said. "And our course and speed?"

"Heading directly for Haverford," Thompson said. "I estimate that we will reach the planned emergence point in approximately thirty-seven hours. But we can alter course on your command."

Joel shook his head. "Weapons and defenses?"

"All unlocked," Thompson said. "We can fly and fight the ship."

Unless we take heavy damage, Joel thought. *We can't hope to keep control while running damage control teams all over the* Uncanny.

He glanced at Julia. "Did you unlock the entire datanet?"

"All, save for the captain's sealed core," Julia said. She sounded annoyed. "There's a very different set of protections on it. I'll crack it eventually, but . . ."

"The captain can be forced to unlock it for us," Joel said simply. He *knew* very little about command-grade sealed cores, but none of the rumors he'd heard were encouraging. If Julia made a single mistake, the entire unit would turn to dust. "As long as we can fly the ship, it doesn't matter."

"I can try," Julia said.

"Let me see if we can get it out of Sir William first," Joel said. He looked at Rochester. "You can handle the helm?"

"Of course, *Captain*," Rochester said. "You had me drilling on it, remember?"

Joel nodded. Cross-training *was* important, after all. He doubted the Admiralty would be pleased when they found out what *he'd* done with it. Thankfully, Captain Abraham and Commander Greenhill hadn't paid much attention to the training schedule. He'd trained up a whole new command staff under their noses, and they hadn't even *blinked*.

"Very good," Joel said. "Take the helm. Keep us on course."

Thompson frowned. "Captain," he said. He swallowed hard. "Captain, we are meant to link up with *Lightning* at Haverford."

"I know," Joel said. "We're going to meet up with her and destroy her."

He went on before anyone could muster a response. "*Lightning* is the one thing standing between us and the ultimate objective," he reminded them. "She has to be destroyed before she can interfere. She has *no* reason to believe we are hostile. We fly up to her and blast her at point-blank range before she can raise her shields."

"This is madness," Thompson said. "Captain, if we alter course now, we will be well on our way out of the sector before *Lightning* has any reason to suspect trouble. We could be halfway across the galaxy before Tyre realizes that there was a mutiny."

"We need *Lightning* gone," Joel reminded him. "It's as simple as that, *Commander*."

He leaned back in the command chair, keeping his face impassive. Thompson might verbally protest, but he was too much of a coward to do anything. Even if he managed to return control of the ship to her rightful captain, he would still have to explain his own conduct. He was damn lucky that his victims hadn't pressed charges. Perhaps the thought of him suffering on *Uncanny* had been enough to mollify them.

"Thomas, assemble the rest of the group and then start isolating the remainder of the crew as planned," Joel continued. There was no point in letting them think the matter was up for debate. "If they are willing to join us, then put them in the lower hold for the moment; everyone else can be held in the main shuttlebay, save for the officers. Leave Marine Country strictly alone."

"Yes, Captain," Rochester said.

Trying to radiate power and ease, Joel grinned as Rochester left the bridge. "Thompson, can you draw a bead on the colonist-carrier?"

"Yes, sir," Thompson said. The tactical display shifted. "Passive lock, engaged; active lock, disengaged."

Joel nodded curtly. "Blow her away."

"Aye, Captain," Thompson said. "Missile away."

Uncanny shuddered as she launched a single missile towards the target. Joel watched grimly as the missile slammed into the colonist-carrier and detonated, blowing the freighter into a fireball that vanished rapidly within hyperspace. He waited, but hyperspace remained quiet. All traces of the colonist-carrier were gone.

"Target destroyed," Thompson said. At such range, the crew would have no time to react before it was already too late. "Captain . . . why?"

"Because they deserved to die," Joel said simply. "And because we needed the target practice."

And to get more blood on your hands, he added, silently.

He smirked up at the tactical display. They were pirates . . . competition, as far as he was concerned. It was a shame about the crew of the freighter, but unless he missed his guess, they were smugglers. No one would miss them.

"Keep us on course," he ordered. Soon the remainder of the crew would realize that something was wrong, but the die had been cast. They were trapped, isolated, and alone. "And start running through tactical simulations. I want a comprehensive plan for destroying *Lightning*."

Thompson looked pale. "And what about . . .?"

Joel rose and strode over to the tactical console. "You will have your reward after *Lightning* is blown out of space," he said. "Until then . . . I expect you to run simulations for the next few hours, then get some rest, alone. Do *not* even *think* about trying anything stupid. Do you understand me?"

Thompson edged backwards. "Yes, sir."

"Good," Joel said. He touched the knife at his belt. "I'd hate to have to cut it off, *Commander*. You can have your fun afterwards."

He eyed the younger man until he quailed, then walked back to the command chair. There wouldn't be any problems from Thompson. The man was a sadomasochistic asshole. He *liked* it when his partners hurt, or bled. Joel had no idea how he'd managed to get through the academy—Thompson was addicted to his sex games—but he couldn't help thinking that Thompson would fit in very well with a pirate crew. He was already diseased.

He won't last for long, Joel added silently. *I won't let him live after Lightning has been destroyed.*

He forced himself to relax as *Uncanny* continued on her way. Taking the ship hadn't been hard once he'd obtained the weapons, but *Lightning* was a dangerous complication. She had to be taken by surprise.

If we can force the captain to cooperate, he thought, *taking her by surprise will be easy.*

CHAPTER THIRTY-FIVE

William felt sick.

It was hard, so hard, to think clearly as he fought his way back to awareness. His entire body felt numb, as if he were caught in quicksand; his thoughts felt sluggish, as if nothing quite made sense. It felt like hours before he was able to recall what had happened, who had stunned him and left him bound on the floor of his cabin. It felt like hours more before he put the pieces together and worked out what was going on.

A mutiny, he thought through a haze of nausea. *The senior chief is leading a mutiny.*

He swallowed hard to keep from throwing up, forcing himself to *think*. The mutiny had to have been planned for a long time. Nothing had happened, as far as he knew, to push the plotters into drawing up the plan and striking within the week. If anything, there had been plenty of good reasons *not* to have a mutiny. Hadn't the crew, under his command, earned a huge bonus? No, the plot had to have been formulated while Captain Abraham had been in command . . .

They want the ship, he told himself. A dozen crewmen could have easily deserted on Jorlem or Vangelis and, as long as they were careful, never be caught. *They want the ship and then* . . ..

He forced his eyes to open and looked around. The cabin lights were dim, red warning signals blinking on and off. They'd put the ship in lockdown, he realized. They hadn't subverted the entire crew. He was relieved and worried in equal measure. If he managed to break free, he could find help . . . but if the mutineers didn't control the entire crew, they might simply space the remaining shipmates as soon as possible. They might have done it already.

William cursed as he tugged uselessly at his bonds. He'd lost the ship. There hadn't been a single mutiny in the entire history of the Navy until now. Even if he regained control, no one would ever trust him with a ship again. Maybe the *Uncanny*'s curse hadn't been beaten after all . . .

He cleared his head. The situation was bad, but that was no excuse for giving in. There would be a chance to break free. And when it came, he had to take it.

The hatch hissed open. He rolled over and looked up just in time to see the senior chief stride confidently inside. A large automatic pistol was positioned prominently on his belt; he carried a datapad in one hand, keying it as he moved into the cabin. Someone had to have isolated the entire subsection of the datanet, William concluded. Even if he managed to get to his terminal, he probably wouldn't be able to use it to call for help.

"Sir William," the senior chief said.

"That's *Captain* to you," William snapped. Maybe it would be better to be submissive, but he couldn't bring himself to bend his knee to a mutineer. "You'll never get away with this."

The senior chief knelt down beside him. "I already have," he said. "*Uncanny* is very tiny on an intersteilar scale. No one is going to find us unless we let them."

Christopher G. Nuttall

"*Uncanny* also requires a constant supply of spare parts," William sneered. The hull would last for decades, perhaps centuries, but the starship's innards were a different story. "How do you intend to *find* them? Turn pirate and raid the Navy's supply dumps?"

"I already have solutions to most of those problems," the senior chief said. He met William's eyes. "And I'm sure you know why I've kept you alive."

William glared daggers at him. "You're going to take *my* ship and turn her into a pirate cruiser," he said. "You've *seen* the aftermath of pirate attacks . . . are you planning to loot, rape, and kill your way across the entire sector?"

The senior chief showed a flash of raw anger. "Of course not," he said. "I have something better in mind."

"Really," William said. He snorted. "You intend to sell this ship to the Theocracy?"

"The Theocracy certainly believes that's what I have in mind," Joel said. "I had to bargain with them for weapons. All the hacks I had planned to take weapons from the lockers were foiled by you."

"You're welcome," William said dryly.

The Senior Chief ignored the jibe. "This ship is the most powerful unit in the sector, excepting only *Lightning* and *Glory of God*," he said. "I intend to take her and put together a vest-pocket empire of my own."

William stared. "You're insane," he said. "Do you honestly believe the Commonwealth will let you get away with it?"

"The first king was a lucky bandit," the senior chief said. "This sector has a great deal of potential, if united under the right hand. The Commonwealth will probably be glad of the chance to open negotiations with a single power rather than a number of deeply corrupt worlds. Think what Jorlem could become if she actually had a *decent* government."

His demeanor changed. "The pirates are just parasites," he added. "Think what *they* could do if their energies were harnessed to a greater goal."

"Like I said, you're insane," William said. "I think you've been on this ship too long and it has addled your mind."

"Perhaps," Joel said. "But really . . . how many of my supporters, do you think, are *colonials*? Men and women who found themselves constantly left behind by the Tyre-born? How pleased were *you*, Sir William, when they gave a command that should have been yours to a girl young enough to be your daughter?"

He smirked. "Why should we be loyal, *Sir William*? The Commonwealth has not been loyal to us."

William's mind raced, trying to keep up with what he was being told. The man was either lying or certifiably mad. And yet, William didn't believe that Gibson *was* lying. *Uncanny* wouldn't be a very effective pirate ship, not in the long run. She could cut a swath through most convoy escorts for a couple of years, but then successive system failures would cripple her. Using her to carve out a small empire might be an effective use of her firepower, particularly if the senior chief somehow managed to conceal his involvement from the Commonwealth. If he could take control of Jorlem or Vangelis . . .

It was madness, utter madness. But the plan just might work.

William bowed his head and took a breath before looking up. "Forget this lunacy," he said. "Surrender now and I'll see to it that you get a life sentence on a penal world rather than the hangman's noose."

"A slow death sentence," the senior chief said sharply. "Sir William, be reasonable. If you cooperate with me, I will dump you and your loyalists on Haverford. You can survive there until you are picked up. If you *don't* cooperate with me . . . we have ways of making you talk."

"I think you need to say that in a bad accent," William said. The senior chief's face darkened, but he said nothing in return. "My implants won't let you force information out of me."

"No," Joel agreed. "On the other hand, a couple of my followers have . . . tendencies that would have got them arrested, if they hadn't managed to evade all suspicion. I'll set them loose on a couple of the young female crewmen. You can watch."

"You *bastard*," William said. "You . . ."

"Perhaps," Joel said. "But really, after spending a couple of years watching how this ship was allowed to decay, I find it hard to care about crossing lines. I will do whatever I have to do."

William wasn't afraid of pain or torture, even though he knew his implants would kill him if it seemed as if he would break. He *was* afraid of watching his crew suffer. He'd grown up on a world where protecting young women was practically hard-wired into the men. To be forced to watch them endure cruelty, to be helpless to stop it . . . wasn't something he could withstand. The senior chief knew it.

"Give me the command codes," Joel said. "You owe the Navy nothing. A man of your talents should be sitting in a command chair of his own . . ."

"I *was* sitting in a command chair of my own," William snarled.

"Yes, you were," Joel agreed. "You should have been given a command chair a great deal sooner."

He shrugged. "At any rate, I have to deal with *Lightning*," he added. "After that . . . well, we'll see if we can make you talk."

William stared. "Deal with *Lightning*?"

"I can't have another heavy cruiser running around the sector," Joel said. "I can take the ship out before she realizes she's under attack. Then there will be no one left to stop me."

He turned and headed towards the hatch. "You can think about it," he called back. "And about just how much loyalty you owe the Navy."

William glared at Joel's back as he strode out of the hatch, then looked frantically around the cabin. No weapons in sight. He needed to break free, but he didn't know how . . . would someone come to save him? Or did the remainder of the crew even *know* the ship had been taken?

He started to roll towards the side table. It wasn't easy to move with his hands bound behind his back, but he made it. The coffee mug Janet had brought him was still there, right on the edge of the table. Bracing himself, he forced his way up and tipped the mug over the side. It struck the deck and broke into more than a dozen pieces, some sharp enough to cut their way through duct tape. Somehow, struggling desperately, he managed to make enough of a cut in his restraints to pull his hands free.

Crap, he thought as he freed his legs. *They'll have locked down the entire ship.*

William checked the terminal, just in case, but it was locked out of the datanet. The two datapads he kept in his drawer were active, yet they couldn't establish a link to the datanet either. He swore and then recovered the pistol from his wardrobe. He headed for the hatch. Someone had scrambled the access permissions so thoroughly, he discovered, that even the captain's override couldn't open the hatch. Plus, there might well be a guard on the far side.

Damn it, he thought.

Despair threatened to overcome him for a long second. He forced the feeling aside as he headed for the maintenance tube and opened the hatch. The air inside smelled musty—someone had turned off the lights—but he recovered a flashlight from the emergency supplies and climbed into the hatch anyway. There was no point in hiding where he'd gone, but he still pushed the hatch closed behind him. It might just slow any pursuit down for a few seconds.

He crawled down the shaft and into an intersection. The lights were working, but the hatches that would have led farther into the ship were sealed. But they were *designed* to be opened from the inside, if necessary. He removed a multi-tool from the emergency kit and went to work, silently grateful for his odd career path. Captain Abraham probably wouldn't have known how to jimmy the hatch if he'd thought to use the tubes to escape.

It occurred to him, a moment too late, that the mutineers might have left a guard in the tubes too, but it didn't seem too likely. The senior chief couldn't have subverted more than a few dozen crewmembers at most.

Some of the worst were rotated out when I took command, William thought. There was no one on the far side of the hatch. *I must have crippled his planning, quite by accident.*

He headed further down into the ship, thinking of his time on the *Uncanny*. He'd been *impressed* with the senior chief. Joel Gibson had seemed ideal, a surprisingly good man in a starship permanently on the verge of breaking apart. William had been relieved to have a competent man in the post. None of the officers had spoken badly of him, so William hadn't bothered to look too closely. Yet, if he had, what would he have seen?

Most of the decay was cosmetic, William thought sourly. The senior chief had probably played a role in that too. Uncanny *looked bad when I took command, but she was in working order.*

The next set of hatches opened on command, taking him down towards Main Engineering and, he hoped, help. There was no point in trying to get to the militia. Marine Country could be completely sealed. William only hoped that the senior chief hadn't tried to pump out the atmosphere and kill the militiamen. If Joel wasn't bluffing about his plans to take out *Lighting*, William didn't have very long to regain control of *Uncanny*.

He's mad, William thought.

He shook his head in disbelief. It was easy to understand the resentment spreading through the crew, certainly prior to his assumption of command. Two-thirds of the starship's crew had been assigned to *Uncanny* in lieu of dismissing them from the Navy. Many of the others were colonials who'd watched helplessly as others were promoted ahead of them. Captain Abraham had certainly done nothing to repair morale or turn his crew into a coherent unit; he'd been more interested in stripping the ship bare for a quick buck. Yes, William could understand why the crew had wanted to mutiny . . .

. . . But to plan to take over the *sector*?

He's cracked, William thought. The plan was sheer lunacy. *He has to be out of his mind.*

He braced himself as he reached the bottom of the shaft. Main Engineering was just below him, but he knew he'd need help to take control. He couldn't believe that *everyone* in the compartment, including Goodrich, was a mutineer. If that was the case, he was roundly screwed. Gritting his teeth, he opened the hatch and crawled out into the corridor. There was no one in sight. But the faint hum of the drives was steadily getting louder. *Uncanny* had to be nearing her destination.

If the engineering crew are prisoners, William thought, *they'll be kept in the wardroom closest to the department.*

He slipped down the corridor and glanced around the corner. A young man was standing guard outside the compartment, cradling an assault rifle in his hands. William hated to think what Patrick Davidson or Major Lupine would have said about his stance—the man looked as if he was *posing*, rather than standing guard—but there was no time. He drew his pistol and walked around the corner.

"Freeze," William snapped. He didn't want to shoot one of his crew, but he wouldn't hesitate to pull the trigger if there was no other choice. If William was recaptured, the senior chief wouldn't leave him alone again. "Don't move!"

The guard stared at him. William tensed—if the guard wanted to do something stupid, this was the ideal moment—as he walked up to the crewman and took the assault rifle. The crewman still looked shocked, horrified beyond words. William stepped back and motioned for him to open the hatch. The crewman paled but obeyed.

"Captain!" Goodrich yelled. He and a dozen other crewmen were lying on the deck, their hands and legs bound with duct tape. "Thank God!"

William nodded to the crewman. "Free them."

The crewman swallowed, hard. "Captain . . ."

"Help us now and I'll speak for you," William said firmly. He wasn't willing to make any other bargains, not yet. "Free them."

He watched, in some relief, as the crewman went to work. As soon as the engineering crew was free, William ordered two of them to bind the crewman and leave him in the wardroom. He then led the remainder out into the corridor.

"They've taken Main Engineering," Goodrich said. He sounded pissed. William was relieved. An angry man would be more helpful than someone who had given in to despair. "Captain, what are we going to do?"

"Recover the ship," William said. He did his best to sound confident. "If we recapture Main Engineering, we should be able to lock them out of the control datanet."

He passed Goodrich the assault rifle, then led the way down to Main Engineering. The hatch was unguarded, but sealed. Goodrich knelt down with a multi-tool and went to work. A moment later, the hatch hissed open. Five of the twelve stations were manned; William cursed as he realized that two of the mutineers were clearly engineering crewmen. The senior chief had had *far* too much time to turn the crew against him . . .

"Get away from the consoles," William shouted, waving his pistol. "Keep your hands where I can see them!"

The mutineers stared in abject fear and did as they were told. William watched grimly as they were bound and gagged, then pushed into a corner. There was no time to do anything else with them.

"The system has been locked down," Goodrich said as he bent over one of the consoles. He scowled. "It's a pretty crude piece of work, Captain, but powering down the ship is probably impossible."

"Shit," William said.

A low rumble ran through the ship. The drive hum rose to a crescendo, then faded back into the background. He cursed under his breath as he realized what the sounds portended.

"I've got a link to the tactical display," Goodrich said. A holographic image blinked to life in front of them. "Captain, we have arrived at Haverford."

William swore again. *Lightning* was clearly visible on the display, holding low orbit over Haverford. *Uncanny* was flying right towards her . . .

Their time had just run out.

CHAPTER THIRTY-SIX

"We didn't know where the goods came from, Captain," Governor Younghusband said. His voice was wavering between defiance and bitter resignation. "But we were in no position to ask questions."

"I understand your position," Kat said. She had been relieved, in some ways, to arrive at Haverford and find that the planet was *not* occupied by the pirates. Nonetheless, the discovery also forced her to play the heavy, threatening a planetary government that was in no state to stand up to a pirate vessel, let alone a genuine warship. "However, I must point out that accepting stolen goods is not conducive to your interstellar reputation."

"I am aware of the dangers," Younghusband said. "But I am also aware of the *other* set of dangers."

"I understand," Kat said. "We will be running patrols through the system on a regular basis."

The two exchanged a few more polite formalities before finally ending the conversation. Kat groaned as she sat back in her chair, feeling frustration mixed with bitter guilt. Haverford was *naked*. Even a gunboat could launch punitive strikes that would bring the planetary government to heel, assuming the government dared to stand up to the pirates at all. Who could blame them for rolling over? Their population was terrifyingly vulnerable.

We just need to expand our convoy protections, she thought. *Make it impossible for the pirates to actually get their hands on the loot.*

Her intercom buzzed. "Captain," Crenshaw said. "*Uncanny* just entered the system. She'll link up with us in seventeen minutes."

"Very good," Kat said. "Invite Sir William to dine with us this evening. We need to plan the next set of patrols."

"Aye, Captain," Crenshaw said.

Kat took one last look at the terminal, then rose. There was little else they could do on Haverford as long as they weren't staying in the system. The planetary government had no technological base and thus couldn't operate even a small starship to protect its orbital space. Given time, Kat was sure, the pirates would move away as the pool of potential targets shrank, but there would be a great many uncomfortable days for vulnerable worlds before the threat was finally gone.

She walked onto the bridge. *Uncanny* was clearly visible on the display, her tactical staff running tracking exercises as she neared *Lightning*. Perhaps there would be time for a *genuine* exercise, Kat thought, as she took her chair. A proper war game would give both crews a chance to shine.

"Mr. Crenshaw, work out a plan for a war game," she ordered. "We can stay in this system for a couple of days, I think."

"Aye, Captain," Crenshaw said.

◆ ◆ ◆

"Weapons locked on target," Thompson said. "Passive locks only; I say again, passive locks only."

Joel allowed himself a moment of cold anticipation as *Uncanny* hurried towards her target. *Lightning* was holding station in orbit above

Haverford, her shields and weapons down, her hull naked, defenseless. He'd run through the simulation a dozen times; if they fired from point-blank range, *Lightning* would have no chance to bring up her shields or return fire before his missiles slammed into her unprotected hull.

"Keep our shields on standby," he reminded Thompson. "Bring them up the moment we open fire."

"Aye, Captain," Thompson said. "Ten minutes to optimal firing range."

"Steady as she goes," Joel ordered. "I don't want them to see *any-thing* suspicious."

"Aye, Captain," Thompson said.

◆ ◆ ◆

"We're approaching *Lightning*," Goodrich reported. "We're already in missile range!"

"They won't fire until they're close enough to be certain of taking her out," William snapped angrily. The senior chief would be at a serious disadvantage if he matched his undermanned ship against a fully manned heavy cruiser. His only hope was to strike as hard as he could from point-blank range. "We need to shut down the power network!"

"I can't," an engineering officer said. William hadn't caught her name. "The command system has been scrambled!"

William entered his command codes. "No change," the officer reported. "The network cannot be powered down. We're locked out of the communications nodes too!"

Goodrich looked up. "We could physically shut down the fusion cores," he suggested. "It would cripple the ship, but it would keep her from launching an attack . . ."

"Maybe," William said. It would be risky as hell, too. "Can we bring *up* the tactical systems?"

"I think so," the officer said. Her fingers danced over the console for a long moment. "But what will *that* do?"

William smiled. "Alert *Lightning*," he said. "Bring them up. A full tactical sweep."

"Aye, Captain," the officer said.

The display flickered and updated. William braced himself. There was no way the senior chief would have risked using active sensors, particularly when he wouldn't have needed them to draw a bead on *Lightning*. But an active sensor sweep would alert Kat Falcone that *something* was up. *Uncanny* had already fired on one friendly ship. Perhaps she would fire on another.

"Get a couple of guards up to the far end of the corridor," he added. "They'll know we have Main Engineering now."

◆　◆　◆

Thompson's console started to bleep in alarm. "Captain," he said, "we just ran an active sensor sweep!"

Joel started. "*What?*"

"Confirmed," Julia said from her console. "Someone in Main Engineering just triggered the active sensors."

"Shit," Joel said. Someone had broken free? Who? He cursed as he pushed the matter aside for later contemplation. The plan had just failed spectacularly. "Fire! Fire now!"

"Aye, sir," Thompson said. "Firing . . . now!"

◆　◆　◆

"Captain," Weiberg snapped. "*Uncanny* just ran a tactical sweep! She's locked onto our hull!"

Kat froze, just for a heartbeat. *No one* in their right mind would run a tactical sweep as a joke. There was too much chance of triggering a tragic accident. *Uncanny* already had a reputation for friendly fire incidents. Had something gone badly wrong over there . . .?

"Raise shields," she snapped. "Evasive action! Stand by point defense!"

"Aye, Captain," Weiberg said. His console bleeped as new red icons flared to life on the display. "Captain, *Uncanny* has opened fire on us!"

"Deploy decoys," Kat ordered as sirens howled through her ship. Her blood ran cold. A few more minutes and there would have been no time to react before the missiles struck home. "Pull us back as hard as you can."

"Aye, Captain," Wheeler said.

"I have target locks," Weiberg added. "Captain?"

Kat hesitated. What was going on over there? She couldn't imagine William deciding to launch a barrage for a *laugh*. No, it had to be a systems failure . . . or what? Had someone else taken control of the ship? She could return fire; she could take *Uncanny* . . . but she had no idea what had actually happened. If she blew the ship out of space, she never would.

"Hold fire," she ordered, finally. "Helm, keep our distance."

She sucked in her breath as the missile barrage roared into the teeth of her point defense, dozens of icons vanishing as they were picked off, one by one. Whoever had programmed the assault hadn't done a good job, she noted; they'd fired too many antimatter missiles in a single barrage. The missiles were so bunched up that one missile being picked off tended to take out several more, setting off a chain reaction. The attacker clearly intended to hit her before she could react.

"They're locking onto our hull," Weiberg reported. "I . . ."

Two missiles slammed into the shields. Kat braced herself as the ship rocked, then let out a sigh of relief as the shields held. *Lightning* hadn't been damaged . . .

. . . but she was still left with one hell of a mess. If *Uncanny* had gone rogue, she had to be stopped, yet she didn't *know* that *Uncanny* had gone rogue.

"Keep a sharp eye on her gateway generator," she ordered as *Lightning* drew back from her sister ship. "If there's a hint she's preparing to jump into hyperspace, inform me at once."

"Aye, Captain," Weiberg said.

"Captain," Crenshaw said, "there were pirate prisoners on that ship."

Kat blanched. Could the prisoners have escaped? It was possible, she supposed, but weren't they supposed to be on the colonist-carrier? Where *was* the colonist-carrier? Had something happened in hyperspace, forcing William to take the prisoners onboard *Uncanny*? Or was the carrier just waiting in hyperspace until *Uncanny* confirmed the coast was clear?

"I know," she said. "If they're in control of the ship, Mr. XO, we can't take the risk of letting them escape."

"*Lightning's* not shooting back," Goodrich said.

"That won't last," William said grimly. "Captain Falcone will know this ship has gone rogue."

He glanced at Goodrich. "Destroy the power conduits," he ordered. "Throw the entire ship back on battery power."

"Aye, Captain," Goodrich said. "But that'll take down the shields!"

"I know," William said. If *Lightning* returned fire, *Uncanny* was doomed. But that was true in any case. "See to it."

He closed his eyes for a moment. Roach had been on the bridge, he recalled, when William had been stunned. No doubt he was a prisoner too now . . . If anything happened to William, command authority would devolve onto Goodrich. The mutineers had to be insane . . . no, they couldn't *all* be insane. By now, they had to know they were screwed.

"I'm going to the bridge," he said firmly. "I want you to cut the power, then concentrate on getting a signal out to *Lightning*. Tell Captain Falcone we need marines."

Goodrich paled. "Aye, Captain."

"And if they counterattack, concentrate on holding the compartment," William added. "Hold it as long as you can."

He braced himself, then headed for the hatch.

◆ ◆ ◆

"Captain," Thompson said, "*Lightning* is keeping her distance."

Perhaps challenging *Lightning* had been a mistake, Joel realized. But the logic had been sound. The Admiralty wouldn't realize that something had happened to both cruisers and dispatch someone to investigate for months. Joel couldn't have a heavy cruiser running around while he was building his empire.

"We should get out of here," Rochester added. "We can't take her in a straight fight."

"Well, then she'll come right after us!" Joel barked. The plan had gone a little off the rails, but it wasn't over yet. He gripped the pistol at his belt, wondering if he'd have to start shooting members of his inner circle. "We have to take her out now."

He closed his eyes for a long moment. "Detach a team from life support and send them down to Main Engineering," he ordered. "I want that compartment retaken before they manage to cut the power."

"Aye, Captain," Rochester said.

Sweat trickled down Joel's back. The plan had *definitely* gone off the rails, but he couldn't withdraw. *Lightning* would follow them into hyperspace if necessary. He'd never have a chance to take control of the pirate fleets and lead them to victory. His empire would be stillborn . . .

No, he thought, grimly. *I've come too far to be stopped now.*

He rested one hand on his pistol. Things had gone wrong, but he could still win. And he would win, even if he had to kill more of his own people to keep the rest of them in line.

"Captain," Julia said. "They're interfering with the main computer datanet . . ."

"Then lock them out, you stupid bitch," Joel snapped. "*Deal with it!*"

◆　◆　◆

William felt cold as he heard footsteps running down the corridor towards him. They had to be mutineers. The remainder of the starship was still in lockdown. He'd considered trying to free more of the crew, or the militiamen, but he doubted he had the time. William reached for his pistol, then stopped himself as the mutineers came into view. Thankfully there was no sign of the senior chief.

"Stop," the leader barked. He stared at William just as the lights dimmed. "Captain . . . I . . ."

William strode forward. "The main power grid has gone down," he said. "Shields and weapons are already gone. There is no way this ship can get into hyperspace before *Lightning* blows her apart. The mutiny has failed."

The mutineers outnumbered him. They could have stopped him at any moment. But they did nothing.

"The senior chief is a traitor," William added. It was as good an explanation as any. "He's a deep-cover agent who intends to hand this ship, and her crew, over to the Theocracy. Do you really want to spend the rest of your days in a prison camp?"

He kept walking forward. "Put down your guns, and I'll see to it that you get to survive," he added. If he knew Kat Falcone, she was already dispatching the marines. There was nothing stopping them from landing on the hull. With main power down, *Uncanny*'s point defense would be down too. "Stay here and you will be collected."

Walking past them, knowing that any one of them could shoot him at any moment, was the hardest thing William had ever done. He *knew* he didn't dare show any hint of weakness. A tingle ran down his spine as he strode onwards, but he didn't turn or walk faster. He just kept walking up to the bridge, ignoring the chatter behind him. The mutineers didn't seem to know what to do.

Get to the bridge, he told himself. *Get to the bridge and put an end to this.*

"Chief," Rochester said. "The captain . . . he's on his way."

Joel turned to face him. "What do you mean . . . he's on his way?"

"He's walking towards the bridge," Rochester said.

"Stop him," Joel ordered. "Get someone to block his way!"

"There's no one in place," Rochester said.

Joel drew his pistol, fighting down the insane urge to giggle. The plan had failed. The plan had failed completely. Everything he'd done to make it work, from assassinating Captain Abraham to convincing the Theocracy to give him the weapons he needed to take the ship . . . it had all been for nothing. *Uncanny* had lost main power; she was floating dead in space, under the guns of another heavy cruiser. He couldn't even blow up the ship and call it a draw! By the time he managed to deactivate an antimatter storage node, the whole affair would be over.

"We lost," Thompson said. "Captain . . ."

Joel shot him in the back of the head. Filthy degenerate. Thompson had his uses, but there was no way Joel would let him live. Now he was an example to the remainder of the bridge crew. Let them see, let them *all* see, what happened to those who defied him.

But there's no point, a small voice said at the back of his mind. It sounded terrifyingly like Thompson. *You've lost.*

He swung around as the hatch hissed open. There had been a guard on the hatch, he knew, but the traitorous bastard had just stepped aside. *Fuck him,* Joel thought, as he lifted his pistol. He didn't need anyone to kill Sir William. Whoever had freed the captain would suffer!

"You're dead," he said. He pointed the pistol between William's eyes. "You're dead."

"It's over," William said. He showed no trace of fear. "This mutiny is at an end."

"Don't be stupid," Joel growled.

"Give up without further ado, and you'll live to see another day," William told him. "The marines are already on their way. You've lost. You don't have a hope of surviving unless you give up . . ."

"Fuck you," Joel said. "I won't . . ."

There was a flash of blue-white light. The world fell into darkness.

William lifted an eyebrow politely, as the senior chief crashed to the deck. Crewwoman Julia Transom—he vaguely remembered her as a tactical staffer—looked back at him, her eyes wide with fear and a strange kind of desperate hope.

"I'm sorry, sir," she mumbled. William honestly wasn't sure who she was talking to. "I just . . ."

"Never mind," he said gently. He looked at the other mutineers. "Remove your interference from the computer network, then open hailing frequencies. I need to talk to Captain Falcone before she blows the ship out of space."

"Aye, Captain," Julia said.

"And then get me a link to the militiamen," he added. "We're going to need them to secure the ship."

He took the command chair, shaking his head in disbelief. Perhaps the senior chief *had* been a deep-cover agent. It made about as much sense as anything else, although finding out the truth would have to wait until the bastard could be interrogated. But then, any *reasonable* deep-cover agent would have exploited his position in a hundred different ways. The grand plan to build an empire of his own? Perhaps it had been true after all.

If Captain Abraham had remained in command, William thought, *Gibson would have gotten away with it.*

Kat Falcone's face popped into existence in front of him. "William," she said. "What *happened?*"

"We had a mutiny," William said. The tactical display updated sharply. A trio of assault shuttles were already on their way. "But I think it's under control now."

"Glad to hear it," Kat said. She sounded dazed. "The marines are still on their way."

"I look forward to seeing them," William said. He knew Kat wouldn't call them back on his say-so. For all she knew, someone could have a gun aimed at his back. "And after that . . ."

He closed his eyes momentarily and then returned his gaze to Kat. "I think I have an idea."

CHAPTER THIRTY-SEVEN

"You need to watch your back," Davidson said as Kat stepped off the shuttle and into *Uncanny*. "There might be undiscovered mutineers among the crew."

There had been seventy-five mutineers in all according to the survivors, all of whom had already been part of the crew when Sir William had taken command. Joel Gibson had done a very good job of picking his targets carefully. Not all of them had fully understood what was going on, but none of them had snitched to higher authority and blown the whole conspiracy wide open. Of course, none of them had had any reason to *trust* higher authority.

They're mostly colonials, she thought sourly. *Crenshaw is going to love that!*

"Kat . . ." William said. He looked tired and worn, a man in desperate need of a shower. "I wish you were visiting under better circumstances."

"So do I," Kat said, offering a tender voice to her friend. The mutiny had been planned long before William had taken command, but that wouldn't keep him from getting a large share of the blame. "Do you think matters are under control now?"

"The surviving mutineers have been tossed into the brig," William said. "They seem to have different ideas about just what Gibson had in mind. Some thought they were turning pirate, some thought they were going to sell the ship, some genuinely believed they could put together an empire of their own. But none of them betrayed him until it was clear the scheme had fallen through."

Kat nodded. "He must have been out of his mind."

"It looks that way," William said. "Everyone agrees he was losing control from the moment he failed to destroy *Lightning*."

"Yeah," Kat said. She hadn't had the *slightest* idea *Uncanny* had turned hostile until picking up the cruiser's tactical sweep. A few seconds of delay and her starship would have been effortlessly destroyed. "He came far too close to success."

She turned to walk beside him as they headed up the corridor, Davidson following behind. "I can leave you one of the marine platoons for the moment, if that's any help," she said. "But I understand that you have something in mind . . .?"

"Gibson decided to dicker with the Theocracy to get weapons," William said. "Only two of his most devoted followers knew it."

Kat nodded. No one in their right mind would trust the Theocracy to keep its side of the bargain. Turning pirate or even building an empire was one thing, but dealing with the Theocracy was another.

"He told them that he'd hand *Uncanny* and her crew over to the Theocracy," William added. "The Theocracy was delighted at the prospect of such an intelligence coup."

Kat winced. Merely capturing the computer files alone would be a major victory for the Theocracy. *Uncanny* didn't know *everything*, of course, but there was plenty of data in routine updates from Tyre that the Theocracy would find very helpful. At that point, they'd have insights into encryption programs, fleet deployments, planned rest and refit cycles . . .

"He told the Theocracy that he was going to take *Uncanny* back to Jorlem and make the swap there," William added. "I was thinking this would be the perfect opportunity to give the Theocracy a nasty surprise."

"Attack them when they enter point-blank weapons range," Kat mused. "Precisely what Gibson intended to do to us."

"Yep," William agreed. "They *did* give Gibson some IFF codes. If we use them ourselves, we can lure *Glory of God* into firing range."

"And engage her well away from Jorlem itself," Kat said. It wouldn't be *that* hard. Hell, the Theocracy would probably be delighted at making the swap well away from any inconvenient witnesses. "What if they refuse to take the bait?"

"We fall back and report home," William said. "If nothing else, we would have definite proof the Theocracy was planning to meddle in local politics."

Kat nodded in agreement. The Theocracy wouldn't have handed over a couple of crates of weapons on spec unless they had plenty to spare. Diplomatic pouches had always made convenient ways to smuggle something down to the surface without being detected, which was why embassies were generally carefully watched. But *this* embassy had been on Jorlem itself. The locals might not have noticed or cared that a Commonwealth spacer had entered the embassy.

"Very good," she said. It *was* too good an opportunity to miss. "How long will it take to get *Uncanny* back into working order?"

"The damage was minimal," William assured her. "My chief engineer wants to spend some additional time checking and rechecking the power links and datacores, but he thinks we can be underway in a couple of days."

"It'll give us enough time to draw up a plan," Kat said. "Did the Theocracy *know* Gibson intended to go after *Lightning*?"

"I don't think so," William said. "I think they would have objected."

Kat was inclined to agree. Mysteriously losing two heavy cruisers would have worried the Commonwealth, particularly as it would have taken several months for the Commonwealth to realize that both ships had gone missing but wouldn't materially affect the balance of power. The Theocracy stood to gain a great deal more if it had one of the cruisers to study, although Kat doubted that *that* would affect the balance of power either. If the latest updates were accurate, the Commonwealth would go on the offensive in less than six to nine months.

Then we won't stop until we drive them all the way back to their home-world and crush them in their lair, she thought. *And that will be the end.*

She turned to look at her former XO. "Do you think you can rely on your remaining crew?"

"I think I have to," William said. "Everyone's very shocked . . . but if Captain Abraham had remained in command, I think a great many more would have joined the mutineers."

William's face was suddenly overcome with gloom. "They killed him," he added. "They assassinated Captain Abraham."

"Shit," Kat said.

She'd wondered why the mutineers had continued with their plan even after a *decent* commanding officer had been assigned to *Uncanny*. Clearly they had committed themselves so thoroughly, they didn't have a choice. The truth would have been uncovered; Captain Abraham might have been a bastard, but the Navy would never have forgiven them for killing him. And even if they had deserted, they would have spent the rest of their lives with a shadow hanging over their heads.

"The Board of Inquiry is going to have fun with this one," she said. "*No one's* going to look good."

"I know," William said, his shoulders falling.

He sighed. "Once we're back underway, we can plan out the operation," he said. "Giving the Theocracy a major beating will do wonders for morale."

Kat nodded. While *Uncanny's* crew *had* had a major morale boost, Gibson had sent morale plunging back down to the bottom. At best, he'd been planning to dump everyone who refused to cooperate on Haverford; at worst, he'd been planning to kill them or hand them over to the Theocracy. Crewmembers wouldn't trust each other for a long time to come *unless* they did something that brought them back together again.

I hope to hell something else doesn't happen after that, she thought.

"Yes," she agreed. "Can you get Gibson to cooperate?"

"Absolutely," William said flatly.

◆ ◆ ◆

"Well," Joel said as William stepped into the brig. "Come to gloat?" He rose and strode over to the force field. "You won," he added. "But it was so *close*."

"Shut up," William said flatly. "I have an offer for you."

Joel lifted his eyebrows. "An *offer?*"

"I could put you out of the airlock right now," William said. "There's no doubt that you and your comrades killed at least nine people, including this vessel's former commanding officer, and committed the worst mutiny in our Navy's history."

"Which is not up against any particular competition," Joel observed. He studied the older man for a long moment. If Captain Abraham had remained in command . . . he sighed, dismissing the thought. "Let us not bandy words, *Captain*. What do you want from me?"

"We can lure *Glory of God* into a trap, if you help us," William said. "If you do, your sentence will be commuted to life on a penal colony."

"That isn't a very good offer," Joel said. "I've heard *stories* about penal colonies."

"You'll be dropped with the majority of your comrades," William said. "If you stick together, you'll have a good chance at surviving the . . . worst . . . of the colony. I'll even see to it that you get weapons."

"Which will be useless when we run out of ammunition," Joel pointed out.

"Some of the really primitive stuff can be duplicated," William said. He stepped closer, his nose practically pressing against the force field. "You had a plan, but the plan went off the rails as soon as I took command. Really, you should have just deserted when we reached Jorlem and vanished. But you tried to carry out the plan anyway. You failed and you were caught. Your only hope for seeing another day is to cooperate with me."

His eyes met Joel's. "You can be dropped on a penal world with your comrades and enough weapons to give you a fighting chance," he said. "Your descendants will eventually rejoin the Commonwealth on equal terms. Or you can be pitched out of an airlock, your body drifting through space until it falls into a star. Your name will be remembered in infamy."

"At least it will be *remembered*," Joel said.

William's face twisted. "You would sooner die than take the chance to build something new?"

Joel looked down at the deck. He *had* failed. He'd known the moment he recovered from the stun bolt that the only thing he had to look forward to was the hangman's noose, assuming the captain didn't just toss him into space. None of his former allies would follow him now. He'd led them straight to disaster. He doubted he could cow all of them once they were down on the surface. He might be better off cutting loose from the rest of the mutineers as soon as they landed and flee into the hinterland.

At least it will be a chance, he thought.

He met his former commander's eyes. "I *will* build something great," he said. "And if there are enough of us, I will take the world."

It wouldn't be easy, he knew. There were no embassies on penal colonies, but he'd heard rumors. The strongest among the convicts ruled; everyone else did as they were told and tried not to be noticed. Some settlements failed because the involuntary colonists didn't know how to grow food and didn't care to learn. His people, at least, would have the discipline to feed themselves . . .

If they don't kill me at once, he thought. *But it is a chance . . .*

"Very well," he said. "I'll do as you wish."

"Good," William said. "And now that that's settled . . . why?"

To remain alive, Joel thought. But he knew that wasn't the *real* question. *Why did I mutiny?*

A dozen answers ran through his head. He'd resented being assigned to *Uncanny*, just like everyone else; he'd resented having to deal with Captain Abraham and his gang of aristocratic criminals. And he'd resented the lack of promotion, the lack of chances to improve his career . . . he'd known, deep inside, that he could be more than a simple crewman on a single ship.

But Joel also desired money and power. He'd known too much poverty and powerlessness in his life.

"We're not that different," he said finally.

William's face hardened. "I'm nothing like you."

"Yes, you are," Joel said. "You're the colonial who became a mustang and slowly, so slowly, worked his way up to command rank. You remained loyal, even though there was no *reason* to remain loyal. I'm the man who saw all of his potential career paths blocked by his superiors, the one who witnessed too much mistreatment to have any loyalty to the Navy. If things had been different, you could have been *me*."

"I am a man of honor," William said tightly.

"Yes, you are," Joel said, "but how long would you have *remained* a man of honor if you had never risen in the ranks? Loyalty is a two-way street."

He exhaled, hard, and then steadied himself. "If you hadn't earned so much loyalty from the crew," Joel admitted quietly, "you would have lost your ship to me."

"Captain," Roach said. "All systems check out A-OK. We are ready to depart."

William barely heard his XO. He was not a man given to brooding, but—no matter how he might have wished to deny it—Joel Gibson's words had touched a nerve. What *would* he have become if his ambitions had been denied? If there had been no pathway to advancement? If he'd been stuck in a dead-end post on a ship everyone regarded as a dumping ground for incompetents, losers, and outright criminals? Might he too have been tempted to mutiny?

Taking Uncanny wouldn't have been difficult, he thought. *But what would I have done afterwards.*

He would have preferred to believe, despite himself, that Joel Gibson had been working for the Theocracy. A major security breach, of course, but such a discovery would have been preferable to learning that some of his own crew were plotting a mutiny. The repercussions would shake the military to its foundations, crushing whatever faith the Navy had in its colonial officers. He'd be lucky not to be dismissed from the service even though he'd recovered his ship. He *had* been in command when all hell had broken loose.

This will lead to more resentments, he thought. *And that will cause more problems at the worst possible time.*

Roach cleared his throat. "Captain?"

William lurched to attention. Woolgathering was bad enough, but being caught woolgathering on the bridge was worse, far worse. But then he was in deep shit already.

"Check with *Lightning*, then open a gateway," he ordered. There was no point in dwelling on what awaited him when he returned to Tyre. "Set course for Jorlem."

"Aye, Captain," Cecelia said.

If we survive the next few days, William thought, *we'll probably be recalled to Tyre at once.*

William watched as the gateway opened, *Lightning* following *Uncanny* into hyperspace as they set course for Jorlem. If they caught *Glory of God* by surprise, they'd have a decent chance to destroy her before she managed to launch a counterattack. There was no way to know just how far the Theocracy was prepared to trust Gibson. He'd certainly never *planned* to hand *Uncanny* over to them.

"Mr. XO, you have the bridge," William said. He took one last look at the tactical display. There was no sign of anything that might keep them from their destination. "Keep us on our current course."

"Aye, Captain," Roach said.

William stepped through the hatch and into his Ready Room. Janet—who had been held in her quarters, along with most of the crew—had placed a mug of coffee on the desk, but she'd made no attempt to clean up the mess. Gibson had searched the Ready Room thoroughly, hunting for . . . *something*. It looked as though he'd tried to crack the safe too, but it had clearly defeated him. William sat down in front of his desk, keying his terminal to bring it to life. He had to write a report . . .

. . . But he was unsure what to write.

He looked down at the blank screen for a long moment. Bad news had been reported to the Admiralty before. Kat had had to write a comprehensive report after the Fall of Cadiz, which had included a description of the precautions she'd taken to save as much of the fleet as she could, but this was different. This was mutiny . . . something inflicted on the Navy by one of its own. Whatever happened, there was no way the Navy would forget this day.

Many other colonials will be treated as scapegoats because of it, he thought sourly. It couldn't be covered up. There was no *way* it could be covered up. *There will be countless new resentments to pour fuel on the fire.*

He cursed Joel under his breath, savagely. Why couldn't he have just deserted? The entire plot would have vanished if the ringleaders had jumped ship. No one left behind would have known enough to resurrect it—or expose it. Captain Abraham's death would have been forever classed as an accident; just one more stroke of bad luck on a ship *known* for bad luck. Perhaps, just perhaps, it would have been forgotten soon enough. Captain Abraham's family probably wouldn't have asked too many questions after the truth about him came out. A criminal in the family . . .

Or perhaps there is some truth to the curse after all. He felt like a heel for thinking it—he had grown to love *Uncanny*. *This is a very unlucky ship.*

CHAPTER THIRTY-EIGHT

"This is either the intelligence coup of the decade," Ambassador Lord Cleric Abdullah said, "or an absolute disaster waiting to happen."

Inquisitor Bin Zaid smiled. His superior—who wouldn't be his superior much longer once news of his success got back home—didn't sound impressed. But then Bin Zaid had been careful to make it impossible for the Lord Cleric to claim more than a tiny fraction of the credit. He'd get *some*, of course; he just wouldn't be able to claim enough of it to keep Bin Zaid from getting the recognition he deserved. His career would take off like a rocket as soon as he handed *Uncanny* over to his superiors.

He held up the datapad. "They took the ship," he said. The message had arrived less than an hour ago. "They are waiting for us to come claim her."

"At a truly staggering cost," Abdullah said.

"It would be worth it at twice the price," Captain Samuel said. Bin Zaid knew the older man didn't like either of the others, but he still sounded awed. "A full-fledged enemy heavy cruiser to study."

He shook his head. "We'll be going out to investigate," he added. "If everything checks out, you can authorize the transfer."

Bin Zaid smirked. The mutineers apparently hadn't taken any precautions against treachery. Infidels could be remarkably trusting at times. If there were *no* precautions, there would be nothing stopping the janissaries from taking *Uncanny* and her entire crew, the mutineers as well as the loyalists. They would *all* be taken back to the Theocracy as spoils of war.

Then, my career will be pushed into orbit, he thought.

"We will also be careful," Samuel added. "This *could* be a trap."

"We don't want to scare them," Bin Zaid said hastily.

"No," Samuel said. "But we don't want to risk my ship, either."

Your ship, Bin Zaid thought. But there was no avoiding the fact that Samuel was in command of *Glory of God*. Even an Inquisitor couldn't overrule a captain without very good reason. *It doesn't matter, as long as everyone knows that* Uncanny *is my ship*.

"We'll depart orbit in five minutes," Samuel said. "You might want to spend the next hour in prayer."

"Under the circumstances, I'll pray on the bridge," Bin Zaid said. "They know me. They'll want to speak to me."

"As you wish," Samuel said.

Bin Zaid smiled as Samuel led the way to the bridge. The starship's captain wouldn't *want* an Inquisitor on his bridge, looking over his shoulder and perhaps contradicting him in front of the crew. But he had no choice. Bin Zaid refused to give up any more control over the affair. Let the Lord Cleric and the captain fume if they wished. This was *his* affair and *he* was the one who would reap the rewards.

His smile grew wider. *And why not? I was the one who saw the opportunity and took it.*

"Gateway opening, Captain," Roach reported. He'd taken the tactical console. "*Glory of God* has arrived."

William leaned forward as a single red icon flashed to life on the display. He'd half expected the battleship-battlecruiser to make the trip in realspace, but common sense had told him that was unlikely. *Glory of God* could be tracked in realspace. The locals might have wondered why she was heading to the system's second gas giant if they'd known she was heading there. They still might, he had to admit, but it hardly mattered. The Theocracy had clearly decided that the prize it had been offered was worth the risk of souring their relationship with the planetary government.

Not that they could do much with the government in any case, he thought darkly. *The president is doing his damnedest to sit on the fence.*

"Send her the prerecorded message," he ordered. "And then wait for her response."

"Aye, Captain," Stott said.

"Passive locks engaged," Roach reported. "Missile launch cycle is active; I say again, missile launch cycle is active."

"Hold your fire," William cautioned. Gibson had faced the same problem back when he'd attempted to take out *Lightning*. Firing too soon would give the enemy a chance to evade and return fire. "Do *not* give them any reason to suspect trouble."

They're probably already suspicious, he thought grimly. He and his crew had worked their way through as many possible options as they could imagine, but they'd been forced to conclude that they would have to play it by ear. *Mutineers offering to hand over an entire starship simply don't exist outside of thriller novels and movies.*

William kept a sharp eye on the display as *Glory of God* closed in on their position. *Lightning* was out there somewhere, under cloak. The plan called for *Lightning* to circle around and engage *Glory of God* from the rear, if she survived the first barrage, but there was no way to know if she was proceeding as planned. *Lightning*'s cloaking device was just too good. *Uncanny* had no way to track her progress.

If we did have such capabilities, he thought, Glory of God *would be able to track her too.*

"Picking up a signal," Stott said. "They're requesting permission to land boarders before handing over the cash."

"Deny it," William ordered. No one in their right mind would abandon their bargaining power so easily. The Theocracy would probably smell a rat if he conceded *too* easily. "Tell them we want the money transferred first, then we'll evacuate the ship and hand over the command codes."

Stott sent the message. Gibson obviously hadn't given much thought to just *how* he planned to hand over the ship, which wasn't surprising. He hadn't *intended* to hand over the ship. Now William had to lure *Glory of God* into firing range before the Theocracy either ordered them to hand over the cruiser or decided to cut its losses and open fire.

They would be right. If the mutineers were still in command, William thought, *we couldn't even turn and run.*

"Enemy ship will enter sprint-mode missile range in five minutes," Roach reported. "I have a constantly updating firing circuit running in primary mode."

"Careful with your hands," William said dryly.

He braced himself. If the Theocracy had been remotely trustworthy, there would be no need for such a complex handover. Gibson and his inner circle could take a couple of shuttles and fly directly to Jorlem, carrying enough money to ensure that no one would ask questions when they docked. But William knew how corrupt the Theocracy actually was. He wouldn't put it past enemy agents to look for a way to keep *Uncanny* as well as the money. Hell, their agents might just try to keep the cash for themselves.

"They're insisting on boarding the ship," Stott reported. "They say we can keep control, but they want to inspect the merchandise before making the trade."

"They're slowing," Roach added. "They may not enter minimum range."

William swore under his breath. If *Glory of God* remained outside point-blank range, William wouldn't be able to destroy her in his opening salvo. That would mean a brutal engagement at knife-range. How could he lure her closer? It wasn't as if the Theocrats would have any trouble shuttling troops over from their current position . . .

"Tell them we've rigged the ship to blow if they try to take control without permission," he said. "But they can land a single shuttle of troops if they wish."

"Aye, sir," Stott said.

"They're coming to a halt, relative to us," Roach said. "We could close the range ourselves."

William considered his next move. If they moved forward, the Theocracy *would* smell a rat. If they stayed where they were, all hope of destroying the enemy ship in a single salvo would be lost. That would risk everything . . .

"Move us forward," he ordered finally. "Fire as soon as we enter minimum range."

"Aye, Captain," Roach said.

◆ ◆ ◆

Samuel glanced at Bin Zaid. "They're moving forward," he said. There was a hint of alarm in his voice. "Is that something you told them to do?"

Bin Zaid swallowed . . . hard. "No," he said. He hadn't issued any orders to the mutineers. "I told them to prepare to receive boarders."

"Maybe they didn't listen," the Lord Cleric said.

"Then tell them to hold position," Samuel said. He raised his voice. "Raise shields! Stand by all weapons!"

Christopher G. Nuttall

◆ ◆ ◆

"Captain," Roach said, "they're raising shields."
"*Fire*," William shouted.

◆ ◆ ◆

"Incoming fire," the tactical officer warned. The display blazed with red icons. "I say again, incoming fire!"

Bin Zaid stared. "What . . .?"

"It was a trap," Samuel said angrily. On the display, *Uncanny* was rolling over to launch a second barrage of missiles. "A fucking trap!"

He glared at his tactical officer. "Return fire," he barked. "Get those shields up!"

"It can't be," Bin Zaid said. He didn't want to believe what he was seeing. His career . . . his plans for the future . . . all gone. The mutineers had tricked him! They hadn't been real mutineers at all. "It can't . . ."

Glory of God shook violently as she unleashed a barrage of her own. Bin Zaid looked back at the display, feeling his entire body shake. The enemy missiles were closing with staggering speed, the point defense grid fighting desperately to take as many of them out as possible. But *Glory of God* had been caught by surprise. Her active sensors were still coming to life. Her shields were still taking shape . . .

"It can't be happening," Bin Zaid said. Had all his plans come to naught? His future . . . had it shrunk to slow torture and execution in a cell? "It can't . . ."

"It can," Samuel said. Bin Zaid looked at him. The captain was holding a pistol in his hand, pointed directly at Bin Zaid's forehead. "And it is."

He pulled the trigger. Bin Zaid's world went dark.

◆ ◆ ◆

"Evasive action," William barked. *Glory of God*'s commander was *wasted* on a semi-diplomatic mission to the Jorlem Sector. What reflexes! Caught by surprise, he'd still managed to bring up his shields and launch a barrage in return before William's missiles slammed into his hull. "Launch drones, hold nothing back!"

"Aye, Captain," Roach said. "Launching third barrage now. *Lightning* has launched her first barrage!"

William nodded as the lead antimatter warheads slammed into the enemy ship. Her shields flickered—they hadn't been fully raised when the missiles struck home—but they held, even though he suspected they'd probably lost several shield generators. She was turning rapidly, bringing her missile tubes to bear on *Uncanny* even as *Lightning* aimed another salvo of missiles into her rear. William had a nasty feeling that her commanding officer was hopping mad. He seemed to be paying very little attention to *Lightning*.

That will change, he thought. *He knows who has to be in command of that ship.*

"Incoming missiles," Roach warned. "Decoys engaging, Captain; point defense going active . . . now."

Glory of God hadn't expected serious trouble, William noted, as the enemy missiles plowed into his defenses. *He* had had *his* missiles constantly updated with new firing solutions, programming their warheads to go straight for their target, but the Theocracy hadn't had time to do the same themselves. A dozen missiles lost their target locks and wasted themselves on his decoys, a dozen more were hit by his point defense and taken out. *Glory of God* had also bunched their missiles up enough that one hit was often enough to take out several other missiles. But the remainder were still coming . . .

"All hands, brace for impact," he warned. "I say again, all hands brace for impact!"

Uncanny rang like a bell as the missiles struck home. William grabbed hold of his command chair and hung on for dear life, knowing *precisely* what would happen if the internal compensators failed. Red lights flashed up in front of him, warning of damage to the ship's internal systems. Even if the raw fury of the antimatter warheads didn't get through the shields, the shaking alone would do considerable damage . . .

"Shield generators two through five have burned out," Goodrich reported. "Major damage to power distribution nodes in sections alpha-three-seven and gamma-three-nine!"

"Injuries reported on decks five, seven, and eleven," Stott added.

"Deploy damage control and medical teams," William ordered. Roach needed to concentrate on his tactical duties. "Continue firing."

He braced himself as *Glory of God* unleashed another spread of missiles. *This* time, he noted, the gunners had had time to program the warheads properly. None of the missiles would be decoyed away . . .

"Enemy ship engaging *Lightning*," Roach reported. "She's coming about to bring her missile tubes to bear."

William sucked in his breath. The enemy ship's ECM was good, better than he'd expected, but she was clearly taking damage. *Glory* had definitely lost at least five or six of her shield generators, judging from the way her shields were shifting and flexing to cover the most vulnerable spots. But she was still firing, still capable of engaging both cruisers at once . . .

Uncanny rocked again. "Fusion Two just failed, Captain," Goodrich reported. "I have teams on the way, but I doubt it can be patched up in time to matter."

After we disabled it ourselves, William thought coldly. *We clearly didn't do a good job of fixing the damage.*

"Do what you can," he ordered.

On the display, *Glory of God* shuddered under his fire. *He* would have seriously considered pulling back and abandoning the fight if *he'd* been in command of the enemy ship, but the Theocrats rarely ran, even when the odds were badly stacked against them. It wasn't something to mourn, normally, but it was a problem now. The fight could still go either way.

"Enemy ship's shields are tilting back towards us," Roach reported. "Adjusting firing patterns to compensate."

He paused. "The enemy missiles are no longer fooled by the decoys," he added. "They're targeting us."

"Keep deploying them anyway," William ordered. Another shudder ran through the ship as three more enemy missiles struck home. "Every little bit helps."

"Aye, Captain," Roach said.

Captain Samuel knew, without false modesty, that he'd been given command of *Glory of God* because he was more thoughtful than the average commanding officer. A diplomatic mission could not run the risk of an officer deciding to avenge an insult to his crew or his faith by planetary bombardment, no matter how much the victims deserved a pasting. He was cold and calculating, cold enough to pull back and concede when he was clearly losing.

He glanced venomously at the dead Inquisitor as another wave of enemy missiles slammed into his shields. Perhaps killing the lunatic had been a mistake. *Glory of God* had walked right into a trap and nothing, not even Bin Zaid's body, would be enough to cool the anger of his superiors when they found out what had happened. *Someone* would have to answer for the debacle and Samuel knew that a dead man couldn't be held accountable for anything. The only way to remain alive was to make the enemy *pay* for luring his ship into a trap.

It was too good to be true, Samuel thought. He'd said as much, but Bin Zaid had dismissed his concerns. *And now we're fighting for our lives.*

The infidels had baited the trap well, he admitted grudgingly. Neither of their ships was a match for *Glory* in a straight fight, but together they might best him. Their first blows had weakened his ship's shields significantly and successive attacks had damaged his power cores. Plus, their ECM was hellishly good. He'd had to have his gunners control the missiles directly just to keep them from going after the decoys and spending themselves uselessly.

"Shield generator nine just failed," one of his officers reported. He sounded nervous, as if he expected to be shot for daring to be the bearer of bad news. "Shield generator ten is on the verge of failing too."

"Adjust the remaining generators to compensate," Samuel ordered. His ship had plenty of redundancies built in, but there were limits. A gap in his shields wasn't a serious problem against *one* opponent. Against *two*? It was a disaster waiting to happen. "And then swing us around to target *Lightning*."

"Aye, Captain," the helmsman said.

Samuel ignored the Lord Cleric's babbling as he thought, fast. Destroying *Lighting* would be a suitable prize, compensation for the staggering damage his ship had already taken. His superiors would accept Kat Falcone's death, he was sure. They'd understand him retreating after smashing *Lightning* and battering *Uncanny* into uselessness. And perhaps, just perhaps, there was an opportunity to fulfill one of the other mission aims.

"Contact the planetary government," he ordered harshly. "Tell them to send out their ships to assist us."

"They won't engage the Commonwealth," the Lord Cleric stammered. He was staring down the barrels of ritual torture and execution, and he knew it. His subordinate had led the entire mission to certain failure. "Captain . . ."

"I don't care," Samuel said. "Get the bastards out here."

A sharp fury enveloped Samuel. His ship was taking damage, and even comparatively *minor* damage was serious, when he didn't have access to a shipyard. Vangelis had the only halfway decent shipyard in the sector, and he doubted he could convince the planetary government to assist him. They'd *know* his ship was badly weakened, her missiles spent on her previous engagement . . .

. . . While the Commonwealth would see the planet's assistance as an act of war.

"Missiles locked, sir," the tactical officer said. "Enemy ship is taking evasive action."

"Fire."

CHAPTER THIRTY-NINE

"Incoming missiles," Weiberg said. "The enemy ship is targeting us specifically."

Kat nodded. The timing had gone a little awry, and they were now locked in a death match with an enemy juggernaut. She would have been happy to pull back and withdraw if *Glory of God* had lost her gateway generator—she'd be stranded until the Theocracy could get a repair ship to the sector—but there was no way to know just how badly they'd damaged the enemy ship. Her ECM was too good for Kat's analysts to come up with any useful information.

"Evasive action," she ordered. *Lightning* had already taken damage, but *Uncanny* had borne the brunt of the enemy's fury. It looked as though that was about to change. "Reinforce shields and return fire . . ."

Kat braced herself as the enemy missiles struck her shields. A low rumble echoed through *Lightning*, followed by a series of alarms. She glanced at the status display and swore. Five shield generators had failed in quick succession, weakening her shields to the point that energy was leaking through them and touching her hull. The damage wasn't as bad as she had feared, but a dozen point defense weapons had been wiped out . . .

"Damage control teams are on the way," Crenshaw stated. "Captain, we have a number of injuries reported from . . ."

"Get medical teams out there," Kat ordered. She would mourn later, if there *was* a later. *Glory of God*, scenting *Lightning*'s weakness, was already launching a second barrage of missiles. "Reroute emergency power to shields, then swing us about."

"Aye, Captain," Wheeler said.

Kat braced herself as another wave of missiles slammed into her shields. *Lightning* shuddered then rocked violently as one of her shields collapsed completely. Wheeler pushed the starship through a series of evasive maneuvers, trying to avoid exposing the gash in her shields to enemy fire, but he couldn't keep the enemy from scoring two more hits . . .

"Hull breach, decks fifteen through seventeen," Crenshaw snapped.

"Evacuate that sector," Kat barked. *Lightning* had taken a beating before, but this was different. "Get everyone out!"

Another shudder ran through the ship. "The enemy ship is closing to sprint-mode range," Weiberg reported. "She's preparing to fire."

"Continue firing," Kat ordered. She had very little respect for Theocratic design teams—she'd seen some of their missteps—but she had to admit they'd done a good job on *Glory of God*. The enemy ship might win the engagement after all. "Helm, put some distance between us and them!"

"Aye, Captain," Wheeler said. "They're picking up speed."

Kat considered the possible vectors. A battlecruiser could outrun anything it couldn't outfight, or at least that had been the rationale put forward by the Naval Design Board back when Tyre had started the massive prewar buildup. But no battlecruiser ever designed could hope to keep up with *Lightning* when she was in good health. Now, though, it looked as if *Glory of God* could match *Lightning*'s reduced speed. *That* meant that her ship and crew were unable to escape . . .

"Deploy mines," she ordered, hoping to win a few additional seconds. "Then push the engines as hard as you can."

More red icons popped up on the display. Two of her drive nodes had failed—a third had been smashed when the hull had been breached—reducing her ship's speed even further. She was *sure* she could have outrun *Glory* if her drives had been in good condition, but as it was . . .

Kat had a nasty feeling they might need to slip into hyperspace to escape. Yet, opening a gateway in the middle of a battle was dangerous. Too many antimatter missiles were in flight.

If we dared close to energy range, she thought, *we might take out their ship at the cost of one of our own.*

Lightning shook, again. "Plasma leak, deck nine," Crenshaw reported. "Two more drive nodes are on the verge of failing."

"Keep pushing them," Kat ordered. The Navy designed its components to take a great deal of abuse. She hoped the designers were correct when they boasted their components could handle more stress than claimed in specifications. "Tactical, report!"

"Enemy ship's shields are fluctuating, but she's still coming," Weiberg said. "She's launching another barrage of missiles now!"

At least she'll shoot herself dry, Kat thought. *If nothing else, the local sector navies will have a chance against her.*

Samuel had never truly believed that the devil took an active interest in human affairs. In his experience, humans didn't need *help* to stumble into sin, but watching *Lightning* evade his killing blows was frustrating. Kat Falcone—and he wouldn't underestimate her just because she was a woman—had *definitely* earned her command. Her ship was bleeding, leaking plasma from at least two hull breaches, but she was still fighting. *Glory of God* was taking a pounding even though she was winning the fight.

And *Uncanny* was on their tail, hammering away at her shields.

"Keep on *Lightning*," he ordered. He'd already expended half of his missile stocks and there were no reserves. One way or the other, the mission had failed. Nothing he could do could change that. "Don't give her a chance to get away!"

A missile slammed into his shields, and he cursed. "Another shield generator has just failed," his XO reported. "Captain, our shields are starting to weaken."

Samuel hung his head in dismay. *Glory of God* was designed to be a hybrid between a battleship and a battlecruiser, but she lacked the heavy armor protecting superdreadnoughts. If she lost her shields and the enemy slammed an antimatter warhead into her hull . . . the entire crew would be answering to God before they knew what had hit them. He was tempted to retreat, but he *couldn't* retreat without something to show for the disaster. The mission had failed . . .

"Hold our course," he said. The enemy wouldn't give him any time to lick his wounds, any more than he would give them the chance to break contact and escape. *Lightning* had to be badly damaged or she would have outrun him by now. "Order the damage control teams to do what they can."

Another shockwave ran through his ship. "Captain, the gateway generator is offline," the XO reported. "It will take *days* to repair it . . ."

If we can, Samuel thought. Suddenly retreat was no longer an option. His engineers were among the best in the Theocracy, but that wasn't saying much. *We might win one battle but lose the war.*

"Keep us on *Lightning*," he ordered. They *had* to kill one or both of the enemy cruisers. "Do *not* stop firing."

"Aye, Captain," the tactical officer said.

William was drenched in sweat as he watched *Glory of God* close in on *Lightning*. Kat's ship was too badly damaged to outrun her enemy. *Uncanny* was closing in on the rear of the enemy ship, but the Theocrats seemed to be largely ignoring her. Instead, they were concentrating most of their fire on *Lightning*.

Smart of them, William conceded. *Playing piggy-in-the-middle just plays to our strengths and their weaknesses.*

Another enemy missile slammed into his shields, flickers of energy breaking through and washing against his hull. *Uncanny* wasn't as badly wrecked as *Lightning*, but she had taken damage. Yet he needed to keep pounding away at *Glory of God*. She couldn't be allowed to overwhelm *Lightning* and blow her into dust.

"They're constantly rotating their shields," Roach reported. "They must have taken a beating."

William wouldn't have cared to put that sort of stress on Commonwealth-designed shield generators, let alone the crap the Theocracy produced. The Theocrats must be desperate . . . He hoped grimly, that it meant that they'd lost too many of their original shield generators. Still, such a state was enough to give them a fair chance to survive long enough to take out *Lightning*, if not *Uncanny*.

"Continue hammering their weak spots," he ordered. If they could take out just one or two more shield generators, part of the enemy shield network would collapse. If he could slip a missile through a gap in their shields, the battle would end. "They can't stand up to this sort of battering indefinitely."

"Neither can we," Stott muttered.

William ignored the remark. He knew Stott was right.

"The enemy will be within sprint-mode range in two minutes," Weiberg reported. The hammering on the shields had become a constant pounding. "Our shields are already weakening."

Kat remained focused. There *had* to be an alternative. There *had* to be a way to get out of the trap. But she couldn't see one. Her remaining drive nodes were already overstressed, her gateway generator was offline . . . and the enemy's shields were holding against her fire. She could inflict horrendous damage if she could get into energy range, she knew, but she doubted *Lightning* would survive the enemy onslaught long enough to get there. The enemy would blow her apart long before she could make it.

At least that ship won't be causing any more trouble, she thought. Even going by the worst-case estimates, *Glory of God* had fired off two-thirds of her missiles. *The Theocracy won't be able to intimidate Jorlem any longer.*

She closed her eyes in pain. She'd finally pushed her luck too far. *Lightning* was doomed; her crew doomed with her. The escape pods weren't even a possibility. Even if the Theocracy didn't start shooting at the pods deliberately, there were just too many antimatter explosions going on for her crew to be safe. She needed a third option and she couldn't see one.

Unless . . .

"Communications, raise *Uncanny*," she said. It was a crazy thought. A *completely* crazy thought. But she was desperate. "I have a plan."

"Aye, Captain," Linda said.

◆ ◆ ◆

Samuel allowed himself a moment of chilly satisfaction as *Lightning* writhed under his fire, her shields steadily collapsing into nothingness. The ship's demise wasn't much—he knew, even if the Lord Cleric didn't, just how badly the Commonwealth was outproducing the

Theocracy—but it would satisfy his superiors. It wasn't what they'd wanted to do to Kat Falcone, yet it would suffice. They'd see it as a fatal blow to the infidels, even though common sense would tell them it was nothing of the sort.

If they'd had any common sense, Samuel thought bitterly, *they wouldn't have* started *the damned war.*

Such a thought would have gotten him executed if he'd dared express his doubts openly. Watching eyes and listening ears abounded in the Theocracy. A crewman who wanted to advance in the ranks could do so easily, by accusing his superiors of heresy and blasphemy. But even the most restrictive societies couldn't clamp down on everything, could they? Samuel couldn't help noticing that the reported battles were all concentrated in the same region of space, instead of a steady advance towards Tyre. The grand offensive had bogged down completely.

Perhaps I should be glad I'm stuck here, he thought. Damaged as she was, *Glory of God* could still overwhelm Jorlem's puny navy. *I might survive the end of the war.*

"Captain," the tactical officer said. "*Lightning* is reversing course. She's pushing everything she has into her drives!"

Samuel stared.

She's going to ram . . .

"All power to forward shields," he barked as *Lighting* picked up speed. A heavy cruiser slamming into his ship would take out both vessels. He wouldn't have thought the enemy commander had the nerve for a suicide run, but *Lightning* was doomed anyway. Why *not* try to take out *Glory of God* in her last moments? "Fire all weapons!"

◆ ◆ ◆

"Incoming missiles," Weiberg snapped.

"Deploy missiles to counteract," Kat snapped. The enemy had been caught by surprise, but they'd clearly already been switching their missiles to sprint mode. Intercepting them was going to be a nightmare as the range closed. "Their shields?"

"They're forcing them forward," Weiberg reported. "Captain . . ."

Lightning shuddered, shaking so badly that Kat honestly thought the end had come. The lighting failed a second later, followed by the gravity. Half the consoles went dim as emergency power came online, the datanet prioritizing weapons and shields. Kat had a nasty feeling they'd just lost everything . . .

"Major damage, all sections," Crenshaw reported. His voice sounded bleak. "Captain . . ."

Kat keyed her console. She had no way to know yet if her plan had succeeded. But *Lightning* was now naked and helpless. Perhaps, just perhaps, some of her crew would survive long enough to be picked up.

"All hands, abandon ship," she ordered. "I say again, abandon ship."

"We got her," the tactical officer snapped. He sounded exultant. "*Lightning* has lost main power. Her shields and weapons are down."

"Lock missiles on her hull," Samuel ordered. "Prepare to . . ."

And then he realized his mistake.

William cursed under his breath as *Lightning* lost main power, her hull starting to tumble through space as her shields failed completely. But she'd made the enemy panic, forcing them to push their shields forward . . .

"Fire," he roared. "All weapons, fire!"

Glory of God seemed to flinch under his fire, spitting out a barrage of missiles in *Uncanny*'s general direction. But it was too late to switch their shields back. Their rear hull was as unprotected as *Lightning* herself, and her point defense was practically gone. William watched, refusing to take his eyes off the display, until his barrage slammed into the enemy ship's hull and blew her into an expanding fireball.

"Target destroyed," Roach said. "I think we won."

"Yeah," William muttered. He keyed his console. "Deploy shuttles to recover *Lightning*'s life pods."

"Aye, Captain," Major Lupine said.

William glanced at the display. *Lightning* was thoroughly wrecked; he doubted the Navy would choose to repair her when it would probably be cheaper to build a whole new ship. Kat had believed, she *had* to have believed, that *Lightning* had been doomed when she'd turned the ship around, gambling that she could make the enemy panic and accidentally expose their hull to his fire. And she'd been right.

Lucky girl, he thought.

He tapped his console again. "Damage report?"

"We took a beating, Captain," Goodrich said. "Fusion Two is definitely going to be offline for the foreseeable future and Fusion Three isn't in much better shape. I'll have a full report for you in the next few hours, but I can confidently tell you right now we are in no state for another engagement."

"Do what you can," William ordered. *Uncanny* would probably have to limp back to the Commonwealth. Vangelis would possibly agree to help, but their shipyard wasn't designed to assist a heavy cruiser. "Let me know when you have a full report."

The display bleeped an alert. "Captain," Roach reported, "we have five destroyers dropping out of hyperspace. They're lighting us up with tactical sensors."

William clenched his fists. The ships *had* to be from Jorlem. "Hail them," he ordered. "Thank them for agreeing to assist with our SAR operations."

"I'm picking up a signal," Stott said.

"Put it through," William ordered.

A man wearing a uniform so fancy that William *knew* he didn't have any genuine naval experience blinked into existence on the display. "This is Grand Admiral Vernon of the Jorlem Navy," he said. "You have breached the neutrality of the Jorlem System. By command of President Alexis, you are hereby ordered to lower your shields and prepare to be boarded."

Odd choice of words, William thought. Or maybe it wasn't odd at all. *He's making it clear that the orders came straight from the president.*

William took a moment to formulate his thoughts. "Grand Admiral," he said. He was staring down the barrels of a court-martial anyway. He might as well be blunt. "Are you aware that my ship out-guns all five of your ships by at least three orders of magnitude?"

Vernon looked irked, just for a second. "By command of President Alexis . . ."

"A full report is already winging its way back to the Commonwealth," William said. It wasn't *entirely* a bluff. *Lightning* had sent a signal to the StarCom as soon as the engagement had begun. "Do you want the Commonwealth to thank you for assisting with the post-battle cleanup or come after you for supporting the Theocracy?"

He leaned forward. "President Alexis will not thank you for embroiling him in war," he added warningly. "Stand down or start a fight you cannot possibly win."

There was a long, uncomfortable pause. William prayed silently that Vernon would see sense and back down. He had no idea just what President Alexis had in mind, but *Glory of God* was now nothing more than space dust. The Commonwealth wouldn't need more than a cruiser squadron to teach Jorlem a salutary lesson. Whatever President Alexis had hoped to gain from working with the Theocracy, it hadn't materialized.

"I will deploy my ships to assist with your recovery efforts," Vernon said finally. "And I congratulate you on your great victory."

"Thank you," William said, silently relieved. *Uncanny* outgunned Vernon's ships, but as badly damaged as she was, the locals might still have won. "It came at a great cost."

He closed the channel. *Lightning* was gone, *Uncanny* was badly damaged, and countless crewmen had been killed or injured. The victory had come at a *very* high cost.

But we won, he told himself. He looked at the fragments of debris floating through space . . . all that remained of the enemy warship. *It could have been a great deal worse.*

CHAPTER FORTY

Joel felt anticipation tinged with apprehension as the landing pod was finally moved out of the station's launching bay and aimed towards the green-blue planet below. The last two weeks had been filled with holographic briefings, covering everything he and his comrades needed to know about the planet below. Bastille, named by someone with a sick sense of humor, was rated marginal, but at least it was habitable. It wasn't *quite* as bad as being thrown out the nearest airlock.

It has potential, he thought, privately.

Speaking to his former comrades had been harrowing. A couple had turned state's evidence, confessing everything in exchange for lighter sentences; others, knowing their hands were too bloody to be forgiven, had turned on Joel himself. He'd nearly been knifed twice before he'd beaten some sense back into their heads. They needed *leadership* if they were to survive and prosper; they needed *him*, the man who had tied them together once before. The whole situation wasn't *ideal*, only a fool would claim it was *ideal*, but it could be tolerated if they worked together.

He felt the pod quiver. They would be landing close, but not too close, to one of the largest settlements on the surface. None of the reports had made their destination sound like anything more than a hellish nightmare from out of the depths of time, a shitty little village held together by spit, baling wire, and brute force. The man in charge was a thug, using his band of hooligans to keep the rest of the population under control. And he lacked vision . . .

We can take over, he thought. He had fifty men and women under his command armed with hunting rifles and pistols. *Then we can start building something better.*

It wasn't what he'd wanted, he knew. All of his hopes and dreams had shattered the moment Sir William regained control of his ship. There were many hard days to come, but they still beat being thrown out an airlock. He'd just have to keep reminding himself of that, when the grueling days came.

"Attention," a quiet voice said, "prepare yourself for entry procedure."

Joel sat upright and braced himself. His new life was about to begin . . .

. . . and, he swore privately, he would make it a better one.

♦ ♦ ♦

"I do trust," the First Space Lord said, "that you have some kind of an explanation?"

He went on before Kat could say a word. "Your *crew*"—his voice dripped scorn—"swears blind that you liberated the cloudscoop personally, risking your life to save the civilian crew from their captors. Is there any actual *truth* in it?"

"It's in my report, sir," Kat said evenly.

"But I am asking *you*, Captain Falcone," the First Space Lord said. "Did you *deliberately* put your life at risk?"

"Yes, sir," Kat said.

The First Space Lord glared at her. "And by what reasoning," he demanded, "did you leave your bridge during a delicate situation?"

"I believed the pirates would need to be tempted with a grand prize," Kat said. "The biggest prize I had on hand was myself."

"The media has already picked up on the story," the First Space Lord said. "Who do you think you are? Captain Dreadnought? Stellar Star, Queen of the Spaceways? Putting your life in danger like that was utterly unacceptable."

"I was aware of the risks, sir," Kat said.

"And your XO filed an official dissent," the First Space Lord added. "Did you know that?"

"I assumed as much," Kat said. Crenshaw had reported his concerns about the mutiny on *Uncanny* to her, pointing out that most of the mutineers had been colonials. She'd eventually told him to shut up during the long voyage home from Jorlem. "Commander Crenshaw questioned a number of my decisions."

He will be reassigned in the next few weeks, she added silently. *He'll be a pain in someone else's ass.*

"If the media hadn't picked up on the story, you'd be facing a court-martial board," the First Space Lord said. "As it happened, the Board of Inquiry has decided that you will face no charges for putting your life at risk."

"Thank you, sir," Kat said.

"Thank me for nothing," the First Space Lord said. "If you pull something that stupid again, Captain Falcone, I'll bust you back to cadet and ship you to the most remote asteroid mining station I can find."

Kat said nothing. She didn't blame him for being angry. If something had gone wrong . . .

The First Space Lord took a long breath. "The destruction of HMS *Lightning* would be a black mark on your record, under other circumstances," he added. "As it happens, the Board of Inquiry has decided that her loss was acceptable. You'll be put back in the command pool without further delay."

In all truth, Kat wasn't sure she *wanted* another command. *Lightning* had been special, and triggering her self-destruct, after the crew had stripped the derelict hulk of anything useful, had hurt beyond all reason. She would hardly be the first officer to lose a starship, but she'd hoped against all she knew that the ship could be recovered. And then she'd been ordered to destroy the hulk . . .

"Thank you, sir," she said finally.

"Admiral Christian is putting together a task force to start the long-awaited counterattack," the First Space Lord informed her. "He has requested that you and your new command be posted to his fleet. Indeed, I believe there may be a promotion in line for you."

Kat swallowed. She was far too young, with far too little time in grade, to be promoted out of a command chair, but she was also one of the most experienced and well-connected officers in the Navy. She wouldn't be allowed to remain a mere captain forever. Her father, if no one else, would want her to take up a higher rank to expand his patronage network within the military.

"You still have your duty," the First Space Lord said softly. "And afterwards . . . well, we will see."

"Yes, sir," Kat said.

She met his eyes. "And the mutiny on *Uncanny*?"

"The Board of Inquiry is still debating the matter," the First Space Lord said. "Too much has leaked out to the media for us to handle it quietly. Assigning blame might take a few months . . . years, perhaps."

"Sir William cannot be blamed for a plot that was devised long before he took command," Kat said. "Or for failing to see it coming."

"That's for the Board of Inquiry to determine," the First Space Lord said. "I dare say you will be called upon to testify soon enough."

"Yes, sir," Kat said.

She felt a stab of pity for William. His first command had turned into a nightmare, even if *Uncanny* had dealt the killing blow to *Glory of God*. Hell, they were even talking about scrapping *Uncanny* rather than making repairs to return her to active service. William would be lucky to get another command . . .

Her resolve hardened. "Sir," she said, "if I'm being promoted, I want him for my flag captain."

The First Space Lord lifted his eyebrows. "And you feel the Board of Inquiry would respect your wishes?"

"Yes," Kat said. She *was* a Falcone, damn it. She might as well get *some* use out of the family name. "He's a more than competent commanding officer, sir."

"We shall see," the First Space Lord said. "It depends on the outcome of the . . . discussions."

He sighed. "You have a couple of week's leave," he added. "I suggest you use it to relax."

Kat nodded as she rose. Clearly someone had already decided that she was going to be put back on active service as quickly as possible. Thanks to the media and her father, she had already become a legend. The Admiralty would think twice about assigning her to a desk job.

"And give your father my regards," the First Space Lord added. "I'll be speaking to him shortly."

"Yes, sir," Kat said.

◆　◆　◆

"It has been decided, after extensive investigation, that Captain Sir William McElney, HMS *Uncanny*, is personally blameless," Admiral Stillwell said. "Save for Lieutenant Commander Leonard Thompson, *Uncanny*'s senior staff and militia complement were likewise personally blameless. The mutiny plot was simply too well concealed for any of the senior officers to be *reasonably* held accountable for failing to uncover it."

William allowed himself a moment of relief. Stillwell's words were about as favorable a ruling as he had any right to expect. He'd been *Uncanny*'s commanding officer. Whatever happened on his ship was his responsibility, even if he didn't know about it. The Board easily could have ruled him completely responsible and ordered his immediate dismissal from the service.

"Conditions on *Uncanny*, prior to Sir William taking command, were disgraceful," Admiral Stillwell continued. "As a breeding ground for discontent and mutiny, they could hardly be bettered. A number of officers have been put under investigation for their role in Captain Abraham's criminal ring, and those found to have close ties to Abraham will be put in front of a court-martial board in short order. Others who turned a blind eye will be severely censured for their conduct.

"In addition, it has been decided that the IG will run regular checks on crew morale and conditions throughout Home Fleet, in hopes of preventing a second mutiny."

He paused. "The issue of colonial officers within the Navy, particularly their involvement with the mutiny, has been passed upwards for later consideration. Such issues are outside this board's remit."

William winced. The mutiny was going to cause problems for the Navy, even with the Commonwealth gearing up for the great offensive. Colonial crewmen would be regarded as potential mutineers, damaging the military's trust in them at the worst possible moment. And Rose MacDonald and the other dissidents were going to have a field day with the story, once the implications sunk in.

"The future careers of Sir William and his senior officers will be determined separately," Admiral Stillwell concluded. "This Board of Inquiry is now brought to an end."

The room buzzed as the spectators rose and hurried towards the exits. William remained seated, feeling unaccountably tired. It *wasn't* the end, no matter what Stillwell said. He'd been relieved of command as soon as *Uncanny* had reached Tyre; now, without a command, he honestly didn't know what to do. And he doubted, somehow, that he'd be offered another command in a hurry. He might be the commanding officer who'd recovered his ship from a bunch of mutineers, but he was also the commanding officer who'd *lost* his ship. The Navy would find good reason to worry about him even if he *hadn't* been a colonial officer.

"William," a quiet voice said, "how are you feeling?"

William glanced up. Kat Falcone stood there, wearing her dress uniform.

"I didn't see you come in," he said. "Did you hear the announcement?"

"You're not being blamed," Kat said.

"Not officially," William said. He shook his head. "The media loves you, but seems torn on me."

"The government managed to ban most open discussion of the whole affair," Kat said. "They didn't want to damage civilian morale."

"I wouldn't have thought they needed to bother," William pointed out. He couldn't keep the bitterness out of his voice. "Civilians *never* understand what is going on."

Kat nodded. She seemed to have grown older in the last few weeks, William noted. But then she'd lost a ship too. Her family connections would probably get her a new command sooner rather than later, but *Lightning* had been her *first* command. No later ship would be quite the same.

"Come to lunch," she said, rising. "I booked a table."

William blinked. "Right now?"

"Nothing will happen for a few days," Kat said. "You have enough time to join my father and me for lunch, I think."

"If you wish," William said. He wasn't enthusiastic, but it was the best he could do. "She was a lucky ship in the end, wasn't she?"

"Yes," Kat agreed. "She was a *very* lucky ship."

ABOUT THE AUTHOR

 Christopher G. Nuttall has been planning science fiction books since he learned how to read. Born and raised in Edinburgh, Scotland, he studied history, which inspired him to imagine new worlds and create an alternate-history website. Those imaginings provided a solid base for storytelling and eventually led him to write books. He has published at least fifty novels and one novella through Amazon Kindle Direct Publishing, including the bestselling Ark Royal series. He has also published twenty-seven novels with small presses, including the Royal Sorceress series, the Bookworm series, *A Life Less Ordinary*, and *Sufficiently Advanced Technology* with Elsewhen Press, as well as the Schooled in Magic series through Twilight Times Books.

Cursed Command is his third book in the Angel in the Whirlwind series, following *The Oncoming Storm* and *Falcone Strike*. Chris resides in Edinburgh with his partner, muse, and critic, Aisha.

Visit his blog at www.chrishanger.wordpress.com and his website at www.chrishanger.net.